PRAISE FOR COLLEEN VAN NIEKERK

"Reading Colleen van Niekerk's *A Conspiracy of Mothers* was a gut-wrenching, emotional roller-coaster experience, with many lines resonating with my own belief that for South Africans to attain restorative justice, we first need to experience restorative memory. Colleen captures all this so well in cameos of captured time, which closely touched many a raw nerve of yet-unhealed wounds that are part of many of our lives. The world of lies and secrets and the pain that goes with it are vividly brought to life."

—Patric Tariq Mellet, author of *The Lie of 1652:*
A decolonized history of land

"Deeply affecting and beautifully rendered, *A Conspiracy of Mothers* is a tapestry woven with sacrifice, suffering, and loss but also with a love between generations of women so deep it invokes ancestral magic that defies the laws of space and time. This story of pilgrimage and reckoning amid the unraveling of apartheid should resonate with anyone interested in breaking down systems of racism and oppression, wherever they exist. A brilliant novel to be read alongside Trevor Noah's *Born a Crime* and Isabel Wilkerson's *Caste*."

—Susan Bernhard, author of *Winter Loon*

A CONSPIRACY
OF MOTHERS

A CONSPIRACY OF MOTHERS

A NOVEL

COLLEEN VAN NIEKERK

Little
a

Published by Little A, New York
www.apub.com

Amazon, the Amazon logo, and Little A are trademarks of Amazon.com, Inc., or its affiliates.

ISBN-13: 9781542023832 (hardcover)
ISBN-10: 1542023831 (hardcover)

ISBN-13: 9781542023849 (paperback)
ISBN-10: 154202384X (paperback)

Cover illustration by Eli Minaya

Cover design by Faceout Studio, Lindy Martin

Printed in the United States of America

First edition

For my father

AUTHOR'S NOTE

While it is my intention to remain, as far as possible, true to the parlance of South Africa, I'd like to elaborate on the racial classifications used in that country and how I've chosen to use them in this novel. There is also an element of sexual violence within these pages for which I'd like to offer context.

The National Party, which formalized already-nascent apartheid into a political and legal institution, came into power in 1948. They passed the Population Registration Act into law in 1950. There, outlined in the neat language of bureaucracy, were the racial groups that all South Africans were subsequently assigned to. After all, one couldn't enact policies of white supremacy if one couldn't determine definitively who was white and who was not.

This clinical act of classification was devastating and far reaching. Families, homes, communities, and individuals were torn apart, as this law and the rest of "grand apartheid's" legislation impacted the full scope of what it meant to be a human being. The consequences of this continue as aftershocks in South African society today. This is especially true of the calamitous Group Areas Act, which segregated physical spaces and communities, towns, and cities. Thousands were forcibly removed from their homes. This particular law meant that those of different races never lived in the same neighborhood and had little to no opportunity to develop relationships across color lines, beyond those based on employment, on roles of master and servant.

The names of the classifications for racial groups often changed in keeping with political and economic drivers as well as international opinion. But the underlying concepts never shifted, and nor did the fanged white supremacy sitting behind them. Yet a number of those dated terms and ways of thinking about and referencing ourselves remain prevalent in South African culture at the time of publication of this novel.

The assumption of homogeneity within these groups is fundamentally flawed. Diversity is not colorful frosting to add to the top of a homogeneous, largely white cake but is literally borne in the bones of every single human being and society. But that's a subject for another day.

Below is a summary of how these groups are referenced, considerations regarding their meaning, and decisions I've made on the same:

Black when it refers to people in this novel is capitalized. *Black* as used here is a unifying term referring to those whose origin is predominantly Xhosa, Zulu, et cetera. It should be noted that Blackness only came into existence when whiteness did. In Africa, peoples considered to be Black have always readily referred to themselves by their ethnic groups and continue to do so where this applies. In South Africa, for example, Black South Africans typically describe themselves as Xhosa, Sotho, Tswana, et cetera. I have done the same in this novel where appropriate. Using *Black* in this way is also a nod to the accepted practice of reflecting the universality of many elements of the Black experience, although Black people are not a monolith.

The term *Black* in South Africa is noteworthy as much for whom, historically, it does not refer to as for whom it does. Excluded under apartheid were those of mixed ancestry and those who can best be termed First Nations (and descendants of the same) in southern Africa.

The term *coloured* was created to encompass these groups. In this novel, this term is not capitalized. This is not intended as a dismissal of these unique South Africans or their complex heritage, with which we have only truly begun to come to terms after apartheid. It is intended to dismiss what this name is: callous language applied by apartheid's architects to create a distinct racial group, purely as a means to achieve the regime's own ends. Determining who was coloured was largely dependent on racism's twin: colorism. Segregating groups by the lightness of their skin created a pecking order, which enabled the government to apply the rule of divide and conquer among those of color. Once internalized, these divisions were often passed down generation to generation.

Among the various criteria applied by bureaucrats to establish one's racial classification was a variety of "tests" taken directly from the eugenics playbook. These determined how near or far from the then-European ideal you looked by assessing the shape of your skull, the texture of your hair, the shape of your nose. Classification often caused an excruciating level of pain for those who found themselves separated from others in their own family, from where they lived, and, in some cases, from the only identities they had ever known.

The term *coloured* does not do justice to either those of mixed race in South Africa or its First Nations. It does not allow these groups to be defined as anything but somewhere in the vague middle between Black, white, Indigenous, and Asian. Much reflection and debate is required within the coloured community to arrive at the answer to what we should call ourselves and whether a term other than *Black* is required. However, *coloured* remains the commonly used term for this group and certainly was in the early nineties, when this novel is set.

The creation of the coloured group, along with every other, presented a raised platform upon which the legally defined white race was placed. The entire power structure of apartheid was centered on whiteness as a pronounced and singular identity. Always capitalized. Always amplified. It is not capitalized in this novel.

The construct of whiteness was positioned by the regime as embodying a civilized and advanced culture to be elevated, a superior race worthy of protection from polluting influences. However, maintaining this construct rested on several legislative acts of exclusion. These created a number of social and cultural realities, the consequences of which persist to this day.

One of the very first pieces of legislation enacted in 1949, one year after the National Party came into power, was the Prohibition of Mixed Marriages Act. It was followed in 1950 by the Immorality Amendment Act. Combined, these laws made physical intimacy between the white race and any other race a criminal offense, subject to imprisonment. The government had of course simultaneously defined who these races were.

These and similar laws rendered the preservation of whiteness a moral imperative. The regime enforced these laws while, immorally, making life a living nightmare for every other racial group. For white South Africans, apartheid's gilded cage offered states of being that ranged from comfortable oblivion to outraged abhorrence. The system offered benefits, though, to those whites who conformed, who stayed within their limits and didn't ask too many questions. Whites, too, were expected to do as they were told.

Perpetuating that original apartheid intent is what capitalizing whiteness in this particular novel would signify. Referring to this group with a lowercase letter doesn't imply diminished regard on the part of the author for those who identify as white. But in South Africa, the weight of capitalized whiteness has bent society in ways that will take generations to recover from.

I have declined, for ease of reading, to use quotation marks or the modifier *so-called* when referring to any racial group.

Systems of oppression never operate on a single plane. They are comprehensive and insidious; oftentimes the oppressed take on the behavior of the oppressor, prolonging the agony. The result of this continual stream of damage tends to manifest in scattershot ways not originally anticipated. In South Africa, this has materialized in an especially horrific social ill: a high degree of gender-based violence. This existed during apartheid. It continues to. While the old regime was by no means the sole contributing factor to this dire reality, it set the stage for it in myriad ways.

Sexual assault is a crime no matter who is on the receiving end of it; it has afflicted people of all classes and colors. Yet under apartheid, only the rape of white women was subject to prosecution, and it was a charge that could lead to the death penalty. For women of color, the regime extended the long, dark night that began with colonization and slavery: sexual assaults within this group went underreported, excused, and barely, if ever, recognized as an offense. The intended conclusion was clear: the bodies of women of color had little to no value.

As a reflection of the place and time in which it is situated, this novel carries an example of this vicious cycle of sexual violence that has extended across generations in many—but in fairness not in all—quarters. Readers, particularly those who have had similar experiences, should note that this novel contains a scene that depicts an act of gang rape upon the protagonist. The trauma she has borne over several years is also relayed vividly through moments of recollection and reflection.

YOLANDA

Night has no color. It has smell, taste, flickering visuals. It is not a void but a time when the presence of other things pushes forward. Darkness sets upon Yolanda, heavy and tight as a vise. Weary, she knows that she will always face the night alone, no matter who is in the room, who is in her bed.

Yet fear rises in her like bile, for this night brings more with it than shadows.

Come home, the voice said, the one she heard after she closed her eyes and lay down on her bed. It was Ma's voice again, wafting in on the wind that raised the tattered net curtain of Yolanda's bedroom like a hand. Two words, drifting in with the scent of fresh rain and wet soil, with the sound of horses neighing in the nearby stables. Rachel, her mother, was beckoning her away from this Virginia hamlet and back to Cape Town's unforgiving shore, as if an absence of eighteen years was nothing at all.

These two words had come over several weeks now, straining Yolanda's worn spirit where it felt held together by rusted rivets, pushing at the tight, painful places within her. The call left her in agony. It illuminated the shards of her broken heart that she'd so carefully papered over. An insomniac accustomed to resting in the security of daylight, she was finding herself too disturbed to get much sleep at all.

Fatigued, she looked up at the ceiling of her bedroom before drifting into an unsettled half sleep. But a cluster of ghouls sat at the periphery of her mind. Exhaustion had drained her of the will to keep them at bay. They were ready to prey again.

Then it came like a switch: the sound of a belt buckle.

Her heart began to race. The shadows at the foot of her bed grew deeper, darker. The belt belonged to Garrick, her boyfriend. He had come in from the stables, into her bathroom. Garrick was a safe harbor for her, yet to Yolanda the sound didn't come from him, not then.

"Help," she gasped, forming white-knuckled fists with her trembling hands. But the ghouls pushed forward. They were standing over her again, belt buckles loosening, hands reaching. They jostled with each other over who was going to go next. They dragged her present self back into the past with them, forcing her, forcing her to look where she didn't want to. Night drew her in.

Yolanda had no idea how long the flashback went on for. When she came to, she was crouched in a ball near her kitchen door, burrowed against Garrick. Her dog was pacing nearby; his were howling on the porch. Garrick had drawn her back with smell. She exhaled into the familiar scent of his body: hay, horses, and cheap aftershave. He'd also lit the oil burner. The air was light with the scent of citrus that she loved. "You're safe," he was repeating. His long legs were curved inward, his body bent over her like shelter. Yolanda relaxed into his embrace. She swallowed her nausea and released her tears.

On good days, she saw the world as an artist. She read the textures of people and places. She observed patterns, inconsistencies, the world's imperfect symmetry. Confidence grew then that she would paint again one day, unmute her art and release the utterances locked in her chest since the day and night she'd screamed and no one had come. On bad days, all of that dissolved. All that remained was a vacuum filled with pangs of yearning and regret, with the ghouls that stifled and throttled.

"How bad was it this time?" she asked.

Garrick shrugged. He had known what to do. He quickened in moments of need: when horses birthed, when the dogs tangled with raccoons. He'd said to her once, "I take care of animals now 'cause there's not a damn thing you can do about people," dismissing his previous career as an army medic. But he was still a man who sensed cracks, who was drawn to brokenness.

"I'm sorry," she said, with the shame calcified within her. "Again."

"Don't apologize, please," he said. "Just remember that even the longest night can only run till morning."

She drew away from his hands as they stroked her back, from the comfort she felt she didn't deserve. Reflexively she tried to wipe spit off her face, spit that wasn't there.

"Come sit," Garrick said, and she slumped into a chair. "You need to eat; chicken OK? I've got some left over in my fridge, got bread too. I'll go get it." He knelt beside her. She struggled to meet his eyes. "You gonna be OK for a minute?"

"I can see the farmhouse from here, Garrick." He frowned, wrinkling his nose slightly in the way that accentuated the curve where it had once been broken. The loose ends of bushy hair lay ragged over his face. She moved it out of his eyes. "I'm OK, thank you. Go."

She looked up at the dusty, empty liquor bottles atop the hutch: a barrier of glass marking the line she shouldn't cross. Here were the old stains of alcohol rings on her kitchen table, and there, in her living room, lay a jumble of cameras and lenses at her workstation. Between it all stood sparse, cheap furniture. *This is what it looks like when your life is like one long wait in an airport terminal,* she thought. *You let go of much more than you keep. This is how it is when you're damaged goods held responsible for the crime you suffered; when the punishment comes, then comes again, like a black hole, taking the years with it.*

Fault and blame. *You asked for it. What did you do to make it happen?* She thought of other women made to walk that plank, eat the silt of those words. But unlike those who pumped their fists mightily against such brutal accusations, she was already in the water, struggling to breathe.

Garrick returned. He moved around her kitchen comfortably. She liked seeing him there yet felt exposed. He had once again seen not only her vulnerability but her terror. Agitated, she took a carton of black Sobranie cigarettes out of a kitchen drawer, fought with the wrapper, then lit one. "God, Rachel," she muttered.

It would be like her mother to remind her of the irony: Yolanda finding refuge here, upon soil where the sediment of African suffering lay so deep that it bled into the very fabric of this place. Yet Yolanda knew she stood apart: she was Black but not the Black of this once-Confederate soil; she was African but not American, an apparition from that unfathomable continent.

"You heard her voice again?"

She nodded.

At first she'd written the call off as guilt and longing made manifest, but it had not relented. Ma called, then called again, her voice reminding Yolanda of who she was. That she had grown up in the grit of a council estate set in the long shadow of Table Mountain; that she would always be a girl from the matchbox houses laid out upon Cape Town's marsh.

"I can't go home. I made a decision, Garrick, back in England, a few months before I divorced and came to New York. Twelfth of June, 1986."

He put a sandwich in front of her, then sat down. He shifted, removing a hoof pick from his back pocket.

"That's pretty specific. What happened?"

Botha, South Africa's butcher of a prime minister, had faced the world that night. Prim, bespectacled, an admonishing white priest. The broadcast showed him seated before the flag of a country that she had been away from then for a decade already. But it was still her country, wasn't it? Although that was not her flag, never her flag.

The prime minister's words made for a crushing hammer that fell upon her like a white policeman's boot on a Black body. He declared a national state of emergency. South Africa, simmering for so long, was now officially at war with itself, the fires of fury out of control. But everyone she loved was on the other end of the flames.

With Botha's stern words, despair fell across Yolanda like a hand over her mouth. Sitting in a damp Manchester apartment, she held her body tight while he made his proclamation. Botha's long reach, the claws driving in, made it hard to breathe. The realization had tightened her chest then that there would be no return for her, not to Cape Town.

She told Garrick of that moment, of how South Africa, rife with her beginnings and endings, had always been near.

"It's too late for me," she said.

"It's 1994 now, not 1986." He meant that apartheid, once an iron-clad institution, appeared to be falling like a sandcastle under a tide. Many had returned to South Africa, released from a different imprisonment than Mandela's but no less ecstatic as the country stood on the brink of democracy. But their joy was not Yolanda's. How could there be joy when she lay at the mercy of night? Night that could come with the lope of a stranger on the street; the stale smell of sweat caught in the bus. The color of someone's shoes; a certain sudden movement in her direction. A baby sleeping in sacred, newborn stillness, someone else's baby, not hers, never hers. Stitch by stitch, thread by thread, Yolanda's own mind would pick apart whatever she endeavored to put together that day, that hour, the very minute before the light departed.

"I'm an exile," she said. "That's the price I pay."

"Why? Why does it have to stay that way?"

She sat back. She withdrew behind the truths she hadn't yet shared with him, including her decision that June night: that she could not return without drawing the fire toward her. The decision was agony, for there was a child left behind: Ingrid, now almost nineteen. The daughter to whom she was a stranger.

Yolanda had drawn a cloak over much of her South African history, keeping Garrick away from where she was most tender. Theirs was a dance weaving between what was known and what was held back, between the intimacies they had language for and those they didn't, not yet. Even though they were growing closer, she could offer him no more, hadn't the capacity for more.

She half hoped for her mother, Rachel, to come into the kitchen and make everything OK. For her to take over with the kettle, fix dinner, hold her. Yolanda had tried to outrun the reach of her mother's lined brown hands, hands that had once stroked her face as if no one else mattered. Ma's warmth lay on the other side of eighteen long years, and that was far, so far to go.

"I need to take a bath," she said to Garrick, touching his shoulder as she stood up. "I'll see you in the morning." He would see himself out, go back to the farmhouse, and give her space. This was the nature of being two damaged people, softly, softly growing closer, pushing and pulling apart. Yet trying.

Running a bath in the old ball-and-claw, she undressed. Her tears made it hard to see. Rachel, memories of Rachel sprang: learning to knit, making toffee apples, riding third-class on the train alongside the ocean. She recalled her mother's gentle correction that no, Table Mountain did not hide the sun every night.

The yearning to be mothered filled Yolanda with mourning. Death must have brushed her parents in the long years she'd been away, but the prospect had always been abstract and weightless. Now Yolanda feared that it was coming for Rachel.

When she'd burned through the cigarette, she lit another before taking off her underwear. She touched her left hip, where an ornate Celtic tattoo painted the letter *I* in a tangled vine of rich color that extended across her abdomen. That particular tattoo hid her stretch marks and marked her as belonging to the one person she'd long accepted would never know her. After removing old silver jewelry from her wrists, nose, neck, and ears, she sank into the bath with an exhale.

Behind her shut eyes, the Cape pushed forward: frigid ocean and hot sun; the evening cool of the Atlantic; people chuckling, *You can't get lost in Cape Town, hey—the mountain is on one side, the ocean on the other.*

"Oh, but you can," she whispered to herself. "You can."

Her mother's house resurfaced, that refuge before the fall, back when she'd been a fearless girl who painted and didn't give a damn what they said coloured girls couldn't do. *Black women's bodies bear the history of the world,* went the caption on a piece she'd created when she was seventeen. Before Stefan. She'd been proud, thought her art a provocative act of bravery in a time of war.

But here she was now, living in small, separate lodgings in rural Virginia, in a house built on the grounds of old slaves' quarters. Her hand was long since empty of the wedding band she'd worn, which had once bound her through a marriage of convenience to a British passport. Dry for a year, she felt hunger for alcohol come upon her in waves, but she fought to let it pass without taking her under. Her fingers brushed the ropes of scars that lay hidden beneath the inked designs on her wrists.

"Ingrid can't know, Ma. I can't do that to her."

Rote words, spoken to the sound of the soft rain against the nearby Blue Ridge Mountains. Words to stop her falling into the black pit that held all she was running from: the smell of salt on Stefan's skin; the feel on her fingers of the red wax her mother used to polish the footpath at their house. She remembered her confusion when, as a teenager, she'd watched her humiliated father weeping in his bedroom, fired from his job for her brother's political interests. Sadness at the dignity of her mother silently cleaning the homes of white women who scarcely remembered her name.

But as she smoked another cigarette to the stub, Yolanda wept, for what if Rachel's call indeed meant the old woman was dying? What then of Ingrid? Yet to go home meant to dig, to resurrect, to bury. It meant hurt.

"I can't do this." Yolanda clung to those words, but Rachel's presence loomed larger than her conviction. There was more to face on that distant Cape shore, more even than Ingrid.

RACHEL

White haired and wiry, Rachel stood at her gate and squinted into the autumn light of the April evening. The turmeric and cumin of Cape Malay chicken curry hung in the air. The wind carried the saxophonic theme of the soap opera *The Bold and the Beautiful* from the house next door while swirling sand and chip packets on the street. A minibus taxi trailed by, its axle dragging beneath the weight of workers returning home. The evening shadow of Table Mountain's southern flank was already long, clouds hovering above.

Rachel stood holding a letter while watching this ordinary world of her endless days. She took a deep breath. Today was different. Today she was resolute that she would not let this world consume her by lying quietly in the council house behind her and having a good death.

She would not be at the mercy of the church sisters with their deferential hats, baked goods, prayer circles, and floral funeral invitations commending her greatest achievements: being the wife of the late George (*God bless him,* the church sisters would say; *he was such a good man, hey, pity about her*) and being the mother of three (*But the youngest, Yolanda, she died in that car accident,* they'd say; *strange business: not even a funeral*).

Rachel set aside the imaginary chatter. Funerals, weddings, births: life always found a way to move on and had done so throughout the decades she'd spent here on the Cape Flats. This stretch of reclaimed marshland, seeded with Black and Brown lives, sat adjacent to the sparkling peninsular city of Cape Town. In this community Rachel was sometimes respected but always feared. As the wife of a churchgoing man, she'd sat alongside them all, another obedient coloured waiting for the afterlife to vindicate the depredations of apartheid they had endured in this one. But that was over.

"You all think you know me and my family: our beginning, middle, and end," Rachel muttered to herself, flexing her jaw. "But you don't." She opened the gate and headed out onto the sidewalk.

The ending of this story, of Yolanda's, she would salvage for her missing daughter. So much of the rest—the life, the joy that should have been theirs—had burned to a crisp in the fires of apartheid.

"Just when you finish sweeping, you need to start again, hey," Mrs. Abrahams mumbled. Rachel's neighbor hunkered over her broom, moving it purposefully, as if it were the tiller of a storm-battered vessel.

"*Ai ja*, same story every day," Rachel commiserated. She nodded toward the grandchild she spied in their house, engrossed in the soaps on TV, California dreaming. "Why is that child not the one standing here with the broom, Marie? You look tired."

"Teenagers," Mrs. Abrahams said, shaking her head. "I can't even ask her to go to the shops for bread and milk, Rachel, or it's a fight. And you know, her mother is working shifts at the factory, so she's too tired for these children."

Nearly thirty years beside each other, and their houses were virtually the same now: only the very old and the very young were left. Gone, gouged, was the generation in between; the Abrahamses' only child, a son, had been in the wrong taxi at the wrong time. Bullet in the neck, dead at the scene. Just one more barely registered death during the chaos of the mideighties, when serial states of emergency, culminating in a prolonged national one, had roiled the Cape Flats.

They didn't talk anymore, these two old mothers, about how time bent them over more and more, shaping them into shields, despite leaving them with fewer of those they loved to protect. Neither found triumph in the jubilant yellow election posters sporting Mandela's grandfatherly welcome to the democratic promised land. Alongside him stood posters from those vanguards of apartheid: the National Party. Their posters were an angelic blue, bearing the bright symbol of the sun. That make-believe offer on cardboard of the sky for the taking could not erase the history that had driven her daughter away. Yolanda's absence was the poison lurking in the unoccupied rooms of Rachel's house, in the wanderings of her mind.

Rachel held her letter like a weapon against defeat. Against the slow, debilitating creep of both bitterness and the early-stage cancer set loose upon her lymph nodes. She walked onward, her gait as deliberate and slow as the Catholics who had joined the Passion procession the previous Friday. Weariness draped her like a shroud. She couldn't tell which burdened her more: apartheid or the struggle for liberation from it.

Her eyes drifted over her suburb of Steenberg as she took in the crudely drawn world apartheid had built. This was the land of the displaced: coloureds forced into cheek-by-jowl homes. Space within and without was compressed by the politics of a regime that insisted that coloureds needed no more, that their ambitions were no greater, than this. So it continued, the grinding war to live between notions of law and order constructed around gradations of melanin. They were a people for whom freedom was a metered privilege and not a right. Here, the shifting sands of the marshy ground beneath them gave way all too often, sinking many aspirations, the whole of it inherited generation by generation.

Just then, a broad-shouldered block of a man carrying a scuffed backpack and a lunch box held shut with elastic bands greeted Rachel.

"Evening, how is Ma today? It's Friday tomorrow, hey. Now there's something to look forward to."

Rachel nodded at him. She'd known him since he was a boy, knew his family and the family in every house she passed.

"Is Ma better?" he asked carefully. "I heard you weren't feeling well again, Ma, with the headaches, those visions and all." He dropped his voice. "I heard someone say you were speaking in tongues, Ma. We prayed for you." Eyes down, he fiddled with his lunch box. Mad Rachel, psychic Rachel, possessed Rachel. They had called her this and more, but what could they know about the weight of her visions?

He stumbled, words caught in his throat, his mind no doubt stuck on the gossip.

She sighed, letting his apprehension fill the moment. "Ask me what you really want to know." And then, before he could speak again, she said softly, "I didn't see anything this time."

He nodded, then turned away, unable to hide his sadness at the particular absence that haunted him. He yearned for what Rachel had never seen in his future: the child he and his wife couldn't seem to conceive.

Oh, children. You were theirs even when they were merely a prospect, an idea. She thought of George, her late husband, and their delight at their three babies. What a distant time; how naive they had been.

The heart attack that had claimed George a few years before was the last of the seismic events in Rachel's life. But always, when these shocks reverberated through her, she found succor in the earth, earth as she'd known it as a little girl, barefoot in a world away from this one. Without him she felt released to take the steps she was taking now, steps that led back to that world and who she truly was. It was a path through what had sat for so long beneath her husband's rigidity and her pain: rage and guilt.

George had only seen Rachel's stillness when they'd met through a mutual friend. He had mistaken the quiet in her for docility. She had seen only his sincerity and charm, mistaking his confidence for self-awareness. Each had clung to what they'd held dear in the other, despite all evidence they were wrong, for that was the way of the time.

Apartheid's mantra of *separate but equal* was something coloureds inhabited. It was often easier to do what was expected, to keep to that mantra, no matter how it chafed. But George had done so with an agreeability that was as corrosive in their home as the government had been.

Time had snatched away the innocence of youth and the concessions of adulthood; this ordinary world had taken them. There had been so much taking. Always more and more, leaving them all pummeled. They felt like the misshapen debris of an unrelenting regime. But today it would stop. No more yielding to the good book, to George's will, to the patience preached by others.

Soon Rachel was at the corner café, with its Coke advertisement on the wall: a blonde woman with unnaturally straight teeth. Soon she was at the postbox glancing at the address on the letter, which she'd written in the neat cursive style she'd been taught as a teenage domestic cleaner. The white lady whose house she'd worked in when she'd first come to Cape Town had told Rachel she was hired because she was a good country girl, because she didn't have the sullen truculence of coloureds and Blacks from the city. If only that white woman had known how wrong she was about her.

After pausing for a moment, her hand trembling, Rachel dropped the blue letter inside the postbox's red maw. Though only a handful of words, it bore promise, the promise of triumph. But the road to that victory, if it came to pass, would be a jagged-toothed thing.

"Come home," she whispered, resting her head against the red box. The words spun with longing and beckoning magic. Her plea created its own current, a wind that carried her message into the distance.

This was all she had for Yolanda, her daughter: spoken words, written words, words infused with the wild root of magic that Rachel had been fed as a child. They would have to be enough. She turned away, back to the sidewalk. Bristling with emotion, she thought of the man who had blessed and cursed Yolanda with more power than any person should have: Stefan.

Stefan and other whites were an unstoppable force dictating the very nature of South Africa, of her family. But Rachel had sent another message days before, this time to him. It was a simple white postcard. An incendiary piece of ammunition fired over the bow. It bore a portent. Soon, one indomitable force would meet another.

Back in the familiarity of her house, cinnamon drifted from the stove's warmer drawer: the dinner she'd prepared for Ingrid, her grandchild. In this kitchen, Ingrid had held on to the legs of chairs as she'd learned to walk. Here, Rachel had given her droplets of Dutch medicine when she'd teethed, when she'd had colic or a fever. That little girl had baked her first cake here, stolen biscuits and cookies, read her books beneath the kitchen table. Step by step, Ingrid had grown into a young woman who looked so much like Yolanda, her mother. Step by step, she'd become an ever-greater reminder to Rachel of everything taken.

Nowadays, dinner with the young woman was a rare event, and Rachel knew that this evening with her would be their last. "No fights. I just want no fighting, Ingrid, for once," she whispered to herself and sat down to wait.

Her eyes flickered over the photographs of her children in the decades-old display cabinet. Its imbuia wood was polished and gleaming even now, at the end. Mark, her middle child, had the only graduation photo, was the only one whose journey to his own family had been captured in its entirety. Gentle Mark, balancing between the stern maturity of Philip, the eldest, and the impetuosity of Yolanda, the youngest. Mark: the one left behind. Rachel had watched his youth evaporate beneath the burden of being Philip's brother and Yolanda's witness.

Philip was proud. In one photo, he stood upright in a school blazer, feet together, looking directly at the camera. Already a commander ready for battle, weighing the frivolity of photographs against other, graver matters. Her firstborn, he was the first of her children to go into exile, though in truth, he had left them years before.

Philip was a boy born with a straight arrow when it came to what was right and what was wrong, an arrow sharpened by indignity. She had shepherded him as a child through where to ride on the train, which shops to visit, which toilet and tap to use, and how to speak to white people—always *baas* and *madam*, eyes deflected downward. A white man on the street had dropped his umbrella beside them once. "Pick it up, *hotnot*," the man had barked at prepubescent Philip. But the boy stood, arms folded, eyes raised in defiance.

After George bent down and handed the umbrella back to the stranger, his relationship with Philip shifted for good. She saw then that Philip could not be a man in the same vein as his father. Rachel had watched the childhood taken out of him as myriad acts like these had planted seed after seed of rage. His departure underground, then across the border, had seemed inevitable from the start.

Beside her brothers: Yolanda's bright eyes and flair. How to look at her little girl without anguish? Rachel no longer knew. She clenched her hands into fists; she could not beat back time. At least George wasn't here anymore to mute Rachel's grief, to tell her to direct it to his Lord, the same god as that of the men who had driven their daughter away.

Watching the footpath outside, waiting for Ingrid to appear, Rachel knew that by telling her granddaughter the truth, by attempting to bring Yolanda back, she would trigger an irrevocable earthquake in the lives of those she held dearest.

"It is what must be done," she said firmly. "It is all I can do."

Truth was all she had left.

For years she'd been forced to sit in silence as her home had been turned inside out, her things scattered under policemen's boots as they'd harassed her family because of Philip. For years, the memory of the night she had found Yolanda lying on the sidewalk, beaten like a dog, had seared her; the girl had been unable to speak of what she'd lived through. No longer, no longer the cruel silence of that time. "I deserve mercy," Rachel said, clutching a fist to her heart. "I want justice," she cried, her whole body aching for these two things that had been denied to her children. She glanced again at Yolanda's photo. Easter had just been and gone. "You deserve resurrection," she whispered.

She had made up her mind. She would no longer wait. She would be the hand that tipped the scale.

A car door slammed.

Rachel sprang up. Ingrid swept into the house with her untamed hair. Rachel glanced at the young woman's telltale green eyes, which pointed to a secret history this girl didn't know. The whiff of chicken fat was still on her grandchild from her evening shift in a fast-food kitchen.

"Some home cooking at last, just for you," Rachel said.

She extended her arms—a peace offering. Tonight, she did not know if there would be forgiveness, but if nothing else, there would be truth. But as her granddaughter returned her embrace, the old woman felt unease. What was the cost of this truth?

"Pumpkin *bredie*?" Ingrid breathed in the stew's rich scent of mutton and spices and gave a small smile. They moved toward the kitchen, where Ingrid hovered like a stranger before sitting down at the chipped enamel table. She folded her arms, her eyes curious. "I still can't believe you drove to Rondebosch to tell me I must come home for supper this week."

"There's no other way to reach you." Rachel shrugged, disguising her fear with ordinary gestures. "When are you girls getting a phone? Are you still waiting for the post office?"

"We applied, but now we must just wait." Ingrid rested her folded arms on the table and placed her chin on them. It was a gesture so familiar that Rachel picked up her oven mitts and turned to the stove in an effort to busy herself and hide her face. The words she needed to say to her granddaughter sat like lead in her chest. She took out their supper and switched off the old stove.

Bredie on a Thursday, fish on a Friday. When her children were little, Friday-night suppers had been fish—a whole *snoek*. George would buy it from the fishermen parked at a nearby intersection, sea bounty spilling from the chassis of vans encased in rust and salt. Mark, Philip, and Yolanda would elbow each other out of the way to help their father brush off the scales. Gingerly, they would touch the fish's eyes and try to scare each other with its head. They were so little.

"Who's that girl you staying with?" Rachel asked Ingrid, spooning steaming rice and stew onto their plates.

"Monica, remember?" Ingrid sounded exasperated. "The one from Mauritius."

"Do you like living away from us?"

"Yes. I like it better than when I was here," Ingrid replied, tying her hair back and jutting her chin as if to make her words more pointed. Her granddaughter's green eyes flickered fiercely.

"There was the unrest, Ingrid," Rachel said quietly. "There was Philip and the police. So many things." Year in, year out, they'd tried to protect this girl from the violence always waiting at the gate.

"Ma, my mother is dead. With the way Pa stopped me from having my freedom, I felt like he put me in the casket with her."

They had come to it.

It was the moment for Rachel to say that they had all been mistaken about Yolanda and Ingrid had been misled. Rachel looked at the storm that was her grandchild. Ingrid wore a white man's image on her T-shirt—who was this Lou Reed, anyway? She had a pierced nose and wore torn jeans and expensive black boots that went halfway up her calves.

But she was here. They were eating dinner together for the last time, and Rachel was so tired. Now, on the last night she was to spend in this house and this life, she wanted this to be a good memory for them both, the last one. Tomorrow and all the days to follow would bring the truth. Her nerve, her will to reveal, failed her.

17

Ingrid was already so angry. What if she never forgave Rachel for the lie of Yolanda? Rachel couldn't let that be her legacy, couldn't allow this to be the memory she gave her granddaughter on this, their last supper.

"It would have helped, Ma," Ingrid said. "If he'd just let me try to be normal. I just wanted a normal family."

"I'm sorry," Rachel said, barely above a whisper. And she was. She squeezed Ingrid's hand and looked at her fresh face. Skin and hair, she thought, the stuff of schoolyard taunts and jealousies, of a little girl who'd frequently been told she looked too white, that she didn't belong amid the cohort of coloureds in their neighborhood. A little girl who'd faced the excruciating bloom of self-consciousness most days. Her grandparents had been so caught up in their losses that they couldn't help her navigate it. Rachel wiped away tears. Ruin, and the kind of pain that battered every day, came all because of skin and hair.

"Uncle Mark and them are back on . . . is it Saturday or Sunday?" Ingrid said, saddening Rachel. This was the pattern learned at George's table: avoid the raw that might tear you apart; talk about something else.

"They're driving up from Sedgefield Saturday, or maybe tomorrow already. I'm sure Tracy wants the weekend to get their stuff unpacked." Rachel watched the realization set in on Ingrid's face: what she'd once known about the family simply by virtue of being in the house was now news about people who were becoming strangers, people making plans she was no longer a part of.

Ingrid took a second helping that she polished off almost as quickly as she had the first. Rachel took small bites, fighting her knotted stomach. She coughed. It was the lingering, hacking cough she now knew was a marker of the cancer that had rooted itself in her body. But she brushed off the querying gaze from Ingrid and this reminder of her mortality. All that Rachel saw before her was that it would never be like this again.

She prolonged the evening, taking out the gas stove to make Horlicks, serving the chocolate-peanut clusters she'd bought especially for Ingrid. Anything to make it last, anything to sweeten the bitter end.

Eventually Ingrid sighed, her belly full. The child was oblivious to what was to come. Rachel looked away.

She had done all she had the strength to. There would be no more dinners between her and her granddaughter. The end of their evening arrived, followed by a hurried kiss, a hug held that bit longer, and then the girl hurried down the same red pathway where Yolanda's feet had come and gone so many times. It was a ragged goodbye. It would have to be enough.

Rachel listened to Ingrid's car whine as it started, then to the night sounds sweeping the street: keening stray dogs, old motors, loud voices mixing English and Afrikaans in slang. The long accumulation of tiny, violent goodbyes had come to this.

All her life Rachel had stood on guard, protecting her children, but none more so than Ingrid: the very product of forces beyond her control. Rachel had been Ingrid's only shield against George's dismissal of a girl born of origins that no one dared speak of. She had protected the girl from the acrid taste and smell of tear gas, the fury of *toyi-toying* marchers now and then as she'd taken the child to and from school. Rachel had even stood guard against the white men who, on occasion, had walked into their house. They'd smoked inside. They'd told Rachel and George that they would find Philip, their terrorist son, that it was inevitable. Rachel had clutched her terrified granddaughter while those white men had strolled through their narrow house like they owned it. Their pale hands had touched everything.

Rachel had let Ingrid down, but she didn't know any other way to be with the girl. It had been her job to keep the child safe, safer than she had Yolanda. Still that hadn't been enough. Rachel's job wasn't over, but she knew what Ingrid needed was to be let go of. A long night waited.

She had told no one of her cancer, told no one that she would not see another dawn in this house. The soft sound of her crying pierced this cruel silence, but the moment passed. She stepped up to draw the curtains and looked out at the slight crescent of the moon, a small beacon in the immense dark.

Knowing that its light fell upon Stefan, too, Rachel's eyes narrowed and hardened.

STEFAN

Stefan jolted out of sleep. A flash had just passed through him, one vivid enough to wake him. Of a movement so natural it had once been muscle memory. Paddling atop the ocean's swell at the back line, having studied the sets. Then the anticipation of the wave's break, positioning for the takeoff. Exhilaration, release, control, submission. All of this encompassed in the single smooth, unconscious movement of popping up on his surfboard. There, in the distance: Noordhoek's bone-white beach laid bare. Here, surrounding him: a wall of green water.

But more woke him than that startling feeling. Stefan sat up and peered into the corners of his bedroom. He felt like he had been watched and knew in an unsettling way by whom: an old woman, *doek* tied loosely on her head. Yolanda's mother, yes, the mother who had once read him cover to cover in a handful of minutes.

"Stef?" His wife, Katrina, moved beside him. "What's wrong?"

He put the light on and found nothing, of course. But still, it felt like the mother had been there, watching like a sentry.

"The children." Katrina sprang up. He placed a hand on her arm, gently, to calm them both.

"It's nothing."

"Did you hear something?"

"No, just had a bad dream." He pressed the heels of his hands against his eyes.

"*Ag*, is it Bram with his grandstanding tonight?" Katrina sighed as she settled back under the covers. "The Blacks aren't coming to kill us. He's just putting everyone on edge."

"It's not your brother or his drama."

Stefan switched off the light and turned his back to his wife. But there was no rest to be had.

Instead, he glared into the dark, troubled. Yolanda's mother? How was that possible? Memories were surging; his mind was letting in questions he would rather not ask. What did one call a surfer who had moved to a landlocked town? Which was the aberration: the suburban father who lay here beside his respectable wife, or the man he had once been, captured by the surges of the ocean, adrift from the sterile world he'd been born into, with its hard lines and inescapable boundaries?

Yolanda sat there, too, on the other end of his discontent. The memory of her intertwined with salt water, with surf, with a life he had once measured in seasons, waiting for winter's storms. Eager for the northwester or southeaster, meticulously fixing dings on his board. Breaking the law with an illegal love affair. Betraying his identity as an Afrikaner.

He tried in vain to push memories of her away, but they lingered, one especially: Yolanda lying on her stomach, with the sweep of her naked brown back exposed. Her face turned to him, chin tilted up, as if waiting for a kiss. She had fallen into a deep sleep, and he'd been unable to take his eyes off her. They had just made love. It was a hot summer's night, and they had been reckless, leaving open the ocean-facing window of his Muizenberg apartment. Eventually he had dozed off beside her, lulled to sleep by the waters rushing to the shore, receding, rushing again. It had been a moment of peace, a moment in which he'd felt complete.

Now, he braced himself as Katrina buried her small feet beneath his, bringing him back to the present. He kept his back to his wife. Shame left him unresponsive.

It had been almost twenty years, but Yolanda was still his secret to keep: the warmth and softness of her, the sharp curiosity and confident ease. It was easy to think of her as a luminous, delicate being, a butterfly in the palm of his white hand. But on that Muizenberg night when he had lain beside her, a woman so starkly different from the one he would eventually marry, he had surrendered himself. He'd been hers entirely.

In 1972, he had returned from the army and bypassed both the waiting arms of his mother and the upward mobility and steady job offered by his father. A civilian again, he left the net of obligations that lay in wait for him at his parents' home and went to live on the other side of Cape Town: Muizenberg, where the waves brought him the quiet that South Africa's slowly escalating border war had taken away. This was a few weeks before he met Yolanda.

He moved into a small apartment rented from an elderly Jewish couple, who regarded his goods with disdain: a pair of large duffels, the longboard he'd had since before the army, and a new, shorter single-fin board he was determined to master. He had been hooked since he was ten years old, since cousins had taken him out at Big Bay a few times and the fear and the draw of the water's immensity and power had settled in him like a barb.

Here now in Muizenberg, in line with Cape Town's segregated spaces, it was whites, most of them English or Jewish, who lived along this bay. The rent was cheaper than at nearby Danger Beach, where he intended to spend his time, and it was easy to get into the city.

Some locals in the lineups became standoffish once they heard his Afrikaans accent. But Stefan didn't care what they called him. He knew how to fight, and the English, those *soutpiele* with their red necks and cricket, looking always north to the mothership of Britain, were nothing. Besides, it felt as if he had gone through the veil at the Caprivi Strip, the deadly stretch of land to the north where he'd served his conscription. He understood how the mere act of being an Afrikaner was an act of dominance. But it was possible to be inside the gilded cage and see it for the prison it was. He'd done so.

Muizenberg's cove was fairly mild, so he appeared before dawn day after day at other beaches around the peninsula, following progressively bigger waves. Eventually he was simply part of the surf community. His passion matched everyone else's: studying the wave patterns and wind; riding an ocean that was indifferent to the segregated beaches at its feet.

Yet even as he earned some money of his own as a handyman, making little use of his engineering degree, he knew that the life he'd fled would never truly release him. His father was giving him some leeway after conscription, but Elsa, his mother, took exception to what she contemptuously termed his "lifestyle." She made no effort at acceptance, which did not surprise him. She insisted instead that he return home whenever she summoned him.

He would have to go back permanently at some point. Initially, that knowledge was a nuisance. After he met Yolanda, it became a grave matter.

In her, he found a complex woman, impatient with the social order of the day, a woman who could conjure magic with a pencil and paper. She would not be taken lightly or easily. He remembered her chewing her pencil tip, looking at him with a crooked eyebrow. Yolanda had little tolerance for the social hierarchy that defined their lives. One morning he returned from an early surf to find her awake in his bed. "This is you," she said, showing him the sketch pad. She had drawn an image of him on the shore, looking out at another rendition of himself on the waves. The expression on each face was that of a man unsettled. "The golden boy who can't make peace with his crown."

Instantly, he felt self-conscious of his blond hair, his blue eyes. "Is that who I am to you?"

"No, but I think that's who you are to yourself. For you the weight is what comes with the pull upward, higher, into the atmosphere, where you can rule. For me the weight is gravity, the push down, into the dirt, where us coloureds and Blacks must grovel. I'm not supposed to dream."

He paused then, looking at her and loving, again, the lucidity with which she saw the world. She had a quality to her, a way of being outside everything he'd known and looking in on it, sparing nothing. "Neither am I, Yolanda, not dreams that take me away from who I'm supposed to be."

"Stefan, it's not the same. You can roam, wherever, however you want. I can't. I'm not allowed here, on this beach outside, without a fine. We can't be real with each other, we can't be true, if we don't acknowledge this."

"Acknowledge how this mess of a country defines us? By laws that don't make sense? Yolanda, look at what you just drew, what you can see. How I see you. This is the truth; being with you is the only truth." He meant it then, knew instinctively that the heresy lay outside their door, not in their bed.

Yolanda often asked him hard questions—questions he'd never considered, but still, she demanded answers. No one had ever asked so much of him, because no one had ever considered him capable of more. But Yolanda did. She gave him books he could have been arrested for. She demanded that he see, through her lens, the theater of violence that was apartheid.

"I don't want your guilt," she said one night. They were camping at a remote bay, isolated and alone. "I want you, but I want you whole, and you can't be whole without being honest." Then she leaned over and drew him to her. "Neither can I." With every kiss that she gave then, with every touch, she made it clear that his desire for her was matched by hers for him. The pressures of conformity dogged her too. She told him about the nice man who lived two streets from her home, whom her father wanted her to marry.

"We know the family. They go to my father's church," she said. "He wants me to settle down, have children. It's time now, he says, as if art and studying are just hobbies to pass the time. I swear, I'll be stuck in the kitchen, the nursery, or the missionary position for the rest of my life if I marry him." It angered Stefan to think of anyone else pursuing her, but what was he to do? What was he to say?

The months of their togetherness stretched into years. Then, abruptly, Yolanda was gone, at the cusp of the moment when she'd told him he might be facing fatherhood. And in that same month, call-up papers came for him. He was sent back to the army inexplicably for six months, not the usual three. Just like that, everything was gone, erased. Muizenberg, with its twin sirens of the ocean and his girlfriend, evaporated.

When he returned from that terrifying military stint, he was numb. But Katrina swept into the void; she was wholesome, she was safe, and she drew him inland to the Orange Free State, a long way from the shore. Married life with her leveled into a routine that everyone seemed to take comfort in: work, family, shopping, trips to Natal and the Drakensberg, Saturday *braais*, Sunday church, lunch and tea with the in-laws, repeat, repeat.

He didn't want to know anymore what his life or country was built upon. Because if that didn't matter, then Yolanda wouldn't matter.

The faint moonlight retreated from his and Katrina's room. The darkness pressed forward. Jaw clenched, he remembered the way his brother-in-law had spoken that night at dinner on Katrina's parents' farm. Bram resembled an ox in every way, from his build to his stubbornness. Stefan thought him too rash. He'd fired and evicted farmworkers with no notice, citing petty theft without proof. The laborers, families in tow, had had nowhere else to go. It would come back to bite him, Stefan was sure.

"I want to clean house before this election," Bram had railed. "These *kaffirs*, they must know who's boss." Bram was always putting blind emotion ahead of pragmatism. But Stefan, who endured reminders that he was an import from the Cape, a place where the law was too soft on the Blacks and coloureds in Bram's view, was never consulted on these matters.

Unable to sleep, Stefan finally got up for a drink of water. In the blaze of kitchen light, away from his wife, his mind wandered again to that night in Muizenberg, a rare one when Yolanda had stayed over. They had to be careful. Most of the time, she had to be out well before dawn, to avoid peering eyes that might alert the police. They were in the habit of exiting the apartment block separately, with a long interval between them.

She only lived fifteen minutes away, but still, as an extra precaution, Yolanda would lie down on the back seat of his car as he drove her home. He had driven through her neighborhood alone a few times, fired by the same curiosity that had led him to meet her in the first place. On those occasions he was careful to tuck his blond hair beneath a cap and wear sunglasses so that he would not stand out. He had no place here. A white man in the township meant trouble.

He remembered driving alone between the plain council houses with their sidewalks of loose sand, the government-built apartments that stood like prison blocks, children playing beneath the endless flap of clothes on the line. He observed what he could of her world at those times, his heart beating as he tried to understand this place where he was the enemy.

Every now and then, he would drive past Yolanda's house. Once, an older woman, her mother, was standing at the gate. She watched him drive by. Her stare unnerved him. He slowed and noticed that her gaze was one of recognition. She could not have known he would be there at that moment, but he nodded a greeting to her nonetheless, accepting that he was too unwieldy a secret for Yolanda to carry alone. Her family knew about their relationship, but it was obvious that his never could. It had frightened Stefan to think of what Elsa would do if she ever found out.

Standing in the kitchen, pouring water from the jug in the fridge, he shuddered to think of the gaze from Yolanda's mother once more: how piercing it was, how it had crossed time and been so present in his mind tonight. He hadn't seen Yolanda on the drive that day. She'd been at her shift at a café in Muizenberg, where men of all shades and stripes would openly flirt with her.

He'd hated going there unless he had to, hated watching his girl-friend being spoken to like she was loose because she was coloured. His powerlessness to dissuade that treatment without calling attention made him retreat to the surf or to his apartment. Burdened, he'd wonder if he was no better than those men. After her shift, all he could do was hold her, settle her down, love her, and let her bitterness at what she had to endure flow. She was determined, though, to earn her own money. "Art supplies don't cost nothing," she said.

Neither Stefan nor Yolanda could ever publicly claim the other. He was careful with friends who invited him on road trips to Jeffreys Bay and Durban, ones who expected him to party with them, with girls. Who knew what? Who could know? This was the weight he bore. Yolanda, too, was often away on weekend trips and braais with family, with those from the church and her community. She was a beautiful woman, beautiful to him, and unattached as far as most people knew. She weighed the same questions. Fits of jealousy between them brought home the fact that the heresy, the power imbalance outside their door, had insidiously made its way inside, into their bed, lingering between them. This was as devastating as the ever-present fear of being discovered.

But that had been long ago. As he stood here in his kitchen, the woman he'd actually married fast asleep, old memories took on new meanings.

He thought of Yolanda lying down on the back seat of his car, headed home. Katrina would never, could never, have done that. He used to think that it was a simple kind gesture to drive her back. Now he wondered how much she had loved him to travel in that way, to take that risk, to be dropped at a station, a street corner, and walk home like he had been a job. How hadn't he considered that before? As he gripped the back of a chair, he realized that the shame that still sat upon him had to be nothing compared with hers.

They'd imagined running away to another country where they could walk down the street together, where they could exist inside the law, maybe one day marry. There were parts of Cape Town where they might have been able to stay under the radar, but his family would never have permitted it, and the law would have been an ever-present threat. Neither he nor Yolanda could conceive of leaving the country. No matter how complicated, South Africa was their home; its shared history bound them.

At difficult times, they vowed to end it, but they were cursed by proximity. Her café was near where he lived. He couldn't stop himself from going to see her, each time promising only to look. Yet with a glance from behind the loaves of bread and sandwiches, they'd found each other again and again, hands touching as she'd come from the kitchen to give him his lunch, him rolling up a handwritten message, brushing her fingers.

Maybe now Yolanda sat in a kitchen somewhere in similar circumstances, contemplating him. The thought filled him with dread and sadness.

Stefan put off the kitchen light and returned to bed. He rested his hands on his stomach, softer now, so different from the defined obliques he'd had as a young man straddling a surfboard, running from the shore.

The curse of thinning hair had passed him by, but something worse than age had drained the vitality, the youth, that once had been his. He shut his eyes. He didn't want to look too closely. He was safe here, with three children he would protect at all costs, in a conservative town in the gold-and-tan heart of the country. Safe from the lure of the ocean. Where had Yolanda gone? It didn't matter. Whatever he'd been seeking once, it was lost to the past.

RACHEL

Once upon a time, Stefan's actions had triggered irrevocable change for her family. Now, the truth of that time would come like a tide and carry them all, including him, beyond the lie. Rachel intuited that this was the road ahead and smiled, satisfied. It was time, time to begin.

She put bottled water and several brown bread sandwiches in an old backpack. From her wardrobe she gathered her old leather hiking boots and one of George's old windbreakers. She took out a brittle leather necklace of beads and shells from a small, worn pouch. As a little girl, she'd worn it while clutching at the skirts of her mother. Rachel and her siblings had lived with that defiant pagan woman in the heart of the Great Karoo, the dry thirstland of fynbos and the scrub that formed the very center of South Africa.

That was her country, not the meager land their council house occupied. The moment was here for her return to it. More than a return to a place, it was a return to the old ways. This was the reckoning road, and tonight, she would begin her last pilgrimage. If she didn't leave now, the cancer, still in its early stages, guaranteed that she never would.

She picked up a large bag from where it sat on her bed. She'd considered giving it to Ingrid at dinner. Out of the bag she lifted a thin, lined book of the sort used in school. A few pages in the front showed careful, separated letters of the alphabet written in cursive. Pages at the back contained sketches of children, classmates from a different time.

Here was Yolanda in her fullness, Rachel thought: grappling with the imposition of structures and duty, words written neatly within lines. But underneath there was always the wild undertow. Always the art.

Rachel left the bag on the bed in the lemon-colored room that had belonged to her girls: first Yolanda, then Ingrid. She placed an old photo beside it, a picture of the dog they'd had when her own children were little. She didn't know who would find these things first, but she hoped they would know what to make of them.

The scent of herbs filled the kitchen as she packed her old pipe and lit it. She had prepared over many days now with the sacred root, consuming every morning, then purging. Clearing her body and letting go, to make room for what was to come. Rachel drew deeply from her pipe, where herbs, including the flowers of wild *dagga*, now burned. She sat in the yard until a feeling of both calm and expansiveness overcame her. This was the last signal to her spirit body that she was ready.

Rachel took off her shoes, then stood beneath the mulberry tree that had grown larger over the years. Yolanda had loved to sit beneath it and draw, the purple juice from berries she'd gorged on staining her face and hands. Rachel drew deeply from the pipe until she felt elongated and envisioned her bones extending into the soil like roots. She had journeyed so often before, but it was becoming different: now that she was dying, she was growing limitless.

But this Rachel remembered, this ability to see farther and deeper than she could otherwise. It was an act of reclamation. It raised her. She smoked, drew deep and exhaled. She repeated a small prayer of honor, seeking grace. Then she sent a different call out on the wind and waited. Breaths passed. Time bent. Then a speck in the sky made her smile. The eagle owl.

The large bird made tight circles in the air until it finally settled on an upper branch of the mulberry tree. It gazed at her. She at it. After another exhale of the wild herb, there was a slight shift, an exchanged nocturnal gaze. Rachel's being settled into the small body, expanding into its borrowed wings. Her own physical body sank against the tree's base as the rest of her became airborne. She became the bird in flight, soaring, swallowed by the night sky.

Now the eagle owl, Rachel veered north, bending and sailing on currents beyond human reckoning, until they reached an unnamed place at the mercy of the Atlantic. A fogbank crept across a vast landscape of quiver trees—their branches growing thick like upside-down roots. A shepherd's tree flowed over and between rocks, its roots and trunk spilling like an arboreal liquid. The fog, that misty product of the currents off South Africa's western shore, swept across pebble fields of jagged quartzitic rock and spanned miles of brown, washed-out bush country and dry riverbeds. Its mist touched a scattering of halfmens trees facing north, each with a branch bent upward—an arm raised in greeting.

Borrowing the bird's sight, Rachel kept seeking, calling. There. The leopard sat on his perch to the east of the arid plain. He tilted his head, observing the desert night below: the pack of black-backed jackals; the distant bark of the hyena. The slightly obscured stars failed to illuminate the dark rosettes that marked him, a tattoo of identity embedded in feline skin. Yet there was no doubt it was him.

The leopard looked up. He had seen the owl, and he watched her land with precision in a nearby tree. Fog and moon formed a daguerreotype of light and shadow, with Rachel attuned to every movement, every element now. She and the leopard looked at each other in an extended moment of exchange. All the elements—the owl, the hoots that relayed what she was asking for, the onward roll of life-giving mist, the entire symphony of this moment upon this land—came together. Rachel watched it stir the leopard. He sat back on his muscled haunches and curled his tail around his body.

Rachel held her faith steady. She needed his help, again. She needed a guide to take her where she was going. Time and again this had been the case through ancient cycles that adhered to their own course, beyond the end of lines and languages.

He looked to the east. Rachel followed his gaze. The contours of the land led to a small, distant town and the home of an ordinary man unable to find peace on this night. While her journey would end there, Stefan's would only be beginning. He would have to reckon with the scales falling from his eyes, eyes that had seen none of the damage he'd left in his wake.

The leopard bowed his head in acknowledgment before descending, elusive, lost to the desert night. The eagle owl whose body Rachel had possessed began to stir. It took wing, bringing her back. Eventually Rachel returned to consciousness in the body she'd left slumped against the earth, hidden by the tree. The grass was damp against her cheek. Her pipe had gone cold.

There was nothing left to do now but leave. She gathered her things and closed the door to the person she had been. The imposing bulk of distant Table Mountain, the wind soughing down the sand-strewed streets—she would never know them again.

The car door creaked shut; she clutched the old leather steering wheel. She started the car and pulled away into the night, leaving the Cape behind. All that she had now was the road ahead. But for once, it was a road of her choosing.

ELSA

To her irritation, autumn's coolness and the pending winter were beginning to claim petals from her proud stand of rosebushes. Setting that distracting thought aside, Elsa van Deventer shut her Bible after quietly reciting the last words of an Old Testament passage. Although her son, Stefan, and her daughter, Amanda, had long since moved on to their own lives, Elsa still rose promptly at six to pray, then plan her days.

Pushing her gray hair back behind her ear, she sipped her rooibos tea and sat back. Drawing over her shoulders the merino-wool wrap that she liked to wear out here on the back patio, Elsa closed her eyes and took a moment to enjoy the guidance that the word of the Lord gave her. It was her constant, this breakfast of humility and comfort, of inviolable principle. Even today, she thought, this glorious Friday morning with its wisps of clouds and the evening that would culminate in the social froth of a dinner party, all of it belonged to Him.

But mundane matters were at hand. Elsa picked up a bunch of mail she'd had no time for the previous day: a scattering of account statements, a pair of fundraiser invitations. Then she turned her attention to her lists, reviewing them to make sure she'd missed nothing. Occasions like tonight's required meticulous finishing touches. It was a company dinner, and guests from her husband's C-suite would be present. There were social gains to be made, and for Elsa, that meant the stakes were high.

Betty—where was this blessed maid? Elsa had told her to come early today; the bathrooms and windows were waiting. She gathered her things and headed inside, the low heels of her slippers click-clacking on the parquet floor. Elsa headed to the kitchen to make more tea. She inspected the living room that Betty had dusted, polished, and cleaned the day before. The maid handled everything except the brass and silver. Elsa never did trust her with those things; she'd pulled on an apron and buffed them herself. Her airy home of exposed wooden beams, restored Cape Dutch furniture, and clean spartan lines was spotless. It was ready for Danie's return from his business trip and their evening visitors.

And yet.

Elsa set her jaw. The country was changing beneath her feet. It was a reality that was difficult to ignore, and so tonight would have another purpose too. She took seriously her duty as hostess to ease her guests' minds away from the threat of the incoming Black government, to distract them from the pervasive malaise and anarchy that this unpredictable time brought in its wake.

A little while later, the intercom's buzz echoed through the house. At last. Elsa released the outside gate and tied her bathrobe, gathering herself to begin giving instruction.

"Good morning, madam," Betty said, the two of them exchanging pleasantries as Betty shuffled into the house, her skin rich with the scent of Pond's moisturizer and woodsmoke. "It's the smell of the Blacks," Elsa used to say to her friends in quiet tones of distaste.

On her first day of employment, Elsa had dismissed her maid's real name, Buhle, as an unpronounceable encumbrance. She'd settled instead on Betty, which she thought suited her.

Elsa clapped her hands together lightly and began to rattle off activities from her list.

"Clean the downstairs bathroom first. Mr. Van Deventer will be back from Joburg after lunch, so lay out his clothes nicely after you make the beds and do my bathroom; I'm going to shower now. Oh, and Mrs. Johanna is coming later on to help with the flowers and the caterers. I'm doing the meat, but the caterers will do the rest. They don't know how to roast shanks properly, those people. And once you've had your sandwich, I'll have my tea upstairs."

As Elsa ascended the curved staircase, she watched Betty's labored shuffle to the laundry to change into her kitchen overalls and take out her labeled mug, plate, and cutlery from the corner cupboard. Betty was struggling with diabetes, and her feet were showing the strain. Elsa wondered what more she could do to help her. It was her Christian duty to take care of the people she employed.

Betty brought in her tea after she'd showered. They both ignored her state of half undress, their relationship long since molded around intransigent boundaries.

"Madam, you dropped something on the back patio, a postcard. I put it downstairs. It is addressed to *kleinbaas*."

"Stefan?" Elsa said, curious.

"Yes, madam, it is one of those plain white Lion postcards."

"That's strange." Elsa frowned. Stefan had moved to a different province after he'd married around fifteen years ago.

"I left it in the foyer for you."

Elsa gave a curt nod, dismissing Betty. Maybe it was an old school friend, someone who didn't know he was in Harrismith. Surely there was a simple explanation.

Soon after, she swooped downstairs, one eye on the clock, the other on her lists. Elsa found the card. It unsettled her immediately. She called her son, reaching him at work. He ran a business selling and repairing farm equipment.

"Stefan, something very odd came here for you. A card, a white postcard, and all it says on the back is *She is coming to look for you.* No one signed it, no return address. And I don't know the handwriting."

Though Stefan was usually preoccupied with his business or family, Elsa heard him stop and give her all his attention. "*She is coming to look for you?* That's all it says?"

"Yes. What does it mean? Who still thinks you live at this address?"

It wasn't so much that he grew silent; it was how. The intake of breath, the moment pregnant with something. Then came the rambling chatter, the poorly disguised discomposure. Elsa knew instantly. The knowledge came with a prickling sensation. The dance around her son was going to have to resume.

After they hung up, Elsa attempted to return to her day and the list of chores ahead. Midmorning, her close friend Johanna arrived. They looked over Elsa's extensive wine cabinet situated behind her husband's bar, picking what would work best with springbok and selecting more bottles from the newly installed cellar. Checking on the marinating meat, they gossiped about mutual friends.

But Elsa's gaze kept returning to the mantelpiece photo of Stefan, his wife, and their children. With tight control, she continued discussing the fig carpaccio and desserts she'd ordered, then directed Betty to get the patio ready so that they could complete the flower arrangements outside—another thing she'd wanted to do herself. All the while the postcard waited for her upstairs, the weight of it threatening her controlled state.

Eventually Elsa settled Johanna with tea before stepping away to her bedroom for a moment. She read the postcard's few words again. She wanted to believe that her gut was wrong, but she knew what it meant with cold certainty. This was a hunt. Which meant she needed a hunter.

She made another call, this time from her bedroom. It was to her brother. He had one of those huge new cell phones. This was urgent enough to try him on it.

"Pieter?"

"El? I'm seeing you a little later, aren't I?"

"Something came to the house today, a postcard."

"OK. And?"

"We need to talk at the party, in private. It's important." She hung up. Pieter would know what to do this time. He had known before.

Elsa caught her own eyes in the bedroom mirror as she tidied her hair. When she was much younger, a rival of hers competing for Danie's interest had said that Elsa's blue-green eyes made her think of a shark. Elsa brushed that thought aside, but the thought of Danie made her pause. Her marriage reminded her of what was at play.

The three women proceeded with the day's work, moving between the kitchen, the outdoor patio, and the dining room; getting the springbok shanks ready for a long, slow roast. As the dappled light of afternoon fell, Danie came home. Since he was a man accustomed to being waited upon, Elsa had Betty prepare his tea and a small snack before directing the maid to set the dining room table. Elsa relished the opportunity to make their world seem normal, unaffected. Danie retreated to refresh and take a short nap.

Elsa sat on the patio with Johanna, and they chatted further while building the single centerpiece bouquet.

"I believe she's divorced—can you imagine?" Elsa wrinkled her nose. "Danie insisted that I invite her, says she's their new sales VP; we can't ignore her."

"Divorced? Well, I suppose that isn't a surprise," Johanna said, her mouth curved downward. "She moved from Joburg, after all, isn't it?"

"Yes, and it's obvious. She runs around with hair as red as my hyacinths; she smokes; heaven knows what else. She was such a spectacle at the company bike race, I'm telling you. Laughing out loud for absolutely everything." The clip-clip of scissors trimming stems filled the pause. "But they say this is the new South Africa, hey. Women like *that*, and Blacks in charge."

"They can call it whatever they want," Johanna said. "It's bad form for a woman to carry on like a man. And if I hear this 'rainbow nation,' 'new South Africa' nonsense one more time . . . there was nothing wrong with the old."

Elsa nodded in agreement, adjusting blue agapanthus and tulips. It was a relief to speak truthfully with a like-minded friend. "Now they want to put the communists and murderers in Parliament with their feet on the table," Elsa said. "You can't just pick these people out of the bush and put them in suits."

"Exactly, remember that Boipatong business? They attacked each other, the women and children even. Never thought in my life that people could fall on each other like animals." Johanna shook her head before saying, "I feel for the women; they always suffer."

"Well, is it any surprise? Look how they carry on. This is how they've always been, Johanna—we just kept them in check all these years."

Elsa called to Betty, instructing her to begin cleaning up the patio area. Elsa hated a mess.

"What an awful episode," Johanna said. "But did they learn?"

"Not at all. They talk about Mandela as if he's Christ himself, as if the man can walk on water. But what is he?"

"A communist, an atheist, and a convict," Johanna offered.

"Exactly, and on top of everything I read he might divorce for the second time." Elsa sighed. "What could anyone expect."

"We've gone from our men like Verwoerd all the way to him. I'm just glad my parents aren't alive to witness this." Bringing Mandela into the seat of government as the country's leader would be the final act of this tragedy.

Elsa thought of her late father; the upcoming election would have left him aggrieved. He used to wear the same boxy black jacket to the Ned Geref's Protestant service every Sunday. The jacket was shiny at the elbows and warped at the collar, but he was fastidious about keeping it clean for church. Her family sat toward the back, removed from the majesty of the organ and the preacher's box, embarrassed by their poverty. But even so, her father would never have tolerated taking orders from a Black man.

Late afternoon drew in and brought the caterers. Betty left, bearing plastic bags with yesterday's leftovers and a few treats for her family, along with liniments from Elsa for her ailing feet. Johanna departed soon after, and Elsa prepared herself and Danie for the evening. Soon, they began to welcome guests, and she attended to them warmly, disguising the fear that had knotted her belly all day. Where was Pieter?

When he arrived, she tried to hide her relief. Her twin brother had the sensible clothing and unfashionable haircut of a bureaucrat. Yet he possessed the presence of one accustomed to authority. He looked like the person he was: a government man, single, childless, wedded to a world of secrets and backroom dealings that was coming apart around him. The Blacks had penetrated the very halls he used to stride, and Elsa could tell that the changes had worn on him. He was thinner, as if political pressures had wrung him out and squeezed him into a more condensed package.

They spoke, and she knew he'd noticed her discomfort, yet he handled the evening as discreetly as she did. Pleasantries and meat falling off the bone; the flow of a well-aged cabernet brought by a friend who owned a vineyard; the burgundy of pinot noir—these things relaxed everyone except her. Once her guests had scattered across the living room and bar area to be entertained by Danie, she said to Pieter, "Let me show you the new tiles in the upstairs bathroom."

They strolled up, chatting until she was certain no one was around. Then, retreating into her bedroom, Elsa handed over the postcard.

"What is this?" Pieter frowned.

Impatience overcame her. Elsa took the card back, hiding it.

"That business with Stefan and the police. You remember," she whispered angrily. She had no time for games.

"Hey?"

She couldn't say the words, just left a blank silence for him to fill. Recognition overtook him, and he chuckled. "You can't be serious, Elsa. You think this 'she' is that girl? You're mad. That was twenty years ago; it's long gone. You're imagining things."

"And if I'm not?"

Her brother looked at her squarely. "How sure are you that this isn't some other 'she'? Maybe Danie . . ."

Her stare cut him short. "I know my husband, and he doesn't have my son's flaws. Danie would never—how dare you say that?"

"I'm just asking. Calm down."

Pieter was doing the logical computation that made him good at his job, but Elsa loathed the dirty tracks down which he often went.

"That woman," he continued. "If she's still alive, she wouldn't dare. You got a postcard, no phone calls? Nothing else?"

"Nothing else."

"Then you're just making an assumption now." Elsa's gaze remained fixed and hard. Finally Pieter sighed. "What do you want me to do?"

"I want to know if that little coloured slut is alive."

Rage that she'd laid to rest a long time ago roused inside Elsa. Stefan had a family now, three of her grandchildren. "I want to know where she eats, sleeps, everything. I want her to stay away from my son. Do you still know people who can help?"

"Of course, but technically, you don't have the law on your side anymore, do you understand? And Elsa, she has nothing to gain."

"We still have everything to lose. Send me someone who can look for her." Her words were deliberate and cool. She set her jaw, exiting the room without another word. Composed as always, Pieter followed.

They paused on the landing, and Elsa looked proudly at the restored wagon wheel displayed above the sunken lounge. It was a souvenir of the 1938 centenary of the Great Trek, a symbolic repetition of the mighty Afrikaner journey inland from the Cape in the 1800s. Like the original trek, the centenary marked the resilience of their people: Afrikaners courageous enough to face the unknown of this dark continent and turn their backs on the duplicitous English.

Elsa remembered watching the centenary's marchers, remembered the muscle and sinew of her father's arms as he held her on his shoulders, her awe at the steady progress of the wagons. That day she'd learned who she was. That knowledge had held her high through all the days that followed. It would do so again.

INGRID

"You surviving?" Ingrid pushed against the huddle of bodies she was dancing in the middle of, shouting over the Soundgarden song crackling through bad speakers stacked against the back of the club. She looked at Monica, her Mauritian roommate, with concern and a speck of envy. A baby doll dress and beads were unusual in this club. Ingrid twisted the leather bands on her arm. Monica was pretty, a word Ingrid never used for herself.

"It's . . . different," Monica shouted back, and they both laughed.

While this was a visit to sate Monica's curiosity about all things alternative, the club was a haven for Ingrid. In the dark, she was safe, safe from asking and answering questions, from explaining herself. She didn't have to elaborate on anything, not her orphanhood, not her backed-up store of anger for parents she'd never had the chance to know. Or how that loss, so central to her life, was an event of which she had no memory. Orphanhood had left her marooned, a strange and solitary creature who did not conform to the stereotype of what a coloured girl looked, thought, or acted like.

Here, among those who wrestled with fitting in as much as she did, it didn't matter, and ordinarily, she would let loose. But tonight she was finding it difficult to feel her usual abandon. She was thinking about Rachel and their supper the previous evening. There had been a restiveness in her grandmother, an undercurrent. Ingrid had attempted to shake it off as tension over her own prolonged absence from Steenberg, but that wasn't it. Something was up. She needed to go back soon, to check on her.

Three songs later, they tumbled outside to stand against the club's blue exterior walls, among the clumps of overheated revelers. The Celtic melancholy of the Cranberries echoed down the factory-lined street, toward nearby downtown Cape Town. With no signage outside, the alternative music den's only decoration was its perennial string of Christmas lights.

"What a fucking racket," said Reuben, Ingrid's oldest friend, after Monica ventured off to find the bathroom.

Ingrid cocked an eyebrow at him. "Don't act like you came for the music. If Monica went to the symphony, you'd be there in a penguin suit."

Reuben gave a slight grin. "Ja, OK. I nearly tripped on the hair of one of those guys inside, is all I'm saying."

"You complain a lot, you know." They made faces at each other and both laughed.

"How is everything going?" he asked.

Ingrid picked up on his hesitant tone. Attending university would take her places, she knew, that Reuben's job at a print shop might not. Her bursary with full tuition had arrived like a magic carpet, sweeping her off to the formerly white university she'd nicknamed Olympus. Being extricated from the supposed badlands of the Cape Flats was remarkable, something to pray about, be grateful for—everyone had told her that. But no one had told her it would feel so lonely.

"They don't want me there, in the class, in that degree." She straightened her T-shirt.

"Well, you can't come back to Steenberg."

"I know." Ingrid sank back against the wall. "Half the neighborhood wants me to succeed at this, because they can't. The other half wants me to fail, for the same reason. I'm on my own either way."

"That's nothing new for you." He bumped her playfully. "I'll get us drinks. What does Monica like?"

"Something that isn't spiked," she joked, then gave him the name of a cider. He walked off. She folded her arms, warding off the memory of a conversation overheard in class that morning: "I thought she worked here," one white girl had hissed to another, thinking Ingrid was out of earshot. "Standards are dropping." They'd both rolled their eyes.

Ingrid exhaled. She watched a group huddle around the club's owner, petting his pit bull. She tried to forget.

"I don't understand your country yet," Monica said, rejoining her at the wall. "Someone just asked me if I'm coloured or Black—I didn't know what to say, so I just said no, I'm Mauritian." She laughed. "He looked so confused."

"He probably was," Ingrid said and shook her head.

"I get that Blacks come from different tribes in your country, but this separation from coloureds . . . ," Monica said and shrugged.

Ingrid took her time answering, bobbing her head to the screech and bass of a song. "It's government engineering," she said. "They put us coloureds higher on the food chain—housing-wise, with schools, work opportunities, and so on. The Blacks—sometimes you'll hear them called Africans—are less well off than us, than everybody. But just like every other race here, they have their own schools, areas, some languages too."

Ingrid continued, "I only really got to know a Black person last year, at work. There's a woman from Langa in the kitchen—Portia, an older lady. She's been there forever."

"What is Langa?"

"A Black area—one of the townships near Athlone."

Monica nodded. "Hey, I was reading about District Six. Did you know it's not far from here? Or it used to be."

"The Eden the coloureds were thrown out of," Ingrid sighed. "Everyone older than me talks that way about it."

The club stood on the fringes of the downtown core, a few miles from what had been a quintessentially blended, Capetonian neighborhood: District Six, mowed to the ground a generation before. Zoned as a white area and condemned to summary execution, to evictions, demolitions, and renaming. Nothing approaching what had once stood there had replaced it. Only a lone church was left standing from the district, a witness to the barrenness of those times.

Reuben returned, drinks in hand. They watched a pair of white girls, either stoned or drunk, who clutched each other, crying.

"*Dronkverdriet?*" Reuben murmured. "Isn't it too early for that?"

"What does *that* mean?" Monica asked.

"Drunken remorse or regret," Ingrid said. "But no, listen to them. It's Kurt Cobain. Just like that he's gone, suicide."

"That can't be a surprise," Reuben said. "There was a man with problems, hey."

"And talent," Ingrid rebuked.

They continued chatting, until Reuben gave Ingrid a subtle hint. Hiding a smile, she left the two of them. She found a spot on the sidewalk where she could stretch out her legs and nurse her beer in solitude.

"Vinyl."

She turned to the stranger who had spoken as he sat down beside her. She resisted the ingrained reflex to pull away from him: he was Black. She'd spotted him earlier, when they'd first entered the club. A lean man, deep-blue jeans, snow-white T-shirt. His foot had been up against the wall, a can of lager in his hand; he'd worn an expression that made it plain he'd rather be anywhere else.

Still, Ingrid's gaze had lingered. There was something familiar about his square shoulders and short dreads, his symmetry and relaxed poise. She'd seen him before but couldn't place where. Instead, she'd dismissed him as someone who'd obviously taken a wrong turn. But now, she recognized him.

"The big music shop in Claremont," she said. "And the stairs."

He gave her a ready smile. "Yes, I saw you one Saturday there. I remember you."

"I was ahead of you later that day, on the stairs in my block in Rondebosch," Ingrid said. "Maybe two or three months ago, hey?"

"That's right. It's where I'm staying for now. Were you visiting, or do you live there?"

"Moved in last year. I live there now. You were carrying a Miles Davis LP."

"You remember," he said with a grin. "I think we have slightly different tastes in music, though."

She gave a shy laugh. Embarrassed, she remembered thinking about him for a moment after their initial meeting but quickly shrugging it off. So far her romantic liaisons had all been excruciating acts of endurance; every shy, solitary part of her had twisted into a knot while she felt compelled to act a part.

"I'm Litha." Despite the harsh streetlight, she could see his eyes. They were brown as the tannin pools on the mountainside, from which her grandmother tended to drink on hikes. He emanated warmth and gentleness, but in the way he carried himself, he hinted at a hidden strength.

"Ingrid," she said, and they shook hands. "What brings you to this den of iniquity, Litha?"

"I brought a friend here, from Salt River. His car was stolen this week, but he met a girl, wanted to see her, so I said I'd drive him." He looked down at her shirt and gestured with his chin. "The Sisters of Mercy, hey, I'm going to guess they have nothing to do with the convent?"

She smiled. "You have strong powers of observation, Litha."

"So? What's a nice girl like you doing in a place like this?"

"What makes you think I'm a nice girl?"

He smiled, drawing his head back.

"What you're really asking"—Ingrid leaned forward—"is why I'm not in a tight-fitting dress and heels, with my hair in layers, jazzing at Galaxy like a good coloured girl."

He laughed. She met his eyes, and it felt as if they were getting the measure of each other. He cocked an eyebrow before shaking his head. "No—I mean, the girls there are also very nice, if you don't mind me saying so. But I don't think that club is the right one for you; you look like you are where you need to be. This music, it is different, though, not normal for us."

"Ah, the grand 'us.'" She swept an arm widely. "Well, 'we'"—she made air quotes—"don't all like Boyz II Men and Toni Braxton."

"Well, now, that's just unacceptable." His tone was teasing, soft. He paused, then stood up with a hand outstretched. "Come. Show me how to dance to this crazy white people's music."

He appeared to be serious. Ingrid blushed, then stuttered, before downing her beer and walking back in with him, Monica winking at her. On the dance floor, he shifted from side to side, bouncing his head like a secretary bird. The drunk crowd surged around them like a single miasmic organism.

Litha had a slightly round belly and an open face. Ingrid got the impression that he was comfortable in his own skin. She looked down at his feet, catching glimpses of white stripes in the darkness.

"Adidas is a bad choice for this place," she shouted into his ear. "There's so much crap on the floor, bubble gum, beer, God knows what, glass."

"Yes, I see you are better equipped." He gestured to her Doc Martens.

"Who's this?" Suddenly Reuben appeared between them like a small stick of dynamite. Ingrid frowned; Litha drew himself upright.

"Just someone I'm talking with, Reuben. His name is Litha. Be nice."

"Oh, is it." Reuben gave Litha a fixed gaze. Litha tilted his head and stared him down. From beside Reuben, Monica shot Ingrid an anxious, confused look.

"Reuben, what the fuck? Don't be so rude," Ingrid shouted. Indignant, she pushed him back. "Go," she said, and Reuben and her roommate moved off into the darkness.

"Sorry," she said to Litha, "he can be such an arsehole."

"What is he? Brother? Lover?"

"Reuben? No, we're old friends, good friends. I think he's trying to impress my friend there, Monica."

She expected Litha's gaze to follow Monica's shapely form, but instead his eyes remained on her. The music slowed down as Eddie Vedder's full-bodied voice rang clear. But the song and atmosphere fell away as Litha moved closer, as she wanted him to. Ingrid heard her grandfather in her head for a moment, swearing her off boys, muttering about her mother's sins. But curiosity and desire held more urgency. Litha's hands touched her waist. She drew nearer to him.

"Hey, what do you think you doing?" Reuben emerged once again and faced Litha down. The men were a few breaths from punches. "Is this *darky* being forward, Ingrid?"

"Reuben," she shouted. "What is the matter with you?" She pushed him away. "He's fine. Why are you being such a dick?"

Eyes blazing, she led Litha outside by the hand. "I'm so sorry," she said, once they were leaning together against the blue wall. "I don't know what his problem is."

"I'm Black; you're not." Litha appeared unfazed. Evidently, this kind of treatment wasn't unusual for him. "Look, I don't want to sound like a forward darky, but can I get you something to eat? Mr. Pickwick's, Kuzma's? I don't mind staying, but I'm not here to fight. And my Salt River friend looks like he is going to be here for some time."

"I just . . ." Ingrid paused. "I didn't drive. Me and my roommate came with Reuben."

Litha shrugged. "You can ride with me, neighbor."

Going back inside right now was out of the question, but driving off with a stranger was a stretch. And he was Black. Ingrid reeled, apprehensive.

Monica approached them with concern on her face, and the three of them spoke. Her roommate's easy banter relaxed Ingrid—she had given Reuben a talking-to, she said. Litha invited her to go with them, but Monica declined. When Litha went inside to update his friend about his plans, Ingrid turned toward her roommate.

"I'm interested, Monica, but . . ."

"What is your gut telling you?"

Ingrid chewed her lip. "Nothing bad."

"I'll come if you want me to." Monica raised her hands in a gesture of surrender. "But with the way you two danced, three is definitely a crowd."

"And you're having a good time with my mad friend, isn't it?" Ingrid shook her head and smiled.

"Yes, is that bad?" Monica said, laughing.

"Well, you saw what you're in for with that one. Good luck."

"You too."

A little later, Litha's car doors swung shut, sealing out the world. Ingrid's fears pressed in, filling her mind with the things she'd been told about Black people. Would he run off with her to a far-flung set of shanties or hurt her in the dark center of Newlands Forest?

Instead, Litha chatted easily and drew her into the conversation. He had an old cassette player in his car. She inspected his mixtapes, gave him her opinion on the music. He said, embarrassed, that he would be getting a CD player sometime soon. Ingrid began to relax. She wanted to blurt out that so much of what she'd learned about Black people she had learned on TV. Coloureds had little good to say about them, and most had few interactions with Blacks, often considering them inferior. But even in her head, it sounded trite. Besides, she thought of her uncle Philip in the armed struggle. She should know better. Coloureds demonizing Blacks was apartheid served cold: the vicious cycle of oppressed groups doing the oppressor's work.

Philip had returned triumphantly from exile only four years before. His was a life given over to the fight against apartheid, something he had no qualms reiterating. She remembered him at the occasional dinner, pounding a fist on the kitchen table: "No more of their bannings and detentions, the torture, censorship, and assassinations. We will be one South Africa. And with all of us unbanned, our liberation organizations will lead the way."

He was a man on a different path. It had been Rachel or Mark, never Philip, who used to take her to school after riots. Sitting in the taxi, they'd weave past tires set alight on the street, tires left to burn in protest against the apartheid government. Ingrid would never forget their black smoke.

Litha parked and looked over, meeting her eyes. Ingrid felt something within her soften. She was brushing against a line, and desire was tempting her to cross it.

"Let's go inside," he said. Soon they were settled in at the diner for burgers and drinks.

"So are you studying?" Ingrid asked. "Working?"

His body changed. He puffed his chest. "I'm doing law at UWC—I suppose I should call it Bush like everyone here does. I did my first degree at Fort Hare."

"You drive from Rondebosch to Bush? Isn't that like an hour each way?"

"I just have to time it right. I'm staying with my brother, in your building, for free, so it's worth it while I look for something closer to campus."

"Lucky you." Ingrid slumped back in her seat. "You get to go to a university where there's more of the grand 'us.' Why law?"

"Well, I grew up in the Transkei. I'm from Lusikisiki, east of Umtata, the capital."

"You're from one of the homelands?"

He nodded, a wrinkle of anxiety crossing his face, as if he was unsure of how this fact would be received.

"I don't understand that whole thing," Ingrid admitted. "I mean," she added hastily, "I know it from school and obviously the newspapers and so on."

Litha laughed, relaxing. "You must think like an apartheid bureaucrat to understand the homelands. When I was growing up, the government forced many men from the Transkei to work on the mines in Johannesburg. When the stories came back, they were bad: unsafe conditions, bad pay, all these things. Many didn't come home. They died working or in the hostels, and the money, it was never enough for the women and children they left behind.

"This is why I want to do law. Our country, the Transkei, it is a made-up one. Our government is propped up by the apartheid government. We are inside South Africa; we depend on it for everything, and it takes what it wants from us. These things are wrong. Even now, with the homelands ending, we must deal with what is left."

Ingrid rested her head in the palm of one hand. Mining was so far from what she'd known in the Cape.

"Honestly," she said. "This country . . . one layer on top of another."

"Yes." Sadness marked Litha's face as he looked down. "All those layers," he said quietly, "are built with people."

They continued eating. After a while, he looked at her and asked, "What about you?"

Ingrid told him about her second-year architecture program at UCT and that she was focused on urban planning.

"That's impressive. Smart girl."

"I don't feel very smart. It's so much work, and every day is literally uphill. I'm struggling to feel at home there."

He cocked his head, reading what she was not saying. "Don't worry about those whites, Ingrid. This is your country; you belong there." She met his eyes and was grateful for his smile. "Why do you want to be an architect?"

"Because I grew up on the Cape Flats," Ingrid said. "With council houses, prefab schools, no trees. We had the bush at our doorstep, unfinished brick houses; some of the very old ones had toilets outside. There were horse-drawn carts on the street when I was small, and every now and then you'd drive past a dead horse. Coloureds got dumped in these places, and no effort was put into where and how people lived. Some people made their places look really good, and not everyone has a council house, obviously, but—" She softened her voice as if afraid now of how he would receive her words. "Design matters," she said. "Your soul responds to it. Assuming, of course, the place you're in acknowledges that you have a soul, that you're not an animal."

"Music, design. You are a woman of big feelings."

Embarrassed, she didn't reply. But as they continued, Ingrid realized that, for all her misgivings, he was easy to talk with and they had much in common. They left the diner, and her mind filled with uncertainties: how to see him again; when to see him; what to do when she did.

They were a few steps outside, making their way to his car, when she felt him press her forward. A sharp scent of glue and unwashed bodies overcame her, but Litha said to run, and without thinking, she did. He unlocked her door and simultaneously shoved her in it and pushed back a child: a yellow-toothed boy wielding a knife that gave off a dull gleam. After a short, terrifying scuffle, Litha rapidly got in on his side and pulled away while Ingrid looked back in shock at a pair of gaunt kids in filthy clothes too large for them, receding from view.

"I didn't even see them," she said, shaken.

"I did when we went in," Litha said quietly, shaking his head. "I don't understand the city; people cut you here for a pair of shoes, a jacket. What kind of place is this?"

She reached for his hand and squeezed hard. "That could have gone so badly."

He smiled over at her, said nothing further. He drove them on and reached their nearby apartment block a few minutes later. They sat silently in the car for a few expectant minutes.

"Thank you for that," Ingrid said. "This is the story of my life, what just happened there. Chaos is always about to come in, and someone, my grandmother usually, protects me. I'm sorry—that's more serious talk."

"One must always make time for your *gogo*. Tell me about her."

She recalled one of her strongest memories: When she was six, her grandmother had let her go to the corner store alone to buy bread and milk. It was hardly an act of independence; everyone on the street, up to and including the store owner, knew Ingrid. Still, savoring the freedom, she would go the long way. She'd gotten in the habit of taking her time, even stopping at a friend's for a short visit, doing whatever she could to delay returning to the house, that heavy house.

"I liked the walk for the same reason I like the club from tonight: no one was hovering over me. But soon after I was six, the unrest really got bad, and they didn't like me walking alone anymore. I'm an orphan, so they were extra cautious." She looked away, not wanting to betray that she'd grown up in a house filled with ghosts. Yolanda, her deceased mother, cast a long shadow. Somehow it had conjoined with her own. The car crash that had killed Yolanda and Ingrid's father, a fellow student at university, had rattled loose any sense of trust her grandparents had had in the world. Then there was Philip. She told him about her revolutionary uncle, who had been absent for most of her life.

"I remember Uncle Mark bringing groceries, just doing stuff, always doing stuff. I would go out with him and my cousins, neighbors, and so on. But I began withdrawing to my room as I got older. I used to have this yellow KIC radio that I kept in my room. That's how I got into alternative music, then grunge, listening to my favorite DJs alone, late at night," Ingrid said quietly.

"What do you like about it?"

"It's been my outlet—music to be angry with. On the one hand, the biggest defining event in my life is the death of my parents; they died when I was a baby. And on the other was the possibility for decades of my uncle Philip being killed. All of this tore my grandparents apart in different ways; I think it killed my grandfather in the end. He had a massive heart attack—he was reading the *Argus* one Saturday and died in his armchair before anyone could do anything. Things changed after that: Ma pushed me to study and so on. But until then they, mostly my grandfather, had tried to keep me safe all that time by almost burying me alive. But you can't protect anything that way." Ingrid trailed off.

"No, you can't."

Ingrid continued. "Reuben used to get into fights protecting me. Girls said I was a green-eyed snake 'cause of my eyes, that I wanted to be white because I'm light skinned."

She didn't know why she was sharing so much with him, a virtual stranger. It embarrassed her. But when she looked up, she found Litha gazing back. He was listening. He did not do what others had done: make light of her unusual circumstances or be ashamed of them. She realized how at ease he made her feel, even now, in the silence that had settled between them.

Eventually he spoke.

"Come to my place soon. I'll play you jazz and the blues."

"And Miles?"

"You must listen to Miles."

Their eyes met. His lips brushed lightly over her cheek, then settled, finally, on her lips. She leaned into the kiss that followed.

Later, alone in her apartment, Ingrid stayed awake for a long time, feeling delight at Litha's proximity in the building and at the prospect of seeing him again.

YOLANDA

Pain had a pattern to it. The bearing of it, that unsteady balance. Then the hurtling down, winded, beneath its smothering weight. You tried to figure out what had been scraped or ripped loose this time. The pattern carved tracks in you. Although you were still here, although you had survived, it felt like a little less of you was left every time, a little more to rebuild.

As the screen door to her porch snapped shut behind her, Yolanda weighed whether she had the will to disrupt those old patterns. She had kept to herself all day, hadn't ridden out on her motorbike, hadn't visited Garrick at the farmhouse, hadn't worked. Instead she'd smoked, sat on her porch. She'd considered the sacred: her mother and her daughter. She'd asked herself what could be worse than the previous evening's flashback.

Even the trip that had brought her here four years ago, a ride out of New York with too much vodka coursing through her body, had not been as bad. Distraught, she'd meant to ride all the way to the Florida Keys that day, then walk into the Atlantic, offering herself as a package of bone and blood to drift back toward Africa. Instead, her bike had failed on the interstate near Virginia's Fauquier County, and Garrick had stopped to help, his mother, then alive, watching from inside the truck. Even then Yolanda sensed that Garrick could tell she was in trouble, that she needed more help than she was going to ask for. There was anguish in him but no malice. There was care. He was the kind of man who gave help more often than he should have.

"Come on, there's a place near here makes a mean pulled-pork sandwich," his mother called. "Come join us. You look hungry." The bike was quickly fixed, but by the end of the meal Yolanda had sobered up. She didn't like riding in the dark, so she lingered, drawn to Garrick, feeling what he felt. She stayed with them that night, relieved to be outside New York's mesh of urbanity. They offered her room and board if she helped his ailing mother with the horses they boarded. She'd stayed.

Now, walking toward the main house as twilight fell, Yolanda knew Garrick had been around all day, tending to the horses, cleaning the stables, fixing things. He'd kept an eye out but left her alone. As she watched him come out with his flashlight and whistle for his dogs, she remembered how long it had taken her to convince him he didn't need to bring a gun out on their evening strolls.

"Virginia is an open carry state," he'd argued.

"You're carrying enough, Garrick," she'd murmured. The Gulf War was still in him.

As they fell in beside each other on the footpath, he simply asked how she was doing, and she gave a small nod, an OK. They often walked like this until long after nightfall, each a prisoner to the same restlessness, the same contested darkness. They could sense the jaggedness of each other's wounds and, despite that, the capacity each still had for tenderness. Often, unwilling or unable to speak, they strolled in silence, sometimes holding hands, sometimes holding each other upright, other times simply beside each other, not touching at all.

"How do you return home, Garrick?" she asked as they followed an old trail toward the hills. "After war."

For a long time, there was only the crunch of his boots.

"A friend of mine," he said at last, "a guy from Harrisonburg—I met him on my first tour. He was part of the platoon I got assigned to, infantry. Like me, he was deployed a bunch of times. He came home to a hero's welcome; he'd moved up in rank by the time he left. His life looked like a postcard: white picket fence, golden retriever, proud wife, one kid, another on the way.

"People fell all over themselves to hire him. He planned to go back to school. Shaft—we called him Shaft; his name was Darren—always had a head for numbers. His health took a beating in Kuwait, you could see that, but he held it together.

"One Saturday morning in July, real early, he got up, put on his dress uniform, went to the shed behind his house, balanced on a wheelbarrow, and shot himself in the head with a .45. No note, nothing, just a wheelbarrow to make sure his wife could move the deadweight of his body."

They stopped. Yolanda couldn't make out Garrick's expression in the near dark.

"He had come home, he had made it, and all he figured in the end is that a beautiful summer's day was the perfect day to die. War fucks you up, Yolanda; there's no question. There's no glory, no swagger. You bring the dust and the heat, the blood, the smell—it all comes with you. Everything sticks to you like dirt.

"I carry every soldier I tried to put back together and the ones I couldn't do anything for. I had to make decisions about people's lives, their limbs. I'll never be clean again; I'll never be who I was." He looked over in her direction. "But I think you already know that." He paused. "What home is for you depends on acceptance: what was gone is gone; you have to build something else. It's a kind of death."

Yolanda knew that his children, to whom he'd had limited access for the longest time after a bruising divorce, were top of mind.

"Shaft's wife and the rest of us would have done anything for him, helped him shoulder it, whatever he needed us to do. If he gave us the chance. But now he's dead."

They stood in silence. When they walked onward, their fingers brushed, and he took her hand.

"Yolanda," he said, "at some point, you've got to trust somebody, trust that they're going to hold you up. And you've got to trust yourself, trust that you'll stand up and stay on your feet."

"But I'm safe here. I know how to do this, be this, live this way."

"OK." Garrick paused. His voice was soft. "But how much living are you really doing?"

They walked toward a rocky outcrop. The past was home. Home meant facing the past. Rachel's two words nudged and wheedled, and Yolanda knew now, in a way she couldn't articulate, that she had to go back. But she had no idea how she was going to do it.

INGRID

Ingrid woke to the sun peeking through her bedroom curtains. In her state of half sleep, she made out the sound of drums, an unmistakably African tempo weaving around a man's bass voice: *kwassa kwassa*. Monica was home. Ingrid found her in the living room, surrounded by books.

"Well?" Monica didn't waste a moment. "How did it go with brother man?" She craned her neck. "He's not in there, is he?"

"Of course not, I just met the guy. And Reuben? Please warn me if he's ever here . . ."

Monica grew coy. "I'm seeing him tonight. So? Obviously it went OK?"

"Sort of." Ingrid relayed the details of their evening and the street kids but struggled to find the words to adequately express the electricity that had passed between her and Litha. Instead, she told Monica about his smile and how, although he took the world seriously, he laughed easily. She'd noticed little things, like how his face was freshly shaved. She could tell it was something that he did for himself every day, and she liked that.

"He sounds a lot less intense than Reuben." Monica sighed and told of her own adventures, growing bashful.

"You like him," Ingrid teased. "Hey, what's the time?" she asked, distracted, looking around for her bag. "I think I'll swing by my grand-mother's before work, check up on her."

She ate and got ready for her shift. On the drive to Steenberg, she decided she would go see Litha the next day, bring some LPs. She turned the thought of him over in her mind; the idea of him lingered, long and sweet.

But as she approached Rachel's, the world came into sharp focus. The front door stood ajar, a group of people scattered on the sidewalk. Mark's sedan was in front of the house. Rachel's car was not. Ingrid tightened. Her throat grew dry. She got out to headshakes, tut-tuts, and quiet consolations. Ma.

Inside, her uncle's pot-bellied figure stood in the small hallway. Mark was on the telephone; he turned to wave. Aside from his voice, the house held an awful silence.

Ingrid hurried past him to Rachel's bedroom. The bed was made, the room neat but empty. The kitchen was too. Dread overcame her as she opened the back door to the yard, searching for the woman who was, in every practical sense, her mother.

"Ingrid." Mark hung up. "At last. I was going to drive to your place later to look for you. When are you people getting a phone?" he asked angrily.

"What's going on? Where's Ma?"

"We don't know." Mark shook his head. "We got back this morning from the trip, I came here, and . . . nothing."

"What do you mean, 'nothing'?"

"The neighbors say the last time they saw her was Thursday." Mark shrugged.

"Yes, I was here with her; we had supper together."

"Well," Mark continued, "Mrs. Abrahams and another woman came over as soon as they saw me, said they were waiting for one of the family." Ingrid sagged with guilt. "Apparently Ma was sick not so long ago, so they were concerned. And the house has been closed; no one answered when they knocked. I'm leaving messages for Philip, but with all this election stuff going on, I don't even know if he's in Cape Town. I phoned the police just now to find out about filing a missing persons report."

"What? But Ma could be anywhere. She's probably on the mountain, picking her plants." A low and treacherous panic began to rise in Ingrid.

"But to not tell anyone, Ingrid, and at her age? You saw her Thursday. What did she say to you; how did she seem?"

Guiltily, Ingrid relayed what she could remember. "She was a bit off, but that could have been anything. Nobody saw the car?"

"No, and there's no sign of a break-in. I told the police about her hiking. They say we must talk with the park rangers at Tokai, ask if they saw anything. Are you sure she wasn't having one of her episodes?"

"She didn't say anything. She just seemed preoccupied." Ingrid grew tearful. She should have been here. She had let Olympus, the bursary, her friends, and even Litha take her away. This had happened to her grandmother while her back was turned.

"Can I leave you here, Ingrid? The neighbors are lining up, and they're going to keep coming. They asked to have a prayer circle. But I need to go get Tracy."

"Ma's not dead."

"Everyone is just trying to help, to do something. People are worried."

He left, and Ingrid sat in the living room, in shock. Neighbors brought tea, biscuits, and sandwiches, seating themselves gingerly, asking if there was any word. Ingrid didn't answer. Hers and Rachel's could be a challenging relationship, but she could not conceive of losing another mother, not like this.

When Mark returned, she decided to go driving, to look for Rachel's car. She felt sure that when she returned, Ma would be back, clicking her tongue at the fuss, inviting everyone to stay for supper.

She drove down street after street in an ever-widening circle. She knew this place—how people carried themselves and who many of them were. Now she regarded it all with suspicion: the local grocery stores, the people walking from the station, the ones who had the benefit of a normality that was being wrenched from her again. She thought with fear of the Cape Flats gangs. They hadn't been much of a feature in her family's life, but they lingered in the underbelly of this place. Had a crime gone awry? Had the old woman been in the wrong place at the wrong time?

Ingrid drove toward Princess Vlei, a favorite location for Sunday-afternoon visits. There, Rachel had always held her as they watched the long afternoon sun burnish the tall reeds. There was no sign of her now. Then Ingrid turned and drove toward the coast, going beyond where the council estate ended and miles of rough, windblown dunes and clumps of hardy bush tumbled toward the ocean.

Standing at nearby Muizenberg Beach, she fought fears of her grandmother lying stricken and unfound, somewhere between the vleis and this, the Atlantic. Yet this old familiar world, the calm cove before her and the reddish-brown mountain behind, was hiding something precious. Ingrid willed time forward, trying to extend the interval before she returned home, to give Rachel time to undo all of this.

The ocean, the mountain, and the world between showed nothing amiss. They didn't reveal any secrets; they didn't confirm or deny Rachel's passing. She drove on to Tokai and Silvermine, areas that Rachel usually favored as entry points for her extended walks on the mountain. "No no no," Ingrid said, frantic, as she drove a winding route along the Back Table, the southern part of Table Mountain. But Rachel's car was nowhere to be found.

Back at the house, there was no news. Stout and stern, Mark's wife, Tracy, had just made tea for a fresh group of neighbors. They were pecking over the details of Rachel's activities that week as if turning over bones. They spoke in the quiet tones of mourning.

Dazed, Ingrid called her work and made excuses. Surely, she thought, this would blow over by tomorrow. She felt covetous of Rachel. All the people clucking their tongues in the living room didn't know her, not deeply. Rachel was her grandmother, the closest thing she had to a mother, her anchor. What right did these people have to sit here, an audience for the show?

She left them, slipped into Rachel's bedroom, and settled under the duvet. She breathed in the comforting smell of the sheets, meaning to shut her eyes for just a few minutes. But when she woke, it was to darkness and tense voices from the living room. Startled, she sprang up—there must have been news. But the words traveling through the compact council house froze her.

"How can you lie to her like this?" Tracy was strident.

"We had no choice at the time, and in the end we were respecting what my sister wanted."

"Mark, she has to know. Your mother obviously left this for her, not you." Ingrid crept up, opened the bedroom door slightly wider. "You people protected that girl her whole life because of what happened, but she isn't a baby anymore."

"You read the letter. You read what Yolanda wanted."

Ingrid jolted at the mention of her mother's name.

"Yolanda, always Yolanda."

"What's that supposed to mean? Look, leave that package in the car, Tracy. I'm not discussing this with her."

"Not discussing what?" Ingrid stepped out of the shadows. "What's going on?"

Mark's nostrils flared, and his dark eyes, usually filled with worry, bore sadness. The front door was closed, the house empty except for the three of them. Tracy's eyes pulled away from Ingrid's with a flash of anger.

"I'm going outside for a smoke." Mark searched his pockets for cigarettes.

"Mark," Tracy said. "I'm getting it from the car."

"I told you to leave it."

"And I'm telling you no." Tracy found the keys, pushed past Mark, and went outside. Ingrid looked at her uncle. In some ways she regarded him as a brother—her circumstances had changed the natural order of things. She trusted him. He would set this right.

Instead he hurried after Tracy and slammed the door. Ingrid knelt on the couch and shifted the curtain, trying to see what would unfold on the red walkway. What more could come undone?

Mark was standing on the *stoep*, still as a stone. Their car's interior light was on. Finally Tracy bustled back into the house. She handed Ingrid a nondescript, large grocery bag.

"Mark should be telling you, Ingrid. It's not my place. But seeing as he's being so stubborn . . ." She paused. "We found this today, on your old bed."

"What is it?"

Tracy didn't offer an answer. Inside the bag were bulging packs bound with rubber bands: photographs, letters, sketch pads and note-pads, rolled-up cylinders, and canvases. The first photo Ingrid found was an old black-and-white of a white man in profile. Blond, he stood on a mountain trail, at a cliff's edge, with his hands on his hips.

The next photo toppled out as if animated and eager to be viewed: here was Yolanda's face, surfacing from the well of history. Laughter was not what Ingrid expected to see in her mother, but there it was, with her leaning toward the photographer as if daring him to take the picture.

Such vivid liveliness was jarring. For so long, death had mingled with Yolanda in Ingrid's mind. She returned to the picture of the man, studying it carefully. Then she picked up a small cylinder, unfolding a watercolor painting of delicate flowers, blushing with pastels. Ingrid's eyes grew larger as she read the words on the bottom: *Stefan—to remember.*

There were two more photographs lying at the top, but they left Ingrid's body braced, her head vertiginous. As if answering the question shaping itself in her mind, the white man had turned to face the camera. He held her mother with the casualness of a lover. Their eyes were bright, their faces flushed with youth.

Ingrid turned the photos over, but there was nothing written on the back. She returned to the watercolor. An unsettling truth assembled itself.

On the stoep, Mark was deep in thought. When Ingrid stepped near, he steeled himself.

"They called me Disa, like these flowers." She held up the watercolor. "Ingrid Disa. This is him, isn't it? My father. Stefan. How come you said all these years his name was James Paulsen and that he was coloured? He was white. How come you never told me that?"

"We could never talk about your father. It's beyond me how photos of him even survived." Her uncle's voice was bitter. "The whole thing was illegal; there was the Immorality Act."

He fell silent, and Ingrid returned inside, relieved that this was the scale of what had been hidden from her but baffled by the intrigue. Vaguely she recalled the act, which outlawed interracial relationships of an intimate nature, one of a battery of apartheid laws hammering human behavior into the government's misplaced ideal. Somehow, her parents had circumvented it. So Stefan was the answer to the question of her green eyes and light skin.

She lifted out an old sketch pad and flipped through page after page of increasingly intricate butterfly drawings. The detail and dimensions were impressive: tails and wing patterns; the shrubs upon which they perched; in a few cases, the hand that held them.

Then, after a few blank sheets, an altogether different subject emerged, and Ingrid reeled.

Sheet after sheet showed miniature dimpled hands, tiny nails, baby feet curled up to reveal puckered soles and impossibly small toes. Someone, Yolanda, had spent several pages drawing them in different ways. There were sketches, tenderly done, of a baby's face and wisps of hair forming a halo. The very last pages of the pad had been torn out.

Ingrid pinched her eyes against the flood. She had been told Yolanda was an artist, and Rachel had shared precious pictures a few times, but Ingrid had never seen herself as the subject. George had refused to have Yolanda's art up in the house. What she would have given to know her, to know someone who could be this careful, this sophisticated, with a pencil and a sketch pad.

After several minutes, Ingrid took out a journal, but as she opened it, a slender cream-colored envelope fell to the floor. It had a British postal stamp and was addressed to Rachel. Ingrid peered into the journal again, then felt a sudden chill. She studied the letter's faint but visible date and the handwriting of the address.

Outside, Tracy had joined Mark on the stoep. They did not look over when she rushed outside thrusting the single page found in the letter at them.

"She's alive," Ingrid shouted.

"Yes," Mark said. He'd been waiting for this moment.

"But you told me. Everybody told me about the car crash. You took me to where it happened on the N2."

His eyes drifted down. "It's not so simple."

Nothing in this family ever was. Ingrid looked at the letter. A tremor had always run beneath the surface of their family. With all the ills they'd suffered, she had simply assumed it was the result of hardship. Instead, everything they were, everything she had become, rested upon a conspiracy of mothers. Newfound rage began to settle in her, driving her to read the letter out loud:

> I know that you're still there, Ma, I know you always. It's been so long now. I didn't know it would be so many years when I left. I am still alive, I wanted you to know that. I think of her and I think of you every minute but to come back now would be selfish, unfair to my little beauty in her lemon Peps blanket, the sweetest love of my life. I have nothing to give her. But every day and every night I'm still your child and she is still mine.
>
> Every door behind me is closed. I'm trying to move on to a different chapter in a new place. I have no choice. To return would be dangerous for all of us. Love her like you know I would. I breathe for her. I live, still, for her. But I don't want my trauma to be her inheritance. Let her leave me in the past.
>
> I love you, Ma.
> Yolanda

"How long did you know? All of you." Ingrid's rage boiled over. "Answer me."

Mark was silent. Tracy stepped back into the house. Ingrid's voice grew jagged. "The date on this envelope is only eight years old. Did you know for eight years?"

"Ingrid, please go inside," Mark said, trying to shepherd her into the living room. "We're not having an argument outside, not with everything else going on."

"I don't care," she shouted. Snot and tears mingled as she wiped her face. "Did you know?"

Her uncle looked away and gave a small nod. "Ingrid, we were all . . . everyone was just trying to protect you."

"I'm so fucking tired of hearing that. From what? From my own parents?" Livid, Ingrid shoved back at him as he pushed her into the house. She felt like a little girl again, dark-haired doll in her hand, staring up at a world whose rules baffled her, like how her grandfather took his teeth out at night but she couldn't, or why stockings made that mysterious sound when women walked. Except she was no longer little, and the world had grown more complex. She could never have imagined a betrayal like this.

"You don't know," Mark muttered. "Everything we went through . . ."

But Ingrid yelled over him, "'Ingrid, you can't walk from the taxi rank.' 'Ingrid, you can't go to the club with Reuben.' 'Ingrid, you're too young.' 'Ingrid, you don't understand; you're not ready; you're not like the other children.' The same chorus, my whole fucking life. Eight years of a lie, eight years that might have changed that. But you decided for me; you all carried on with your grown-up lives, patronizing me with your made-up shit."

Helpless, she tried to strike him, but he easily caught her wrist. Tracy had retreated to the shadows.

"Where is she?" Ingrid pressed. "Only Ma could have left this stuff. How come she didn't just give them to me herself? Where is she? Where is my mother? Why did they leave?"

"I don't know, Ingrid. I don't know where Yolanda is. The letter was from England."

"Why did Yolanda leave?"

"She is still my sister; she would never have wanted you to know. You read the letter—she wanted you to leave her in the past."

Ingrid tried to maintain her balance despite the pain she saw on his face. "Stefan," she whispered. The name from the painting.

"Yes. Stefan van Deventer. That bastard."

"Van Deventer? He was Afrikaans—he was a *boer*?"

"Purebred. Your mother couldn't have made a worse choice."

Betrayal yawned, an ugly chasm. "He's a boer, so I'm . . ." She couldn't bring herself to finish the thought. "Are you saying my father is in Cape Town and no one fucking told me?"

"You watch your language. This was almost twenty years ago. No one knows where he is, and believe me, he's a dead man if I ever meet him. Ingrid, I don't have the answers you're looking for."

She fixed her eyes on him. "But you knew the most important thing, Uncle Mark. My parents weren't dead, and you lied, you of all people. You didn't even tell me his real name. I called him James. I imagined my life as Ingrid Paulsen. Do you know what it feels like to be an orphan, to long for this thing you never had?"

"Oh, for God's sake." Mark stubbed out his cigarette and pointed at his wife. "You started this. Give me the keys."

So he, too, was leaving her. Everyone had. And they had lied, everyone she loved, everyone who was nearest. There was no place for her here. All that remained was a dead house, a kitchen emptied of togetherness, no more than the outlines of a hollow truth.

Ingrid grabbed her bag and ran. Somewhere beyond the maelstrom in her head, she heard Mark calling. But there wasn't safety there any longer. There wasn't home. Her mother wasn't dead, nor was she missing. A man she might have passed on the street was her father.

Shut in her car, she sloped forward, brought low by shame. The infant detailed on the sketch pad lingered, a cruel reminder that her mother lived, breathed the same air, but had chosen to share none of it with her. Ingrid drove away sobbing. How long had the world been watching, whispering, everyone aware that she wasn't an orphan, just an illegitimate and unwanted mutt of a child?

YOLANDA

Seated beside Garrick in his truck, Yolanda unfolded a torn-out sheet of paper. It had yellowed and speckled with time, but the drawing of a baby in repose—ten tiny toes, hairs that she'd captured for fear of forgetting—was still discernible. It was the first thing she'd taken when she'd left the Cape, and it was the first thing she'd packed, now that she'd be returning. She nestled it in her handbag beside her British passport. The drawing was all she'd carried of her life with Ingrid.

They were headed to Union Station in Washington, DC, where she would catch a train to New York, spend a few days with friends to figure out flights and money, then return home, to Cape Town. A single suitcase in the back held a few changes of clothes.

"You didn't have to do this drive," she said to Garrick. "Sunday is your one day off. I'd have figured something out."

"It's no bother."

Yolanda stared at the faces of his smiling children on the dashboard, photos worn by sunlight and time. Acrimony with his ex-wife had left Garrick isolated from his kids. She felt his yearning for them; she commiserated, but unlike him, she had made an unforgivable choice. She did not claim clemency, merely accepted that she was dead to her daughter. That was how it had to be.

Until today.

"You look like you could use a cigarette," Garrick said. "It's fine; just roll down the window."

Anxiety sat fat in her gut, though she hadn't registered its presence until he spoke. She dug in her handbag.

"Are you going through Heathrow?" he asked a while later.

"Probably. May as well do a layover, see people who I haven't in some time." She glanced at Garrick's look of worry. "My ex isn't one of them, Garrick."

Drumming her fingers on her leg, Yolanda thought of her English ex-husband with his Caribbean roots, a man caught up in empire. How she'd scolded him once: "Africa is not a music concert or a flagpole for you to hang your salvation on. Real people live there." Anger at him had come too easily. She knew, now, what she didn't then: that she couldn't offer him the intimacy that he craved. She had none left after Stefan, after the cops, after the car. Depression, numbness, and frigidity had wedged between her and the rhythms of their damp British existence. In an ever more unstable spiral, she'd begun to grasp at whatever made her feel something, anything to get away from stumbling between secrets.

At anti-apartheid rallies that stretched from Manchester down to London, she'd learned to hide her complicated past. People didn't want to hear it. Besides, she was a Black woman, and Black women were meant to endure with grace, not rage with passion. People wanted an illusion from Yolanda—back then, a solid block of Black solidarity—and not the truth.

Everyone had fawned over her as a supposed political exile; her ex-husband had adored his Nubian queen. *I'm not that at all; I'm a woman who's abandoned her child,* she'd wanted to tell them, to scream at him. Apartheid presented clear black-and-white lines of victim and transgressor. There was no room in the conversation for gray.

Garrick slowed and pulled up to a little café advertising night crawlers and deep-fried mozzarella cheese sticks. "Get you anything?" he asked.

"God, yes, coffee and something to eat." She stood outside the car and finished her cigarette, trying to relax the knot in her belly. Garrick returned with greasy breakfast sandwiches and burnt coffee.

Yolanda dropped her head back as they ate. "I'm going home," she said. "There's never been a better moment. If I can't do it now, well . . ."

"South Africa." He paused. "All I know is apartheid and Mandela. We had segregation here—"

"Still have." Yolanda cocked an eyebrow.

"True. Well, what does return mean for you now?"

She sipped her coffee, said, "For almost twenty years I've been adrift, away from my broken-down, made-up, stuck-together tribe, my family, my people. Like every family and every group, we carry this unique imprint of race and of apartheid's vicious damage. I don't have an answer for how I'm going to be in that space, how I'll reenter it. But I'm going."

They finished breakfast and got back on the road.

Pensive, Garrick rolled down the window and let in the cool of the morning, the bracing breeze.

"What are you?" he asked a while later, his serious eyes meeting hers. "I know you call yourself Black, but you're not like any Black person from around here."

It was a question always on the tips of the tongues of Americans she encountered, but there was nothing mocking or casual in his gaze. Yolanda weighed her response.

"I'm coloured," she said.

"You're what?" A look of shock and confusion flashed across his face.

She laughed. "I know, I know. The word makes Americans cringe. But in South Africa, people who are mixed race are called coloured."

She put a hand on his arm to allay the look on his face. "It's different from the way the term was used here, Garrick." She paused. Although across continents, *coloured* held different meanings, in neither country did it bear respect. "We're kind of a creole people: Asian, European, and African, blended. The apartheid government treats us as a separate group to everyone else. It's in their interests to do that."

"So over there you're not considered Black?"

"Not by the government. To be Black in South Africa means you have a traditional tribal background. But for coloureds, our origins are in Cape Town, from the fact that it was, is, a port city on the shipping route between East and West, with a native population on land. There was slavery, colonization, genocide, the usual ills. Still, people mingled; a unique culture resulted. But why are you asking me this? And now? Are we finally going to talk about your family photos, your brother?"

"I figured that as you're heading out of the country, it's the perfect time for this kind of heart-to-heart."

She smiled, sensitive to how difficult talk of his younger brother had been for his mother and was for him.

He continued. "I never spoke much with you about my dad. His family is dirt-poor Appalachian from Tennessee. Growing up, he used to tell us what the folks in the hollers where he grew up were called: Portuguese, Cherokee mix. Some looked Spanish, olive skinned, dark, or red boned. Some looked African."

Yolanda watched his face cloud and grow more serious.

"Pa was working at a county fair when he met my mom. They loved horses, but there was more to it. Mom used to say they connected because they were both a shade off. Her people are old Virginia stock, one of those families that had a plantation, were once gentry, and thought they'd arranged themselves cleanly between the legitimate white kids and the Black, slave-born ones. Then David was born."

She remembered the haunted face of the man who had come to their mother's funeral. Garrick and David had appeared sad with each other over more than their orphaned state, their father having died many years before. She'd felt surprise at David's thick dark hair, the rich brown of his skin.

"Your mom loved to pack up everything and go north to see him."

"She did right: collard greens, cornbread, even fresh milk and eggs; she never did trust grocery stores where he lives in Baltimore. When he was born, Mom's family was real quick to blame my dad; they said to her, 'That's what you get for mixing up with coal-country dirt, all kinds together like pigs at a trough and not a dime between them.' Dave and me got into lots of fights at school. After Pa died, I made him stay here till he graduated high school; then he was gone."

Garrick squinted into the distance, sadness overtaking him. Yolanda touched his arm, and he placed a hand over hers.

"Do you talk with him much now that she's gone?"

"Less so. Without Mom, our differences stand out: He doesn't like that I served a government he thinks is bent on annihilating its people of color. I don't like that he identifies only as African American. He's white too. We got hill people, slaves, southerners, everyone, in our line. We're as American as they come."

Yolanda sat back, absorbing his words. She noted again his pitch-black hair and light skin, the hooded dark eyes shot through with gray. "Garrick, your brother is a Black man, in a way you'll never be. You'll never inhabit the same America."

He looked away from her. When he turned back, she read on his face that he already knew this, was cut deep by the separation it meant.

"Does he have a family of his own yet?" she asked.

"No idea. I think we're his secret. Race, blood, it all seems to make people carry secrets."

Yolanda heard herself inhale. Stefan. Cape Town. She drew back, retreated into the thicket of her thoughts. Fear, fear of what she was doing, of where she was going, overcame her.

"I don't know if this is it," Garrick said. "If I'm never going to see you again."

"Garrick—"

"Hold on. I want you to know who I am, who my family is, before you go. But there's more: I want you to know that I see you, Yolanda, as you are. I see that desolate look when you have no idea how to make tomorrow a different day. I know how that feels. I've watched you notice the way light falls. You look at the leaves when they're turning in the fall with this intensity, like you're trying to remember every shade. You don't even realize you're doing it, but I see it.

"Sure, you take great photos, but don't you think I see the art on your wall? You don't have a TV, for Christ's sake; who doesn't have a TV? You have all these posters of other people's art, big coffee-table books filled with it, so why don't you make art anymore? Why are you just looking at it like someone who's lost?"

"Because I can't." She raised her voice, balled her fists. "OK? I can't."

"OK." He was conciliatory. She lit another cigarette.

"I've told you before, Garrick. Go find a nice southern girl in pearls, someone who'll be good with your kids, who knows how to make a low country boil and ride a horse." She drew a deep breath. "How could you want something as damaged as me?"

"You know that I'm no different."

She smiled at him, a solid bough of a man.

"Are you coming back?" he asked.

Would she? Two decades away from her only child; would she leave her for even one more day if she had a choice?

"I don't know. I surrendered the right to go home a long time ago. I don't know what happens next."

She turned to the open window, shielding herself with her shoulder from what lay unsaid between them.

"Look," he said. "I've got two kids, two jobs, a crazy ex-wife, and my family's land that I'm holding together with duct tape and a prayer. But I will be here if you come back." He took her hand and held it tightly. "I'll be here."

His affection, and what ran deeply beneath it, gave her pause. She placed her other hand over his but kept her eyes on the road ahead.

RACHEL

The leopard was coming.

All through the drive north from Cape Town, Rachel had known this.

During the slow creep of night, she'd rested intermittently in her car, continuing always toward the spine of red-and-orange mountains. Morning found her at the outskirts of a town that was little more than scattered patchwork houses thrown against eroded hills. She parked. Backpack and jacket in hand, she left the keys in the ignition and walked away. The car would be dismantled or taken, its plates removed before the day was done.

Resolute, Rachel faced forward, refusing to look back down the road behind her. The route from here was a pilgrimage she would complete on foot.

Two bottle stores and a butcher shop marked the dusty main street. She knew where she was. The skyline was unchanged from when she was a young girl. Much of the town was new, but the landscape was old, human enterprise merely fleeting when measured against the spread of time the peaks towering in the distance had witnessed.

A pack of boys surged by on rusted BMXs, moving loose and fast. Some pedaled awkwardly, knees at the handlebars; others were upright, leaning forward, bodies arching toward the horizon. They wore dirty pants and torn, old shorts, but their faces were turned up toward the sun, open to the day. In a place where Rachel knew unemployment and alcohol had stalled her people, the responsibilities of manhood would fall upon these children too soon. Yet they appeared gleeful and free. Young and full of verve, still beginning.

Yolanda, Philip, Mark, Ingrid.

It was then, thinking of her children and that grandchild, that Rachel looked back. She held out a single wrinkled hand. She would not cry. She had mothered not one but two generations, and mothering meant you had no choice but to keep going.

She reached the end of the main street and turned toward the valley, the old farm. Her fatigue was constant, another reminder of her untreated lymphoma. Last month, the nurse at the day hospital had offered her another box of pain pills, asked how she was doing, said that it was time to visit a doctor at the big hospital, Groote Schuur. They were going to make an appointment for her. That had been the last bit of impetus Rachel needed.

At the top of the mountain pass, she rested. Table Mountain stood small in the distance, a beacon, a reminder of the seasons of gain and loss that had come upon her in its shadow. But before all that was this: open land, the cartography of life she and her siblings had created based on rock and bone, song and mother. Home was more than place. As she began to make her way down into the valley, that knowledge was both agonizing and liberating. She let the fullness of a country afternoon wash over her.

"A lifetime ago," she said to the buchu scent, the orange sand before her, "a little girl came over this pass in a donkey cart."

As a child, it was the only way Rachel had known to be in the world: tucked between her siblings on a patched-up cart, riding with their mother across the great arid plain of the Karoo. "We are the Nama," their mother, Sara, would say fiercely, in Afrikaans, claiming the language and daring the narrow boer idea of what an Afrikaner was. "This is our country, never mind what the white man says. You must know it." Her mother would speak about this southern African First Nation as kin, rattling off stories of those she remembered, with urgency. Wearing a flowing dress in a dated style and a head covering, her mother delivered babies, brought herbs and healing to the sick, kept her children close and on the move.

Sara's eyes were lit by the campfires, around which she danced on hard feet, bare even in winter. She twirled her children on nights of stars, singing proudly in a clicking tongue almost no one remembered, distracting them from the forbidding cold. She taught them about plants and herbs, about the land, about entire peoples rendered ghosts.

But Rachel remembered the frostbitten morning, their stomachs gnawing, fingers on fire with chilblains, when her mother had told them she was abandoning the cart and settling down on a farm. She had met a man there while helping a laboring woman. Their new father and new circumstances both proved ill fitting. The farm offered the *sjambok* of obedience, that leather whip that spoke for the white baas, driving furrows of servitude into the laborers' backs, their foreheads, their lives. Rachel winced, remembering the punishments her stepfather had meted out for their lack of discipline and manners. This man, remunerated for hard labor with a low wage and alcohol in a bag, a *papsak*, had no other realm of authority in his life.

But Rachel and her siblings didn't care. It was impossible to make them. They had laid claim to the stars, to the very bones of the earth, and no one could tell them otherwise. They were pagan children, lost in the mountains, close to the elements.

Rachel, being the youngest, had little recollection of her real father other than his laugh, booming and joy filled. An undisclosed tragedy had taken him away; he was simply gone.

Now, she wiped the sweat from her forehead with a handkerchief. All of that had long passed. She entered the embrace of those all-enveloping mountains anew, strode down to the valley where the farm of her youth had been. Peaks with a near-magnetic presence watched her from across the bowl. Within their depths were the tracks that drew her. She felt the leopard, a presence like a hum, a vibration quivering through her teeth and bones. It had begun: the leopard, the ancestors, the memory of the clicking man.

The day Rachel had met the clicking man, she'd been ten or eleven—no one was ever quite certain, with her nomadic childhood, of her exact age or birth date. It had been a Sunday afternoon. Her feet had stirred the orange dust, her bare legs charcoal brown in the glare of the sun, her hands hard and white from the dried stickiness that came with gorging on a hidden stash of pineapples.

Taking a shortcut through a field of winter melons, she stopped short. A stranger stood next to her stepfather, peering into their hut. He was a small man, bare chested, with tightly coiled hair like Rachel's and leathery skin like her mother's. Her stepfather lolled beside him in a hungover doze.

The stranger noticed her but said nothing. He wore animal skins over his waist, a quiver with arrows, and beads around his neck, but little else.

A prickly sense of fear ran down Rachel's spine: What was his intent? Where were her mother and the other children?

Her stepfather sighed and shifted in his chair. "Oom Hendrik," Rachel called to him, shouting until he opened his eyes. She gestured to the man. "Your friend, he looks like a bushman. Why is he so quiet? And where are his clothes?"

Hendrik grunted, a sound of incomprehension and irritation. "What are you talking about, Rachel?"

"Don't you see him? The man next to you?" Even as she spoke, her voice dwindled away. Hendrik clicked his tongue and looked around, seeing nothing.

"I'm going to beat you if you keep talking nonsense. I'm sleeping. Go play." Hendrik dropped his head back and drew his hat over his face, dismissing her.

His threat should have scared her, but she was oblivious to the bruises and cut skin from her last beating. Instead what Rachel remembered was the small sound of incredulity in the back of her throat, the sudden sense of aloneness that left her chilled despite the day's heat.

The stranger had noticed her eyes upon him, and as her stepfather closed his eyes, he came closer, speaking in a tongue of clicks. He spoke with her, but then, that first time, she didn't understand. Eventually he walked away, and her eyes followed him.

When she spun back, she saw her mother coming toward her with a small knowing look on her face.

"I wondered if one of you would have the gift," her mother murmured.

He returned, the clicking man, again and again. Other people besides Rachel and her mother were oblivious to him. But Rachel observed how they treated the space, the air that he occupied, as if it had weight. Unconsciously they gave him room.

This first bout of her visions was coupled with an onset of illness that settled in for weeks, leaving her incapacitated. She was different, she learned then. She would always be apart. She had an ability that some trusted but all feared. Everyone except her girl, her Yolanda.

Decades older now, standing in the dusty valley of her childhood, Rachel stumbled, bent anew by her daughter's long absence. Time did nothing for mothers to dull the pain of a child's tragedy. Raising Ingrid had simply blurred the pain's sharpest edges.

Yolanda had known her mother was not mad. She had accompanied Rachel on walks on the mountain, had tended to her when Rachel had lain at the mercy of her episodes. In her pain, Rachel remembered explaining to Yolanda that she could see not only the surface of life but the breadth and depth of its tapestries, the worn macramé that made up the network of existence. Sometimes she saw sharp, swift movement in the water and oncoming jaws: circumstance rising to paralyze, to bite or consume. Sometimes the news was good. But it was not always clear; it was not tidy and linear, and it had failed her when she'd needed it most.

At the old farm, gnarled and untended trees greeted her. The abandoned laborers' huts stood a respectful distance from the ruin of the farmhouse. A fallen roof with a single wall was all that remained of their old hut. The dilapidation seemed appropriate. Settlement had brought ruin to her family, to her people. Rachel recalled the endless rows of oranges and melons, the overpowering scent of rotten fruit, the drudgery of picking that had worn away the horizon from her mother's eyes.

Still, they had left. After one too many beatings, her mother threw a pot of boiling water at her stepfather, gathered her children, and walked off. But their itinerant life was not the same; they were aware now of their poverty, and their mother had aged. For the first time ever, they worried about her.

Rachel and one sister made their way to the Cape. Her two other siblings found work farther north. Midwifery continued to be their mother's calling. When Rachel's sister had announced that she couldn't adjust to city life and was returning to the Karoo, Rachel remembered the isolation she had felt. That feeling was cemented in the last decade, as her mother and siblings had passed away one by one. Now, only she was left.

Looking at the old farm, Rachel took it all in, recalling who had lived where, the topography and characters, their feral dogs, the rhythm of this life. Her temples throbbed. Frightened, she looked to the hills beyond. The mountains sat, behemoth-like, behind each other.

"Rachel." Sara's voice carried on the breeze. She turned sharply. Her blood quickened; the very earth beneath her feet beat its heart in resonance with her own. A tremor rippled in her bones. She breathed in hard before composing herself and looking ahead.

For a moment she was at a loss—paths overgrown, nothing as it had been. Then, as she picked her way through brush and bush, she began to hum. At first she sang a jumble of strung-together melodies, a melee of sound. Not yet harmony and not yet the words she sought—they would come later. In Afrikaans, the staccato of "Boesmanland"; the drawn-out syllables of "Sarie Marais." English wound its way in, from the sweetness of "Baby, It's Cold Outside" to "Strangers in the Night." Her mind swirled with music.

While she made her way along a path found by sense and memory, words and tunes continued to intermingle, blend. They broke and drifted. Rachel was searching for the right note, the correct timbre and pitch. The words, the milk-and-honey bath of them, brought comfort, enough for her to keep moving through the rocks and up the kloof.

Slowly, something took root. She began to sing with a missionary's devout air and clarity of purpose. Her song was full, her words mellow and condensed. She was settling into a meditative state. She knew the way, here from Gousblomkraal se Kloof up and around the peak of Witberg, over the Suurvlakte and into the land of high and forbidding peaks. There stood lacerated rock faces, ragged and torn by the wind.

At night the distant scamper and cough of baboons came and went. Rachel did not sleep but drifted, dizzying nausea accompanying her visions of the ancient tracks. Some were faint and others lost, but as time passed, the lines stood clear along the land. Others had walked them millennia before, others whose whispers came lilting to her on the breeze.

The next day Rachel walked onward, moving between increasingly precarious rock scrambles and bursts of vivid restio flowers. Every so often the sound of trickling water rose above her melody, and through it all the wind was a constant. With her changed gaze, everything in the world was at once observed and enlarged.

"I am here for those who have come before," she said, whispering a solitary prayer. The clicking words of a different tongue, an ancient time, came of their own accord. She was their ready current. In her nightmares, these words had slipped from her mind, become too slick to grasp, thin as weak tea. Rachel had awoken cold and afraid, for if the words went, she would go with them, her very essence dissolving amid the forceful stream of newer languages. Those tongues, brought by Europeans, could never be a substitute. They were the voice of the outside looking in.

Time fused into a singular state where everything was known and seen, where the past stretched long as the Gariep River in the north and the future reached its hand toward the glistening promise of the ocean.

The dull, compressed heaviness of a migraine began to form. Soon, Rachel knew, jagged triangles of piercing light would gather on the outer perimeter of her vision. Soon she would want to cleave her head open from the pain. She abandoned her boots and pressed her toes into rocky soil, feeling her foot bones dig into the earth, exhaling with the joy of it.

She sang with open release now, words not heard for centuries in this place. The grieving sorrow of a wrecked people, the call of a buried language and all who had been nursed and nurtured by it, seared through her. Yet she was alone. There would not be a hearkening back to a glittering past for any of them, not for the ancestors and not for her. There could be no undoing of what had been broken. Only a bid to set it right.

Feeling the earth and rocks carefully with her bare feet, she moved ever upward. The discipline of mountain walking had left her strong. Still, her eyeballs sparked with every step. She wanted to dash her head against the rocks just to release the pain. Her sight had begun to change; her scrying eyes pierced everything, seeking.

By the time she came upon the giant eye of the cave, buried in the orange-and-red rock, night had long since fallen. Rachel looked up to the Southern Cross and Southern Pleaides. Foot over hand, she entered the damp interior of the cave, felt the earth fall away to hollowness and cool air. Her song echoed against the depths, returning a multitude of voices that welcomed her inward.

She clambered over the loose boulders to reach a warm and sheltered place at the rear, redolent with the deep, musty odor the cave held in its bosom. There she waited. She was deep within her mind and far beyond its perimeters at the same time.

The vision that came upon her was dark: music, the sound of a man singing to himself as he assembled a gun. Rachel couldn't see his body, only his gloved hands moving with skill and certainty. She could hear a snatch of his voice, singing, but the words escaped her.

Then he was gone, and the sandstone cave was all her eyes fell upon. She collapsed into slumber, woke to far-off light. She had no context for her vision, nothing to connect it to, but this was typical. Still, it was disturbing to consider that violence lay down the path that any of them were on now. She ate the last pieces of her bread and moved to the cave's lip, encircled by the wild heights of the peaks. Throughout the long day, she held to her peace as best she could. Evening brought a chill, but that wasn't why she began to tremble with electricity, the hairs on her neck rising.

"Ma." The rich baritone echoed as the man emerged from the cave's belly. He moved with feline grace despite his old, broken clothing and worn, unlaced boots; a bag was on his back. He looked like a farm laborer.

"Jan." With outstretched arms, Rachel greeted him. He had inviting amber eyes that grew bigger as she stared into them. "You came."

"Yes. You found me. You remembered how. Not *klein* Rachel anymore, hey."

Hearing her name spoken in the guttural country way, she smiled.

"That small wild child from the veld," Jan continued.

Something distant—and yet so near—was rending. The journey had begun, but so had the mourning. Rachel hung her head. She knew that Jan was reading her road, the one left behind and the one to come.

"These tracks, Ma," he said, "the ones you called me to lead you on, they only go one way. This is the last journey you will take. It is the road back to the ancestors. Do you understand this?"

"Yes."

"Why are you here?"

She looked at the disappearing sun. For her, the close of this day held an ending grander and more poignant than any other.

"You keep your children safe, Jan, or you try. My mother did." She sighed. "But then you can't do it anymore. In a way they are gone from you forever. All my life I was told I must accept, accept, make peace. My sons will be OK; I know that now. But I can't let her go, my daughter. I don't have that peace, Jan. I will have justice for her. It is why I am here. Two decades lost: that has been the cost of what I couldn't see. And I am dying. Slowly, but still."

Jan nodded, said simply, "I can smell the cancer."

"I want to set right what I can before I am too weak. I want to fight for Yolanda."

"There is more to come, Ma. Neither your story nor hers is done. But it will come at a price."

"I know, Jan. It is a price I have already paid."

They sat in silence for a long time. "Sunset," Jan said. "This one will be something to see."

His tone eased her. From the bag he carried, he raised the stringed bow of an instrument and began to blow into it as he played: the goura. The sound sparked memories of vivid stars in the time before the farm, of dancing, of rawness. She looked at Jan's right hand. The missing top digit of the little finger had marked the clicking man. It also marked Jan. They were of her people.

She watched the sun grow grander in its final moments, setting the world ablaze, reaching for the heavens one last time.

Jan was playing the land, a haunting tune that reached past rock and bone to the marrow of the earth, binding its living soul to his call. The lone cedar tree on a ledge below changed with every stroke of his strings. Bursting its bark, a branch reached toward them, grew large enough for them to step upon. Her heart taut with pain, Rachel watched the last of the sun leave.

The tree bore them through the rear of the cave, rock shifting and folding around them. They went deep into the bosom of the mountains, where the oldest tracks lived, the ones left by those long gone. The tree withdrew. Jan fell silent. Then he led Rachel along a path that might have been but was no longer once they passed.

"Ma," he said. "I will guide you one last time. We will do this together."

She gripped his hand, holding it lightly as it softened into his leopard tail, knowing she could not look back, go back, undo. Mending and magic waited. There was the chance, at last, to come home.

ELSA

André Kuiper smoked a pack of unfiltered Camels a day. It was a habit Pieter said he'd acquired years before on the border. This explained both the hovering reek of ashtray that pervaded the government office and the distaste Elsa felt toward him.

A receded hairline left Kuiper's face open and elevated. Beneath his brow, he had sun-lined skin, rugged with the pockmarks of adolescent acne and the markings of a life at war. His beard was well trimmed—incongruous, Elsa thought, for a man like him—and his white cotton shirt sat around his muscled neck with the crispness of a papal collar. Irritatingly, persistently, he tapped his foot to some unheard melody.

Seated in Pieter's cavernous office on Plein Street, alongside the Houses of Parliament, Elsa looked out at the billowing clouds drifting across Table Mountain. Kuiper had swiveled his chair to face her and her brother, as if he were interviewing them. For several minutes he'd stared disconcertingly at Elsa. Not lost on her was the jarring irony of the first time she had sat here regarding this matter, before her brother's large desk, her handbag perched primly on her lap.

"Well, I don't think we need a long meeting, especially on a Monday morning," Pieter began. "Kuiper, we need your specific skills."

"Why and for how long?" It was the first time he'd spoken, and he did so only after a short pause. His question was directed at Elsa. But she set her jaw and refused to look at him.

With a lazy movement of his head, Kuiper turned to Pieter. "My bags are packed, you know. Early retirement to an undisclosed location."

"We will pay. I know how precious your time is," Pieter said with a modicum of sarcasm. "Elsa, would you like to explain?"

She brushed away the unsettling feeling Kuiper gave her, the sense of a cocked trigger. She looked at him with determination hardening her every fiber. "I want you to find someone for me, Mr. Kuiper." His inspecting gaze left her feeling foul. She would bathe as soon as she got home, but for now she continued to stare him down. "I have reason to believe she's a threat to my family."

Quiet hovered. How much information would she have to give up?

Her heart had thumped nineteen years ago, too, when Pieter had delivered his opening words. He had stood behind his desk then as well, in this room of old wood and stature, his barrier against the world. Captain Fouché from the police, newly met, had sat on the broad sill at the rear of the room.

"Elsa," Pieter had said gravely, "Stefan is in a little bit of trouble."

"What do you mean?" she had stuttered.

"There's a girl . . ." Pieter's voice had trailed off awkwardly. Elsa remembered the panic she'd felt.

"What did you do to her? This 'someone' you want me to find." The query snapped Elsa back to the present. Kuiper, smirking, looked her dead in the eye.

"Excuse me?" Elsa drew her head back and eyed him coldly. "I think you misunderstand, Mr. Kuiper. We are the ones being threatened by her."

"When did you become a judge, Kuiper?" Pieter interjected.

Kuiper didn't respond. Haughty, Elsa took the postcard from her handbag and gave it to him. "We got this in the post on Friday," she said as he scanned it. Elsa noticed the animalistic way his eyes took in details.

"Local card, postmarked last Monday," he said. "And?"

And? Untidy history dangled off the question. *And?*

In this same room, Captain Fouché had sat on the sill, body drawn away from something untouchable. *And?* A large brown envelope had lain on this same desk, as Fouché and her brother had spoken their allegations and indignant desperation had poured out of her.

"El, we have photos; there is evidence. Fouché told me months ago, but I didn't want to believe him."

Guilt and fury had enveloped Elsa then, as if she'd been the one charged. The charge was of raising a son who had done the unthinkable, the immoral. A son who was a race traitor.

"I had the photos taken myself, sister. I hired someone; I didn't want to bother you. But everything is true."

"He wouldn't." The nauseating taste in the back of her throat— she remembered that well. "What are you talking about? I don't understand."

And? "Elsa, he broke the law." She had glared at her brother and Fouché.

January 1975, a warm, summery day, the office silent. It had been soon after Christmas. *And?*

Boxes stood high against the wall behind Kuiper now, but the portrait of Vorster and the mounted display of an old Vierkleur flag were still there, witnesses to this devilish business of lust that could drag them all to hell. That day, in Pieter's office, Elsa had looked at the large brown envelope with an emotion unusual for her: unmitigated fear.

Now, she raised her aged eyes back to Kuiper with indignation and exhaustion. "And what?"

"Lady, you're going to have to give me more information. There are approximately forty million South Africans, depending on who you count. Fifty percent are women. Where am I supposed to begin looking for 'her,' and what must I do when I find her? And I will find her." His last words snaked around the others.

Straight lipped, Elsa took another envelope out of her handbag and handed it over. Kuiper removed the single old photograph it held and examined it intensely. All the while he was humming to himself. Elsa was eager to rid herself of this unsettling man.

Glancing at Pieter, she knew that he, too, recalled the awful revelation he had made in this room, so long ago. This photo had been in that brown envelope then, which had sat large and bulging with other photographs her brother had been unwilling to show her.

Then, she had been adamant with Pieter. "I want to see," she'd insisted. "You want to arrest my son on a charge that I don't believe? It's absurd; he doesn't have any reason to get involved with a coloured." Shrugging off disbelief, she had drawn herself upright, tall. "I want to see them."

When he'd said, "Elsa, it's not fit for a lady to look at," her response had been a face of stone. Eventually her brother had opened the brown envelope and handed it over.

Even now, the grainy photos were burned into her consciousness. She had looked at every one in turn, marveling at Stefan's utter stupidity. Here was his car in front of a house she didn't know. Pictures of a girl in a dowdy uniform in a café. The girl had a distinctive chin, a pert nose. She was attractive, but there were hordes of coloured girls with the same tousle of hair and brown skin. Beauty could never hide the flaws of the coloured character. After all, what could one expect from a race of leftovers?

Then came the picture of her son in his awful beach togs at the same café, talking with the girl in earnest, sandwich in hand. The reel unfolded as if at a cinema: a stolen kiss; a shocking picture, snapped through a bedroom window, of sleeping bodies, naked, entwined; hands that should never have been held; smiles that had no place in this world.

Stefan walking with his arm around a white woman she didn't know, while the coloured girl walked alongside them both.

Finally, the photo that disturbed her most: Stefan, on a distant hillside, looking rougher, wilder, than she was used to, with his arms wrapped around the girl. He looked untamed, but there was a lightness on his face, a joy Elsa had never seen. In that single moment of theft, hatred had coiled its tail around Elsa.

"Pretty girl," Kuiper said, looking at the picture. "But what is a fine lady like you doing with an old photo of a coloured girl at a train station?"

He looked up at Elsa. The foot tapping, the humming, had returned.

"Stop, Mr. Kuiper, with your feet," Elsa said.

"I like music, Mrs. Van Deventer. Keeps me moving."

Pieter asked, "Kuiper, are you looking for money or for cause?"

"Both," Kuiper said with quiet disregard for Pieter's tone. Elsa glared at him.

"The cause is none of your business," she said.

Kuiper stared at her, bemused. This, her darkest secret held at bay for so many years, was nothing more than a game to him. "What's her name?" he asked.

"Her name is Yolanda Petersen," Fouché had said that long-ago January. "She's a student at that coloured bush college. That place in itself is a problem. The terrorists are hard at work on that campus, let me tell you. She has a brother who's of interest to us, a troublemaker. Philip Petersen."

The photo Kuiper now held had been newly taken then. It captured Yolanda in an ordinary moment, at a railway station, looking down the track, her blouse's collar sitting askew. Elsa had looked at her as if she were roadkill. A swelter of anger had built inside Elsa like magma. At the thought of her son and family being so defiled, it crested and broke.

"We've just arrested her." In the long blank that followed Fouché's words, Elsa realized with horror what they meant to do next.

"You can't," she said, standing up. She could see everything she had built, the distance she had put between herself and her childhood of patched clothes and hole-ridden shoes, evaporating in the heat of scandal. "You dare not arrest Stefan, Pieter. I will deal with him, but please, do you understand what it would mean?"

Fouché looked sheepish for a moment, Pieter more calculating. Elsa continued, "He is a young man; he made a mistake."

"Elsa, Stefan hasn't been very careful with his personal life." Vaguely Elsa registered that, unlike her, Pieter did not take exception to Stefan's behavior, only his lack of discretion.

Fouché stood, smug. "We can't arrest this girl without arresting him also. Such an offense, and carrying on for so long. When did your son move to Muizenberg? It could have been from then already, more than a year before we started following them. We came to Pieter when we knew who he was, or both of them would have been arrested long ago. We can't just give him a warning and a fine."

"You're the police; you can do whatever you damn well please," Elsa snapped. "The day that my son's name appears in the newspaper with this little mud parasite's face next to his—my brother, my husband, and I, we will come for your head and your boss's head, do you understand me?"

She made sure her gaze was as sharp as her tongue. "Fix this, I don't care how, and leave my family and my son out of it."

Spinning on her heel, Yolanda's photo still in hand, Elsa had held her composure, though her mind had spun with options for drawing Stefan back in, back onto the ledge from which he had launched himself.

Now, Kuiper nodded slowly as Pieter said Yolanda's name. "Lovely," he said. "A lovely name for a lovely girl."

Elsa raised an eyebrow. She had been assured that he was excellent at what he did, but here, talking to him, she had doubts.

"Mr. Kuiper," she said, her voice edged with anxiety. "Find her and watch her. There was a time when one had the law on one's side and all of this wouldn't have been necessary. Naturally now, with the kaffirs and hotnots, everything is chaos."

A delicate pause fell between them as Elsa and Pieter waited for a sign of his assent.

"Where does your son live, or is it your husband? Is this the weekend special of one of them? A bastard child, what?"

Elsa was outraged that he would salt her wound with such abandon, but instead she drew her face tight as a drum. She glanced at Pieter, who appeared tongue-tied.

"Do you know who my husband is, Mr. Kuiper? Who we are?" she said.

Kuiper turned his head and looked at her lazily. "I'm going to do a bit of guesswork and say it's your son, although your husband might surprise me."

Pieter intervened. "Kuiper, that's enough."

"Do you know what year it is, Mrs. Van Deventer, what month? Do you know what *chaila time* means? It's what the workers say when they're going home, when the day is over and the work is done. When it's time to leave and pick up their pay packets, they chaila." Kuiper's voice was unruffled. "These coloureds and Blacks, the hotnots and kaffirs, the unwashed masses on the Cape Flats, maybe even this girl's people, they are the bosses now. They run the show. The world is changing, just like that." He clicked his fingers. "Chaila time is coming for your husband and his cronies, for all of us. Remember that."

He straightened up, businesslike, and put the postcard and photo in a back pocket. He seemed suddenly disinterested, the meeting exhausted of its drama.

"I expect ten thousand in cash within a week. The address is Nine Palm Straat, Ruyterwacht. The person who answers the door is called Blommie. Blommie will count all the notes. I don't take checks."

Taken aback by his briskness, Elsa looked to Pieter, but Kuiper continued, "Your daughter, Amanda, lives in Durbanville. Two kids; same job and husband since high school. Your son, Stefan, lives in Harrismith; he's married to Katrina Odendaal. They have three kids. Your husband is Danie van Deventer. His father was a wine farmer from Paarl. You were originally little Elsa du Toit from Epping, whose daddy was a railway worker. Little Elsa who hit the big time when she became Danie van Deventer's secretary."

Elsa's jaw worked, but she had nothing to say.

"Pay me on time," Kuiper said. "I expect the next ten thousand within a month, same place. The job will be done by then. I will phone you if I need anything. My name is Johan; I work for Van der Merwe and Son. You're planning to do some landscaping."

Pieter was smiling slightly and shaking his head. "I presume you'll see yourself out, Kuiper. You know where to find me."

"Of course." He was almost at the door.

"How do I know," Elsa said, stuttering against the slipperiness of something careening out of control. "How do I know you're not just going to walk away with my money?"

"Mrs. Van Deventer." He turned to face her. She realized as she watched him move, watched his gaze, that there was something predatory about him. "I'm a professional. Besides, all that you have to remember is that I know. I know something that is important to you." He pointed at her, emphasizing his final word. "Pay me on time, and remember that."

He left. Exhausted, Elsa fell back in her chair. Pieter poured her a shot of whisky, assuring her that Kuiper was unpleasant but worth it. She pinched her eyes shut.

Back then, it had been sobering to learn her own son had lied to her. To know that she had raised a stranger; that even on the occasional Sunday when he'd been home, sitting alongside them at an otherwise normal braai with others in their circle, he had been sleeping with that woman, maybe even the night before. They had given him free rein after the army, had let him have some time away, and he had abused it. The rot of Muizenberg carried over to this very moment.

But the end justified the means, Elsa thought. There was no question that it had then, and it would do so now.

INGRID

Yolanda's watercolor flowers hovered in Ingrid's mind as she lay on her bed. Monday morning unfolded beyond her drawn curtains, but she didn't move. Disa. She thought of her middle name and remembered the first time Rachel had told her about the flowers. Delicate, they grew only in hidden kloofs on Table Mountain in the summer, her grandmother had said, and even then they were difficult to find.

It had meant nothing until now. The flowers' impermanence had been another brick upon which Ingrid had filled out the hollow shape of parents who'd been snatched away by a tire blowout. The lie.

The night before, she'd stood at her living room window, looking at the train tracks that ran near her apartment. It was the Simonstown line. Cape Town's downtown, a prosperous slice of white industry, lay on one end. But along the other side was the world she came from: the southern peninsula, the Cape Flats.

In the months since she'd moved to Rondebosch, watching the train had provided comfort. At peak hours, coloured life would pour out of third class: men standing at open doors, women sheltered farther inside, trying to relieve their bunioned feet. Familiar chatter would drift up to Ingrid's open window, and with it, small signals in slang and gesture that she understood. She'd spy a scattering of Brown people in the first-class carriages, too, looking well dressed and occupied.

On mornings when she had to steel herself to face the climb up the big hill to university, or on those afternoons when that climb had meant so much more, that train line was like a cord connecting her to where she came from. The journey she was undertaking felt like moving from the bustle of third to the relative isolation of first class.

But last night, she'd looked at the tracks through tears, hugging herself. The railway was silent, its brown arms extended into darkness. The cord was cut. She was an impostor, a boer's illegitimate half breed, a traitorous mother's dirty secret. Bad seed fallen from a bad tree. Just like the mother who'd birthed her, Rachel, the only mother she'd known, had run. Had fled rather than face her directly. Ingrid was alone, an illegal creation born into shame.

Now, standing in the bathroom, she gripped the sink. Her trembling hands touched her face. Whose eyes did she have? Whose nose? Which part of herself should she hate more: the mother who'd thrown her away, or the father who wandered these same streets, who couldn't be bothered with her in the first place?

She was lost. No longer just a little different from her peers. Now she was something more ominous. Library trips with Pa, Ma letting her make the jelly for trifle at Christmas—the whole of it had been an act, a plastering over. She did not belong in this family. She belonged to no one.

Back in her room, an angry stew of music thundered from her stereo. The classes she was missing, the unfinished assignments—it all seemed to add to the burden, to make her feel that she in turn was betraying something. But she couldn't see a path to correcting all that had been overturned.

Monica returned home in the evening, shouted to Ingrid that she needed to get up. Ingrid had told her only of Rachel's disappearance, not the revelations about her parents. The hole of abandonment she faced, with its black, slick walls, was too frightening to discuss.

"Leave me alone," she said as Monica entered the room, opening the curtains and windows.

"No. Come, you need to chop vegetables."

Groaning, Ingrid reluctantly joined her in the kitchen, until a knock on the door froze her. Mark and Tracy had visited the previous day, and she'd told them, through her locked bedroom door and a stream of flustered tears, to go away. She hadn't the stomach for more.

Monica answered the door, and the sound of Reuben's voice propelled Ingrid back to her bedroom. She locked the door with a click.

"Ingrid, I'm not going," he said, standing directly outside.

"Reuben, what do you want?" Ingrid asked.

He paused, then said, "Ingrid, look, I know the whole thing. Mark told me. He's upset."

"*He's* upset," she muttered but unlocked the door. Reuben made himself at home on her bed. Ingrid glared at the bag he'd brought in.

"What did Uncle Mark tell you?" Ingrid asked. "And why do you have that bag of my mother's stuff?"

He was uncharacteristically solemn. "That your parents are alive. He gave me this, said maybe it will help you get used to the idea."

"Are you serious?" Ingrid sat on a chair, facing him. "Do you know what they did to me, Reuben?"

"Well, obviously the accident was a lie."

Monica came nearer, leaning against the doorjamb. Reuben held a hand out to her, affection softening his face. Ingrid sighed. Now that they were together, telling one was as good as telling the other. Rage churned in her gut as she recounted everything she knew of Yolanda and Stefan.

"I don't know who these people, my family, are," she finished. "Who holds back information like this for so long?"

Monica looked between Reuben and Ingrid uncertainly. "I know this really isn't my business, but you don't have all the facts, do you?"

"What difference would the rest of it make, Monica?" Ingrid said. "What kind of grandmother lies about something this important? What kind of woman throws her child away and pretends to be dead for two decades?"

"Maybe someone who didn't know how to be a mother in the first place, who wasn't ready?"

"But your father, the boer . . ." Reuben's voice trailed off.

"And a boer is?" With her long braids bundled up in a headscarf, the look of confusion on Monica's oval face was clear.

"An Afrikaner," Reuben said sharply. "Or the police—we use the term for both groups 'cause they're basically the same thing. They're the people who created apartheid and made life a living hell for everyone who's not white."

"God, this country is complicated." Monica sighed, shook her head. "What I'm studying in sociology is nothing compared to what I have to understand outside it. In Mauritius, well, we don't have this history. Anyway, I'm going to leave you two; I don't want to step in. I'm worried about you, though, Ingrid, that's all."

She left, and Reuben turned back to Ingrid. "You're missing the point: These people are alive. You don't need to imagine your parents anymore, like you did at school, sitting around feeling sorry for yourself. Are you saying you'd rather have a dead father than an Afrikaner?"

Ingrid looked out the window. She didn't have an answer for him.

"Look." Reuben sat up. "We coloured, we already mixed, and mixed includes them, whether either side likes it or not. There's nothing we can do about it. A lot of us talk Afrikaans anyway."

"But Reuben, this isn't ancient history. This is now; it's me. I have to think about this guy in a safari suit, with *veldskoene* on his feet and a comb in his sock, on top of my mother. His people hunted my uncle like a dog; they harassed my family, murdered coloureds and Blacks.

They terrorized us with fucking tanks. How could she do that to us? How could she do that to me?"

"Find her. Ask her those questions. Or ask him. Apartheid is over, hey? Everything doesn't have to be hush-hush anymore."

She folded her arms. "I can't go knock on the man's door and say, *I'm your daughter. No, we've never met, and no, I don't know if you even remember my mother, the coloured woman you used to be involved with.*"

Ingrid stared out the window. The sun, despite its brightness, brought her no real warmth.

"Ingrid, I know you better than anybody." Reuben's voice was soft. "You can't avoid your problems by barricading yourself away. You need to act; you need to do something."

She turned to him, her irritation and frustration plain. "I have my plate full just carrying on with my fucking life."

"Yes, and shit happens. I know things with your family have been difficult, but Ma has always loved you. She's the reason you got a license; she's the reason you moved out. I think she wants you to find the answers on your own. People keep talking about Ma like she's mad. She's not. She knows what she's doing."

Ingrid thought of their last supper and the plain moments they'd shared over pumpkin bredie. "Oh, I know she does," she said. "She lied to me deliberately. All this time. Then left me this bag, just left it like I'm nothing to her, and walked away. She couldn't even face me."

"But that's not true. This can't have been easy for her, either, all this time. All I'm saying is, if Ma left this for you, then she's still trying to tell you something. Half the Cape Flats is looking for her. If she wants to be found, she will be. You have other stuff to figure out." He came to stand beside her at the window. "Let me ask Jerome, my cousin. He's with the post office. We'll see if we can find this Stefan."

"Reuben," she snapped, "there must be twenty, thirty Stefan van Deventers."

"So? We phone them. There must be something unique about him, some way we'll know he's the right one." Reuben pointed to the parcel. "Maybe there's a clue in there."

"I want nothing to do with that bag," Ingrid said, turning away. "Or the man."

"Then I'm looking." He gave her a moment to counter him. When she didn't, Reuben went over and began to peruse the package's contents, item by item.

"By the way, Friday night. I'm sorry for that," he said, looking up from a handful of photographs. "I just wasn't sure if you were interested in that guy."

His words reminded Ingrid that somewhere beyond this was Litha—Litha, who made her feel safe. She tried to remember his apartment number.

"Your mother was pretty," Reuben said quietly, holding up a picture.

Ingrid narrowed her eyes. "I don't give a fuck what she looked like. She's nothing to me, not now."

"Don't be so quick to judge." Reuben continued to sift. "Well, this is unusual," he said, brightening. "He surfed. I didn't know the boere surf. Check this 'Whites Only' sign. This is Muizenberg back in the day. Look at the big old board."

Ingrid would not turn to see the photo.

"OK," Reuben said. "I'm going to phone Jerome when I get home, let you know what he finds."

He stood and walked out, and she heard him fall into conversation with Monica. Giving a deep sigh, Ingrid lay back on her bed.

Reuben's pragmatism had outlined what, for him, was a clear course of action, but it wasn't so easy for her. Wherever she looked, she faced the uprooting of indelible truths around which her life had formed. There could have been a different way. Mother, father, her, together. It had been possible. But she had not been enough to make any of them stay.

Dinner was eaten in a daze. Ingrid felt overwhelmed, unable to see above the waterline. An impulse overcame her to get away from everything: the people presenting problems, creating solutions, acting like it was all so simple when in reality it was *her* world turning upside down. She needed space. She wanted Litha. After Reuben and Monica settled on the sofa, Ingrid grabbed some records and walked to his apartment.

He wasn't home, but his brother, Tsepho, said he'd be along shortly. Ingrid waited inside while Tsepho busied himself in his bedroom.

Absentmindedly flipping through her albums, she ran her finger over the sleeve of Prince's *Lovesexy*, remembering her grandfather's fury when she'd brought it home. "He's disgusting," the old man had scolded, pointing a finger at the cover featuring the naked artist. "*Sies.*" She remembered the questions she hadn't asked Pa: *What are you so afraid of? Who don't you want me to be? I grew up under a shadow, and that's your gift to me: Yolanda, that long shadow.*

She heard the front door open. "Miss Vinyl," Litha said, beaming as he came in. Briefly, he switched to isiXhosa to chat with Tsepho. As he did, Ingrid realized she was sitting rigidly, with her arms wrapped around her records.

"I hope I'm not intruding." She was trying to sound more nonchalant than she felt.

Litha flopped beside her on the sofa. "No, of course not. I've been thinking about you. Besides, you're saving me from starting to read about constitutionality. But this"—he tilted his head at her as she sagged forward—"is not a happy visit?"

Tears dripped. "No," she said.

He drew her close, something that she hadn't realized until then she needed. She reveled in the feeling of his hands on her back. "I'll make tea, or do you want something stronger? Why don't you put something on the turntable?"

Ingrid went through her LPs blankly, settling on Depeche Mode. Where were the words to describe her situation? Was it simplest to say she was a bastard? A mistake? She curled herself into a ball, let the music wash over her.

Returning with a beer, Litha put a hand on her knee. "Tell me," he said. "Talk to me."

"I don't know what to say," she said. "My family . . . families are supposed to be that foundation you stand on; they're not supposed to be the reason you don't have one."

Litha said nothing, but his face told her to continue.

"I could have had something else, a more normal life, with people who loved me, who wanted me. Like I imagined when I was small."

Ingrid slowed down, trying to catch her breath and make sense. She described everything that had unfolded. As he had in the car, Litha listened attentively.

"I keep coming to you with my heavy shit," she said. "You must think I'm all over the place. I just needed everyone I know to leave me alone. I didn't know who else to talk to. I can't go home. Ma's not there, Litha." Her voice shook. "She left me too."

"You can stay here." She lay on his chest, sobbing as he stroked her hair.

"My parents . . . it feels like I've lost them all over again."

"But you haven't. It's quite the opposite now. Don't push them away out of fear. Your grandmother, maybe she will come back. Maybe your mother will be with her."

Ingrid shook her head, sat up, and wiped her face with the backs of her hands. "I'm not ready," she said. "If that happened, I'm not ready for her. She threw me aside like I was nothing. Maybe my father just didn't know, but Yolanda . . . she made a choice."

"Don't give the boer such an easy excuse." His voice hardened. "They hold all the power." She shuddered at the realization again that Stefan's Afrikaans heritage flowed through her veins.

"I think the answer is to get out of Cape Town," she said, testing out her resolution with words. "Yes. I'm not ready for a family reunion, for Yolanda reappearing like she's a superhero for staying alive. Maybe my grandmother is also coming back. But I can't sit here and wait and pretend everything will be wonderful, that I'm grateful."

Litha got up and switched records. Ingrid caught a glimpse of russet skin as he bent down. She imagined that he was Xhosa through and through, standing firmly on the clean lines of clan and tribe that she would never have. The fantasy of a real relationship with him felt like another casualty on the altar of apartheid's threshing board.

A woman's voice spread like soothing balm from the speakers, singing about tupelo honey. Ingrid played out Yolanda and Rachel's return in her mind, the way the family would orchestrate her life again. But as they had found with Philip, not all things could go back to where they had been decades before.

"Where will you go?" Litha asked, breaking into her thoughts.

"Windhoek, Durban, I don't know. Away." She shifted on the couch, putting space between them. She would spare him the awkwardness of saying he wasn't interested in such a messed-up woman, spare herself the embarrassment of being rejected.

"Ingrid, you must know that with the elections . . ."

"What?"

"How often have you left Cape Town?"

"I've gone up the Garden Route before." She shrugged.

Litha smiled. "OK, that's not far enough. Cape Town is not like the rest of the country."

"You think I can't take care of myself?"

"I know you can. It's whether other people will take care of you that I don't know. Some places, they are dangerous."

When Reuben returned two days later, clutching a phone number and address and saying he'd found the right Stefan, a man in Harrismith,

Ingrid took it as a sign. This was her destination, her route out of the Cape.

"I'm going to the Orange Free State this weekend," she said to Litha that night over coffee. He had visited her for a long spell the night before, heightening her confusion about what was happening between them. "My father lives there. I'm going to find him."

His face dropped. "*Hau*, Ingrid, you can't go there, not now. That place is the last stand of the boere. It's not safe."

"I'm not doing anything political, Litha. I'm going to meet my father."

"But that is political." Frustration flashed across his face. But she had made up her mind. "How are you going to do this?"

"Translux. I'll take a bus to Durban, then figure it out from there. My car won't survive the long road."

He leaned forward, studying her face. "So you are going to where the Zulu and the Afrikaners each are based, and both of them are fighting against the elections, against the new South Africa? You're going toward the violence?" It was the most serious she had ever seen him.

"If you're so worried, come with me. I looked on the AA maps. A person can do it in a weekend if you leave on a Friday and drive."

"What if it takes a day or two more? What are you going to do about university?"

"I've already asked for a leave of absence because of my grandmother." Silence spanned between them. Ingrid shut her eyes. "It's fine, Litha. I'm not your girlfriend; we're not anything. I'll figure this out."

He continued to study her quietly. Then he shook his head.

"I'm coming," he said. "But I'm driving, and we're going through the Transkei, up the coast. If we're going up-country, there is someone I'd like to see on the way. Friday, we'll do it; we'll go."

Taken aback, she nodded but could not resist a smile. She would get to be with him.

Long after he'd gone, Ingrid lay, wide eyed. Between Litha, her mother, her father, and her disappeared grandmother, her life was shifting into a shape she could not recognize. The stakes had grown; the outcome was obscured. The journey would be about more than Harrismith and Stefan. There was a tightening, sinking feeling in her chest. But maybe, Ingrid thought, if she pushed through, she and Litha together, maybe she'd find room to breathe.

YOLANDA

Table Mountain rose in the distance, with the presence of a mother waiting for her brood to return underwing. Seeing its profile through the airplane window, Yolanda felt herself grow greedy for the wild thicket grass, the fecund valleys, the kloofs. There it all sat, between the broken rock faces that stared, scarred, at the ocean.

Home. It had not been real until now.

"That really is something," the teacher next to her said in breathy Californian upspeak.

Yolanda gave a slight, distracted nod. "My daughter is down there," she said to herself.

"We're all going to remember this month: April of 1994," the teacher continued.

Yolanda knew what she meant: South Africa was a hairbreadth from a different reckoning with itself. A couple of weeks from now, for the first time in its life as a republic, there would be universal suffrage. But the excitement of that prospect was displaced for Yolanda by the gravity of realizing she was now at the point of no return. Besides, she had been gone so long that as she watched Cape Town approach, with the sweeping view of its parts known and unknown, it felt like someone else's country.

"That Mandela is such a dignified man," the teacher was saying.

"Absolutely," Yolanda replied on cue. "We've had fifty-odd years of apartheid; twenty-seven of them Mandela spent in jail."

It was the kind of blanket statement that drew everyone into the feel-good, history-making nature of the moment. Yolanda had heard the same kind of thing over and over again since she'd left Union Station. While trying to patch together money for airfare and finding a flight to the place everyone suddenly wanted to visit, she'd followed the newspaper reports in New York and London. But she didn't need to read their background on apartheid, the history of how it had been fed by the bitter feud between the British and the Afrikaners, at the expense of everyone else. She'd lived it.

In those papers it was so simple, so neat—without Philip, her lost brother; without loss; and without Stefan, there, on the other side of it all. Without the way he would stand with his broad feet in the mud and grass of Table Mountain, entranced by the sight of the distant ocean while curious about the fate of the elusive ghost frog; a man engrossed in the wonders of the world, in her. There they both had been, tangled in the agony of what they could and couldn't have. Each had waited for the moment they would need to lie on an altar of sacrifice, seeking absolution.

Reaching for a tissue, Yolanda brushed her hand against the yellowed sketch in her purse. There could be no absolution, not for her. Not for anyone.

The teacher babbled on. The many triumphs of this moment were sweet, but heartache was sewn into it. Yolanda smoothed her shirt. That was not what the teacher wanted to hear. She was asking about Cape jazz and a club called Manenberg's. She wanted to know about township food and the colorful quarters of the Bo-Kaap. Like many, she sought the emerging rainbow nation, a neat and uncomplicated African tapestry.

Preparing to land, the plane dropped its wheels. Yolanda drew herself upright like a flower at dusk. In her head, she began reciting the speech of return that had run in her head for so many years, echoing words that had once gone dry, with no one to receive them.

She had decided to say only the minimum: that politics had driven her away, but now they could move forward. Her family could be happy, the past no longer relevant; it had to be possible. Still, she hadn't called ahead to announce her return. What could she say? To whom, and how?

But there was one act she needed to carry out alone first. She entered the terminal clutching her British passport and accepted her visa stamp stoically. She emerged alone, finding herself between other people's relatives and friends.

Within the hour she was driving a rental car. Following pathways of familiarity and memory, she oriented herself by the sun and the mountain. Yet she was terrified, driving through suburbs whose names she'd not said for a lifetime. She peered at the faces of men on the sidewalk, petrified by the prospect of recognition. One of them might walk up to her car, and the nightmare would begin all over again.

"Stop," she said to her racing heart and the sweat that poured out of her, to the adrenaline and trepidation. God, she hated cars, hated feeling like a foreigner looking in.

Yet she knew this soil too well. Hers was a country of casual, random violence and casual, random joy. That was her refrain for those abroad, the ones who could move on in a breath to something else.

Street names pecked at the edges of her mind. She should be remembering them, felt compelled to, and yet . . . it had simply been so long. Around this corner lay Halt Road, surely, where the air in a cloistered takeaway shop was heavy with vinegary fish and chips. But no, she was mistaken.

She drove onward, knowing and dreading where she was going. More than Stefan's bed, more than the police cell, this place was where the end had come, the one that stalked her. The visit could be a complete failure. If the ghouls came, if the horror from the back seat of the car resurged in her mind, what would become of her? No one really knew where she was.

But she wanted to do this: face it, package it, set it aside, and carry on to the Mardi Gras reception of her dreams. Soon she would be sitting around Rachel's kitchen table with her mother and daughter, completing the circle.

The grounds of her old university were calm. The campus was empty of demonstrations, of tear gas and armed policemen. The old hall bore no posters of Black fists, no brimstone rhetoric. The air was filled with the snap of dominoes. A sprinkling of students wandered about; they looked bored and preoccupied, like young people anywhere in the world.

In that distant time, this place had boiled and spluttered with dysfunction. Yolanda remembered flying through here with a paintbrush and an attitude; she remembered the girl she had been. Now, she hurried out back to her car, unable to speak as she looked at the grasslands and bush beyond the campus. Those marshlands would never be empty for her. Terror dripped from memory's fronds, and memory, despite the decades, always threatened to reshape itself into the present.

Clinging to the steering wheel, she sped onto the highway toward the city. Straight ahead, Devil's Peak showed its horn to the heavens. She exited onto Main Road, where the throng of taxis surprised her. There, on the busy, ordinary street, she felt herself relax. Old men in hats pedaled ancient black bicycles behind narrow men on racing bikes. Office workers clutched bags; teenagers slouched by. Yolanda felt the familiar wind and smiled.

Hugging the mountain's green belt, she drove south. Beyond Constantiaberg's vineyards, the land opened up. The trees grew sparser, the earth browner. The suburbs here were, she recalled, white. She waited at a dropped boom gate over a railway crossing. Across the tracks lay the other half of a world bifurcated by the railway line: the coloured suburb of Steenberg, with Retreat beside it. Here the wild world of the marshes she remembered from her childhood, which used to be tucked between vleis and gravel roads, had been beaten back by zinc walls and more houses than Yolanda remembered. The main arterial roads were the same, but the slow pace of decades before was no more.

Like a strand of hair snagged on a branch, Yolanda found herself caught on a memory. It rushed back with a hum that she didn't entirely realize she was singing. The memory was of a radiant day spent at home with her mother. It was a Saturday, so they had cleaned together. Rachel polished the path outside while Yolanda washed the kitchen floor. There was joy, despite, or maybe because of, the ordinary moment. Rachel's upturned smiling eyes had watched Yolanda open the curtains facing the stoep after she turned up the old record player. Where had her father and brothers been? Yolanda couldn't remember.

Shirley Bassey, the powerhouse British singer, was the voice that had belted through the house as they worked. Yolanda remembered how proud her mother was of her Shirley albums, how fascinated Rachel had been that a woman whose skin color matched her own could offer such commanding performances. "She's enough to make even kings kneel," Rachel had said proudly, as if the singer's accomplishments were for all Black women.

Yolanda played album after album for Rachel that day. She loved watching her mother light up, work with pride in their house, even as she gave Yolanda a break to sit in the yard and draw. They'd cooked together later on, and the smells of fried onion and tomato with spices blended with the other elements of that memory.

Try as she might, Yolanda couldn't recall what they'd said to each other that afternoon. But the mood and the music, Rachel's warm, dry hands on her own, those stayed with her.

Never, Never, Never had been the newest Bassey album then. Yolanda found herself singing now, tripping on the album's title song, recalling feelings: the first burn of love, the surge of boldness. So many rules were being broken, but it wasn't her fault that he fit just right.

There was a rawness with Stefan; he was learning to swim his own currents. Rawness from that first moment, when she knew she was sinking into a togetherness that could break everything apart. But it would have been a lie to walk away because of something as superficial as the color of his skin.

Of course, it hadn't proved to be superficial at all.

Driving into her old neighborhood, she looked around with the wonder and regard that were the sole preserve of the homesick emigrant. This was not Africa through a television lens but her old community. As she maneuvered through several wrong turns, she remembered: here was where the Hernandez family had stayed; on another corner was Mrs. Jacobs, the schoolteacher. Nearby were friends that she used to visit after school. The favored street for hopscotch and marbles was no more. But despite the changes, this was the only place in the world she could truly say she was from. It was rooted in her marrow.

The luxury German car parked outside her old house jarred her. Yolanda sat in her car with her head sunk back, observing the home she'd grown up in. The house itself now seemed smaller, humbler, but that was not what mattered. *Come home,* the call had said, and here it stood: home. Yolanda took it in, eyes heavy with fear. "I took too long," she scolded herself. Constriction set upon her. This was the very moment when everything could change. What if they'd moved? Did they believe she was dead?

"I walked away, no explanation, no mention of coming back," she continued. It was possible that they had simply buried her symbolically and moved on. She could not entertain the thought that had lingered since Rachel's voice had disturbed her: that death had visited her childhood home. Many things were possible, but as with anything, a step forward was required. Yolanda inhaled sharply. She got out of the car. She lifted the latch at the old gate.

The front door had been standing open. A tall man came outside, his triceps bulging out of his black blazer. He carried a rifle openly, ostentatiously.

"Can I help you?" he said.

Yolanda stumbled on her words, shocked. "I'm here for Rachel and George Petersen. Do they still live here?"

She had been so sure they hadn't moved, sure they would have remained here, just for her, just in case. But that wasn't what her intuition told her. Something was wrong.

The man looked confused. "Who are you, lady?"

An angular figure came out onto the stoep. Yolanda stood with her mouth open. It was typical of her brother to wear a work jacket; there was always an air of industry about him. "Philip."

"Yes, can I help you?" He was brisk, formal, with the forward-bending demeanor of an impatient, busy man. His hair was closely cut. A Rolex hung heavy from his wrist.

"It's me."

He grew pale. Recognition widened his eyes. "Yolanda?"

"Yes." She took another step on the red path, but the man with the triceps stopped her, gesturing for her to raise her arms. Taken aback, Yolanda found herself being quickly searched. She froze there and then, recoiling at the rough feeling of his hands. Philip appeared unconcerned and soon pulled her into a tight embrace full of confused, shocked laughter and tears. Philip made sounds of disbelief; Yolanda stood still, stunned. Yet she looked at the open door, every fiber in her body on tenterhooks. She told herself to ignore this bad omen, the appearance of the last family member she wanted to see, as well as him allowing a strange man to set his hands on her. She told herself to be grateful that Philip was alive.

With her entire being she reached into the house. *Rachel, Ma. Be here, be home, be alive. Be with me.*

"My God," Philip said. "After all this time."

They walked inside, Yolanda trying not to pull away. She was about to call out for Rachel when Philip's words halted her.

"We haven't found her yet. I was in the Transvaal, Pretoria. This election is keeping us going twenty-four seven. What is today, Thursday? Well, I could only come back to Cape Town two or three days ago. Naturally we're in shock."

Yolanda's eyes adjusted to the small, dark living room. Her gaze seeking, wanting. The house's silence pressed upon her.

"Philip, what are you talking about?" she asked.

He frowned. The well-worn lines on his face marked his age. "Aren't you here because of Ma? Someone must have reached you. I mean, I don't know where you've been. I'm barely here. I just got bits and pieces about you, never the whole thing. But I assumed Mark or somebody . . ."

Yolanda thought of the insistent call she had heard. Her mind scrambled.

"Ma is gone, Yolanda. She disappeared a week or so ago." Philip flicked his hands like a magician performing an act of illusion. "There's a big manhunt on. I'm using all my resources, of course, so we'll make headway. I'm actually just here now because I'm waiting for the police chief to come and give me an update." He shook his head as if suddenly realizing that there were other questions to be asked. "If no one called you, why are you here? Where have you been?"

Yolanda's eyes teared as she took in the living room furniture, still in place; the photos, telling the story of a family from which she was largely absent. Her eyes searched among them until she found a school portrait. Her daughter had become a beautiful young woman.

She drew a deep breath.

"I haven't been in touch since I left in '76, Philip, not with anyone." Confusion creased his forehead further. She watched his body language, the slight withdrawal of his upper body, the glance to his bodyguard. He was suspicious of her.

"Did you know our father passed away?" he said. "A few years ago now. I had just come back into the country."

His words came like a hard blow. Over the space of so many years, death must have edged in. Yolanda had known that logically but never accepted it.

"What happened to you, Yolanda?" Philip persisted.

But Yolanda was not ready to answer that question, at least not with him. "No one knows if Ma is OK or not?"

She felt like flotsam tossed down a street after a parade, except here the celebration had not come to pass.

"No idea."

"What about Ingrid?"

He flicked his eyes down, shrugged. Yolanda read in his body language that he and her daughter weren't close. "She's off on her own now, living in Rondebosch." He looked up, fixed her with a hard stare. "Yolanda, who sent you?"

"You think I'm here as part of your war games, Philip? Get over yourself." She got up, paced. She wanted to cry out loud for their mother.

"Sounds like you were overseas," he continued.

"Don't make chitchat with me, not now."

The vastness of lifetimes apart made for a vacuum of incalculable scale between them. She felt it acutely.

"Where did you go?" Yolanda finally asked. "You were underground and then . . ." She could say no more. 1976 had been a year of extraordinary suffering.

"Exile. Angola and Botswana, at first. We had to go after Soweto, the uprising; we didn't have a choice—the regime went into overdrive. I always tried to stay on the continent, but then, you could never stay anywhere for long or get too comfortable. Their reach was wide. I've been on the road for twenty years."

"Me too."

Philip folded his arms. "You left a child behind, Yolanda."

"You left a family behind, Philip. You left us expecting to bury you, every goddamn day. I have no doubt it was the same after I left. Don't point a finger at me."

"It's just amazing," he continued, narrowing his eyes, "that of all the times you come back, it's now, when Ma's disappeared into thin blue air."

"Careful, Philip, you're sounding like a lawyer," Yolanda said and stepped outside to light a cigarette.

"So you don't know anything," he said, coming up behind her.

She drew in nicotine, trying to soothe the part of her that wanted to crumble. "No." She said it firmly, but she knew that something was taking place, an unseen dance unfolding. "I came back to see Ingrid."

"Why didn't you do it sooner?"

Yolanda remembered leaving Cape Town like a woman throwing herself on a funeral pyre. It was the second time she had known what it meant to want to die. Thinking of all that had transpired, she owed Philip nothing, least of all an explanation.

"I had my reasons."

"You walked away."

"You have no idea, Philip."

"Oh, I know all about Stefan van Deventer."

His words dug into where she was most tender. Philip like a train, Philip like a pit bull, clamping his principles in his jaws.

"I didn't realize that news traveled to the underground. I thought you forgot there was anyone besides yourself during your GI Joe years. The underground cadre, dragging his family through the wringer." Yolanda spoke softly but sternly, out of respect for how her mother had wept in the night at the kitchen table, longing for her eldest boy.

Philip laughed hoarsely. "I didn't betray my people, betray the cause that was life and death for us."

"I loved him." She locked her brother in an unwavering stare. "You don't think that was life and death for me? You don't know anything about it. You barely know me. You were too busy waiting for the red tide to carry you to victory. One that you can enjoy now with a Mercedes-AMG that could feed a township."

He came up beside her. "Don't you dare. You ran from your responsibilities after making a mess; I ran into the fire. You don't know a damn thing."

"You think I don't know what exile is like? Do you think I've been on vacation for twenty years?"

He shrugged. "It certainly looks like it."

The trigger was pulled. She slapped him in the face. He grabbed her wrist, and his bodyguard ran toward them, but Philip told him to stand down. Yolanda wrenched her arm free.

"Fuck off, Philip. I see that two decades hasn't made you any less of a pompous prick. So sorry I lack your black-and-white view of the struggle. How clear it must have been for you up on your noble steed, leading the masses with your banner held high."

He glared at her. "Don't you ever raise your hand to me again."

She stepped closer, until they were nearly nose to nose. "Or what? The worst has already happened to me, my dear brother, but you weren't here for that part, were you?"

Philip's posture stiffened. "You've got no respect." He spoke with the same force he had always set upon the world. "None. Not for yourself, not for your country, not for your family. But this is how you wanted it, hey: you don't do any of the work, our parents struggle for years to raise the child you threw away, and now, when all of that is done, when democracy is around the corner, you come back for the easy life."

Yolanda looked him in the eye. "She has a name, Philip. It's Ingrid." She reached for her cigarette, turned away. "You can't say her name? Because, what? The movement, Black consciousness, everything collapses because the father of your niece is an Afrikaner?" She jabbed at him with a finger. "I knew who I was; I followed my truth. Do you think I got off scot-free?"

"I heard you got roughed up. What did you expect after where you made your bed?"

"Roughed up?" She strained to say the words. She wanted to beat her fists against his chest, to beat him back into exile so she could be left to mourn the lost promise of this moment. "You of all people don't get to judge me. It's all so easy for you, isn't it, so crystal clear, who was right and who was wrong. But don't worry. Now that you, the fighters of our great liberation, have the keys to the castle, your complexities will show. Every miserable shade of fucking gray. I made my choices, and I own them. I get to live with them every day, every night. And you? How well do you sleep at night?"

They looked at each other, chests heaving. Her fury at her brother had brewed for decades.

"Why did you even bother coming back?" he asked, acrimony twisting his face.

"Funny." She cocked a hip. "I was going to ask you the same damn thing."

She rubbed her palms over her cheeks and grabbed her purse. Brushed by Philip, got into her car. She sped through traffic, her hunger and anger pushing her in equal measure until she found a random place and sat at its cheap pine bar and ordered a double vodka, neat.

She knew that down this road lay a drunken night with someone she didn't yet know. But it was easier, so much easier, than that empty house, the irreconcilable past. It had been a mistake to return here; she was a relic from history, erased. She should have stayed that way.

The barman delivered her drink, and the clear liquid sat in front of her, so available, so easy to have. She wanted it, pressing her palms down hard on the bar, her neck strained. *Just a sip,* she told herself, *just one, I won't even finish.* She could all but taste it.

She turned for a moment to light a cigarette. As she pinched her eyes, drawing deeply, it was Garrick who came to mind, his open, even gaze that took in all of her. She saw little splayed hands tucked in a lemon-colored blanket. Neither time nor distance had dimmed her love for the girl she'd named Ingrid Disa.

Yolanda thought of her mother and what Ma would want her to do. She had crossed a line in coming to this bar, in allowing this moment. She faltered, afraid to so much as look at the glass. It would take courage to get up and walk out, to find her daughter, find her mother—more courage than Yolanda thought she had. The drink would rob her of her only chance to be a mother to the girl, now, when her daughter needed it most.

Her arrival would bring a new kind of devastation to Ingrid, the kind Yolanda had wanted to avoid. But the sliver of a chance to be something other than a stranger on the street was worth it. Whatever havoc she would bring, Yolanda knew she needed to do it clear eyed and sober. Ingrid would have questions, and she deserved answers. Ignoring the drink, she finished her cigarette, threw money on the counter, and walked out.

RACHEL

Humming, Rachel tilted her head at the peculiar sight of the Knee Knee None. The creatures stood in the distance, slanted like praying mantises. They huddled in the shade of an acacia tree. Their long bodies were human but for the missing knee joint.

When she was little, Sara had told them about these creatures from stories her own mother had heard from the !Kung. "They are people thin as reeds," she'd said, "but harmless. Every night they eat the sun; every morning it comes back."

This was how it was in the land Rachel found herself: strange wandering bands of creatures, animals as capable of speech as Jan, animated objects. Navy sky bled like ink into sunburnt day, only to be swallowed whole by the fire of sunset. Linear time folded over, grew thin in places. Whole seasons shifted around them. The past or hints of the future poked through.

Now and then everything tilted so that they walked on the stars and looked up at the earth. Rachel thought her stomach was going to turn inside out until she remembered her stomach wasn't really here, not anymore. Nor could she taste the residue of the bulbs Jan had given her at the start of this journey.

Her body lay, in a trance, in the round belly of the painted cave to which Jan had led her. Now, adrift in this otherworldly place, she held on to the only manifestation of herself that she knew. But she was well beyond Rachel. She could become big, small, winged, or scaled; a *rooikat* with her belly to the ground or a black eagle, beady eyed in the skies. All her potential, her memory, her self, was here, vital and full. And along with it, a deep presence and knowing that came from her wellspring.

Impressions of the dead overlapped with those of the living. Would George seek her out? What would she say if his spirit found her?

It had never been easy with him. He had loved her and the children, but he'd wanted them to be tame. He'd wanted a family like the one he'd grown up in, a family that accepted without trouble that the white man and God were basically the same thing. George had likely died disappointed, desirous of some imaginary reward that would come from being a coloured man who did as he was told. Rachel wondered if most of her children deviated from conformity because of him or because of her.

Jan walked with his leopard tail pointed up like a flag. As they approached the Knee Knee None, he assumed his human form. One of the strange half humans approached, his legs like sticks, his long face ponderous. After an exchange of greetings, he asked, "Where are you going?"

"We are going east, to the place of the ancestors. Ma is returning to them."

As he spoke, a stirring began in Rachel. Instinctively, she lifted her head, as if to sniff the air. Song, a thread of a song, came to her.

The Knee Knee None looked at her, as if he knew what she was sensing.

"There is a water hole. It is close. You must go there." He gave Jan brief directions and withdrew, wishing them well.

Effervescence, like petals of light. That was what it felt like. Joy, unadulterated. As they drew nearer to the animal and bird sounds that indicated the watering hole, as the song's words came to her lips, Rachel sped up. She knew what it was; she recognized the song. Disregarding the hippos and bowlegged antelope, she squinted and scanned the pool's banks. Small sandy islands were scattered in the middle, empty. All but one.

She shouted, and it all fell away, every cross-questioning doubt, every pang of absence. Yolanda stood upon the island.

The effervescence in Rachel transformed, became a swarm of butterflies that trailed behind her. She splashed through the mud and the muck. Animals parted before her. Her daughter's shape and face, so much older, yet still similar to Rachel's own, turned to her. But the image of her girl then wavered and lifted into the air, until finally, Yolanda disappeared.

Rachel cried. Her girl had heeded the call to return to this soil. She was near; she had listened. But Rachel wasn't there, in that world, in Steenberg. She fell to her knees on the muddy bank, digging her hands into the sand. Again, her girl was alone.

Jan drew her up, absorbing Rachel's wails and sobs. They settled beside each other, and Rachel watched the swirling, unbridled butterflies on the wing. The song wove through her, light and bright, bringing with it the memory of a peaceful Saturday with her child.

Then it was gone. Desolate, she gripped Jan. "I came too soon," she said.

"You came when you were ready. The timing is not a coincidence."

"Jan, I want to be with her."

"You are always with her." He waded back through the water. "Come," he said. "Follow me."

He led Rachel on. They skirted around a *voortrekker*-style wagon that stood forlorn and abandoned, without horses, oxen, or *laager*. The air was still, yet the wagon's dirty cream cover flapped in its own wind. Jan watched the place hawkishly.

They moved across open bush, toward a large stand of trees. "Come, let's sit here," Jan said.

He was still a long time. So was Rachel. She was deep in thought, consumed by what might be unfolding in her little council house. The languid rays of the sun settled into her bones. The tranquility of the bush drew itself over her like a quilt and took the edge off the anger, the fears, the tender memories. Yolanda was home. She and Ingrid would find their way to each other.

But Rachel knew that that road would not be simple.

"I can feel Yolanda's pain, Jan," she said. "And her love. Like she's in me, growing still. Ingrid, she is also in pain."

"Your grandchild, the little one, she is on a different road."

Rachel considered the stones she had cast, the ripples waving through her children's lives. The white postcard and then, days later, the blue letter. Lastly, the items she'd left behind, the bundle she had watched over and clung to for so long.

"The child would have been lost, Ma, if her roots remained hidden. How can she move forward if everything behind her is a lie?"

Rachel asked: "Are you talking about Yolanda or Ingrid?" They exchanged a smile. "That child of mine, Jan, she is such a bright light. She draws the other to her. Danger came. I couldn't warn her. It just came, it came." She stopped, clenching her hands. "I couldn't see it."

"It wasn't your fault, Ma. It wasn't for you to control."

"But I am her mother." Eighteen years of agony, and the pain was just as fresh. "I felt something, like a fog, an ugly fog. But I wasn't strong enough then."

The contours of her grief and guilt were as well worn as the path to her house. What more could she have done? She'd asked that question every day of Ingrid's life.

"I failed Yolanda, Jan, and she suffered. And then I couldn't see beyond the loss to give Ingrid what she needed. So I failed her too."

Jan sighed. "For your own blood, there are some things you should not see. You would act on that seeing; you would remake their road." He looked over at her. "As you have done now, Ma."

She squinted into the distance, seeing all the way back to the night when her faith in people had ended. "I couldn't forgive myself, Jan, for my weakness. So yes, I fed the magic, I walked in the mountains, and I called for it; I built it up, and I used it."

Something brushed her ankle and startled her. She looked down at her feet and saw a seed that had fallen from the tree. It was jumping.

"This tree is the tambouti," Jan said. "A moth puts its larvae into the seeds when they are still green. After the seed grows and falls, the larva moves. It makes the seed hop around."

He pointed upward.

Reflected against the uppermost gray bark and the variegated underside of the leaves was a woman's face, fluttering between daylight and shadow. An old white woman, well kept, bun on her head.

"What do you see around you, Ma? Look closely."

Confused, Rachel studied the face, the tree, then the larger thicket, which was an abrupt formation on otherwise flat land. "These trees are all the same kind, I think."

"Yes. The tambouti doesn't like other types of tree," Jan said. "It has a poison in its sap; it makes you sick. The tree puts that poison into the ground to stop other types of trees or bushes from growing near it. So the tambouti stands alone, or it stands only with other tamboutis."

Rachel stared up at the old woman's wavering face, puzzled.

"You are a mother," Jan said. "Fighting for your children. But you are not the only one. There is another mother. She is like this tree. You, Ma, are like the quiver tree, hardy, a survivor. In times when there was nothing, when there was a drought for your family, you persisted. This tambouti woman, she is also a survivor. But she keeps to her kind; she pushes away what she sees as different."

"I don't know her. Who is she?"

"Stefan's mother. You focused your anger on him, Ma. You see him as the one who did wrong by Yolanda, the one who has to pay. But I tell you, as much as you fight for Yolanda, his mother fights for him, to make him a tambouti. Because of that, a real danger is coming."

Rachel grew alarmed. "What do you mean?"

"A man. A man of music. He will bring truth but also pain and death. This tambouti woman has brought him onto Yolanda's road."

His words lit a fire in Rachel. She remembered her vision: gloved hands assembling a gun, singing. "Music?" she whispered.

"There are ways we can shield her from this man, but you can't hide her from herself, Ma. Yolanda is not safe, not within, because of what she will not face. And the inside becomes the outside. There is a road she must take now, choices she must make."

"What can I do?" Rachel asked, terrified.

"You must let your fears go, Ma. You must trust your child. Your anger is also your fear. You are afraid that as a mother, as a woman blessed with the gift, you have failed. This has made you angry, and you believe you must set it all right. You can't. Ingrid and Yolanda have work to do. You cannot do it for them."

Jan's eyes glowed softly. "Stefan is afraid," he whispered. "The tambouti woman, she is afraid, too, and angry. Her fear will drive her; her anger will cause her not to see.

"There will come a moment when what you see and what you do about it, Ma, will be important. But if your anger is there, you will not see clearly. You also have work to do."

He touched her arm.

"You have to make peace with your own tracks. We will keep walking," he said, standing up. "We will not be alone for long."

They continued in silence, Rachel weighing all he had said against all that she had done. She thought of the helplessness she had felt so often in that council house's dark quarters, the slow grind of living in a world that thought and treated her as lesser. Balancing against that helplessness had been an act of strength.

As she walked taller beside Jan, she willed for her girls what she had begun for herself: the strength not to have the past dictate the entirety of the future.

Twilight came. Rachel wanted to sit, to be, to reach out to Yolanda. She settled upon a grassy tussock beneath an impressive baobab, crossed her knees, and shut her eyes. She did not see what came behind her.

The twisted, malignant force crept along the ground with speed. It clawed into her back. Then the first blow came.

INGRID

Ingrid rolled up her window to block out Friday morning's crisp, cool air. "Driving someone you don't know across the country is a big deal, Litha. I appreciate that you're doing this."

When she looked at him, the seriousness on his face froze her.

"Well, I suppose I can tell you now." Sunlight had yet to tip over the barrier of mountains that cordoned the Cape off from the rest of the country. Momentarily his face dipped into shadow. "It's much easier this way to steal you. We are going to my village in Pondoland; you will be my third wife, but don't worry: you'll be my favorite."

His smile lit his eyes with a mischievous glance. Ingrid slapped his arm.

"That was worth it for your face." He grinned naughtily.

He moved his hatchback into the right gear as they began the climb up Sir Lowry's Pass. Steenberg fell away far behind them, and Rachel came to Ingrid's mind. More than leaving home, she was leaving her.

On impulse, Ingrid had grabbed Yolanda's package on her way out the door. It was a burden she wanted to escape, but in the end she found it impossible to leave behind.

"Let's stop here," Litha said, breaking into her thoughts. "At the viewpoint." He swung right at the final curve, into the parking lot.

The shadow of the mountain range towering behind them chilled the air. At their feet, the Atlantic filled the breeze with hints of ocean salt. Ingrid watched whitecaps roll in along the extended shore far below. Table Mountain stood guard in the distance. The little house she'd grown up in felt farther and farther away.

Here, in this slow, steady place, how could her life be so violently reordered? So many chess pieces rearranged by the unseen, and mothers lost in the chaos of it, lost and lost again. Ingrid turned, trying to hide the conflicting emotions no doubt crossing her face, but Litha was observing her. He slid his arms around her from behind, blocking the cold. She leaned back into him. This, too, was a journey: beginning to learn how his body felt.

"Ingrid, what you are doing is important," Litha said into her ear. "For us, the amaXhosa, our ancestors are essential; they built the road we walk on. We go to them first; we praise them first; we acknowledge them. I can't imagine how it is not knowing your clan or where you come from. I hope you will find that, some of it, with your father." She felt him smile. "But it's also an excuse to spend a weekend with you."

Ingrid wrapped her arms over his. Finding Stefan might have unpredictable consequences, but it was her decision to seek him, hers alone.

"Does he know you're coming?" Litha asked.

"No. But even if he isn't there when we arrive, I want him to know that I exist. That I am here."

As they returned to the car, she gave Table Mountain a last look before they drove into the rugged brown-and-green spaces beyond the Cape.

"You said we'd overnight in your town," Ingrid said. "But also, there's someone you wanted to see?"

"Yes." Litha gave a long sigh. "I have a son, a five-year-old. His mother and I are not together; we have not been for some time. He lives with her, close to my family, who help with him."

"Oh." Ingrid was stunned. "Isn't this going to be weird, me showing up with you while you visit him?"

A Conspiracy of Mothers

Litha shrugged. "You will be our guest, and my family will make sure you are treated well. We will get there tonight." He paused. "I know it can be off putting"—he glanced at her cautiously—"that I'm a father. I wanted to tell you now, before . . . anything. I want you to know so you can decide. Other girls, well, let's say it hasn't always gone so well."

Ingrid nodded. "Thank you." She fell silent for a long spell. "Families are complicated; I know that better than anyone. But you being a dad—which is a weird idea, I'll be honest—doesn't change that it feels like I've known you for so long, much longer than a week."

She interlaced fingers with his and smiled at the warmth on his face, the warmth she, too, felt.

Ingrid continued, "Does your son look like you? 'Cause your brother, Tsepho, he doesn't really."

Litha laughed. "I forget sometimes to change what I am saying . . . Tsepho is actually my cousin. In my culture, some family members who you call cousins, we call sisters or brothers."

She nodded. All this talk of family was weighing upon her. Unlike her, Litha had one he could trust, people that he wanted to spend time with.

As if he'd read her mind, he took her hand. "Having a big family with expectations doesn't always make things easier." His face grew serious, but he said no more.

Without the clutter of the city, the land opened up. In the distance, bright-yellow canola fields shone iridescent against the hills. Litha pointed to the hulking figures of cattle and sheep, described how one took care of them. This agricultural landscape was more akin to the world he had grown up in than Cape Town, Ingrid realized.

Eventually, they slipped into silence, and she curled up and shut her eyes in the warm sun. Knowing that Litha was here steadied her. But still her mind drifted to her mothers—they held her; they would not let her go. How well did she really know these women?

There were things about Rachel that Ingrid had always feared: the coming and going of her severe migraines; occasional bouts of what they all assumed was mental health trouble; her reputation in the community as a psychic. There had been odd, inexplicable things that Rachel should not have known but did; strange chatter with the unseen. Yet she had also been the homespun mother of comfort and care that Ingrid had known all her life, just as she'd been over pumpkin bredie at that last dinner together.

A recollection from that night made Ingrid think: for a moment, over the stove, Rachel had gazed at her with an uncharacteristic look. Ingrid hadn't thought much of it at the time, but it occurred to her now that her grandmother had been afraid. Peering out the window at the passing landscape, she felt instinctive longing for Rachel but also fear for her and what that gaze signified.

"Are you hungry?" Litha asked, interrupting her thoughts. "There is a Golden Egg here. We can get something to eat."

Ingrid nodded. They approached the roadside eatery and parked alongside a long-distance bus disgorging an army of people. Their bacon and eggs arrived while they sipped coffee at a table.

"Is your clan name and surname the same thing?" Ingrid asked.

"No, but the clan is more important," Litha said. "It's a bit complicated for us. My mother is Zulu, but my father, he is Xhosa, Pondo, to be specific. So we were all raised in the Xhosa ways."

"How does that work? Even I know the Zulu and Xhosa are enemies," Ingrid said.

"I wouldn't say enemies, but it's not easy." He sat back for a moment. "My grandfather on my mother's side, he didn't like the idea of my parents' marriage; he is a very traditional man. Negotiations took some time and *lobola*; it was high, a lot of cattle. Now and then, there can be challenges between the families.

"With all the violence now, when I hear about the fighting in the mining hostels, when the murders in Thokoza happened, the Zulu and

Xhosa killing each other left, right, and center, I couldn't pick a side. I'm Xhosa, but I can't ignore my mother and her family. Part of why I came to Cape Town instead of going to Joburg and Wits"—Ingrid nodded at his mention of the university there—"is to get away from that conflict. Cape Town has other problems but not that particular one."

They finished their breakfast and got back on the highway. Ingrid almost didn't notice when the car began to stall, but suddenly Litha was fighting the gearshift. She could hear the engine shutting down; the car began to drift. Litha forced it onto the shoulder.

"Oh my God." He smacked the steering wheel and pointed to the dashboard. Ingrid's eyes widened at the temperature gauge, which sat squarely in the red zone.

"What's going on?" she asked.

"Let me try it again." Litha tried to fire the ignition, but the car was unresponsive. He sank back. "This is bad."

Any further efforts to coax the car into any sort of cooperation were in vain. Litha opened the bonnet as Ingrid stepped out. He cursed in Xhosa. A gaping hole was steaming furiously where the radiator cap should have been. Litha sank down in the dust on his haunches.

"The garage early this morning," he said. "I forgot to put it back. I can't believe this. My engine must be one big block of metal now. Hau, how can I be so stupid?"

His head fell. Ingrid groaned. "Fuck, I'm sorry," she offered. "You wouldn't be here if it wasn't for me."

He shrugged. "You didn't fill up the water. That was me." He stood up. "I need a mechanic. The next town, Swellendam, is big. Chances are we'll find someone there. We can hitchhike."

They gathered their things out of the car before turning toward the highway.

"I think," Ingrid continued, "that your ancestors are trying to warn you that I'm bad news."

He said nothing but curved his body toward her, and she saw in his eyes that even if that was so, it didn't matter. Her desire for him was another kind of undoing. Standing at the roadside, as trucks and disinterested cars torpedoed by, they shared a single, raw kiss.

She curled her fingers over his as they turned, bags on their backs, Yolanda's bag at her feet. Thumbs outstretched, ready to face the road ahead.

Nearly an hour later, a white Volkswagen Kombi van came to a halt, and a thickset figure peered out, inspecting them both.

"Where you people coming from?" the driver asked in strained English—he was clearly Afrikaans. A woman leaned over to look from the passenger seat, and Ingrid spied a blonde head in the back.

Litha relayed the details of their journey to date.

"OK, well, we can get you to Swellendam," the driver said. "We live in Heidelberg; that's near there."

Ingrid exhaled with relief.

"Hannelie, come now," the woman commanded the girl in the back. "What are you sitting still for? Open up; let them in."

The daughter, Hannelie, was tall and well built, her hair neatly cut and her face lightly made up, despite her bare feet. She rearranged the bags to make room for Litha and Ingrid in the row of seats behind her.

"My mother with all these things," she said and shook her head. She shyly inspected them both, but her eyes rested mostly on Litha.

The door swung shut. The Kombi pulled away. Ingrid glanced back at Litha's car and the highway leading back to the Cape. More and more things left behind.

The woman in front turned to look at them. "My name is Mrs. Marais," she said, touching a hand to her chest. Charm bracelets jingled on her wrists. "This is my husband, Mr. Marais, and that cheeky child of ours is Hannelie, my youngest." She spoke with a singsong tone as her daughter rolled her eyes.

Mrs. Marais had an open face and bouffant hair, a dramatic foil to her stolid husband. Ingrid introduced herself and Litha, feeling all the while that they were being examined. Beside her, Litha sat stiffly.

"What is taking you both out of Cape Town now, with all this election stuff going on?" Mr. Marais asked, giving them a look in the rearview mirror.

"Family," Litha said quickly. "We both have family commitments."

"Oh, I see," Mrs. Marais said. "I would rather go the other way, I must say. Cape Town is such a nice place."

She regaled them with details of their visit. Hannelie occasionally chipped in, offsetting her mother's animated descriptions with withering scorn. There was an ease to the family that made Ingrid think of Yolanda's materials. She peered out the window, trying not to dissolve into tears.

"Well, I must say, it's something different to see an interracial couple," Mrs. Marais said with a puff of pleasure. "This is the time of the rainbow nation now."

She looked at them hopefully, and Ingrid glanced at Litha, the both of them blushing. Every part of her body touching his felt electrified. But his face was stony, difficult to read.

"Ma," Hannelie scolded. "Don't be so embarrassing."

"Ag, no shame, I'm just saying it's nice, they a cute couple. Our people are all coming together now at last."

"We are just friends," Litha and Ingrid said simultaneously and glanced at each other, amused.

"Oh, oh, I'm sorry; I misunderstood." Mrs. Marais fell silent but smiled knowingly. Soon after, she piped up, "Where are you sleeping tonight?"

"We don't know yet," Ingrid responded.

"Towing that car to Cape Town is going to cost a lot of money," Mr. Marais said and shook his head.

"We will make a plan." Litha's tone was that of someone who'd been challenged.

"You don't know any people in Swellendam?" Mr. Marais asked. They shook their heads. "So if you don't get a mechanic, what are you going to do?"

Ingrid felt Litha's body tense.

"Why don't you just come home with us?" Mrs. Marais blurted, to the surprise of all. "You can overnight, and we can drop you in town tomorrow to find a mechanic. We know some people who can maybe help. Charl can do something, Tienie," she said in response to her husband's gaze. "We can phone tonight."

"My brother is away on a hike, so we have space," Hannelie said eagerly.

The kind offer hung awkwardly in the confines of the Kombi. The buts were difficult to articulate, bulging with everything Ingrid thought about Afrikaners. They were people who, in every conceivable way, were empowered to tell her how to live.

Mrs. Marais bore none of that authority yet held all the privilege. Still, whatever this was, there was no real reason to turn them down. She and Litha had nowhere else to go. Despite the anxiety on his face, she accepted the offer for the both of them.

"Wonderful. I'll cook us something *lekker*," Mrs. Marais said. "You must be hungry."

A couple of hours later, they left the national road for the wide streets of Heidelberg. The town was an idyll of trees and modest but large houses. A pristine church with a formidable steeple predominated. Ingrid considered how the light fell differently in the countryside; longer, softer rays lit upon the open spaces and lingered there.

As they drove, she was surprised to see coloureds walking, pausing, waving. White people did the same. Now and then Mrs. Marais asked her exasperated husband to slow the Kombi to chat with this person or that, irrespective of color. These easy interactions were not what Ingrid had expected. Maybe country life was different in this way too, she thought, slower, with the towns smaller, the people closer.

Litha was unmoved, distant and watchful as Mr. Marais turned up the driveway of a corner plot. An old oak guarded the beautiful, large garden. A stoep ran all the way around the house, providing a ready path to follow the sun.

Inside the high-ceilinged living room with its dark wooden rafters, their hostess's ebullient hand was evident in the bold floral upholstery, dappled wallpaper, and swirled patterns on the curtains, rugs, and doilies.

"Make yourself at home," Mrs. Marais said. "Hannelie, put that kettle on for tea, come now. Oh, if you need the toilet, let me quickly show you where."

Ingrid was settled into the bedroom of the Maraises' absent son, while Litha was given the sofa in the living room. Mr. Marais excused himself to take a nap while Hannelie assembled a tea tray. Soon, the four of them sat on the stoep, a breeze rippling through the oak leaves above. The moment was civil and polite, but coolness had come to prevail on the hastily assembled company. Mrs. Marais launched into a barrage of nervous questions about family, studies, and their journey, but the ensuing chatter felt tense. She was more circumspect with Litha, articulating her words as if unsure his grasp of English was sound.

Ingrid noticed, too, the furtive, almost feral glances that Hannelie gave Litha. She thought of how Reuben had treated him and wondered how often it was like this. Litha in turn had withdrawn; she couldn't read him.

When Mrs. Marais drew her daughter away to help prepare dinner, Ingrid strolled behind Litha to the perimeter of the garden. "You OK?" she asked.

"I'm just worried about my car there on the highway."

"Well, we're lucky, hey—it will get sorted out tomorrow hopefully."

"I suppose so." He sounded uncomfortable, detached; he was silent for a long time. The air and the garden were serene and still. But then he spoke between clenched teeth.

"This was the dream, Ingrid. This life, nice big house, everything tame and in its place, the government keeping it like that for them. This is what it was all about."

She frowned at his tone. "What are you talking about?"

Litha spread his hands. "This life was never supposed to be for our people. Just them, the ones who don't belong here."

"Litha." Surprised, she dropped her voice. "These people have been nice to us."

"It's white guilt, Ingrid, picking up the coloured and the African from the side of the road; it will make a nice story for their friends. They can say, *See how liberal we are; see how far we have come.*" She searched his face and saw hurt beneath the stoicism. "So much suffering for a few people to live like this," he continued.

"But they aren't the only ones with nice houses, Litha," Ingrid said. "There's coloureds in Punts Estate, Fairways, other nice places in Cape Town. Surely in the homelands some people live well also?"

He gave her the saddest of smiles. "Ja, no, that's true, but we are poor in the Transkei, many of us, poor in the ways that matter in this kind of world. We don't really have a proper economy. All of that, the Bantustans, the *dompas*, it was all for this."

"But those things are over now."

"The Transkei and Ciskei, Bophuthatswana, the homelands are reintegrating with South Africa, yes, but over . . . I don't know. Is it?"

"We're standing in their garden, not working in it. We're going to eat their food and sleep in their house."

He shrugged. Ingrid could tell Litha thought her naive.

"We are the only ones who belong here, Ingrid. These people must go back where they came from. Maybe it's different for you. To them, you can be in places like this. But me, no."

She was stunned. "Am I just coloured to you? Stupidly sitting on this apartheid food chain?"

He looked at her, wide eyed; her words had jarred him. But incensed, she continued.

"Of course, only you Blacks call yourselves the Africans. I guess that says everything we need to know about the rest of us."

The wind wove through the oak tree's leaves. The still country afternoon of bicycling children and neighbors watering gardens while stealing glances at them unfolded.

"Ma was right," Ingrid said, taking a few steps toward the house. "She always said apartheid is a cage, but only you can decide if the bars will exist in your mind." She stormed back inside.

The Maraises offered the use of their telephone before dinner. Litha rang his family, then a friend in Port Elizabeth. His demeanor softened as he spoke; he was distinctly at ease with his own language.

Ingrid considered calling Rachel's house. The desire for news about her grandmother was strong, but not greater than the anger still percolating within her that Rachel, even at their last supper together, had withheld the truth. In the end, she compromised and called Reuben, then faked a conversation long after his mother told her he was out and the dial tone buzzed in her ear. She wanted to pretend, for all present, that her family knew and cared about her whereabouts, even if the reality was quite different.

After dinner, everyone settled in for the night. Unable to sleep, Ingrid felt alone and deserted in the alien bedroom. Her exchange with Litha had erected a wall between them. Wide awake, she looked at the large grocery bag. Should she delve into Yolanda's past?

A sound broke her train of thought: a bedroom door creaked open, and Ingrid spied bare white legs, moving like a ghost's beneath a nightie. Hannelie. The pitter-patter of her feet led to the living room, and Ingrid could hear whispers, voices.

"That stupid girl," she breathed. She knew what it would look like if the Maraises caught their daughter with Litha, even if Hannelie was the one who'd instigated it. She knew what might happen to him. She flew up, making as much noise as possible. After heading to the hallway, she searched for and then switched on the light. Hannelie jumped backward.

"Everything OK?" Ingrid asked. "Sorry, just came to get some water."

"Yes, I was just seeing if he was warm enough." Crimson, Hannelie marched back to her room, avoiding Ingrid's eyes.

Mr. Marais's voice rang out: "What is going on there?"

"Everything is OK, Pa," Hannelie called. "I was just checking that they have enough blankets." She retreated to her bedroom and shut the door.

"What was that?" Ingrid whispered to Litha. His torso was discernible in the half dark as he leaned, topless, against the sofa. Her breath grew shallow at the sight of his body. She was aware that she wore only her T-shirt and underwear. She felt every part of her tighten.

He shook his head. "That white girl, she wants to get me killed." He paused, reached out his hand. Ingrid took it but let the silence sit between them. "I'm sorry," he said, kissing the knuckles on her hand lightly. She kissed him fully, the afternoon's words and anger falling away. It was complicated today, and it would be so tomorrow; she knew this now. None of that changed, though, the fact that she simply wanted him.

Still, she whispered good night and returned to her room. She lay awake for a long spell before thinking again of her family. First her mind and then her hand wandered to the bag. She argued with herself, knowing the images and the words would unsettle her. But eventually she switched on a night-light and reached for the photos she had found that first time. The images of Stefan and Yolanda so plainly in love ripped at something in her. Staring at them, she felt the scale of her distance from her mother.

As she put the photos back, though, her hand brushed a small, hard canvas. She lifted it out. She struggled at first to understand what she was looking at, but as she ran her hands over it, she realized, in a way that left her chilled, that the bruised and beaten face staring back at her was Yolanda's. Disturbed, she set the painting down. Maybe there had been something else, something darker, that had made her mother run, a dangerous truth that made the lie worth keeping.

KUIPER

People are transparent buggers," Kuiper muttered. "They think they're not, but eventually they show their hand. Just once. That's all it takes."

He read people like he listened to classical music: until he understood the layers upon which a crescendo was built, the arrangement, why this instrument was used for that solo. People's gestures and expressions were the same, a fine symphony conducted moment by moment that told you their whole story.

Yolanda was no different, he thought, turning up Bach as he drove. He'd watched her come home to Steenberg, alive and kicking. She had the air of a quiet storm about her. He noticed the light silk scarf around her neck, her jewelry and heeled leather boots. The girl in Elsa's photo was very much a girl. This was a woman. She was attractive, yes, but there was something else about her he couldn't put his finger on. A worldliness, a weariness.

He first saw her, the real Yolanda, when the bodyguard frisked her. The brother Philip's countersurveillance was patchy; Kuiper managed to watch the red path, to trail his binocs up to Yolanda's face as she arrived. He saw the horror when the rugby-prop-size chap placed his hands on her. It was more than discomfort or indignation. He made a mental note to chat further with Pieter, to plumb one or two more local sources about her.

Kuiper had followed Yolanda to the bar. Through a window, he'd seen the lust in her eyes for the drink she hadn't had. He'd smiled. Just like animals in the wild, a watering hole was where things got insecure. This was the land of predator and prey. She would falter. Drunks always did. He only needed to mark time, then, until the inevitable.

He considered Philip Petersen, the brother. Kuiper knew his name; he knew all those ringleading terrorist motherfuckers. Philip had been involved in the trouble in the seventies. He'd gotten snapped up by the so-called movement, then gone underground, popping up across the country like an angry little mole, inciting the natives. Finally he'd disappeared, gone to join his banned organization outside South Africa, to sit, smoldering, in the bush.

Now Philip was hot currency in a fast car. Targeted for a senior leadership role and a rapid ascent through those same musty halls of Parliament he and his buddies had decried as the den of an illegitimate, slaughtering regime. Kuiper didn't consider himself a sensitive man, but he'd looked at the chrome finish on Philip's car with envy. Instead, what did he get after decades of service? He, André Kuiper, was the Parabat who'd jumped out of planes, fought through *vasbyt*, sat with the heat and the flies and the isolated nothing of army bases up north, and spent the eighties trying not to get killed in the stinking, murderous townships. He'd done all that because this was his country, and it was all that he had, and he was going to defend it to the bitter end.

Now what? *No, look,* they'd said, *there's a place for you okes in the new defense force. Ronnie Kasrils may be the new minister; he'll want instructors for the troops and whatnot.* Ja, sure. Kuiper shook his head. Security was always necessary in Africa; he could probably work something out, but he was a man who'd stayed alive because he was careful. He knew he'd made enemies.

It wasn't the politics of a Black government that bothered him most. Everybody fought their position; that was how war worked. He'd just never seen the Blacks do a good job. Look at Rwanda. Someone had just shot a plane full of their people out of the sky; now that whole place was falling apart.

No, what bothered him was the act of opening the gate and handing your keys to the enemy as reparation for supposed crimes. This was war. If you did that, your head was almost certainly going to follow. No, he would leave South Africa. His former bosses were shuttered on their farms and estates, beyond reach. Papers had been destroyed; they swore up and down that men like Kuiper didn't operate at their command, never had. Legal teams circled them protectively like great whites.

And here he was, reduced to contending with this woman who had sat out the whole thing overseas. She got to come back, after most of the blood had been spilled, while her brother joined his cronies and ran the show. Kuiper would execute this job for the money. But he couldn't disguise his displeasure at having to do a thing so clearly beneath his talents.

After the bar, Yolanda had gone, teary eyed, to the house of the other brother, Mark. It had been clear she was staying there for the night, so Kuiper had driven on. He'd spent the next day talking with a few people, learning valuable information. Now, as Friday evening drew near, he pulled his van up at his destination, a pay phone in a different suburb, and dialed.

"Mrs. Van Deventer."

"Yes, who is this?"

"Why didn't you tell me anything about the child?"

ELSA

The words fired from Kuiper's mouth into Elsa's kitchen. Danie was inside, watching a show on M-Net. She moved wisps of hair from her forehead, looking at the tray before her. It held cups for what would prove to be a much-needed nightcap.

"Mr. Van der Merwe?"

"Yes, Mrs. Van Deventer."

"It's late. What do you want?" She resented his intrusion on her quiet Friday evening. "I can make an appointment with you for next week." She clicked her tongue. "Let me quickly find my diary."

"Mrs. Van Deventer," he said, and she hardened her jaw at how he rolled each syllable. "Listen carefully." A protest formed on her tongue, but he continued, "I'll ask you only one more time: How come you didn't tell me about the child?"

She shut the kitchen door and said in hushed tones, "I don't know what the hell you're talking about, do you understand? And believe me, I don't have time for this kind of rubbish."

"Mrs. Van Deventer, or rather Elsa—*Mrs.* is so very formal, don't you think? Rachel and George Petersen have been raising a child who is apparently the orphan of their own daughter, Yolanda Petersen. The father, some people say, was a student from the same university. Some, not all."

His voice dropped.

"The story was that Yolanda and the father, James Paulsen, died in a car crash in 1976. The orphan, Ingrid, is almost nineteen now, and she's the spitting image of her mother except that, you know what? She reminds me of you, Elsa, eyes and all. You know what I mean?"

Elsa dismissed him, dropping a spoon on the floor. "Coloureds grow like weeds. That woman could have slept with anyone and probably did."

He laughed. The words he was stringing together led, by logic, to a neat conclusion. But she wouldn't permit it, not here in her kitchen where Stefan and his sister used to sit and have chocolate Maltabella for breakfast, knobs of butter melted on top; where they used to chase each other after school, apricot jam smeared on their fingers and mouths, laughing.

"Elsa, why do you think those people exist in the first place, these coloureds: a little bit Black, a little bit white?"

She lowered her voice, cupped her hand over the telephone to keep Kuiper's acidity from entering her home. "Are you trying to tell me that Stefan fathered some coloured child in a township? Are you mad? You've just told me about—what was the father's name? James?"

"Elsa," he hissed. "There's people on the Cape Flats with long memories and other versions of the truth. This James Paulsen is fiction. I've checked at both the universities here, even Stellenbosch, just to be sure. The car crash is also fiction. One thing that's clear is that Yolanda disappeared in '76, after that mess in Soweto, the uprising, as they call it."

He continued. "Let's think about this: a young man, around twenty-four years old. He's been in the army, a *tiffie*—oh, sorry, that's the Technical Services Corps for you civilians. He got to use that fancy mechanical engineering degree of his in the army. But women were scarce on the border. What is the one thing he wants to do as much as possible with his new bird there, slumming in Muizenberg, when he gets the chance?"

Danie entered the kitchen for a glass of water, and Elsa gritted her teeth into a smile, intimating the call was friendly gossip. Once he left, she shut the kitchen door once again and unleashed her fury across her granite countertops.

"How dare you? How dare you phone me with such a load of nonsense?"

Kuiper snickered. "I'm the least of your problems, Elsa. That girl, that supposed orphan, left Cape Town this morning, hopped in a buddy's car and went up-country somewhere. Now, why would a girl in the middle of a heavy degree at university and a family crisis pack up and leave? Who is she going to see and why?"

"What crisis?" Elsa asked, gripping the edge of the kitchen table.

"Rachel Petersen, her grandmother, is MIA. Even I can't find her. These women have a habit of disappearing. But that isn't the best part of the story. Guess who arrived, like Lazarus back from the dead, in Cape Town yesterday? And she was—how do the English say? Hale and hearty. Yolanda Petersen."

How much worse could this get? Elsa searched her kitchen, frantic.

"Are you ready for the next episode?" Kuiper continued, with a small chuckle. "The one where that girl from the train station decides to look for her child? Where the child lands on your son's doorstep, looking for her real father?"

"Stop the girl, do you understand me? Stop her from getting anywhere near my son."

"This isn't a 'buy one, get one free' kind of arrangement, Elsa. You didn't hire me to deal with Ingrid Petersen."

"You want more money, isn't it? You're not getting another red cent from me."

Her emphatic voice only elicited another chuckle. "Ja, well, blissful ignorance was always the state of you people out in the suburbs, living lekker while we fought for you. Remember one thing: I make the terms of this contract. Take a look in your postbox tonight, Mrs. Van Deventer."

The click of the telephone was abrupt. Elsa finished the tray and tried to shut out of her mind all that he had said.

But watching television beside Danie, she thought again of the photograph of her son, the one that had rankled all those years ago in Pieter's office. She'd sat in her car for a long time that day, realizing that what she felt was grief. Stefan had become his own man. There had always been a little distance between them; affection was never her strong suit. But he was still her boy, and she loved him and hated that now she could not hold him close and set everything right. She had wept, thinking of him on holiday at the beach. A little boy, just a salty bundle of tears after a bluebottle jellyfish sting. He had sought out Betty, the maid, instinctively; only she could make it better. But once he'd realized she was nowhere in sight, he'd turned to Elsa, and she'd done all she could, always wanting to do right by him.

That boy had been dislodged by a young man with the mercurial, radiant light of youth on his face; a man possessed by a coloured—possessing her. In the days that had followed that meeting with Pieter, Elsa had wrestled, Bible in hand, with difficult questions: Was it something she had done as a mother? Hadn't she forged the arrow of her boy straight and true? How could he curve so flagrantly away from the protection of the wagon wheel?

She'd settled on the only possible truth: what a woman could do to a man between the four posts of a bed. Elsa remembered her own youth at secretarial school, boarding with a pair of women—poor young girls pooling their resources to survive. Each had had a meager wedding *kist*, trousseau enclosed. Held like an old-fashioned chest at the Union Pacific dock, ready to set sail on the rescue ship of a respectable marriage.

Sure footed, cleverer than the rest, Elsa had secured the job she'd wanted at the right company. With a deftly cut skirt, she'd caught

Danie's eye. One of the others had snared a married man, who'd fallen for the bedroom charms that hid her avarice. Elsa reasoned that Yolanda was no less of a cunning Delilah, luring Stefan like a siren calling sailors to the rocky shore.

The ecstasy on his face in that old photograph was a lie. Coloureds drifted from Friday to Friday without morals, without compunction. They were parasites, clumped like fungi in their separate areas. Their women walked in rollers and petticoats, bra straps out for the world to see. A rootless, toothless bunch, hollering down the street for drunk men and rambling children.

No, Elsa knew lust alone had motivated Stefan. After all, once Pieter had pulled his strings and Stefan had gone and returned from the army, she had watched him gravitate to someone new. In the aftermath of her meeting with her brother, she'd turned to her social set to find a distraction. By and by, Katrina Odendaal appeared at their Sunday lunch table: a girl from a wealthy Free State wool family, alone at Stellenbosch University, was one in need of chaperoning and care. When Stefan returned from the border, cleansed and set straight, he found Katrina frequenting their house. Pieter told Elsa the police were moving on, making other plans. Stefan, now living at home, tended to disappear into solitary solemnity. Elsa didn't ask after the cause. She just presented Katrina and steered the inevitability of the Lord God's will into being.

It worked. The drift vanished from her boy's face. Marriage within a year materialized and, with it, a route away from the Cape and that damn ocean, to the farm of his fiancée's family. Over the years, Elsa watched the couple bloom and felt vindicated. Stefan had sinned, but he'd found his way back into the fold and made them proud. Yolanda had been eviscerated.

Danie switched off the television. Elsa looked at the photos on the mantel. There was her son; there was the small scar on his face from a childhood game of catapult gone awry. Her boy who brought insects and snakes to the back patio, who was unafraid to dig in soil or climb trees and grab whatever he found with his bare hands. His hair was thick and full, a strawberry-blond mop. His back was broad, his body muscled. She was proud of the man he had become. She had never told him that she knew about Yolanda.

Katrina stood beside Stefan in the portrait, a dark-haired, petite woman with the harried look of a mother of three. A flush of red always colored her cheeks, a legacy of the many winters she'd endured on her parents' farm.

There were things about her daughter-in-law that Elsa didn't like; for one, she and Stefan were too easygoing with their maid. The husband was God knows where, so this Black maid lived in servants' quarters on Stefan's property with her own child, a little boy. Much to Elsa's chagrin, Katrina took the little boy to school and collected him, just as she did with her own children. The family refused the use of the terms *madam* and *master* in the house. Never countering Elsa to her face, Katrina nonetheless made it plain that she thought the titles theatrical nonsense, that Dikeledi and her child were part of their household.

Despite Katrina's too-wide interpretation of Christian brotherliness, Elsa valued two attributes most in her daughter-in-law: she was an uncomplicated, even-tempered woman, and she adored Stefan. She suffered from what Elsa thought of as the tyranny of plainness; she would never be stylish, but she was a fastidious mother and maintained a good home. She made Stefan happy. Together, they were the foundation of a family. Nothing could unseat that.

Only—

Early the next morning, Elsa drew a large envelope out of the postbox. In her sewing room, Stefan's old room, she cut open the envelope with her craft scissors and drew out a new set of photos. There she was, a young girl, standing outside an apartment block, walking out of a grocery store. Elsa squinted, inspecting the child's light skin. She discerned the lines of her nose and cheekbones, peered at eyes as light as her own. The resemblance was unmistakable.

It was only then that Kuiper's notion of Stefan's child assembled itself into a possibility. It was only then that Elsa felt fear. It would be enough for this child to stand there with those eyes and that skin and say *maybe*. They would all take a treacherous tumble down to the place where Kuiper's inferences about Stefan sat, evil and dark.

Elsa's mind spun. What could she do?

She began with a light mention to Danie at lunchtime. By that evening she had settled him on the idea that a short visit to see Stefan wasn't out of the ordinary. When Danie asked, "Why so soon, Elsa, so unexpectedly?" she softened, pleaded, "I couldn't go at Easter because of your dinner party. Do I need a reason to go see our grandchildren?"

She left the next day, after church. The girl might get to Stefan before she did, in which case Elsa prayed that her son would do the intelligent thing. But the insolence of the mysterious "she" from the postcard had ignited a fury in her. Elsa would not stand by if catastrophe descended. The tumult of distant history would not be allowed to pick her family apart.

YOLANDA

There's no sign of anything criminal." The policeman looked down at his shoes as he spoke. "There isn't really anything we can do, you see, in such a case."

Seated between her brothers in Rachel's living room, Yolanda guessed that, at some level, the man knew the ramifications of what he was saying.

"What do you mean, 'such a case'?" Philip's deep frown matched the flintiness of his tone.

"Mr. Petersen, it looks like your mother left of her own free will. She's not a minor; she can go wherever she wants."

Yolanda stalled the inevitable explosion from her eldest brother. "What about Table Mountain?" she asked. "She used to spend a lot of time there, even when I was a girl."

"Lady, we already heard that she likes going for walks and things. We worked with the rangers to comb the usual areas. There's no sign of her. And her car, it isn't in any of the parking areas, so now we really looking for a needle in a haystack."

Philip straightened up. Mark sighed deeply. Yolanda wasn't in the mood for the showdown. She excused herself and retreated to the yard with a cigarette. She willed Rachel's voice into her mind, seeking guidance, assurance, answers. But there were none, and the absolute silence that came instead felt like brushing a raw wound.

The policeman was right: all of them were seeing what they wanted and not what was. Their mother had walked away. It was the truth, Yolanda sensed, but there was more. A creeping dread pointed to things at play that none of them could discern, not yet.

Though she was staying at Mark's house, he'd said nothing about Rachel beyond the obvious. Their chatter had focused on his family, on Yolanda's return and her life abroad. She had said nothing of the voice that had beckoned her back. It sat lodged in that private space between mothers and daughters.

She had returned to Rachel's council house with Mark earlier in the day. People from a long-ago life who had heard of her return had crammed the house with curiosity and goodwill. To keep the peace, Philip had sheathed his sword, and so had she.

But where was Ingrid? Friday had passed with no calls, no visit, and now it was Saturday. She must have heard about Yolanda's return, even without a telephone at her apartment. And surely Rachel's absence was a concern for her? Minute by minute, Yolanda had sat, waiting, wanting their reunion to be here, in this house, this kitchen. But that moment had not yet come to pass. There was no indication that it would. She would have to force it. Having decided on an altered story of exile, one that obfuscated the worst truths, Yolanda resolved to go to Ingrid's apartment in the evening. She needed to see with her own eyes that her daughter was OK; she needed her girl's presence to balance the leaden weight of Rachel's absence.

Mark joined her in the yard, shaking his head. She heard Philip's voice thunder from the living room.

"Honestly," Mark sighed. "Sometimes I don't know if he makes everything better or worse."

Yolanda smiled. "He only goes in one direction, Mark. Straight ahead and over. Just like when we were kids."

"Ja, but everything has to be a show, like he's making up for lost time. He did this with Daddy also. Made a big drama of the funeral." Mark curled forward, leaning on his elbows.

Yolanda sat silently, then replied, "At least the old folks had you, Mark. They didn't need any more of Philip's problems. Or mine." Her head fell, and her tears splashed on the ground.

"Yolanda, you did what you had to do. I was here. I remember you sitting in that exact same spot like a zombie. Ingrid would be crying inside, and I could see on your face you couldn't even hear her. One of us would have to go and sit with her, and the other stay with you."

"Except Daddy."

In the days after the assault, her father had taken to holding her for long spells, as if pouring every beat of his love for his only daughter into her. But then he'd withdrawn, fallen back behind the whispers in the neighborhood. She was spoiled goods; she'd slept with the enemy. He'd begun to push her away as much as Rachel had fought to keep her together. Yolanda drew deeply on her cigarette.

"At least the mulberry tree is still here, hey," she said.

"The way we used to eat them . . ."

"What a mess." She paused. "How much does Ingrid know, Mark?"

He shrugged. "We told her there was a car crash, you and him. That's all. After . . . after a few years it was just easier. We couldn't make her wait for you."

"Of course," she said, disappointed that she'd been made a ghost and yet relieved that her daughter had not lived with the cruelty of deliberate neglect. Besides, a car crash was an appropriate analogy. "So she doesn't know about him?"

"Stefan?"

"Yes. That was always just my cross. And the rest of it, what happened to me. Does she know? Please tell me you didn't tell her."

Mark's body tensed. He was holding something back.

"When I finally thought I could do it," she said, keeping her eyes on her brother, "when I wanted and needed to come back, the national state of emergency was in effect, to make a bad situation worse. And I figured it was getting to the point where it would be selfish of me to turn her world upside down. But really, I wasn't ready, not even close."

"You're never ready, Yolanda, for your children." He hadn't answered her question, but she let it be. They would discuss that another time. Ingrid awaited.

"Will you take me to see her?"

Mark nodded. "I'm surprised she hasn't been here, very surprised. She and Ma have had ups and downs but always been close. What are you going to tell her?"

"That I was in exile and her father is dead. That it's possible to move forward. I've done it, or at least I've tried. That all I've wanted all this time, is her. She needs to know she was wanted."

After they returned to Mark's house, Yolanda couldn't decide what to wear. She squeezed her eyes shut while applying makeup and forgot everything she'd planned to say.

They said little on the way to her daughter's apartment. Outside the locked security gate, Mark reminded her to breathe. Something could come of this, something good. She balled her hands as he rang the bell.

A young woman with long braids opened the door. Yolanda blinked. This was not her child.

"Hi, Monica," Mark said.

The young woman frowned. "Come inside," she said. "Is it Ingrid? Is something wrong?"

"No, we just came to see her," Mark said. Monica drew her head back.

"I don't understand; she's not here. You know that, right? She left yesterday."

"Left? For where?" Mark said, his mouth ajar. Yolanda leaned forward, certain she'd misheard.

Monica's eyes moved between their faces. "I know she's upset, but . . . it's been very difficult to talk to her since this thing happened with her grandmother."

"Yes, but we're trying to find Ma, all of us. Where is Ingrid?" Yolanda fought to hold on, to not collapse into the sweep of sadness.

"Monica?" Mark pressed.

"She met someone." Monica held out her hands, placating him. "We were out dancing. He seems nice; he lives in our block. She left with him yesterday. Like I said, she hasn't been herself. But you need to talk with Reuben."

Yolanda watched what appeared to be guilt change the girl's face.

"You know where she went, don't you?" Mark said.

"Please, it's not my place to share. You need Reuben."

Yolanda looked at Mark's exasperated face. "Can I see her room?" she asked abruptly, walking toward the hallway. Monica nodded and led them.

"Sorry, Monica, this is Ingrid's mother," Mark said. The girl appeared unsurprised by this news, which disturbed Yolanda.

Posters on the wall of Ingrid's room caught Yolanda's eye: Ian Curtis, half-illuminated, had pride of place, the words *Love Will Tear Us Apart* emblazoned below him. Lenny Kravitz, in fur coat and dreads, was tacked to the side. An album lay on top of the stereo: *Dry* by PJ Harvey, the words *Sheela-Na-Gig* written on a Post-it stuck to the sleeve.

Yolanda stood there, reckoning with her daughter's life. She touched the architectural tomes and book bag, the large board and tools set aside for drawing. She looked at the jumbled records and novels, brushed her fingers over the clothing in Ingrid's wardrobe. Here there was more silence; here there was another absence.

She'd elevated Ingrid above all the suffering in her life, but it wasn't enough. The hollowness of this moment ground that in deeper.

Back in the car, her disappointment drained out in sobs.

"I'm sorry," Mark said, trying to comfort her. "This is my fault. I told Tracy; I told her not to give Ingrid those things." He drew a deep breath. "She knows, Yolanda. I'm sorry; I know it's not what you wanted. It isn't what we wanted."

"How much does she know?"

He described the package of items from Yolanda's life before. She listened with the prickly sense of being played. Rachel.

"So Mommy did all this deliberately. I sent the letter just before I left England. My divorce had come through; I was so homesick, and I couldn't come back then."

"I promise you that we did our best to shield Ingrid from your past even before that letter. There was talk for a while about you, but then people moved on. We didn't want her to have to account for herself to strangers, for people to make things up like that she was born after the rape, put that into her head."

"I understand; I wouldn't have wanted that to be any different. But now, now she has everything."

"She does. Philip doesn't know about the parcel," Mark said. "I didn't want to tell him; you see how he is. I'm sorry I didn't tell you all this; I thought maybe if Ingrid saw you, it wouldn't make a difference anyway."

Yolanda slumped back. "Ingrid knows. She knows we all lied. She must think she's some kind of horrible secret." Yolanda placed a hand over her mouth. Again she thought: *Rachel, what have you done?*

"Until she comes home, we won't know what's going on in her head. But I'm telling you, there's trouble everywhere. The Zulus don't want to participate in the election. Did you hear about Bophuthatswana? They don't want to integrate; three hundred people are dead from the fighting. I hope Ingrid isn't going anywhere near that mess."

"This Reuben person . . . ," she said.

Mark nodded and started the car.

Maybe this was just a quick getaway to scare them, Yolanda thought as they drove. Retribution for the pain. Myriad thoughts ran through her mind. As they neared Reuben's, she dried her face.

The front light of the small house was on. A boy let them into the small living room. Mark stood still as Yolanda paced.

The mother appeared. Thick armed and clearly accustomed to taking charge, she filled the living room with her presence. She had a pleasant, round face, wore a checkered headscarf and a housecoat. A crucifix hung around her neck. An array of boys, presumably her other sons, tumbled in behind her.

"Mrs. September, sorry to disturb so late," Mark said. "I don't know if you remember my sister."

"Yes, man, I heard the news about you coming back. Yolanda, my word, praise God," she said and clasped her hands together.

"Sorry again, Mrs. September," Mark continued. "Can we talk to Reuben?"

Mrs. September looked at the eldest of the boys in the pack, a curly-haired young man. "What did you get up to now?" she asked him.

"Reuben, we're looking for Ingrid. Apparently she left Cape Town and no one knows where she is but you," Mark said.

"I told her to tell you." Reuben had barely glanced up since they'd arrived; Yolanda could tell he wasn't sure what to make of her.

"Tell us what?" she asked, disguising as best she could the feeling of slipping into a well and watching the light dwindle away above her.

"Her father," he said, then repeated it more loudly at his mother's insistence. "I said maybe she must go find him; she wasn't sure, but she's got his address."

"What?" Mark's face fell.

"Stefan?" Yolanda said at the same time, appalled. "Stefan van Deventer? But he was from Cape Town."

Reuben shrugged. "He moved. He's in the Free State; that's where we found him. We phoned to make sure."

"'We found him'?" Mark fixed him with a stare. "Who's 'we'?"

The boy's only response was a hung head and red face.

"Reuben, answer him," his mother said.

"I helped her," he mumbled.

"Reuben, damn it, man, are you stupid? This isn't a game."

As Mark yelled, Yolanda stood in shock. Stefan: absent, gone, yet somehow claiming their child.

"The whole country is about to go and vote, and Ingrid is driving into the mess with someone she met in a club?" Mark's voice was rising. "The Blacks are killing each other everywhere between here and wherever the hell that place is. The boere are in their *volkstaat*, ready for war. What were you thinking?"

Yolanda shut her eyes. She could not yet process what it meant to have this information, to have Stefan present again, but she needed something that tied her to the child. Her child; hers, not his. When Mark was done, she asked a single question. "Do you still have his address and phone number, Stefan's?"

Reuben leaped up with visible relief and disappeared into a back room.

Mrs. September shifted uncomfortably. "I'm sorry, Mark. You know these young people today, they just do what they want. I'll talk to him." Hand to her mouth, she frowned. "But she phoned here, yes, it was Ingrid. Last night. Reuben wasn't here, and I just thought she was at home. She didn't talk long, didn't say where she was or anything."

Reuben returned, flapping a piece of paper. Yolanda took it, thanked the Septembers, and hurried her brother out the door.

"How the hell did this happen?" she roared as they drove. "How is my child halfway across the country and my mother God knows where? Ingrid should never have got my things; she'd have been better off not knowing about the past at all. Fuck, where is my child?"

"Yolanda." Mark's voice had gone low, emptied of anger. "We tried our best to protect her all these years, to get her into university, give her her own life."

Yolanda could see the exhaustion in him.

"All these years," he continued. "And we always missed you, you and Philip both. Did you have a plan? You and Stefan, when you found out? Does he know about her, even?"

Flower petals down her neck and over her belly one night when they dreamed of the travels they would take outside South Africa: sushi in Japan, boating down the Amazon. Dreams. She remembered sinking in the sand dunes with Stefan under a full moon, sitting well away from his car; a bottle of Tassies between them, the cheap red wine spilling into the sand.

Then the ghouls said months later in wild marshland farther on: "Come, come dance for us like you dance for your white boyfriend." Beasts tightening their circle around her.

"No," Yolanda said, her voice unsteady. "We were young, dumb, and those were dangerous days to be young and dumb. But I'm going to find her, if I have to go all the way to his door."

Mark shook his head. "Stay here; wait. She'll come back. This country is changing, Yolanda. You don't know it anymore."

"I don't care. He doesn't deserve her. He hasn't earned the right to father her, to have her show up on his doorstep."

Mark put his hand on her arm. "Let's go home."

They returned to his house, and Yolanda retreated to her bedroom, exhausted. She couldn't, wouldn't, give voice to the suffocating possibility that her daughter had known she had returned and left because of it. That notion wrenched and tore at the seams along which she held herself together—seams that had already been worn down by Rachel's voice, pleading with her to come home.

Night shifted between dreamless sleep and waking to an unfamiliar, unsettling dark. Yolanda found herself asking why she had come back.

Her disappointments strung together in a paralyzing daze as the next day unfolded.

"This is just a scare tactic, Yolanda. She'll be back soon. It's Sunday; the weekend is winding down. I'm sure she won't just stay away like this, with everything with Ma. This just isn't like her," Mark said as they sat together in Rachel's kitchen.

"If this isn't like her, then how do you know what she's going to do next or when she'll come home?" Yolanda asked. She regretted that she hadn't fortified herself with booze, that she had left the vodka sitting at the bar.

"I need time alone, Mark," she said to her brother when evening came and there was still no sign of Ingrid. "I'm staying here. I'll get the rental car and stuff and come back here. Philip said he was staying in town."

She wanted to find something: a *smokkie* selling illegal alcohol, a bar, somewhere to look away from the nothing space where her mother and her daughter should have been. Beat by beat, she clung desperately to the lessons she'd learned in the months she'd worked to remain sober. At Mark's, she gathered a small bag, then forced herself to go directly to Rachel's. There, as night fell and quiet descended, she sat alone, the emptiness sitting within her as she sat within it.

She ran her fingers over the photos of her daughter in the display cabinet. She smoked two cigarettes in the yard, her spare hand gripped into a fist. After coming in, she sat on the sofa, thinking, *If only one of them would come home, if only . . .*

Exhaustion overcame her, and she slipped into a sleep that was blank but for a single lucid dream: She felt her body raised from the blue depths of the ocean floor. Light. Her translucent limbs came toward the surface with a growing sense of rapture. Breaking into the day with a splash, looking toward a long shore she didn't recognize.

Ingrid was there, on the shore. Bursting with delight, Yolanda swam toward her.

But a forest looming behind the beach drew her child like a magnet. The girl kept turning her head toward it, as if she heard someone calling her. Yolanda's lungs burned like embers. She grew desperate, stroked harder and harder. Cold set in as she realized that the forest held peril. She called and splashed but could not reach the beach, could not stop her child from running into the impenetrable woods.

Suddenly the shore was emptied of life. Ingrid was gone.

Yolanda's eye caught the swish of a tail: a leopard perched on a branch. The animal looked at her, cocked its head, and spoke. As it did, the cold of the ocean settled deeper and deeper into her bones, until she felt it at the very gates of her heart. The leopard's words slipped away from her but left an imprint of warning.

When she burst awake, a thin film of sweat coated her body. Yolanda called for Ingrid. A dreadful danger was coming. Her intuition of this cut through the despondency that had sat upon her all weekend.

Whether Ingrid would accept her or not, she needed to know that her girl was safe. It was six in the morning on a Monday, but all she could think of was dialing Stefan's house. She smoked before and after a shower, drank two mugs of black coffee, waited until nine. She found Reuben's note and dialed.

To her relief, a woman answered. "Hello?"

"Hello, my name is Yolanda. I'm an old—"

The woman hung up. Yolanda frowned. She dialed again, but no one answered. The same paralyzing fear that had swept in with the dream ran its icy fingers over her.

She waited half an hour, then tried again. "Hello," said the same woman's voice.

"Yes, my name is Yolanda; I called earlier for Stefan van Deventer. Does he live here?" A dissonant pause, crammed with static; Yolanda wondered if the connection was bad. "Hello?"

"Why are you phoning here? What do you want?"

The woman sounded livid. How was that possible?

"Who is this?" Yolanda asked.

"You've got no business phoning here, do you understand me?"

"What? Wait, where is my daughter? Where is she?"

The woman clicked her tongue before slamming the phone down. Yolanda stared at the buzzing receiver before hanging it up gently. She dialed again, then twice more, only to get a busy tone.

Many things about Stefan had been out of view from her, yet she'd known his world well. But that had been twenty years ago. That woman had appeared as unsurprised as Monica had, but now Ingrid was somewhere on the other end of this.

She called Mark, explained that she was leaving immediately, going to Stefan's. He tried to talk her out of it but failed.

Her family was spread out on a razor's edge. Her decision was made.

Although she had heard Rachel's voice calling her across an ocean, she couldn't hear the sound of an engine murmuring nearby. Didn't see that a street over from the council house, a man had taken off his headset. He tapped a photo of Yolanda on his dashboard. "Here's the trigger," he was saying to himself, "finally pulled on the threat."

STEFAN

He needed space, silence, to consider this coloured boy coming to claim him as his father.

When the boy had phoned last week, asking if he'd once surfed in Muizenberg, Stefan had been caught unawares. Preoccupied, he stumbled into the admission that, yes, he'd lived there years ago. But then the boy said he knew a woman, someone who'd known Stefan well during that time. Stefan hung up, but it was too late. The acknowledgment of who he was and where he lived now could not be taken back. *The child,* he'd thought. *My God, she had the child after all. And he knows where I live.*

The dreams of her that had bothered him at night had been a warning. After all their ducking and diving, avoiding arrest and disclosure, a young man he didn't know from a bar of soap was going to show up on his doorstep and drag the whole affair out of the shadows. It would happen in front of his three children, his wife, and his town, a place where few had tolerance for transgressions of color, especially now.

And he couldn't get away, couldn't leave for a long hike, because his mother was visiting. Although she'd declared her arrival with little warning, they couldn't deny Elsa, didn't really have a reason to. She'd flown in the previous evening. Katrina's glare said the hike was going to have to wait.

So here he was, out for an evening jog with his ridgeback, on the land near his house, contemplating how he was going to keep his life together when all hell broke loose. He'd left Elsa at home, braiding his eldest daughter's hair, Katrina fussing over the pots in the kitchen. It couldn't be a more ordinary scene.

Stefan clenched his fists and ran faster, pushing himself, his jawline hardening. He didn't want to think about Yolanda. That chapter in his life had to remain so foreign as to be another man's memory, a different man's body.

Muizenberg. He never said much now about those days or his love for the surf. It embarrassed Katrina; "It was his hippie phase," she would say with a light laugh before moving the conversation along. When he'd moved to the Free State, he'd left his boards with his mother. He was unwilling to sell or give them away but didn't doubt that Elsa would. He didn't have the heart to ask, and she never mentioned them again. Everything in his life had since gone in the opposite direction from Muizenberg.

But having Elsa here now in his house made him remember why he'd moved away to that bay as a young man. It had always been suffocating to live with her, stumbling between boundaries, choking on privilege. He wondered when it had begun, that dissonant feeling of looking for something he couldn't wrap a name around.

Surfing had reset his world in his early teens by making the ocean a wilderness for play and exploration. But before all of that was Betty. He thought of their maid, who had been with them since she was a teenager, and the gardener they'd had then, the odd occasions when the police had asked for their papers. As a child, this puzzled him. "Are they going to take Betty away?" he asked his mother once. Elsa said simply that Betty and the gardener were Blacks, so they couldn't just go walking and working in the white areas.

At night, Betty went somewhere else, somewhere outside the white areas, while he stayed behind. He couldn't have been more than six the first time he had the sense of being penned in, of wanting to get out. Stefan recalled the day he'd decided to follow her home, remembered the sudden compulsion to see what happened beyond the white areas. He'd made it as far as the bus terminus in Bellville, a terrifying place, but he'd held the coins he had taken from his mother's purse in his hand and waited in a long line because everyone else was in a line too. People turned to look at him. The bus driver said a lone white child on his bus was trouble and refused to let him board.

Betty noticed him, from a different line, and hurried to take his hand. He remembered how she'd taken him home, gentle with her kleinbaas. She was deeply concerned and apologetic in the face of Elsa's fury. She left late. Elsa wanted to fire her, but his father said it was the boy's mistake. Stefan burst into tears that softened everyone's anger. He was sad because Betty had missed her bus, and now she had to do that long walk and wait in line again.

Yes, that must be it, he thought, his heart pounding as he ran. The first time he'd hid these feelings. He couldn't tell his parents how terrified he'd been of Betty never coming back from that alien, other landscape. His own world was one of order, steady yet constrained. Betty was the one who took care of him. She animated his life with her care, made him yearn for something quite different.

How did it go then? Puberty came with a desire to set his own terms, to figure out what they were. Drinking at braais and camping with friends was one thing, but it was on the mountains and mostly in the ocean that he felt genuinely alive. He tolerated rugby—he had no choice—but his heart wasn't in it. He earned money for his own jalopy. He began to savor being alone, took occasional overnight hikes, but mostly spent weekends surfing—at Blouberg first, then elsewhere.

University provided a stay of execution, but then the army came and changed everything. It declared him unequivocally an Afrikaner, a member of a nation at war. Stefan was nothing special, first in the field workshop, then on the front line at the Caprivi Strip. A trained engineer, he fixed machines, sometimes gave instructions under fire, preserving weapons of war in order to keep people alive. But as he fell into the grind of a vast machine that wanted him to be a good soldier, that didn't allow him to question or object without consequence, the last bit of obedience was wrung out of him.

Even as a boy he'd known intuitively what he had to do to earn respect and love: silence his curiosity about why their world worked the way it did. "You have everything ahead of you, my boy," his parents had often said. As he'd aged, he'd learned the subtext: *Don't fuck it up.*

Muizenberg undid all of that. After the land mine at Caprivi, he couldn't maintain the pretense. He wanted to have the ocean on his face, for it to somehow make him clean, help him see again. That day, the day when the season of Yolanda began, was one of several when he let his curiosity, his need to go beyond his world, come to the fore.

He used to roam the whole stretch of coast then, from Fish Hoek, dabbling at Kalk Bay Reef or Dangers, over to Noordhoek Beach, which he favored.

That morning, as he stood outside his place with a coffee, he could tell that there wasn't much swell. It was the middle of summer, a windless, sun-drenched Saturday. The summer waves typically held none of the power that winter storms brought. He decided on a paddle from Dangers Reef, skirting Muizenberg and heading east. There was a beach break out there, at the coloured beach, one he hadn't surfed yet. It would be a long paddle, he'd have to come to shore to rest, but he'd never done it before and had time on his hands.

From out in the ocean, he spied the whites all the way until Muizenberg Beach but moved beyond where the **WHITES ONLY** signs ended. He came closer to shore again. Brown bodies began to appear on the beach and in the water. This was a stupid idea, he thought. He imagined how they saw him emerging from the deep: the capricious, conspicuous blond wearing nothing but board shorts.

Eventually he spied all the signs of a good wave. He paddled out, rode it in, then paddled out again, watching his observers from beyond the low break. There were no other surfers out. Finally, another wave brought Stefan to the shore, where a thrilled group of children greeted him. A boy touched his board, asked questions. Soon Stefan was showing him how to balance on it, telling him what the board was made of, why it was so long, and what the purpose of the single fin was. Stefan explained where he had come from. He remembered the inevitable question of how surfers peed.

The beach looked rough; none of Muizenberg's amenities were here. There were no policemen in sight, no lifeguards. Stefan felt isolated. A group of men sat on one of the dunes, watching as the band of children around him grew. Soon he was showing the children how to stay afloat in the shallows and trying to explain how to read the waves. Stefan remembered a sense of vindication. He'd set aside the misgivings he'd been fed, which had been watered his whole life.

In the middle of it all, he saw her walking toward them. They all saw her. She wore a large hat and sunglasses; she carried a towel, a sketchbook, and a small satchel. She had one of those Indian-print hippie skirts cinched up on her hips, and he could see her well-defined calf muscles. But there was something more: a body she moved with ease, even pleasure, as if she herself were shifting through water. She kicked the sand and the waves like a child.

She sat down a ways away, settling wide hipped and alone on her opened towel with the grace of a butterfly lowering its wings. One of the children offered Stefan a sandwich from his mother, which he accepted. He considered the situation. It would be foolish to try to speak with her so openly. He knew that interracial liaisons happened; everyone knew that. Even so, the Immorality Act could cause serious trouble.

Time passed; the children drifted off; the men on the dunes shifted on their haunches, their faces hardening. Stefan had to go back. But first he had to say something, and his opportunity was narrowing. Despite the risk, he sat beside her in the sand.

His opening words weren't memorable; he was never good at those things. But he remembered the mole on her neck, the pink top draped off one shoulder. Her small bare feet and her neatly painted toes. He wanted to stroke and hold all of it. When she took off her glasses and hat, he recognized her: she worked at the café close to his apartment. She looked completely different there, tucked away in the kitchen under a headscarf, a uniform, and a whole array of inhibitions.

Yolanda showed him her sketches, and as she spoke, he knew that he was falling into something he couldn't describe, breathing her in and wanting more. Something caught alight between them, like it had always been there, waiting for the right moment. She didn't call him *baas*; she didn't seem especially impressed by his presence on their beach. When a man from the dunes came over to ask Stefan what he thought he was doing, she was the one to tell him to mind his own business. Then she turned to Stefan with a coy raise of an eyebrow and asked what, in fact, he was doing here.

He'd said the first thing that had rushed out of him: "I was looking for you."

Stefan thought back on that day with sadness now. Similar moments of being so casual and so close in public lessened afterward. He used to think that he was altered from then on by how near he could be to her, whether or not he could hold her. But that was the blind desire of a boy.

He turned to run on a gravel road, agitated by the memory of how he used to make love to her far from human view, in the mountains, where their cries had gone unheard. Then there were the risky nights in other places: along the shoreline, in his parked car, in his apartment, on blankets far off in the dunes. It would have been one thing if this were only about the pleasure of a woman's body, the tenderness of it, where it curved and tightened, puckered and folded. But there was more between them from the outset. It was raw and unvarnished. It had depth.

There were close calls with the cops, and they developed a sixth sense for people who looked at them twice, who appeared too interested in each of them. But there were good days, some of them even in the café. For a few moments when the place was quiet, they were free and normal. The manager, a white woman of the liberal English variety, knew about them and didn't care; she covered for them. She went so far as to pretend to be his girlfriend when things grew uncomfortable.

But his mother insisted that he be home some Sundays for church and lunch. He had to be well behaved; he had to set aside a crucifying sense of damnation. He sat at the foot of the pulpit, with his parents, his sister, and his brother-in-law seated in the same pew. The *dominee* railed from on high, while Stefan wondered if the smell of Yolanda was still on him, remembered the taste of her. He was not a good man. They wouldn't want him if they knew.

Everything soured as their relationship reached its third year. The anguish between and within them wouldn't settle. He learned that Philip, Yolanda's brother, had been forced to go underground. He was being hunted by the state. Yolanda worried and raged; it became apparent that they could not escape the long shadow of the politics of the day. Stefan knew then that this simple act of having his skin next to hers tainted them. She became withdrawn. Her period was late.

Before he could digest what that meant, she fell away, back into her country, so separate from his. They told him at the café that she didn't work there anymore. The manager said simply: "Stefan, there's trouble. You should stay away." Then, unexpectedly, he got called up. War in Angola was imminent. Every white man he knew, for whom conscription, followed by periodic call-ups, was mandatory, expected to go there. He had to bear arms for a cause he didn't believe in. Still, gutted and conflicted though he'd been, he hadn't objected to going, and he hadn't chased her. He hadn't had the courage to go to her house, at least to tell her he was leaving. He'd taken his things back to his parents' house. He'd had to let her go.

It was for the best. He'd tried to convince himself of this over the years.

Stefan stopped running. He stood at a fence and bent over. He sank his head against the post, using his T-shirt to wipe sweat from his face. If this boy came to his door, if he found him, Stefan couldn't deny what had happened. But he wanted to keep his family whole, protect his children from his mistakes. There wasn't room for sentimentality these days, with the elections, the violence, people leaving for Perth.

And where was Yolanda? Would she follow her son? It wasn't a welcome thought. He hadn't room to entertain it, couldn't.

He jogged back to the large house that, like his wife, was his shelter from those raw days. The prospect of Yolanda disturbed him almost more than the illegitimate son. He was haunted by her; there was no other word for it. Waking up in the dark because he heard her laughter rippling like a brook. Falling asleep to the vivid memory of stepping into a cave on Table Mountain, out of sight; the intensity of not just kissing but bonding in that absolute dark. He had never been closer to another being, not ever. Still, he'd set it all aside for decades, treated it as forgotten, irrelevant. But it would not remain so.

He opened the door to his mother's clucking and his wife's fussing. The familiar sounds helped to draw a comfortable numbness over it all. Maybe he was mistaken, and nothing would come of his fears. He had kept that period of his past out of view for all this time. He would continue to do so. There was no room in his home or his heart for that child or Yolanda.

RACHEL

Filthy Black vermin." Disgust made every word a punch. The blows hit Rachel with force. Dazed, her breath knocked out of her, she lay facedown in the dirt. She felt a foot on her back.

"Good Christian souls, just a few thousand of us, was all it took to make something of this country. But you lot—" The stranger kicked her. "You squatted here like the dumb animals you are for hundreds of years, wiping your Black arses in the dirt, doing nothing."

Word after word ground into her like a fist. The shooting pain was acute. "Jan," Rachel croaked in shock.

How could there be hurt like this, here? How could any of this be happening? She felt the pain light up the well of her memories. Of holding Ingrid for the first time, the feistiness in her full-throated newborn cry, the foreboding when bent and elderly Sara, who had just delivered the baby, had said, "There is fire in her—good. She's going to need it." Of one of the last fights between Philip and George, the old man berating his son for bringing home liberation-movement pamphlets. "We're one police raid away from them putting us all in prison," George had shouted. And Philip's response: "Rather that than live like you, old man. Your whole life you work for them, day in, day out, yes baas, no baas, like a fool. Daddy, you're a stooge, an Uncle Tom, and too blind to see it."

Family. Rachel's heart brimmed with love and terror. Those emotions surged, overtaking even her shock at the brutal attack. She rolled onto her back to look her attacker in the face. He was older, unshaven. A white man, dressed as a relic from another era.

Beyond the baobab, she spied a wagon and movement beside it: a woman, huddled with two children. But it was the man who transfixed her, the white man with a soiled hat. Bitterness and rage pulsed in the veins of his neck, curled his lips and sharpened his eyes. His ugliness had a texture, a coarseness she could taste. To him, the mere fact of her presence was enough to earn this punishment.

"You lazy, thieving, slaughtering kaffirs." Another kick to her gut. Blood, her own, sprinkled on the ground, dribbled from her mouth. But as the droplets reached the sand, the grains moved. Rachel heard something else, a sound that was from neither Jan nor the man.

Curled up, she hacked, coughed, and fixed fierce eyes on her attacker. More vile words spilled from him, but something was happening, a transformation that overtook his aggression. Color ebbed from his skin. His body crooked forward. The gleam in his eye at the power he wielded caused those same eyes to bulge into black, pitiless holes. He hunched over the violence he bred as if it were a baby he might nourish and clasp to his bosom.

But then, as Rachel watched his brutality consume him, the pain within her diminished. The sand beneath her shifted, grew animated. She felt vibrations. Whispers swirled in the air, a swarm of sound.

"I died with rats running over my legs, Ma." A disembodied male voice spoke, laced with anguish. "The diarrhea never stopped; I was too weak to fight the infection. They stopped feeding me; they waited for me to die."

A woman's voice, wafting by: "It is a thing, Ma, when all your bones are not together. When your grave is a shallow hole in the ground and the hyena eat the last of you. It is a thing, Ma."

Other stories drifted on the wind, accounts of lives and deaths that grew in scale, that drew down deep into suffering. As these stories layered upon each other, Rachel felt distinctly that the troubles of her own family stood against a much larger backdrop.

"Come, Ma." Jan, at last. A shift in her being; a movement out of the form she had taken. She was being carried in Jan's body now, Rachel realized.

"You are safe, Ma. I am here. Look."

Something was changing with her old body. The white man, buckled into a brute, had resumed berating it, kicking and beating it, despite the swirl of sand and the churn of voices. But Rachel's old form was transforming, too, becoming the man when he'd been human, before he'd changed so horrifically. Soon the man was punishing a being that mirrored him.

"I don't understand, Jan. Is he trying to destroy himself?"

"That, Ma, is the question. After all, anger and fear are two sides of the same coin," Jan said and told her to look again.

Her old form disintegrated into the soil. The whispers and voices began to attach to limbs that grew from the sand, a multitude of bodies forming, rising up. They emerged from behind the wagon, the trees. They were human. Their faces and bodies wore the misery of those robbed of life, opportunity, decency, and wholeness.

They encircled the man and his family. Despite his curses, the rage and the fists he threw at them, the circle tightened. With stones and tree branches in their hands, they moved like a wave around the pale figures.

Justice, Rachel thought with satisfaction. Payback.

On his knees, the man returned to his human form. He seemed diminished. He turned to his wife and children, shielding them as they cowered closer. Stones flew. Blood appeared on their clothing, and Rachel's satisfaction ebbed. What would be gained, even here in this elsewhere place, from more suffering?

One of the white children peered up. She saw the surprise on his little face: that life could offer an experience so bleak, so irredeemably violent. The shock of what was being taken away was evident in his eyes; the realization already there, bitter bread for one so young. What was taken would never come back.

"Stop," Rachel commanded. With that single word, she separated herself from Jan, took up her body once again. The figures the sand had spawned were lifted by the wind, blown into her, and their stories with them. Woven into her journey now were their trials.

She did not stand alone, Rachel realized. She never had. But what had fueled her, her desire for revenge, would render her the same as her attacker. It would make her less than human.

With the roar of the crowd gone, Rachel observed the white man. His ripped clothes, his aged body of skin and bone. He was a spent figure.

"Mercy, Ma, please," the woman asked as she gazed at Rachel, her eye sockets hollow with hunger. But it was not food and drink these beings lacked.

"I have granted it," Rachel said. "But I ask you, where was mercy for me?"

The man stood and looked at her with new awareness, for Rachel, too, had changed. Emboldened, she had become larger, somehow. She was unafraid and knew innately that he no longer had power over any part of her.

"Mercy in this place," the man said, "is for the birds."

"No," Rachel said. "Mercy makes us human."

A pause. The man turned his head, speaking to the bush veld.

"What does home mean, Ma, to you?"

"It is my people," Rachel answered. "It is the place I know like the back of my hand. It is where I want my bones to rest."

"Yes. This land, to which we gave everything, it gave us our wagon of plenty." He turned his eyes away. "We built something here. Then the Blacks slunk in and took it all from us in one night. Man, woman, and child."

"But you accumulated by theft; you shared nothing," Rachel said. "You built your house upon that of your brother, upon his selfhood and tribe, his history."

"We were told it was our right. This is our home, too; we have nowhere else to go, and yet we are lost here. So every Black I see, my anger leads me on with its own force. And every time, they come for us. We can never die; they can never rest. It is our cycle."

"No. It is your choice," Rachel said.

But the family drew away, broken people hauling their destitute wagon for all eternity. From the dreadful darkness of its interior, the children eyed her. The one whose face she had spied earlier gave a small wave, and Rachel smiled. Even children's spirits held a glimmer of hope for a different future.

"Who will win, Jan?" she asked of her companion, who had come to stand beside her. Together, they watched the retreating wagon. "If the power to assault, to control, is all we have, and there is nothing left to reign over?"

"That, Ma, is the legacy of the wagon. You are here, Rachel, because you also believe you are on a righteous path. But do not follow the same tracks. When he lived, that man justified himself with the bones of another and called it destiny. He is blind, Ma. Do not be. You dream of retribution, but you must not blind yourself with savagery. That is a game at which everyone eventually loses."

In the silence that followed, Jan moved through the veld's long grasses, back to the baobab. It was enormous, its girth wide. Layers of bark bursting from bark hardened its trunk, made it appear impregnable. Jan looked up at it.

"This tree, Ma, it is a being of generations. Of wars and the end of eras. Of migrations, those of people and those of animals. Time, human time, like the life of the wagonman, is a blink to it." Jan waved a long stalk of grass in time with his words. "Still, battle after battle that man will fight. Like a drunken general, he will think himself to be invincible, immortal like this tree, even when the truth says otherwise. And so it is with the tambouti woman too."

Rachel came beside him as he paused. Both of them looked up at the high, gnarled limbs of the tree that dwarfed them. Rachel placed a palm upon it, digesting his words.

"Ma," Jan said softly. "The return home you seek, the road back to the ancestors, you cannot walk that road arming yourself with your discontent. You know more now. You have seen wider than your family, into the stories of others. Like this tree with its breadth, extend yourself now beyond your narrow needs. Think in generations.

"If you do not, you and the tambouti woman will be the same. And you will descend, taking your children down too."

Rachel reflexively touched her stomach. There were no bruises or welts anywhere upon her, nothing but the memory of the attack. The pair stood together for several long moments of quiet, until Jan breathed in deeply, shifting shape. He angled his long feline neck so that he looked at a distant point, far from the tree. "More awaits, Ma, beyond this veld."

Although the wagon was long gone, Rachel thought again of the children riding within it. Children and ancestors, past and future made present. Jan cocked his head as if listening to her thoughts. He stepped forward. A single out-of-place fern appeared where he had been. "All of them await us, Ma, children and ancestors. But first, we seek a giant," he said and beckoned Rachel to follow.

INGRID

Yolanda sat heavily on Ingrid's mind as she sat behind Litha in the back of an old Jetta driven by his friend Khwezi. She couldn't stop thinking about that self-portrait. The image of her mother's damaged face that Ingrid had found in the bag, uncovered at the Maraises' house, was one she returned to again and again.

It presented the gaze of someone whose heart had been carved out and flung in the dirt, someone too afraid to look at what was in front of her. It told Ingrid that maybe her mother's abandonment hadn't just been recklessness and self-interest. Maybe there was something else.

But that was even more disturbing. What had driven her away? What had made Yolanda paint something so painful? Ingrid shook her head. She wished she'd never found the painting.

She tried to focus on the people milling along the worn streets of Motherwell township, but it didn't help. All that the world unfolding outside told Ingrid was that she was moving into foreign waters, traveling on currents and winds she didn't recognize. Meanwhile, Yolanda was turning Ingrid's past into another country. The painting poked at her, whispered to Ingrid that her rage at Yolanda was premature. Something evil had driven the woman away.

Litha's car had been towed back to Riviersonderend, his worst fears confirmed: repairs would not be minor. He'd offered to put Ingrid on a bus back to Cape Town, but neither of them wanted her to go. It would have been the responsible thing to do, but she'd made up her mind. She was going to Stefan.

And there was Litha. She wasn't ready to leave him either. After they'd all attended to the car, the Maraises had dropped them back on the N2. Together, Litha and Ingrid had hitchhiked earlier this afternoon to Port Elizabeth, which lay farther along the southern coast. In the late afternoon, they'd entered the city aboard a long-haul truck whose interior was a shrine to Ferrari. Khwezi had been in nearby Motherwell for a family function. He'd collected them at a bus stop in town.

Throughout the trip, when she was sure no one was watching, Ingrid reached into the package Rachel had left her. Setting the self-portrait aside, she looked for more between love letters and old photos. She fished out a battered journal full of images drawn in pencil and smudged. The first was a face she thought for a moment was Rachel's, but the similarity ended with the almond-shaped eyes and cheekbones. This older woman, with her few teeth and lined face, stared Ingrid down from across the ages, eyes burning off the yellowed page like hot coals.

A landscape unfolded in the remainder of that journal: *dongas* and hills; small fires; country people and shrubs scattered across wide-open spaces. Snot-nosed children and adults weathered by the passage of time. Yolanda had a precise hand.

Farther inside were a few undated paragraphs:

I never met my grandmother until now. We are somewhere near Vioolsdrif, where the ground makes a crust like bitter old bread in some places, and in others, the sand flows like water. Ouma is letting me stay here until after the baby is born. Ma doesn't want me in Cape Town since the arrest. She's scared of the police. I can't blame her. She put me in the car, and made Daddy drive me here as soon as the police sent me home. She says Ouma is a midwife anyway, she can take care of me.

I feel like I'm being punished for Stefan. I miss him so much; he must be wondering.

Ouma lives alone without electricity and makes a living selling herbs and treating people. Now and then she goes away to deliver a baby—it can be a day, even a week—but no one worries me except to make sure I'm OK. She makes sure I get 3 meals a day and makes me walk a lot. People know I'm here and because of her, they bring all kinds of things—herbs, bread, fruit; they're all poor and this land is so dry, I don't know how they do it.

Ouma starts the fire or the paraffin stove at five o'clock every day come rain or shine, she beats the beans for our moerkoffie by hand and gets the mielie meal on the stove. She checks the baby and me every day. She doesn't say a lot and doesn't ask me a lot either. So far she has taught me how to make fresh bread over a fire and a good potjie with basically anything, including rabbit, which we have to catch and skin.

Here I am, on the edge of the Orange River somewhere in the desert. Ouma calls the river the Gariep. Ma has made me disappear.

Another betrayal, even there, at the start of her life. No one had told Ingrid this, that she'd been born into the knobbly hands of a great-grandmother she'd never met. She felt like a dirty little secret, marked by distant dust.

Ingrid returned to the same self-portrait once again. The face puffed, purple and black with bruises, the lips cut, the eyes filled with tears. It was an invasion, violent and haunting. The inscription on the back read:

Blackface golliwog
Give a dog a bone
This is the woman
Who never came home

Here was the crucial piece of a story she didn't know. Not just Yolanda's story but, she suspected, also hers.

Ingrid looked around at Motherwell again, the makeshift hair salons and bent figures in shacks dark as night. It felt safe and numbing to know no one. Children without pants and adults in old shoes wandered beneath the low, dangling cables that formed a celestial web over this world. On the odd corner, men huddled, one of them peeing into a ditch clogged with dirt.

"Smileys," Litha said, pointing at a roadside food stand: a cooked sheep's head locked into a grotesque grin.

"Have you ever seen one?" Khwezi asked, although she could tell he had seen the answer on her face.

"No," Ingrid said. "We have parcels and footlongs, gatsbys and things like that in Cape Town. I've never eaten anything's head before."

Khwezi laughed. "The cheeks are the best."

She thought of the little white gods in her class at university and wondered what they would think of that. Her eyes moved to Litha. Once again, she thought, his roots held firm. Hers were a tangled mess.

An old Peugeot went by, its headlights big as bowls; it was nearly as slow as the occasional horse-drawn cart. They drove on, into what seemed to be an older quarter of the township, and the shacks tapered away. Brick houses appeared. Khwezi slowed and parked as Ingrid stretched, feeling the last of the Saturday-afternoon sun.

"This is Khwezi's grandmother's place," Litha said. "It's her birthday." The smell of braai thickened the air; the meat had clearly been grilling for hours. Cars lined the street and driveway; people came and went.

"Leave your things in the back—we will get it later. You will stay here tonight; they said they will make a plan for you."

Once again she was at the mercy of the road and those who gave her shelter. Of Litha, who had been courteous with her, and warm. They were circling each other, Ingrid thought, tugged by something irresistible.

Loud greetings of "*Molweni*" and "*Kunjani*?" rose up when they entered the house. An assembly of Black women held court in the living room, and some clapped their hands at the sight of Litha. A bespectacled old lady was helped to her feet, and she embraced him warmly.

"*Kunjani kuwe?* Such a big man now," the elder said.

Ingrid looked down at the torn black denim of her jeans, her ever-present boots and grungy T-shirt. Would it be possible to sit this out in the car? She glued her eyes to the floor.

"This is uIngrid," Litha said and gestured for her to step forward.

"Kunjani, come inside, welcome," the old woman said. Ingrid felt acutely aware of stepping over lines, of somehow embarrassing Litha. But the old woman grasped her hand warmly, peering at her through Coke-bottle glasses. Ingrid took to her immediately.

"This is Ma Thembi, the birthday girl." Litha smiled. The old woman gave him a playful smack on the arm.

Enamel-backed chairs were delivered from the depths of the house, and a string bean of a girl brought out two glasses of orange Fanta on a tray. Ingrid watched Litha launch into isiXhosa, switching now and then to English for her benefit as he relayed the tale of how they had gotten here. Unable to participate, she could do no more than watch him. In Heidelberg, he had been so silent, a strange phantom. Here, he was rooted like an oak, animated and expressive, clear about who he was in the world. Such belonging was not hers to have, not with that damn package she bore.

More people appeared in the living room. A dimpled man, Khwezi's cousin, greeted Litha with a complicated handshake and embrace. Litha introduced him to Ingrid, then said, "I'm going to greet some people in the yard. I'll be back just now."

Ingrid nodded, despite the anxiety she felt at being alone.

"Now what is your name?" asked the Fanta girl. But a woman came up behind her and shuffled her along before Ingrid could answer. The woman scanned Ingrid up and down. It was evident, in the turn of her lips and her raised eyebrows, that she didn't like what she saw. Her hair fell against her skull in an elegant, straightened sweep. Her beautiful printed chiffon shirt flowed over tight taupe pants; she wore expensive shoes.

"I'm Nomhla, Khwezi's wife." She spoke in a clipped, formal manner. "The braai is almost ready; these men, they take so long. Then we can eat." She paused. "So you are a friend traveling to the Transkei with Litha?"

"To Durban, actually, to see a friend," Ingrid lied. She felt instinctively that this woman would pick apart any hint of romantic affection for Litha.

"You met him at university, I suppose?"

Ingrid nodded. Ma Thembi clicked her tongue. "You ask a lot of questions, Nomhla. She has traveled all day; let her rest."

"Sorry, Ma." Nomhla withdrew, and the old woman winked at Ingrid, who smiled gratefully.

The singsong of polite chatter continued until they were summoned outside, to a table covered with meat fresh off the braai, potato salad, samp, and other dishes. Ma Thembi and the other elderly people were served ahead of everyone else. The yard was a bazaar of noise and male voices. Ingrid spoke with Litha briefly, before returning to the living room, where lunch was followed by sweet hot tea, cake, and sticky doughnuts.

"I can't eat any more," she eventually had to tell Ma Thembi, who laughed and slapped her own hefty thigh.

"Where do you think these come from, my dear? You are too thin. Eat!"

Ingrid blushed. Litha came inside and squatted beside her, a beer bottle in his hand.

"Sorry, there are a lot of people to catch up with. Come join us," he said. "You shouldn't be so shy."

She got up to follow him, feeling as if every pair of eyes in the living room, especially Nomhla's, was upon them.

The men gathered around the crackling fire were animated and glassy eyed. Introductions were made, and Litha supplied Ingrid with a beer, clinking her bottle in a toast. Rhythmic music that she recognized as *kwaito* came from a stereo. Ingrid answered more questions: why she was traveling, where she was going, if she was coloured, if she was married. She spoke as gracefully as she could, wondering why on earth so many people wanted answers from her now, when she had so few to give.

"Do you want to take a walk?" Litha asked when their drinks were done. They headed out, Ingrid reddening at the catcalls and whistles from Litha's friends. The streets were lively with the promise of a Saturday night. Weary dogs and occasional chickens skittered as they strolled.

"How do you know Khwezi?" Ingrid asked.

Litha smiled slightly. "Our families have known each other since we were small. And we became men together, you know."

"Initiation?" Ingrid blurted, and he nodded. "Oh." She blushed. "I mean, I've read about it in the paper, but that's all I know." The Xhosa tradition signaled the advent of manhood. She raised an eyebrow. "Circumcision, that must hurt."

"Well, we don't talk about it really," he said, and she felt again that she was brushing up against the strange boundaries of his world.

"Will you ever come back out this way to stay? Everybody knows you. It must feel good to be home."

He grew pensive. "I have my feet in two worlds now: Cape Town, city life; and then Pondoland—that part of the Transkei where I'm from, the country." His voice softened. "Each of them expects me to only be passing through the other, to settle into being either a traditional Xhosa man or an urban one. It was not a dilemma I was expecting when I left home."

They headed up a small hill that gave them a slight vantage point over the compressed streets. Litha sighed heavily. "My father, he has already given all of us a piece of land. He doesn't like the city; he wants the family together; he wants the old ways to stay."

Ingrid frowned. "But what do you want?"

Litha was silent for a while.

"To fix my car and keep driving with you," he said, looking ahead. "To Mozambique, Tanzania even, all the way to Kenya and Egypt."

His words took her by surprise, and at the same time, she smiled at the idea of driving with him through Africa.

"Ingrid," he said, as if growing accustomed to the sound of her name. "I was thinking about you today." He turned to her. "Last night, after I saw you, after Hannelie." He brushed her face with his fingers.

"What were you thinking?" she asked, aware of her hardening nipples.

"That I don't know why I can't stop thinking about you," he said.

Between them stood the family and clan he could take for granted, and her own, which she couldn't. The dogma of culture and her growing awareness of the weight of race crowded the moment of his lips touching hers. But she wanted wholeness; she wanted to be held; she wanted him and his body to stand between her and her uncertainties. And as their arms snaked around each other, as she felt hot and wet between her thighs, she simply wanted him.

She sank into the kiss. She was falling in love with him despite her life coming undone. As they returned to the house and slipped back into the fray, she knew this to be true. He wanted her, he wanted to be with her, and that single thought eclipsed everyone else in her life who did not.

Night drew near. A room was made up for her, while Litha was given a sleeper couch. In the dark, Ingrid's thoughts paced. Desire carried her past her inhibitions and the realities of her family. Yet even as she rose on its crest, guilt came; getting involved with Litha like this, it was the wrong timing. But she didn't want to be alone, not with Yolanda's picture, not with all that lurked in the darkness.

The house had long fallen silent when she arose. She tiptoed to Litha and found him awake, led him to her room. She undressed, feeling bold and exposed, wanting to be naked, to come clean in some way.

She couldn't frame the reasons in words, but she and Litha needed each other. The night offered shelter from scrutiny.

Even as she explored his body and allowed him to explore hers, she felt them both reach beyond the physical. They had sex with urgency, but the longer spells in between brought a deep, powerful feeling of bonding with another human being. Ingrid could not explain to herself why she was with this unlikely man in this unlikely place. She simply needed to be, wanted to be, even though everything around them held darkness.

RACHEL

The landscape around Rachel and Jan changed, the brown wave of savanna grass growing taller, greener, more lush. More ferns and fallen logs appeared underfoot, and the travelers found themselves flanked by trees Rachel had not seen before on this journey, ones that grew ever thicker and taller.

Jan had said little since the incident with the wagon people, leaving Rachel alone to reflect. Retribution felt like a hollow promise: she had seen now where it led. Instead, she thought of the expansiveness of time and space, the complex web of life, the baobab. She saw the unvarnished, undiminished whole; threads and patterns woven into choices. This knowledge brought with it power and an understanding that the events of her life were held in the context of a much larger tableau. The council estate had made life feel small; the hatred inflicted by one person could do the same. She was leaving that behind.

The forest thickened; it grew mysterious and disorienting. Jan held his head low; he seemed to be hunting, stalking. The air was damp, the earth dark and rich. Water droplets hung off ferns that stood waist high. Shadows moved.

They both slowed when they heard the voice. It was a faint, drifting thing that grew in sound and tone until a person assembled herself around it: an old white woman in farm clothes, wrapped in a thick woolen cardigan, her checked apron covered in dust. She wore scuffed veld boots, the kind one used for outside work. Blood was spattered across her face and clothes, but she didn't bear any wounds that they could see. A life balanced between hardship and the strength it took to endure it marked her face and the way she carried herself.

"He is a good boy, my son," she said as they neared her. "Please don't hurt him. He's only doing his job, what they trained him for. He just wanted us to be safe, that's all."

"But there is blood," Rachel said.

"He didn't mean to," came a mechanical answer. "He just wanted us to be safe, that's all. He is a good boy."

Rachel frowned at the woman, confused.

"He is a good boy," the woman repeated. "He is a good boy."

Jan turned away, saying nothing, and Rachel followed. The old lady shadowed them for a while, until her pleas became as thin and indistinct as her body and she drifted off like a fog between the trees.

"I have seen enough blood for today, Jan." Rachel sat down on a large blown-down tree trunk. She paused, then said, "When that wagonman beat me, the pain I felt was monstrous. So now I'm asking: What did Yolanda encounter that day, that night? Was it the same kind of evil? How could I have drawn her back here, back to where that horror lives? And Ingrid. What will the tambouti woman do to her?"

"Trust your children, Ma. Trust what you have taught them. But come, that ghost woman feels to me like a warning. Something is happening with Yolanda." He tilted his head as if listening to the forest itself. "Someone is waiting, someone who will help us."

They moved on, Rachel holding within her the stories brought by the voices of wind and soil. Yet she feared the story she was closest to: what would become of her daughter and granddaughter.

In front of her, Jan stopped, sitting back on his haunches. "Giants are coming," he said. "But not the giant we are looking for."

Before she could ask what he meant, Rachel felt herself being watched. She looked up into a large, ancient eye.

The elephant moved past with the elegance of a dancer. Beside and behind it, barely disturbing the forest, were others of its kind. Rachel held its gaze. The regal animal gave her a look of empathy and awareness, as if it knew how far she had come and understood the nature of the journey, the hardships it entailed. Rachel bowed her head in greeting. This other matriarch slowed momentarily to do the same.

Moments later, they were gone, and the forest was still, as if they had never been.

"Who are we looking for, Jan?" Rachel asked.

"A friend. He is beckoning."

Dewdrops brushed against their limbs. Half-hidden serpentine shapes moved between rocks covered in red-and-gray lichen. The trees grew bigger, moss and branched leaves making a canopy.

"Yellowwoods," Rachel said. "I haven't seen those for a long time."

"And stinkwoods," Jan said. "Over there."

They crossed a chilly crystalline river and climbed up a small ridge. Sunlight threading through the trees momentarily blinded Rachel, but she squinted and gasped at the sight before her: a towering tree, its bark calloused, its trunk large as a boat. It appeared older than anything she had ever seen. As with the baobab, the age of a tree of this size had to be measured in the movement of peoples, the crossing of oceans.

But Rachel frowned, certain her eyes were deceiving her. A head had appeared, between the tree's branches, and a pair of eyes peered down at her. These did not belong to an elephant but to a man.

A figure emerged, and her jaw dropped. She had never seen an animal as magnificent as the one before her.

One of his hooves was bigger than both her feet together. His dense reddish-brown coat rippled like water; he had a strong neck and the giant torso of a man, but the rest of him was a horse. His red beard and wild, matted mane hung in loose locks. His face was square and solid, his dark eyes grave but gentle.

The centaur gave a great sigh. "Jan," he said, and his rich voice echoed. "At last we have found each other. We don't have much time."

Rachel frowned. The creature spoke with an American accent.

"It is time to go, yes," Jan said.

"To Yolanda?" Rachel asked, longing in her voice.

"Yes, but there is danger, Ma," Jan said. "From the man of music. We can shield her. We will draw shelter over her."

"What do you mean, Jan?" Rachel flicked her eyes from one to the other.

"Climb aboard," the horse-man said, bending his forelegs to lower his body. "There is a gap where you can cross her path. I will take you."

Still a leopard, Jan crouched and then sprang onto his back in one fluid movement. The centaur twitched but held steady. He turned his head, and Rachel looked at his gentle face, his large brown eyes. With one of his massive hands, he offered her assistance; Jan, human once more, reached an arm down too. Together, they helped Rachel climb on.

In front, she was near enough to see the centaur's large nostrils contract as he drew in long breaths. A lighter coat covered his upper body. Most impressive were his ears, which, more than any other feature on his head, resembled a horse's. They were large and flicked toward sounds as he traveled over the forest floor. Rachel dug her hands into his ample mane and held on.

"Why are you helping us?" she asked.

"For my son," the horse-man said. "My Garrick."

"I don't know him."

"Yolanda does. He is still in the world of the living, waiting for her. He loves your daughter. This aid, this is the least I can give."

Rachel was stunned. So much of Yolanda's life had been predicated on the consequences of her romance with Stefan. The idea of another love, flowing from a different person entirely, was unexpected. Her girl was not alone.

"Garrick." She repeated the name, felt the energy of his father course through the horse-man's body: a humble, loving man, and principled. She reached with every part of her heart toward the girl who had, at last, come home.

YOLANDA

Doubt clouded the road ahead of Yolanda. Fatigued by jet lag, she clutched the steering wheel too tightly. The past that should have been a memory receding in her rearview mirror was, instead, accelerating into view. Heavy with it, she was going to beat a path north, up the N1 highway that ran like an arc across the country, and straight to Stefan's door.

Speeding through the Huguenot Tunnel and the fortress of peaks beyond, on into the fecundity of the Hex River Valley, Yolanda cursed. She should have sought out a motorbike and left this damn rental car behind. The car's confines began to press upon her. Tight. Discomforting. Loaded.

Opening the windows gave her a bit of breathing room. Again and again, she pushed away the ghouls breathing down her neck, threatening to occupy the back seat, making the car smaller and smaller, waiting to drag her back there with them. But the farther she drove, the more the distance and heat, the jet lag and decades-old weariness made a dangerous soup of her mind.

She set her jaw, narrowed her eyes, and lit a cigarette, hoping the haze of smoke would bring clarity. Reunion, redemption—she needed to hold fast to the notion that these things were possible.

Stefan. She couldn't grasp the beauty that had once been there. It was hard to even imagine now: How they'd laughed together, what it was like to be playful with a man, to love deep and full. To know what her body felt like before it was ground into the dirt. How he had looked at her. How it had felt to know no one else could stir that kind of sparkle in his gaze.

Memories came. An argument as they drove down the highway, about Steve Biko, Mandela, Robert Sobukwe: who was inciting whom; was it incitement or people trying to climb out of the prison of their suffering? She remembered Stefan saying many months later: "We are forcing these men to be lesser people, to not be men at all. And they are refusing. I would do the same." He said it softly, a quiet admission to himself that came before a long silence. He left later to surf. She knew he needed to be left with the weight of his realization.

Slow dancing in the house of a friend in Obz. It was a date night: hours of solitude with doors and windows locked, curtains drawn, the scratchy white noise from the vinyl of a Rabbitt album, her head on his chest until he lifted her up at the waist and she wrapped her legs around his body.

Getting caught outside his apartment by an inquisitive neighbor. "She's just the maid; I'm taking her home," Stefan said, transforming for a moment into a stone-cold Afrikaner, a baas. Brisk, businesslike, they'd left, and Yolanda hadn't returned there for two months.

Those memories were hard to hold on to; they were soiled. Yet Yolanda had known her truth then: she'd loved him; she'd known who she was. That kind of conviction had taken courage she didn't believe she had anymore.

Kilometer after kilometer brought her farther into the immense brown heart of the Karoo. She felt temporary against this expanse that was an ancient testimony to time. Road bled to bush, which shimmered into sky. She was alone in her country's beating heart, confronting the mirror offered by the solace of this place.

Ahead, she spied a railway station platform, deserted. It stood like an old man, bearing witness to a time when he'd been strong and useful to the world. It made her think of her father, of what apartheid did to men and how it damaged the very idea of being a protector, a provider.

Yolanda drove down a gravel road and pulled over. She walked a long way toward a rock formation, sat, and finally allowed the mourning for her father to begin. Occasional cars passed, but the wind was her only steady companion. It dried her tears but drew out her heartache, rendering her as desolate as this very place. She willed Rachel's absence not to signal another death.

She wasn't sure how long she'd been sitting there when the vision emerged from among the *koppies*. It drew first her sight, then her body, until gradually every part of her, every sense, had turned toward the exuberant, unexpected scene.

Dust formed a trailing jet stream behind the distant, speeding horse. He was not saddled. Two small figures sat on his back, clutching him tightly. Riders and horse formed a spirited dervish, moving for the simple joy of it across the heat-locked land.

The horse ran with glorious abandon. Transfixed, Yolanda read the light and the lines, the sheen of his muscles and how they rippled with vital power beneath his skin. Desert bushes quivered as the horse's legs moved past them in a fleeting symphony. She stared long after the animal had disappeared into the distance, the earth and the day shifted by its presence.

Garrick, she thought suddenly. He would have loved this sight.

Once, her first instinct would have been to draw what she saw; she had never been without a sketch pad. But that was no more. She'd stopped painting and drawing soon after the assault. She tried, but all that came out of her was ugly, and the mere act of expressing it was a torment. An unfiltered connection used to exist, with highly valued oil paint, always-available pencil, watercolor mess on her hands and face. When she was a girl, the canvas had always been in her mind. She'd let herself be carried. Unexpected turns would show the unforeseen. Her own inner symphony would harmonize the elements she crystallized into a picture.

Her mother had understood that ability and nourished it, taking her everywhere, from the tapering ends of the Cape Flats to the wild, unforgiving quarters of Cape Point. Rachel had taught her to defend her craft, for it was her own, and when the world had exploded around them, it had formed the solid ground upon which to define who she was.

She remembered the jerk of the train on Saturdays, before they'd walk up past the white beach toward their own shore. She'd rest her head on her mother's lap and look up at her face. Rachel's scarf was tight, her skin like copper, a faint line of strength along the jaw. Her eyes held more than the stern line of her mouth revealed. Ma, her eyes that shone down on her like stars, was undeniably beautiful.

Deep in the Karoo, Yolanda walked farther from the road and the car. The land held no revelations beyond the settling haze of the horse's dust.

How little room there was for regret under this sun. The same sun had set, night after night, on Yolanda sitting at a bar or a pub: honey nectar, sweet elixir, just to take the edge off, just to make it go away. But hadn't she earned the right to her imperfections and weaknesses? When her heart felt like a spray of shattered glass, with every piece reflecting something else, hadn't she the right?

In this desert, none of that mattered. Here, day would pass into night and continue, beat by beat, on into an infinity that had already seen so much sorrow. It would pass beyond hers too. It was calming to consider that her tragedies were nowhere near as large as the expanse of time that swept through this country's great, arid heart. Calming to know that through it all, someone outside her mattered and needed her to move beyond the sorrow.

Yolanda continued to walk, passing between hardy bushes, deep in thought, drawn forward by the elemental energy with which the horse had left her. In the hopes that she might once again glimpse the animal, she trudged up a nearby koppie. The hilltop was of orange-brown sand and stone, scrubby bushes clinging to it like barnacles. Standing at the top, the thought of the horse's strength and presence, still remembered, brought her to tears. Feeling vulnerable and entirely, unnervingly alone, she sat heavily upon the earth.

"Ma," she said. "Come home, please. I can't say goodbye to you, not like this. Daddy, I'm sorry; I am so sorry."

A melody suddenly carried on the desert air: the tinkling of tin cups colliding and a voice speaking Afrikaans. Standing up, Yolanda looked behind her.

An old couple made their way around the base of the hill, a raggedly dressed man and woman, their shoes broken, their clothing not much better. They labored, carrying tied bundles on their backs. Each of them had a can of water strapped around their body.

Yolanda wiped away the last of her tears and put on her sunglasses.

"*Middag*," the man said, ascending the hill. He greeted her in English as well.

"You're carrying a lot of things, hey," Yolanda said.

She swore that she heard him say, "So are you."

"Where are you walking to?" she asked.

"Home, just going the long way. You know the *karretjie mense*?" he asked. "The cart people? Well, that's who we are. But the cart's wheels aren't working, so ja, well, now we walking."

The man had a kind face. His hair was a woolly, matted gray beneath his cap, and his yellowed teeth were gapped. There was something faintly feline about him, Yolanda thought.

"You must excuse Ma." He gestured to the woman beside him. "She is a mute."

The woman gave Yolanda pause. She couldn't place her finger on why—something about the way she moved and held her head, about the way she looked at Yolanda with her wrinkled eyes.

"Where you going to?" the man asked.

"I'm looking for someone," Yolanda said slowly. "But I don't know if I'm going to find her."

"She is here?"

"Not in the Karoo, no."

"She is here," he said, insistent, then paused. "To be found again must mean that someone is lost."

Yolanda's smile was slight. "I don't know who is more lost, her or me."

"Maybe you will find each other. There are many ways to be lost, and many ways to be found." He off-loaded the bundled bag from his back, then helped his partner. Yolanda saw the softness as he helped her sit. The tall, dark woman was shy, avoiding her eyes. Together they were gentle and steady; the pace and nature of the Karoo emanated from them. They wore a world of care in their bent hands and shrunken faces, but there was a reassuring humility and generosity of spirit there too.

"You learn a lot in this place, when you don't have things to distract you," the man said.

"That is the gift of silence, isn't it," she said, and he smiled.

"Yes," he said. "Helps us all listen better."

She enjoyed the moment with the cart people awhile longer, then bid them goodbye, the woman giving her an unexpected, tight hug. Yolanda looked ahead to the long ribbon of highway. She gave the strange pair a last, lingering look, then walked away.

RACHEL

It was not Yolanda the pair watched. The man of music, back in his own car, had attached himself to his target once again, like a long dusk shadow.

The spirits of Rachel and Jan moved past the hill, the figures they had assumed dissipating back through the fold in time and space through which Garrick's horse-father had carried them. They shimmered like heat haze back into the rocks and sand, the stones and silence.

They had come to offer Yolanda shelter. Now they followed filigree tracks scratched on the earth's belly, tracing the faint marks of hooves in the soil. In this way, they were pointed back to safety; they were not lost between the worlds.

Rachel's heart hung low with the weight of everything clawed back from the precipice, the awareness of everything that it was too late to save. It was fitting that she had seen Yolanda here, where their people had once walked with the unassuming presence of children. But innocence passed like sunshine. Rachel's eyes grew heavy and dark.

The man of music would not relent.

She looked ahead. There lay the sickle.

KUIPER

Yolanda had been right there, sitting on that hill in the wide open, as if she were waiting for him, inviting him near.

He had watched the whole business of her walk into the veld with curiosity and glee; he wasn't one to let a chance pass. Accidents were like luck: a matter of opportunity and, simply, timing. A knife would make enough of a warning. A few words, maybe the odd caress, would be enough to direct this *poppie* back to Cape Town and, if he was lucky, back on a plane.

Of course, he wasn't one to negotiate. She looked like the kind of woman who could kick up a fuss, and in that case, the knife might have found other uses. He knew the single event sitting at the core of her; he owned her now. Still, although this woman had entered the country with little more than tattoos, nice jewelry, and black cigarettes, the sum of her was more than that, and he couldn't put his finger on why.

No matter. She was his in a way that she would never be anyone else's. As for Rachel Petersen: well, that mystery bothered him, but probably it was a case of an old woman who had lost her marbles, gone *bossies*—couldn't say he blamed her.

Following Yolanda out of Cape Town, Kuiper had settled in behind his prize, his eye keen and fixed on the road ahead. But nothing could explain this business at the koppie. He'd sat a distance away, watching her with binocs, ready to move nearer and see if they could have a little chat. He was at ease with tracking and the hunt, but still, the moment came with a rush of blood and power. Hunting required ritual, and for him it was song. Today: "Ruby Tuesday" by the Stones. He'd hummed the melody in his mind as he made his way quietly across the hard-packed sand to where Yolanda sat, angelic.

He couldn't have turned away for more than a breath. But when he looked up, she wasn't there.

Had she seen him and scampered like a bunny? He'd heard nothing. Her car remained exactly where she'd left it.

Was she down the other side of the koppie? No, nothing. He could have sworn he heard voices, but everything around him was clear. The woman was gone.

He walked back to her car; looked underneath, inside; even rifled through her handbag. Still nothing. He looked back at the koppie and tried to figure out what he was missing, but nothing was disturbed, and there was little in this barren land for her to hide behind, especially so quickly.

A large owl stared down at him from its perch on a telephone pole. He gave it an irritated glance. Kuiper was angry now. He walked back to his van, scratching his head.

What had he missed? Nothing led anywhere that made sense, so he waited and watched. He knew how to do that. On the border, he'd gotten used to doing it even when everything ached: Your mind ached because the *terries* were only a few clicks away and you were trying to push out of your mind the mess of one of your infantrymen, his body at irregular angles, lying dead between them and you. And the flies, the fucking flies just kept coming. Your body ached because your shoulder wanted to explode from the R1 rifle you'd propped up. But you waited because, at the wrong time, moving meant dying.

Kuiper opened his cubbyhole and pulled out a cassette tape. Prokofiev. Around him, the van was neatly arranged, weaponry stored under a floorboard, gun barrels cleaned. A garbage bag in a corner held remnants of food and drink. He was a systematic man. There had to be systems, there had to be structure, or the world would collapse into disarray.

When he was young and eager to earn his place in the military—volunteering, not waiting for call-up papers, mind you—he'd believed that its power and structure were noble. Entire lives depended on its order. Demobilization had ended all that, of course. But old habits died hard.

Funny to be back here. He was unsentimental about the Karoo. Bleached-white bones and the blood of birthing animals had left him that way: the stuff of his farming childhood in the northeast of this land. This place gave little and took everything.

He thought of the lone stand where his family's farm, now sold, stood and where his father lay buried. It was a helluva cold place of enamel mugs filled with the potent black coffee his mother had made in the morning before the farmwork had begun. In the summer, there was unrelenting heat, days that just stood still; nothing moved. He remembered splashing in the small dam on summer nights after the workday.

Handsome Drakensberger cattle had been prized then. When he was a boy, his mother once scolded his father that the cattle meant more to him than his only child. His father said nothing. The scrape of his chair was enough. By the time he stood over her, his mother's hands were already shielding her face. Kuiper recalled the piece of beef in his mouth once, the one he'd struggled to chew when the beating had begun.

Only child, only son, he learned at that kitchen table that the only thing that mattered was survival. Everything was a battle, and there was always a border, a fence to stand behind. What lay beyond it were the maladies of Africa. But by Kuiper's reckoning, that barrier was an illusion meant to make everyone comfortable. African soil rooted them all indiscriminately. African rain, just like the heat of its sun, fell on everyone without favor.

The day came when Kuiper left his home, passed beyond the farm's fence to the actual borders with Angola, Zambia, South-West Africa, to face the communist malevolence that festered in those countries. Even as a *rofie*, new to the game, every fiber in him lit up the first time his battalion took live fire. He was alive, truly alive, and this was the life he wanted. He had only felt that way once before, when he was fourteen years old, *naaing* for the first time. She was a daughter one of the laborers had offered to him like a present. He had taken her in the shed several times until he'd gotten bored with the same old, same old.

One day, long after the military had claimed him, he returned to the farm to find his long-widowed mother clutching the kitchen table, keeping her rifle at the ready. The place was falling apart. She couldn't stay there alone. Despite her pleading, he knew he wasn't his father. He didn't have that fortitude, that single-minded dedication to the land. He wasn't going to watch the cattle and sheep—their hooves, their eyes—and try to read when the rain was coming. And it would have been a disservice to turn the place into a bed-and-breakfast just so the formless milky-white thighs of Joburg people could sit at the kitchen table, inhaling authenticity. He sold it instead, posting his mother to relatives in Oudtshoorn and dismissing the laborers to their fate at the heel of the great Karoo. Everyone, including Kuiper, had become nomads, without a place to return to.

And here he was again, in this godforsaken desert where everything either evaporated or petrified. Some people came here to get lost, to leave things behind. Most moved through, bored in the bubbles of their cars. The Karoo brought a certain kind of stillness and silence; it unsettled people. It was a place of bones.

Kuiper had learned about blood here, on this soil, not at the border. He'd learned how to hold a rifle from his father and, from the laborers, how to tell the small hoof of the klipspringer from the wide track of the eland. He learned to track, to shoot, and what to do with the kill. At the border, city boys would heave at the sight of blood and bodies turned inside out. Kuiper had learned young that some animals were meant for slaughter. He was a boy when he first caught the metallic scent of blood. He was a man when he learned that to kill was not nearly as awful a thing as the people who had benefited from his defense all those years now said it was.

"What the fuck?" The words burst from him; the hairs on the back of his neck stood up.

There she was, walking out of nowhere, back to her car, as if she'd been there all along. The blood drained from his face. Binocs up, he scanned their surroundings but found the world unchanged.

She started her car. He narrowed his eyes. The challenge had been accepted.

INGRID

The undercurrent swelled up and pulled Ingrid backward. She swam against it, set her feet back on the shore of South Africa's vast southern ocean. Again she slipped, fell, and laughed wryly at the many ways in which she was losing balance.

Litha sat nearby on their borrowed picnic blanket. They were at a remote beach, empty but for the two of them. Ingrid shivered in her soaked T-shirt and underwear. Looking at the rough orange rock jutting out where the sands tapered away, she imagined fifteenth-century European sailors, their lips blistered, their teeth loose, from months at sea, emerging from the break as easily as African warriors might emerge from the land.

Time, Litha had told her, had left this place unchanged. The same could not be said of the two of them. She was in deep now, going to his extended arms, letting him peel off her clothing. Her skin sparked at the grains of sand on his hand, the brush of his lips on her body. She savored, once again, the delicate feeling that was taking root between them and flowering.

Lovers. They were lovers now, and she liked the word as much as she liked him: the gestures he made; the way he used his hands when he spoke, extending his words with his body. And that body: the muscles along his arms and shoulders, the eyelashes that were even longer up close. It was all becoming welcome and familiar to her.

Half in the sand and half off it, their bodies melded together. They released themselves into each other and into this moment. Passion had burned a clear-cut path through prejudice, making way for something altogether different.

Afterward, they lay beside each other, their feet off the blanket, toes toying with the sand.

"I've never had a day like this with a woman, Ingrid," he said. "It's different with you."

"I've never had a day like this with a woman either."

He punched her shoulder playfully.

Crossing the Kei River border post the previous night and entering the Transkei had made Ingrid feel as if she was in Litha's country now, on his ground. There were lines she, too, was crossing; a home, a known state, that she was leaving. Snacking on leftovers from Ma Thembi's party, they'd arrived at Nomhla and Khwezi's house quite late. Litha had arranged to borrow the car for a day of sightseeing. Ingrid's rush to find Stefan was slightly cooled. Litha and the here and now pushed everything else out of sight.

Early this Monday morning, Litha had navigated rutted and eroded country roads. They'd passed turquoise huts set against green hills; cattle that he said were like traffic lights here; and people who waved, each without fail. He'd brought her to an otherwise nondescript path, down which they'd scrambled and slipped to reach this secret cove.

She shivered. Litha draped an arm over her.

"Nothing will be the same again after this trip and this election. You and me."

"How do you feel?" Litha asked carefully.

"Like I'm on a cliff."

"Well, don't jump," he said, pulling her near and resting his chin on the top of her head. "Don't leave me."

Ingrid drew herself tightly against the security of him. She pushed aside the growing cloud hanging over her: a fear of Yolanda and, the nearer she came to him, fear of Stefan and the consequences of this journey. A reckoning was coming, she knew. But how would it play out?

As the sun lowered, they scrambled back up the goat path to the top of the cliff. At the house, they joined Khwezi and Nomhla for dinner. Their little girl was staying with an aunt to make room in their small house. Nomhla maintained the same frostiness toward Ingrid as when they'd met in Motherwell. As they ate, Ingrid caught Nomhla watching her and Litha as if calculating something. Ingrid straightened her T-shirt and sat upright, as if better posture could hide her grunginess.

"You must be excited to see your friend tomorrow, Ingrid," Nomhla said. "In Durban."

Ingrid shrugged. "Yes, yes, of course."

"I spoke with Zintle today, Litha. You know, while you two were out." Nomhla cast Ingrid a look that made her freeze. "She says Andile can't wait to see you, and of course, she is excited too."

Ingrid cast her eyes between them, reasoning that Zintle must be his little boy's mother. She watched Litha, but he just gave a small shrug and carried on with his meal.

"Andile is his son, chubby little five-year-old, so cute," Nomhla said, expressly to Ingrid.

"I know," she answered.

"Sis Noms—" Litha began, but Nomhla cut him off.

"Is it true, Litha? I heard that the uncles are discussing again whether to start marriage negotiations. They say this matter must be resolved now for you and Zintle." Nomhla looked at Ingrid coldly. "I suppose you people don't have traditions like we do. I can explain how it works if I must."

Khwezi dropped his silverware and began to angrily scold his wife in Xhosa. Everything around Ingrid fell away. Litha met her eyes. Anger flared in them.

"Negotiations? Marriage?" she said.

"Ingrid, it's not like that."

"Are you getting married?"

"No. Nomhla is speaking out of turn. We should talk alone."

"No." Ingrid whipped up and headed to the bedroom. Litha followed her, while Nomhla and Khwezi continued to argue at the table.

"Ingrid, let me explain."

"What?" she said, scrambling to gather her things. "How you screwed me for fun on the way back to your little family? You're getting married. My God, how stupid am I."

"I told you the truth; it is not like that, not at all. You don't understand."

"No. You don't." She threw Yolanda's bag at him. The letters, photos, and paintings scattered and rolled like dead leaves. "My life is shit, and now to make it worse, I see that I am my mother. I've got the same fucking bad judgment. I should have stayed with my own people."

"Ingrid, please." His voice cracked.

"Go home to your family, Litha, to your fiancée or whatever the hell she is."

Somewhere beyond the roar in her head, Litha was talking, explaining, hands moving, pain in his eyes, but she couldn't latch on to any of it. She needed to get out. She grabbed her purse and a few other random things.

"Get your damn hands off me," she said when he tried to stop her. She stormed out the front door, into the Umtata night. Litha called, followed her for one block, then another, but she didn't turn back.

Once out of sight, she stood on a street corner and sobbed, bending down under the sheer weight of her pain.

Is this what it was like, Yolanda? she thought. *For you and him? Am I cursed because of you?*

Litha had only just been with her; they had only just begun to figure out each other's contours. Yet humiliation pressed in, shame at her naivete in thinking she could build this fantasy with him. With the anchor of Rachel gone, she was lost somewhere between mother and father, home and elsewhere.

Again she heard her name, but she wiped her face and kept walking. A barking dog drove her from one fence into the street, and she avoided the eyes of a group of people walking by. Finally, she muscled up the courage to ask how to get to the main taxi rank. Two hours later, she was squashed in the rear of a minibus, vaguely aware that she was headed east, toward Port Saint Johns. There was talk of unrest, of clashes and sporadic road closures farther on, near the Natal border. But the taxi was full. There had to be safety in numbers.

Night on the unlit coastal road was dark. It suited Ingrid, as she was lost in thought, hiding tears. They had been driving for perhaps an hour when hooting came from behind and grew louder. The commotion and chatter inside the taxi rose in volume. The driver accelerated.

"What is it?" Ingrid asked those around her. "What is going on?"

"*Haibo*," said a woman not much older than her, wearing a head wrap. "Maybe they want to rob us, or could be trouble again with those Zulus." She clicked her tongue. "Me, I don't know."

Bright headlights fell upon the disarray inside the taxi; the passengers grabbed at their things and tried in vain to duck down, away from the windows. Pinned in place, Ingrid twisted, watching the pursuing car race nearer. Movie clips played through her head, images of gunfire, of cars forced off the road. Black men like bogeymen.

As the car came alongside the taxi, she squinted. It was Khwezi's car. Litha.

At the front of the taxi, she saw an arm go out of the driver's window. Khwezi's headlights illuminated the gun that the driver was trying to point backward.

"No!" Ingrid shouted as loudly as she could. "Hey, what are you doing? Stop the taxi—please, don't shoot him. I know him."

In a panic, she kept calling, fighting to get up and over the other passengers.

"Do you know this car?" the head-wrapped woman asked.

"Yes, yes, it's my friend; please tell the driver not to shoot."

In a loud voice, the woman directed the driver in Xhosa. He pulled his gun inside. Khwezi's car had fallen back abruptly; no doubt they had seen the gun as well. Everyone looked at Ingrid with questioning faces.

"Please, please don't shoot him." Her whole body shook with adrenaline.

"Why are they chasing the taxi?" someone asked. The taxi driver had not yet stopped but was slowing down, his face a mask of irritation.

"For me," Ingrid said meekly. "Just for me."

The driver pulled over to the shoulder, and everything froze. Ingrid was red with embarrassment, unsure what to do. Stuck in the back, she could hardly move.

She heard a car door slam and, in the headlights, made out Litha's figure. He came to the driver's window, greeting the man apologetically. Then he pulled the minibus door open and apologized to the passengers. In the dim light, she saw the emotion on his face that he was struggling to control.

"Can we talk, please, Ingrid?" he said. "I'll take you wherever you want to go afterward; just don't leave like this. You don't know this place."

The taxi driver began to scold both of them. An old man beside Ingrid said, "You must maybe let your boyfriend explain."

Her pride would have her stay and send him on his way. Dismissing him, and judgment from his friends—all this felt justified when she was coloured and they were Black. But that was nowhere near the truth of their togetherness, hers and Litha's. It would be false to pretend it was.

She climbed out. The driver undid her bag from the pile on top of the minibus and passed it over. Then the taxi pulled away, leaving them in silence, the only light that of Khwezi's headlights.

"How did you find me?" Ingrid asked.

He pointed to the taxi's distant red lights. "The taxi's name there, on the back window. S'bu's Vibe. People at the rank noticed you."

Ingrid pulled away when he reached for her. "Is Nomhla lying?"

"No, she isn't, but she is exaggerating. There is talk of marriage; there has been since before Andile was born. But it isn't what you think. I'm not engaged. I have no plans to be. Nomhla is close to Zintle; they have their own ideas about things. But my life is not her business."

A car drove by, illuminating his face. Turmoil drew lines on his brow.

Khwezi called from the car, "Lovebirds, we need to get off this road. I don't like it. This is a bad time to be out at night." As they hastened inside, he added, "Cattle thieves, taxi violence, politics. All bad. You were going into the lion's den there, Ingrid, closer to the Natal border. Let's go back. I will deal with Nomhla at home."

Back at the house, Ingrid strode past Nomhla, who sat fuming in the living room. "Get the kettle on, Noms," Khwezi snapped as Litha spoke with them quietly in Xhosa.

Ingrid retreated to the bedroom. Yolanda's items and the other things she had forgotten had been gathered into a heap on a chair. Litha entered with a cup of tea. He offered it to her, then sat down gingerly on the bed.

"Zintle became my girlfriend when I was in standard nine," he began. "She was in standard eight. She fell pregnant in matric, in the middle of the year, so she could at least finish high school. I was already at Fort Hare. She wanted to stay home with the baby, get married, even have another one. It wasn't what I wanted. We were on and off for a while, but it was obvious we didn't want the same things. The furthest she has traveled in her life is Butterworth. She likes the rural life. I'm not saying that's a bad thing, but it isn't what I want."

"But you have history with her. She's obviously close to your family."

Litha gave a deep sigh. "Yes. You are in the land of the Xhosa now, Ingrid. Our culture is about the people, the clan, family, more than the individual. When a woman has your child and you are unmarried, you pay damages to her family. Because of my studies I couldn't pay much, so I have an obligation still. Zintle's family has been reminding us of this and suggesting that we just marry and settle on lobola; then they will accept less for damages. That would make it all easier. I would be lying if I said I didn't think about it. She is a good mother and I love my son. Besides, it would be comfortable and what many people want."

"But not you?"

"Not me. I have known you for a week, Ingrid, and even in that time . . . you and I are closer, deeper in a way. I can't turn away from that."

"Who are these uncles?"

"Just the men in the families who begin the negotiations that start this process. But they won't do it until we agree, and I haven't. My parents understand what I want to do with my life; they know that she and I are not together anymore. Still, there is my extended family, and Zintle's family also, all with their own opinions on the matter. We can't ignore them. My family has to manage all of this carefully, for Andile's sake. For mine."

Silent, Ingrid nodded. While she'd listened to his words, that wasn't what she was observing most closely; his body told her more than his voice. She read the distress on his face, saw the longing in the hands that she could see wanted to touch her, reassure her. A realization was coming clear, but she held herself still and waited for him to finish.

He slumped forward. "This is not simple, but it also isn't as complicated as Nomhla is making it sound. Zintle and I are not together. I wasn't intending to have you visit Lusikisiki as more than a guest, and that would have been fine. My family would have treated you well.

But now Nomhla has poisoned the well. She's made you sound like a woman of bad character."

Ingrid searched his face. "I can't go, can I?"

"Not now. But that means I can't go either."

Ingrid reached out and clasped his hand, brought it to her face, drawing a deep breath.

"I need to say something too, Litha." She paused, arranging her thoughts. "I've been angry at the world because it changed, because people had the audacity not to be simple. I've been so focused on my pain, on the disruption in my life, that I never stopped to ask how much disruption I was causing you. You have no car because of me. Now, you can't see your son. And I treated you this evening like a cardboard figure, a man who could only be what I wanted him to be. Which, I guess, is how we've always been taught to think about Black people. I don't understand all this negotiating in your culture. It sounds expensive. But"—she gripped his hand tightly—"go home. Go and see your son. I'll be fine."

He drew her near, and she leaned against him, slipping an arm around his body. "You can't go to the Free State alone, Ingrid; that's suicide." At her groan, he added, "I said I would take you to your father, and I will. I have family in KwaZulu anyway. I'll go home on the way back, get you on a bus back to Cape Town. I'll talk to Khwezi. I'm sure we can use his car." He drew back and looked at her. "It will be OK. It will give me a chance to talk with everyone at home."

"As long as things with Andile are OK."

Litha shrugged. "We'll be fine. I don't know if Nomhla will be when Khwezi is finished scolding her. She really overstepped. But are you ready for tomorrow, for Stefan?"

Ingrid shook her head. "I don't know. I found a self-portrait of my mother. It tells me that even this lie of her death, it pales in comparison to a bigger, uglier . . . something. Did he know, and can he tell me?

Were they protecting me all this time? I don't know, but it's time for me to look, no matter what it is."

They kissed, setting aside the vagaries of the world outside. Later, Litha made arrangements with Khwezi for the use of his car, then returned to curl up beside her. As his breath deepened into sleep, Ingrid lay awake, dazed at the rapidity with which her life had become unrecognizable. All that she saw behind her were gates that only opened one way: having passed through, she could not go back. The intimacies she'd shared with Litha; the genie mother, released from her bottle; the mystery father, no longer a daydream but a stranger she might have passed on the street. Ingrid rose to visit the bathroom.

In the hallway, she paused. A heated conversation was underway between Nomhla and Khwezi, and it carried from their bedroom. She heard Nomhla's sharp voice as she switched between English and Xhosa.

"His father will never forgive him, Khwezi. His family will be scandalized. He can't take that girl home. Look at her. Where does she even come from? And what kind of young girl goes traveling up-country alone, sleeping with a man she just met? You know these coloureds. And his mother adores Andile. That little boy will always be Litha's firstborn."

"It is not your business, Noms."

The pair reverted to Xhosa. Ingrid returned to the bedroom and looked at Litha with heavy eyes. Pulling his body close, she held him as if this were their last night together. Some of Yolanda's things were still on the chair, lying like small ghosts in snatches of streetlight. Their painful revelations had left a mark on Ingrid, but what had been the cost for Yolanda?

It was as easy to judge you, Yolanda, she thought, *as I judged Litha. But is it right? Is it fair?* Head on her pillow, Ingrid was no longer so sure of the answer.

RACHEL

The heavy curtain of night fell around Rachel, and she was glad for it. It allowed her to shield her agony from Jan, although to do so was likely pointless. What couldn't he see?

Rachel sensed that she was weakening. The illusion that she, the centaur, and Jan had created had come at a cost. Energy was leaving her. In her physical body, the cancer was accelerating.

But even as she wept, she felt joy. She had seen her girl, and Yolanda's mannerisms were the same. She still pushed her hair back, as if trying to see more clearly. The familiarity of the way she cocked her hips and kept one hand lifted, its fingers curled, beckoning. Rachel knew these gestures in a way beyond words, in the way of someone who'd watched that body grow and form.

"She is not yet free and clear of the past, but"—Rachel's voice cracked—"there is strength in her, and I have to trust it." She paused. "If there was just more time . . ."

Jan caressed her with his tail. "There are things, Ma, that are beyond time."

They journeyed on in stillness, through rockier terrain, the air growing cooler around them. "Where do I go from here, Jan?" Rachel asked.

"You stay where you have always been, Ma. Alongside your family."

The chill in the air grew. Gooseflesh prickled Rachel's skin. Jan froze, and so did she. He crouched. Turned. His glinting eyes shone under the full moon as he looked behind them. Fearing what she might see, Rachel held still.

A movement came: a shifting, dragging sound. They remained dead still as a figure emerged from between the rocks they had just passed. A scent came of smoke and burning rubber. The figure wheezed like an asthmatic. It pushed anguish ahead of itself with such force that Rachel fell to her knees.

Jan padded closer to her. Sound hovered in a cloud around the figure, sound moving like a swarm. It tore into Rachel. She heard the voices in that cloud clearly. A moan began deep within her body. Beneath the moon and the stars thrown up against the sky, a young man came into view.

His penis was so outsize it dragged in the dirt. Around his neck the remnants of a car tire smoldered. A bony claw of a hand brushed at the tire, as if to assure him that it was still there. His body lurched forward at an angle, a defensive, shamed posture. A small bag hung haphazardly over him. Rachel fought hard to steady herself and control her shaking.

The cloud of sound abated.

"I seek forgiveness, Ma," the man said.

"You broke into my daughter and left nothing. Nothing!" Rachel shouted. She made fists. Her knuckles whitened. She remembered her own screams and cries as she'd lifted Yolanda off the sidewalk. Everything lost, fallen down and drifted into the gutter, like ash.

"She betrayed us, they said. They said that we must find her and make her pay."

"Who said that?"

The man shrugged, his clawing hands reflexively reaching for the tire. Guilt shaded his face. "There were lies and spies in those days."

"At least justice came for you," Rachel said.

"This is justice, Ma: The police, they arrested me. I tried to do the right thing for my people, to be part of the movement, the armed-struggle side. I went to a meeting, but the police raided it; they caught us. They said to me, if I don't cooperate, it will not be so good for my brothers and sisters. My parents, all of us living on next to nothing, they would take even that away. I continued my actions as a comrade, but they turned me."

He spluttered as he spoke; he cried. And all the while he picked at the tire like a scab.

"We knew Yolanda, Comrade Philip's sister." Rachel blanched at the familiarity of his words. "Nice-looking girl, but full of herself; always with her art, acting like she was better than us. Cheeky girl. When they came to me and said she had betrayed us, that she was with a boer, I hated her for what she had done to the people. Because she chose him over us." His stare became lost, vacant. "They said she must pay, and so . . ."

Rachel pulled herself upright and grew tall, much taller than normal. She looked at the malformed man with eyes of swelling rage. He stumbled to one knee. Tears made their way down his face and dropped into the dust.

He was a tool, Rachel thought, used and thrown to one side.

But even so.

Air swirled around her, full of all she could no longer contain: the pain, the cost. The breeze picked up its pace. The gusts grew stronger.

"You took her away." Rachel's voice boomed into the distance. She wanted it to echo in every cell of his hideous body. She meant to bury this pitiful creature, to fill every part of him with the fury she had carried since that night. "You took her from me. You showed no mercy."

Restored to human form, Jan put a hand on her arm. The tempest did not sway him.

"Release him," he said.

She saw in the leopard man's eyes the long arc of time, stretched like a skin over millennia, far beyond the single night that had swallowed her family whole. She remembered the baobab. Her anger tapered. The winds settled.

"Ma, they came for me," the man said. "The people found out that I was betraying them. They came in the night, in the township. They were ready with the petrol. They chased me; they had the tire necklace, the matches. Lies and spies, ja. So you are right, Ma: justice came for me, but it came without mercy."

Rachel looked at him and saw that even death could not relieve his pain. Not the ordeals he'd instigated, nor those he'd endured.

"I take no comfort in your state," she said. "But it is the price of the road you have taken. Forgiveness, release: you have no right to ask for those things."

"Look at me, Ma."

Rachel stared at the ravaged figure. His body was a map of the worst acts of man. The acts, large and small, that had reshaped her land, much as the act led by this very man had reshaped her family. No one had won. Everyone had lost.

"I see you." She stood in a long silence as he collapsed. "Forgiveness is not mine to give. You will know when my daughter has set you free."

He nodded, grasping hands clasped together as if in prayer. Then he stood and reached into his bag, offered something to her with both hands.

"It is a rain horn, Ma. Make rain for Yolanda. Help her wash the whole thing away."

Rachel took the horn from his trembling hands. She gave a nod. Jan beckoned her, and they walked onward.

Atop a nearby tree sat the eagle owl. The bird watched them for a few moments more before it soared into the night. Rachel turned and watched it go. Behind Rachel, the crooked figure of Yolanda's attacker had turned to see it too. Small, he looked like a lost boy. He was someone's brother, Rachel thought, someone else's son.

Her journey was nearing its end. Jan had given her all he could. It was for her to decide now how the rest of the road would unfold. Rachel looked up. There was the sliver of a new moon.

"My daughter. What will she do now?"

Jan walked on before responding. "What she has been afraid to do. She will become a mother."

YOLANDA

A brooding storm darkened the horizon toward which Yolanda drove. Fatigued, she watched the buildup of clouds and gave up on the idea of driving through the night. Instead, she looked for signs to the nearest town and sighed with relief when one appeared. A bed was within range and, with it, a break from the clamor of thoughts in her head.

A butcher shop and a church dominated the main street of the town, which formed a small island upon the Karoo's ancient plain. The air was electric with the promise of a thunderstorm. Yolanda found a room at a small motel, then walked to the only restaurant that was open.

Settling into dinner amid a handful of other patrons, her eye lingered for a moment on a man who came in, who glanced over at her with interest. He caught her eye, but she looked away. She was starving. Once she sat back, sated with her food, she realized that her starvation lay beyond her body: emptiness and hunger for tribe were overtaking her. Yearning for Rachel and Ingrid had grown acute with every passing mile. Her longtime consolation, that the two of them were together, that Rachel would protect her child, had evaporated. There was little that was certain now, other than this push to find her daughter. Yet Yolanda knew that, as with any journey, it was never possible to leave yourself behind.

The search for Ingrid was extending her further than she'd thought she could go psychologically, physically. But she had to keep it together, keep at bay not only the jet lag but every screaming fear within her. She didn't live a life where she had the benefit of only imagining what could go wrong. She knew. Weary down to the bone, she ached for Rachel, who was somewhere unknown; for the smell of Ingrid, her baby, a smell she couldn't remember anymore. To have come so far and still have no reunion made the ache deeper. There was no guarantee that anything would come of this at all. She searched for a cigarette in her bag.

What if she was too late? What if her journey didn't matter? How could she attempt now, in this way, to matter to a child she'd had no hand in raising?

A cigarette lighter startled her. The same man she'd noticed earlier was beside her, offering a light. She thanked him.

"Mind if I join you?" He sat at her table as she gave a small nod. "Captivating, isn't it, the coming storm." There was gravel in his tone.

Intrigued by him, by the promise of this segue away from the darkest reaches within her, she took in his streaked blond hair, the markings on his face, the glass of alcohol in his hand. In her solitude, Yolanda realized, in that dreaded car, desperation had crept up on her. Her eyes hovered on the liquor, the shades of amber refracted between pieces of ice. Scotch.

"The Karoo is like this," he added, "like being at sea, storms and all."

"You've been at sea?" she asked, forcing her gaze to the main street outside, imagining the landscape of flattened hills she had passed through earlier. Yolanda filled her mind with their lines and colors, with everything except the whisky she could all but taste.

"Only once, in another life. Never done it since, no. This land is hard to let go of." He took a long, lingering sip. "Africa is such a dangerous place, isn't it," he continued. "Anything can happen."

"Many places are like that," she said, taking a long, controlled draw on her cigarette. "But danger is a question of appetite, isn't it?"

He gave a sideways grin. "Some would say it's a question of aptitude." His voice grew low, husky. "But you sound as if you've crossed the waters. Your accent is difficult to place . . . America? England?"

"Everywhere."

The ice clinking in his glass made an inviting sound, and Yolanda couldn't resist another glimpse. She used to say when she was drunk that she was wearing happiness, pulling that illusion like a coat over the vacant places within her. *Drink,* she'd tell herself. *After all, who cares?* But Garrick did.

"Well, it would be negligent of me to leave such a lovely lady without company," he said.

Yolanda smiled. "And they say chivalry is dead."

"Not at all," he chuckled. "A man has to have manners."

"Oh?" Yolanda cast her eyes his way, drawing deeply on her cigarette. "And what is it that a woman is meant to have?"

She blew smoke over him. His eyes gleamed, amused. "If women were simple, I might have an answer for you."

"Really? Men are not as straightforward as all that," Yolanda said. "Men, too, have secret lives."

"That may be, but women have the mystery, and that is all you need. Keeps us boys on our toes."

Yolanda laughed.

"Let me buy you a drink," he said. "What's your poison?"

Yolanda stalled. She took another long drag on her cigarette. She hadn't the courage for this journey. She wasn't anyone her family could love: the daughter Rachel had nourished, the mother Ingrid had no doubt imagined. She was just a middle-aged alcoholic, a drifter with the past always at her heels. Accustomed to building arguments like these, she knew that it would be easy to do this, comfortable, especially when everything else was so hard. Still, she looked out the window: Ingrid was out there, and Garrick much farther beyond.

"No, thank you," she said.

The storm above began to rumble and churn, as if the gods were gnashing their teeth. In the distance, she could spy clouds boiling with thunder in their bowels. Lightning ran across the sky in loose, illuminated threads. The church spire stood white and immaculate before this storm, which came from a different, pagan god.

"What do you do?" she asked.

"I'm a professional hunter. How about you?"

"I'm a photographer. I do landscapes, weddings, whatever pays the bills."

"Debts, yes, those always have to be settled." He took out a cigarette of his own, broke off the filter, and leaned in to light it with hers.

"What brings you all the way out here . . . ?" she asked, gesturing for a name.

"John," he said.

"Yolanda," she replied.

"Work," he said. "You?"

"Family," she said. "Taking the long way round to see them."

"There's a lot of that these days, a lot of people coming out of the woodwork."

"Or crawling into it," she said, and he laughed. "Which are you?" she asked.

"I don't crawl," he said.

"You must have family, though, someone with whom to sharpen this wit of yours."

He shrugged. "Attachments are complicated."

They were words that had once served as a siren song for her. She had walked this path often, one where the thought began to form as it did now, not so much in her mind as in her body, of a quick fuck, a night composed of the three pleasures before her. There was a time once when she had buoyed herself in that way, afraid of being alone, of what she would face in the solitude of her own bed. Back then, she'd accepted that she was too damaged to deserve a man's commitment. Too complicated.

He looked at her. She met his eyes. His eyes wandered down the line of her neck toward her breasts. She turned toward him, titillated not so much by him but by her own ability to have him now, if she wanted.

"What's so funny?" He tilted his head at her. "You're smiling."

"Oh, just thinking about how charming you are. Your mother must be proud." He laughed at her, a full-bodied laugh that nonetheless sounded mocking.

He shook his head. "Never been a mommy's boy."

"Mine made us *vetkoek* on a Friday night when I was small." Yolanda diverted herself back to thinking about Rachel, the memory of her mother frying the sweet dough bread. As a little girl, Yolanda would devour her share, which would be smothered in apricot jam. She'd sit on the sofa between her brothers, jiggling her short legs with delight.

Something flickered across John's face for a moment, a hint of softness. She intuited that a similar memory sat there for him too. But soon hardness came upon him, a hardness that unsettled her. And it brought with it a shadow, an impossible one, darker than any shadow should have been.

"Oh, Yolanda," he said. She froze at the too-familiar way he said her name. He leaned forward and rested a firm hand on one of her knees. "I see what he saw in you, Stefan." His words snaked over to her. She was petrified. His muscular hand moved over her thigh, reminding her, in a flash, of other hands, unwanted hands.

He spoke in the same low voice. "But I know, Yolanda; you see, I did my homework. I know what happened on the way to the train station from university that one day. I know what kind of woman you really are. You can't make history disappear."

She tried to hold on to what he was saying, but the implications of his words were too large. "If you scream, you won't make it out of this town alive. I'm warning you," he said softly. "Go home; go back to America. Leave Stefan and his family alone. Because otherwise, I will find you again, and I'll bring my friends. After all, that's the way you like it, isn't it." With a last caress under her leg, he drew his hand back. He stood up and leaned over her. Adrenaline and fear made a heady cocktail in her frozen body.

He drew her face close and did so gently, as if they were lovers. "Such a stupid cunt," he whispered in her ear. "Why don't you get yourself a drink, maybe two? You're not worth killing, not worth the mess." He took her hand, slipped something into it. "Do me a favor and take care of that yourself."

With that he left with disarming speed. Cool. Efficient. Gone.

Terrified, for several moments she stayed where she was, before slumping back in her seat. She was shivering from head to foot. She turned her hand over to find a razor blade still in its wrapper. She ignored the server who asked if she was all right, the woman's concern drowned out by the small plea in Yolanda's head that grew in intensity: *Where is my child? Where is my child?*

Yolanda paid the bill, then ran outside as fat drops of rain fell. But it was far too late; he was nowhere to be seen.

Running, retreating to her motel room, she locked, chained, and drew a chair in front of the door. Pain felled her. Pure, dark, malevolent pain, thick as treacle. It made her gasp for air. She rubbed her legs where he had touched her, bristling at the power in his hands, at the cursed sense of helplessness. In a tight bundle upon the bed, she felt the swooping sense of night rising from her dark places. Her mind pushed forward the memory: reptilian men pawing at her body. Their fetid breath enveloped her once more. Her pain had a bare menace to it, real teeth. It gnawed, digging within her, finding her bones. The rain fell harder.

Outside her door, outside the motel, John filled the world with his presence. Inside this room, her head betrayed her, regurgitating the assault that his touch had brought forward, that singular attack from so long ago. Her mind went over it from this angle and that, feeding on it, again and again. The bones stirred.

Yolanda ran to the bathroom and vomited before drawing herself into a ball between the porcelain toilet and the yellowed bath. Surely the bright light would make the gnawing stop. Helpless in the face of the dark swirl, she clutched the edge of the tub, shivering.

There was nothing to draw her away from it. This man, this sting in the tail, had hit her hard enough to take her back there. There was nothing to draw her eye away from what lay beneath. Garrick was not here. She was alone. She was a young woman again, begging for mercy. "No," she said in a small voice. Terror shortened her breath. She crouched, taut, her heart racing, her mind trying to reach for the light even as it was drawn down to what sat deep and squat in the caverns of her heart. She felt in her shaking body the cry that had been stuck in her throat since that day upon the wilds of the Cape Flats.

That day. Ingrid had been six months and sixteen days old. An ordinary visit to varsity, trying to get a job on campus and enroll for part-time study, trying to get to the train station and home to the child she was nursing. Being shoved in a car and punched in the face when she bit one of the reaching hands; being held down as they tore her clothes off and took turns on the sticky leather back seat.

Out in dunes near the ocean, Yolanda had been thrown out of the car and kicked. The five of them had made a sport of erasing her. She vomited again as she remembered the murderous eyes of the one who'd spat on her after he'd raped her. He'd called her a snitch, a traitorous *impimpi*. Yolanda had cried out then, again, fearing that she might not live through the night, might never see her child once more.

Now, she slipped down beside the toilet and wept for the girl forced into the car that day. She'd calcified, never died, never grown. That night, motherhood, along with so much more, had been stolen from her. The violence of the act had left room for little else.

Under the bathroom's yellow light, Yolanda lost track of time. Sweat left her cold. Blood rushed past her ears, but she held on. "Even the longest night can only run till morning," she repeated softly, imagining Garrick's long arms and his embrace. How many times could she fall? How many times could she be so afraid to be something other than what they had made her that night?

She sucked in air through her teeth. She knew what it meant not to care whether she lived or died. Only one thing mattered now. It lay outside her, outside the pressing tide of history. One word formed after the keening wails, and the clapping of her hands on her face stopped. *Ingrid.*

Out there, in the unrelenting rain, beyond the borders of her paralyzing fear, was a child who deserved more than she could offer. But it didn't matter. She was the girl's mother. Both of them had to come out the other side of this.

She gripped the edge of the bath. "Come on, get up," she commanded herself. "You stand up and fight."

She raised herself into the tub and filled it. She was exhausted and bathed quickly, afraid she might sink in and drown.

Afterward, she curled up tightly on the bed, entirely drained of energy.

Memory barged into her dreams: her ex-husband with his inky eyes and trimmed beard. That first time, when he had come to stand beside her in a Soho club at a live show. They'd watched a man with wide sunglasses possess the stage with an earnest bent back and a slide guitar. Her ex's words drifted into her ear, marked by the cadences of his Mancunian accent.

"Home haunts everyone," he'd said. "And the blues is wake music, vigil music, except the vigil never ended, just wound its way into this: the spirituals, hollering and chanting, the music of cold hard feet walking a long way. People exiled by money and greed, unsure of the direction of home, trusting only in the salvation of God."

The scene drifted: to a night spent crouching over the alcohol she no longer hid, while he paced and preached his own gospel.

"We sing hymns to heaven for this thing called home that we don't see, but we cling to it; we hang on to it like faith. We belong there; we have this sentiment of belonging and familiarity for a place we remember. But we forget, don't we, that it didn't freeze in time waiting for us to return; it didn't wait. So we sit with this inconsolable love at the mercy of all those paths of promise that petered out as some ships left, as other ships came to shore."

And then those words, the ones he'd spoken toward the end of their time, a year before she'd left him. He'd said them tenderly, words like the stroke of a light hand. "Yolanda, I love you more than you love yourself."

As he'd spoken, she had looked at the IV drip in her arm, her bandaged wrists; the hands she'd wanted to sever because they were mute, dumb instruments, unable to paint. With every cut she had done no more than crucify the both of them.

Now, waking to morning light, Yolanda drew herself upright. It was possible to die, yes; death, too, had teeth, and they had brushed their edges against her time and again. But she was not going to die today. She dressed and pulled herself together. Night fell away behind her as she looked out the window to a world washed clean. She didn't know where he was, didn't know if he was watching. She didn't care. She had long since flicked the razor blade into the trash.

She made one phone call, to Mark, giving him Stefan's address and directing him to get Philip there. Ingrid's life depended on it, she told him.

Downstairs, she persuaded the receptionist to arrange a motorbike for her. A cousin of one of the staff arrived midmorning, demanding more than his sport bike was worth, but she didn't care; it didn't matter.

"If I drive back out of town like I'm going toward Cape Town," she asked the cousin, "can I cut over on the farm roads to get back toward Harrismith?"

He was puzzled, clearly wondering why the N1 highway route wasn't sufficient, but her demeanor didn't invite questions. They found a piece of paper, and with a pen, he marked out a route that she could take.

"Is this bike going to get me to Harrismith?" she asked as they walked to the bank.

"Lady, how do you mean? This is my baby. Of course it will." He puffed with pride. "But do you know how to ride it?"

All she did was smile. "I need your jacket and helmet too."

The rain returned. She rode carefully, pulling over at random intervals to see who came by, whether anyone stopped. She welcomed the taste and smell of water on her face when she opened her visor. It was cleansing.

All was clear ahead of her and behind. When she swerved off the highway onto the gravel back roads that took her east, she was terrified but unaccompanied. In a groundswell, every emotion from the strange violences that had ended her youth washed over her. She held firm, clutching the handlebars.

"Stefan, she's ours," she pleaded to the sky. "Don't hurt her, please."

In the farmlands and open wilderness far outside town, she wound from one path to another, artery to vein, until she was back at what looked like a main road. The rain had stopped. It would be a few hours yet from this point, the cousin had said, but his route would take her there. Yolanda dropped her visor once again, looked into the bright sun ahead, and rode as if hellfire lay behind her.

KUIPER

In the opposite direction, parked out of view on the N1 headed to Harrismith, Kuiper had spent the morning watching the highway. He was angry, annoyed at Yolanda. He'd approached her because he had to see for himself what it was about her that could make her disappear, then reappear. Yet there was nothing untoward about her. So who was this woman?

Hoping against hope that this little pursuit was over, he drove back into town. He kept an eye on the road but saw no sign of her car. When his eye fell on the motel parking lot where it still stood, he weighed things carefully: Was she as weak as he'd thought? It was unlikely that she'd not checked out by now, and she could not have walked out of town. The car wouldn't have taken her far; he'd made certain of that. But then, it didn't seem to have moved at all.

Cagey, he weighed the options before entering the motel and speaking politely to the receptionist.

"I'm from a car-rental company, just following up on a call. Can you tell me where the woman who rents the car outside is? Yolanda something."

As the flustered girl relayed everything about Yolanda's departure, he grew furious. How had she evaded him again? How dare she? He wanted to grab the receptionist by her collared throat. He despised Yolanda then, for having the gall to think she could escape him.

He would get to Stefan's house before she did. He'd put an end to this. He had had enough.

INGRID

I think we will be seeing more of you, my dear." Khwezi winked at Ingrid before Litha backed his friend's old car out into the street at seven in the morning. Nomhla, as expected, was absent from their goodbyes.

Litha pulled away, his face a map of emotions. As at the very beginning of their journey, they were together and alone. But between them now was everything they knew and felt. Ingrid read his face, trying to unravel the delicate net of obligations that beset him.

They wound through Umtata's downtown area, which was near empty at this early hour. A dark feeling grew in the pit of Ingrid's stomach at the prospect of leaving the town and reaching Stefan.

"What is going on in Natal?" she asked. "Why does no one want to go near the border?"

"You said you know a little about Zulus, hey?"

"I know Shaka Zulu; there was that show on TV." Images from the lavish, vaguely remembered production about the life of the famed warrior king swam through her mind.

"The Xhosa and Zulu are brothers in a lot of ways; even our languages are very similar, but we were different enough for the apartheid government to drive a wedge between us. I hear bad things about Rwanda now, about the Hutu and Tutsi; it is like that in a way. Now that wedge is deeper: the Zulu don't want to be part of the election, they don't want to be part of the new South Africa, and they don't want the Xhosa to tell them what to do. uMadiba—we call Nelson Mandela this, it is his clan name—well, he is Xhosa."

"But what's the alternative?"

Litha shrugged. "More blood, more protests. We can't continue to be a country of homelands, but now we fight because everybody wants to be in charge." From her view the conflict in her country and in her family had always run along straightforward lines of black and white. In both cases, the reality was more complex. In her enclave in the Cape, the horrific unrest in the Transvaal, the violence that brewed along ethnic lines, had appeared distant.

They drove on, the landscape on all sides a lush green once more. "How do you feel about the violence? How does your family handle it?"

"My mother is a teacher. She tries to educate; she believes that is the right path. It's the killings that are difficult for her, when the marches happen, or attacks in the township. There's so much violence. But she says if our family can remain together, then there's hope."

Ingrid heard in his tone his protectiveness of her.

"And you?" she asked.

"I am Xhosa. For me it is settled. I accept that I have roots on both sides, but a man has to stand with both feet somewhere. And I would defend my mother to the death. So would my whole family. All this violence is stopping us from looking at the real enemy: the boere."

"Ja, hey? Like Daddy dearest."

An hour later, they were forced to stop at the first of several police roadblocks, and their car was searched for weapons. Harried policemen asked abrupt questions, particularly of Litha, regarding his politics and background. Ingrid caught the men looking at her curiously.

"Why are you coming through here now?" they asked her. Ingrid, her heart racing as she took in the size of their guns, relayed the details of their journey from Cape Town. She saw the men turn away, cackling about the two of them in Afrikaans.

"We're not here for any trouble," she called. "We're just passing through, like I said, to get to Harrismith."

One of the policemen smirked at her. "This is not the time for a sightseeing trip. Trouble is going to find you."

Still, he waved them on but rerouted them off the highway, down a country road. The road to Stefan grew ever more precarious. The new route meant moving through the heart of Natal, skirting Lesotho, and bypassing the Midlands, which, the police had warned them, was a site of considerable unrest.

At a gas station, Litha spoke with the attendants who filled their tank, and learned of where the hot spots were that day and the best route to take. Later, they saw a village set against a distant hill, smoldering, part of it in ruins. The air was tense. Every face they passed returned a hard, suspicious gaze. Armored vehicles flanked the highway when they rejoined it.

"This is like the protests in Cape Town, the rallies, the tear gas," Ingrid said. "Seeing tanks like this makes me think of all that, of people's anger and that smell of things on fire, your eyes burning. Everybody was just *gatvol*; we'd had enough."

Litha nodded. "Not everybody wants this new South Africa."

YOLANDA

If she'd been there, Yolanda would have shared Litha's observation. She'd taken a wrong turn somewhere on the back roads of the Orange Free State. Idling, trying to get her bearings, she heard the distant howl of dogs and the rumble of an engine. Squinting, she made out a group of khaki-clad men on the back of a flatbed, rifles held at the ready, dogs sprinting beside them.

She spun dirt, skidding the 800 cc bike, pushing everything she could out of it. There wasn't time to consider that her life depended on this, the engine of someone else's bike, or how unnerving it was that an array of predators was pursuing her. She didn't decelerate until she could see nothing behind her but her own dust trail.

"O little fucking star of Bethlehem," she said, eyes locking onto a distance marker. Fifty kilometers to the small town of that name.

Coming up on it an hour later, she exhaled, long and slow. She tried to gauge whether to pee, eat, or get gas first, but it soon became clear that staying for too long would be a bad idea. *Seething*: that was the word for what she felt in the air and read on the faces of people walking down the town's main street. Licked wounds and suspicion, buoyed on an undercurrent of resentment and apprehension, all directed at her, at anyone who was not white.

The yellow election posters sporting Mandela's face were nowhere to be seen here. Instead posters in Afrikaans made it clear: this was a different country.

The woman at the café where Yolanda bought a sandwich was polite but asked pointedly what she was doing here and described, with little impetus, how she was stockpiling flour, sugar, and canned goods.

"My husband already got a cabinet full of guns," she said proudly in choppy English. "Ja, 'cause those kaffirs, they coming to kill us in our beds, you mark my words."

Yolanda ate in silence. Ingrid was somewhere behind this wall of blind ignorance and prejudice. Armageddon, the night of long knives; she'd read once about this reckoning for which guns and Bibles had been nursed so long, filling these people with paramilitary ambitions and adrenaline. Yolanda imagined men of the old Boer Republics huddled together with renewed righteousness and purpose, determined to keep the protective barrier of their laager intact.

But Stefan, she thought. What on earth was he doing here? What would he do with their child bringing him the worst of news at the worst of times?

Yolanda filled her gas tank and sped out of town. Fear dogged her all the way to Harrismith. She navigated its wide streets, breathing in the light, sweet country evening. It was restful and still here, making her think of towns in Virginia with their large, well-tended properties and family cars.

When she found Stefan's street and saw the face-brick house tucked behind a wall, she set her jaw. Her history with him sank out of focus. Ingrid was all that mattered now.

She parked her bike and looked up at the untrammeled sky, where she saw a large owl sitting on a phone line. Its head was retracted; it appeared to be in a meditative pose. The sight steadied her. She walked up to the house and knocked.

The maid who answered gave her a perplexed stare.

"Is this Stefan van Deventer's house?" Yolanda asked. "I need to see him."

"He isn't back from work yet."

Footsteps approached. Yolanda's face hardened. In Muizenberg, Stefan had warned her of those few occasions when his parents had deigned to visit. Occasionally, he'd ended up at the beach with them, and Yolanda had watched Elsa from a distance. She remembered the woman's open discomfort at the beating sun, the sand on her feet, her son's embrace of what she sneered at as squalor.

Now those eyes shot venom at Yolanda.

"Can we help you?" Elsa asked sharply.

"I'm looking for Stefan van Deventer."

"What for? Who are you?"

"I'm an old friend, passing through the neighborhood."

"Well, he's not here." Elsa advanced to the door as the maid stepped back.

"I guess I'll wait."

"I said he isn't here. What business do you have with him?"

Yolanda stared her down. "You answered the phone, didn't you? You know who I am."

Elsa sprang forward. She filled the doorway, hands on her hips, her bun high on her head. Yolanda didn't flinch.

"You've made a big mistake. Leave and don't bother coming back," Elsa said.

"Like I said, I'll wait." Yolanda spun on her heel.

On the street, resting on the seat of her bike, she lit a cigarette. Her road had wound so far, but it didn't matter, not as long as it led to her child. She rested her eyes on the owl until someone drove into the street: a short-haired brunette. Yolanda spied small children in the rear of her large car. They pulled into the driveway, and a girl not much younger than Ingrid got out, followed by a pair of feuding little ones and a Black boy.

The woman, no doubt Stefan's wife, came around to the gate and frowned at Yolanda. "Can I help you? We don't allow loitering here."

"I don't think you can help," was all Yolanda said. She didn't want trouble, just her daughter. The woman stumbled over a few words before going inside in a huff.

It was just a matter of time until Stefan came home, and it was clear Ingrid had not yet been. Yolanda finished her cigarette. When she looked up, another car had entered the street, on the opposite end, driving in the hesitant manner of someone looking for a particular house.

She smiled and cried all at once, unable to take her eyes off the girl in the passenger seat. Ingrid. Earnest conversation ensued between her child and the driver, followed by fidgety glances toward Stefan's house. When she noticed Yolanda, Ingrid's face changed. Yolanda's heart rose.

KUIPER

B ut they were not alone. Kuiper was observing the street from a nearby double story he'd broken into, the dogs shot, the maid bundled downstairs in a heap.

He'd waited here for vindication. He'd watched her arrive, while calculating who was in the house, where the daughter and her grandmother might be. He'd picked Yolanda's song, a newer one, "Exit" by U2. Appropriate for this *cherry.*

The only trouble was the owl. It had been sitting in the same place all afternoon. Another owl. What were the odds? And this blessed bird kept looking directly at him, like it knew he was there.

Ignoring it, he'd repositioned himself so that his rifle had the greatest possible range across Stefan's street. He liked the way it sat on his shoulder, the familiarity of it, its weight. Through its scope, he'd seen Katrina's frowning forehead as she'd had her words with Yolanda, who'd sat atop her bike like the queen of England.

When Ingrid arrived, Kuiper's grin widened. His eyes narrowed as he traced Yolanda's jawline and neck with the rifle.

Yolanda walked toward Ingrid, hand over her mouth. It was time. He hummed her bass line. Slightly shielded by the window netting he'd bundled to one side, he shifted and addressed the rifle anew. Sinew interlocked with metal. The gun was at an oblique angle, but he could make it work; her lyrics were already on his tongue.

YOLANDA

It was less than an instant, but Yolanda caught the reflection of sun on glass, sun on metal. In that fraction of a moment, John's hand was once again on her leg, the ugliness of terror in her chest. She was in Steenberg, dreaming, as the leopard flicked his tail in warning.

The owl hooted. The earth slowed to a single breath. A scream rose from that hidden, private place where Yolanda had always held her child.

"Ingrid! Run!"

She turned just as a shot tore through the evening, and her left shoulder exploded. The impact threw her backward, and she hit the ground hard, winded.

He was here. He was going to rob her of the thing she'd sought most, now, when she was nearest to it. Shock overcame her, before pain flared and made her writhe. But she urged herself to move. She dragged herself toward the curb and the sanctuary of a parked car, gritting, biting down. Another shot narrowly missed her. She raised her head to see Ingrid dropped into a crouch beside her own car, her driver friend shielding her. No more than ten meters between them. Ten sorrowful, impossible meters. Yolanda realized she might die here, before she could speak with Ingrid, before she could acknowledge, describe, explain.

Every filament around the wound in her shoulder now felt like it was on fire. Her arm hung uselessly. She'd known pain in her life, all types of pain, but this was something different. Yet she knew she would rather die than watch him kill her girl.

Suddenly, someone appeared beside her: Ingrid's friend, a young Black man. He moved her sprawling legs out of the street, saying something in a low voice, one of his hands behind her back, another below her knees.

"No." She tried to push him away. "Ingrid, please, go back."

"Is it Stefan?" the man asked.

"No, it's something worse."

More shots rang out. They dropped their heads as glass rained down. With a jolt, they felt the car beside them tilt. Gone were the windows and at least one tire.

KUIPER

Kuiper was patient. Over the years he had learned a sniper's diligence: to wait until his targets assumed they'd outlasted him and changed position.

But this evening he couldn't help but be unnerved. The owl hadn't stopped looking at him. Kuiper was fed up. He repositioned and settled his scope.

"*Los my fokken uit,*" he cursed. He fixed his rifle, adjusted it for distance, and shot the owl. It was almost comical, how its body blew up into a stained, feathered cloud, like a *Tom and Jerry* cartoon. Pleased, Kuiper returned his focus to the street.

But it was to the sight of Stefan's open gate and a body disappearing through it, which he just missed with his next shot.

How was it possible that even here, within a kilometer, that bitch could continue to evade him? He had enough ammunition to destroy every organ in her body, and his desire to do that was so hot he could taste it. But first he would get her on her knees, begging for the mercy he had no intention of giving.

He packed away the rifle, put a Beretta in the holster around his waist, and slotted another handgun down by his ankle. He made his way downstairs, onto the street. All was clear, though the police were probably on the way. This was too much noise, too much drama. He approached Stefan's house, saw the blood on the handle of the gate, smiled.

He raised the latch, heard the dog in the yard, and saw the three of them, like kittens in a bucket. Ingrid and the kaffir were on the stoep, banging on the door.

But Yolanda, well, the woman had nerve. She half knelt in the path, her body drawn to one side as if her shoulder were heavy with lead. Pale, she fought to pull herself upright when she saw him, her expression bold, unsurprised.

"John," she said. "Miss me?"

YOLANDA

Yolanda's heart drummed, blood leaking, shoulder shooting pain through her body. She steadied herself with all the scraps of control she could muster.

"A flesh wound. Too bad."

He stood over her, hands on his hips. She feared if he so much as breathed on her, she'd fall over.

She prayed that Stefan would do the only thing he'd ever have to do in his life for their daughter and come home from work—that he wasn't part of this.

"Leave Ingrid alone," she said. *Just buy time,* she thought. *Hold on a bit longer.*

Kuiper came close enough for her to catch the scent of him. She fought every urge: to drop, to vomit, to fold.

"That, my dear, is not your call to make."

"Whose call is it?" she whispered. She fought not to think about the sensation of a thousand needles radiating through her upper body, or the shock that she dully realized she was in. The blood on her skin felt slick. "Stefan's? His mother's?"

Kuiper leaned toward her. "Did you really think a joyful reunion was going to happen, Yolanda? That Tutu could clap his hands, Mandela could wave his flag, and you could come in from the cold? A new family warmed up and served like instant noodles."

Her knees buckled. She was slipping away.

"My family isn't your concern," she whispered.

He pulled out the Beretta. "Oh, I don't think so."

She heard Ingrid scream, heard her friend shout no, and then her daughter had sprinted to stand beside her. Yolanda pushed her child back with a shaking hand before turning to face Kuiper.

"Go to hell," Yolanda spat in Kuiper's face. He wrenched her good arm, twisted it behind her back so that they both faced Ingrid. Yolanda cried out, and her knees caved. Ingrid's face went pale, her gaze horrified. Kuiper forced Yolanda upright, but she was weakening, growing light headed. "Ingrid. Go, please."

Ingrid's friend had come to tug on her arm, but the child wouldn't budge. Kuiper brushed against Yolanda's back with the cold steel of the gun's barrel. She felt his lips against her neck.

"There was one thing I've been meaning to ask," he said loudly. "Does this bastard child of yours know about the rape? And was it four men or five? That's the only thing I couldn't verify. Or did you enjoy it so much you lost count?"

Yolanda drew a single breath. There it was, out in the day. Thick black shadows rose up in her mind, and her head fell forward for a moment with the weight of the shame she knew so well. She saw shock whiten Ingrid's face; she saw her child's tears spring. She felt her own.

Yolanda clung to the thing she'd held on to since she'd left Cape Town: she was Ingrid's mother. She sucked in air through her teeth.

"Fuck you," she said over her shoulder.

"You coloured girls are cheeky, hey," Kuiper said. "But you're forgetting who has the gun, my dear." He pressed the barrel hard against her back.

"And you're forgetting who has the balls."

"Tell me," he said. "Did it hurt more that they were your people? Your brothers-in-arms, your comrades?"

At the edges of her consciousness, death was baring its teeth. But Yolanda knew she had to fight against fading, against the haunting that hunted her. She would not die under shame.

"Pull the trigger. Do it," she said, heaving. "You with your big boots, just another Security Branch fuckup. You think you're stronger than me? I've been dead before. I've had to wake up and decide to breathe, that I want to live. But you, you just know how to kill; all you know is death. There is nothing you can take from me. Do it."

KUIPER

He was a soldier, not a murderer. He followed orders. He was a disciplined man who'd wanted the money from this job, not the hassle of disposing of a dead body. But this woman, this woman who wouldn't stay down or go away, who disappeared and then came back. He could have snuffed her out with a quick jerk of the neck, a blade between the ribs. He could have had her. Why hadn't he? What was it about her?

All Kuiper's discipline and all his caution wavered—this family, that fucking owl, had chewed away at it. He raised his gun, lifting it over Yolanda's shoulder. He pointed it at Ingrid.

As if she had known what he was going to do, Yolanda jerked forward against his arm, wresting free of his hold with a force he didn't anticipate. Bodies fell. He pulled the trigger. Glass shattered, followed by an agonized scream.

But in the instant it took Kuiper's finger to release the trigger, it was as if gauze had been thrown over the world. The face-brick house, the screams and scuffles, the ongoing barking of a dog—it all mixed into a muffled, drawn-out sound. Yolanda, Ingrid, they disappeared. Instead an old coloured couple came into view: dumb country types holding their hands behind their backs like they were on a Sunday stroll.

They looked at him as if they'd been there all along.

The grandmother, Kuiper thought, pleased that the puzzle was solved but mystified by how she'd gotten here.

Yet his gaze was drawn to her old face. Rachel's eyes held him, reminded him of the owl's. He couldn't look away. Her sight crawled into his head, her eyes looking through him at all the bad shit he'd done in his life, and he grew ashamed, angry. It felt as if she were opening him up and seeing what had wired his head together. He wanted to cower and crawl away.

It began then: his skull, the crawling within, like it was occupied by the busy bodies of lice. The sensation grew maddening. The lawn was gone. A cracked wasteland lay around him, inside him. Thirst and hunger hit him violently, along with panic and emptiness. He gripped his hands into fists. Surely he had been drugged. Where was the house?

The grandmother watched him, unyielding. "The inside becomes the outside," she said.

Then he saw them coming toward him, arms outstretched: his parents.

"André, *seun*," his mother said, dressed like she had been every day of her miserable, plodding life. His father stood with the gaping hole in his head where Kuiper had shot him. One shot, plastered over with a lie about a hunting accident.

What else could he have done? He was a boy bred on fists, tired of seeing his mother beaten in one corner while he waited his turn in another.

Kuiper tried to crawl away on hands and knees, but everywhere he turned, they appeared, all four of them. The grandmother's eyes burned with a low glow. Clawing at his face, he found it impossible to turn from his father, who looked at him like he was a lost cause; from his mother, whose sad gaze said Kuiper was the only cause she'd had left.

The gun, the gun. He reached for the gun at his ankle, pulled it up to his head, and made it all stop.

STEFAN

Stefan flung his car door open to the sight of feather, bone, and blood upon the sidewalk. The blockade of people and sirens had alarmed him. But this disturbing sight, this bad omen, spurred him to run. His children, where were his children?

A colony of hadedah ibises flew low overhead, their incessant caws startling him further. Cops and neighbors engulfed his house: a cordon, lights, someone in uniform at the front gate telling him he couldn't enter, not until he told them who he was. Emergency vehicles lined the block; people littered his lawn. Near the gate lay a figure, facedown, covered. Stefan was horrified by the bloody mess of brains the sheet could not hide.

A few feet farther on a woman lay like a blood sacrifice, another woman bent over her, both their faces obscured.

The head of the bent woman shot up as he entered the property. She was young, and she looked at him with pain and recognition. Something about her face was familiar in an inexplicable way. But then his eyes drifted down to the woman, limp in her arms, and the noise and pandemonium receded. In that stark moment, everything fell apart.

Yolanda was dead. She was here, but she was dead. A moan crept to Stefan's lips, a cry of "No!" formed with more than his mouth. He knelt, agony cresting in him. It couldn't be. This couldn't be how it was going to end.

"She's alive," the girl was saying. "I felt her pulse here, on her neck, but it's faint. She's lost a lot of blood."

Yolanda's beautiful face, the face that had lain beside him night after night, trusting him, loving him. Stefan bent forward; he couldn't help but brush her cheek, through the grit and blood. He had failed her.

But as it had been twenty years ago, there were eyes on him, and they burned.

"Stefan!" Katrina screamed. "Your mother!"

Stefan staggered toward the house, heart pounding. Devastation leveled him with every step. Katrina grabbed and held him. Paramedics swarmed the living room, and it was only as they shifted that he saw why they were there: his mother, laid out on a stretcher. They were on the verge of carrying her out.

"Ma!" he shouted.

"Are you the next of kin?" a paramedic was asking.

"Yes, I'm her son."

The man spoke rapidly. "She's alive, but there is severe blood loss. We are taking her to hospital." The man turned back to the stretcher. Stefan saw blood-soaked bandages wrapping Elsa's head. He gasped.

"What happened?" He pressed the paramedic. "Please, tell me."

The man gave him a cursory, irritated glance. "Gunshot wound to the face—her jaw is shattered, looks like the jawbone splintered up into her left eye. Please talk to the doctor at the hospital further."

Stefan couldn't comprehend what they were saying. The trauma upon his mother's body left him shocked, silent.

"I'll go," Katrina said, gesturing to Dikeledi, the maid, to go sit with the children. "Stefan, with the cops and everything, you stay here. But then come to the hospital quickly, please. Maybe they will need your blood. Stefan, look at me."

She shook him. Shouts from outside, the girl again: "He didn't do anything. No, you can't arrest him. Litha! Stop, you racist fuckers."

Stepping outside, Stefan watched his unconscious mother being carried off, as the paramedics descended on Yolanda.

"Do you know these people, Mr. Van Deventer?" a policeman asked him, but all he did was shake his head. "The white man had no ID. He shot himself. The other two look like mother and daughter; the African is the boyfriend of the girl. We bringing the whole lot in for questioning. We still confirming IDs. Don't know what this country is coming to."

Mother and daughter. Mother and daughter. The young woman's familiar face. The rest of the man's words rolled off Stefan. Robotically he returned inside, embraced the kids. He saw the broken window, the glass on the floor, the blood between the shards.

When he glanced up again, his eldest child, his and Yolanda's, was there, standing at the door. He didn't even know her name, but now he saw himself in the shape of her brow, her mouth. Her fiery expression was her mother's.

"I wanted to meet you," she said as he walked up to her. "I thought you could tell me what it was like, what the disas and the butterflies meant. That was why I came. But all I did was lead her here. She may die because of me. She may die because of you. But you're just going to walk away again, isn't it? Isn't that what you do?"

"There's been a big mistake," Stefan said. "I don't know who you people are."

It wrenched him to lie to her face, to see an echo of himself, an echo of Yolanda. But what was another lie, after all this. She didn't understand. How could this child understand?

"You're a fucking coward," she said, then left.

He stood, aghast.

"Ulrika, I'm going to check on the dog," he said to his other daughter, the teenager he had treated all this time as the oldest. He mustered authority, ignored her expression. "Then I'll go to the hospital. Dikeledi, do they have sugar water yet? Please, and pack clothes for them. I'll drop them at their grandparents' on the way."

He went to the yard and crumpled to the ground, out of sight, head in his hands, while the agitated dog sprang over and around him. There was no one he could tell about his heart breaking, about what it felt like to have had all that was buried deepest in him thrown out on the street. He couldn't begin to grasp what had happened to his mother, the price she might be paying for his actions.

Self-loathing from twenty years ago returned in a wave. But the reasons were different. Now it was the immensity of the pain he hadn't expected to feel or cause throwing him off-balance. The deception of pretending to neither know nor care when the very thought of the light being taken out of Yolanda's eyes was destroying him.

Decades, a marriage, a home. All of it was only a pause in the intimacy he'd coveted, that he'd lived with Yolanda, a thing only they knew. Her hair soft against his face, her art painting a wider world than he had ever known. There weren't words he could wrap around it for these people. For himself.

But he was the man of this house. His spoken truth was the only truth. He returned inside, drew the lie of his ignorance over the shattering he felt. He dismissed Yolanda's child as hysterical, mistaken. He arranged everything, gave the police free rein of the property. And then he left, praying for his mother, stepping over his hidden fear for Yolanda's life.

ELSA

Surgery after surgery continued. Elsa drifted in and out of sleep and anesthesia. With each wave, through weakness, exhaustion, and the lightness brought on by painkillers, she spied different members of her family in the room.

Eventually she gained consciousness. Danie, Stefan, and her daughter, Amanda, were standing away from the bed, in conference with a set of doctors. Elsa heard clips only, medical terms distilled at Danie's insistence into plainer language: yes, her jawbone had been rebuilt, but no, her left eye could not be saved.

Calculating what it all meant, she scanned the hospital room with her good eye. It was the ultimate sacrifice, the ultimate alibi. Who would question the integrity of her family now? Reassured, she dozed off.

A vivid dream overtook her. She looked around her room, seeing with both eyes, the whole picture restored. The room was empty, until an old woman entered, someone she didn't know, a coloured woman with eyes that held her in a magnetic and unwavering stare.

The coloured pulled up a chair and sat beside her—the nerve. She placed what looked like a seed on the nightstand, a pod that moved of its own accord, unsettling Elsa. The woman wore a doek, and she was a plain old thing, her skin wrinkled with age. But there was nothing defeated about her, none of the bowed-down state Elsa expected. She meant to reprimand the stranger for her audacity but found she could not speak.

"So this is how it is," the woman said, "when you win every single battle but lose the war. I thought I lost my child. We wandered in darkness for a time, unable to find each other, yet we were together, always. But you. You will lose your boy for good. That day is coming."

The woman leaned in closer and whispered: "For the rest of your days, Elsa, you will have half the sight and twice the vision."

With that, she got up and left.

RACHEL

Rachel turned away from the vision she'd created, the truth she had handed Elsa, and looked to the veld. It drew her back in. She savored the smell of sun-warmed grass, the feel of the long stalks on her hands. She gave a last thought to her blue letter, sent on its way weeks before. *Find your way,* she said to it. *Find your way to Yolanda.*

"It is done, Ma," Jan said. "It's time to come home."

She was ready.

Gemsbok on a nearby ridge turned toward them. One by one, the large-bodied antelope trotted toward her and Jan. Their white-ringed eyes and black snouts looked like masks; their big vertical horns slanted up and backward. They meant neither her nor Jan any harm.

She watched them and thought of her journey. Her energy was wavering, her body losing its fire. She shifted nearer to Jan, who remained still. He was calm, expectant.

"Don't run," was all he said.

The gemsbok came closer. Some drew themselves upright onto human legs, their front limbs reshaping into arms. Rachel couldn't read their faces or eyes, which were as black as night. She couldn't read anything on the winds that sailed around them.

Past them, up on the ridge, she saw a different animal, a bigger antelope, fat bodied, its horns shorter than those of the gemsbok. An eland. But commotion and dust distracted her, and when she looked up again, it was gone.

A tight circle of regular gemsbok and half-human ones now surrounded her and Jan. Before Rachel could wrap a clear thought around the feeling that had begun to take form within her, Jan and the gemsbok bowed their heads.

The circle opened.

Rachel's hands flew to her mouth when she saw who was walking toward her.

Her mother, Sara, was still proud. She'd always been larger than life, as if fire spread outward from her being. Death had done nothing to dim her fierce eyes. She wore animal hide, strings of porcupine quills and ostrich-shell beads. Her arms were extended, something draped over them.

She came nearer, and Jan lifted whatever it was off her arms. Rachel embraced her mother then, holding on to her, let everything sail out: every touch of grief, every whoop of joy, every moment of letting her children go and forcing them now to let her go in turn. She used to cry alone about Philip and Yolanda, hiding all the deep cuts, how raw it felt to be so petrified for your children. Were they alive? She'd asked that question every day, unsure she could live if they were not breathing. Now she wept with the release of one who no longer had to do this.

Her mother held her tightly. This love was absolute.

Then, gently, Sara undressed Rachel, taking off every item Rachel wore until the sun beat down on her naked form. Ceremonially, her mother took the animal hide she had carried from Jan and wrapped it around Rachel's waist. She lifted a string of beads from her neck and placed them around Rachel's. Lastly, she lifted another item Jan held, a beautiful tan-and-black kaross, and hung the cape over Rachel's shoulders.

She placed a hand on Rachel's cheek. Rachel placed her own over it. So this was how it was. Love prevailed.

Then her mother turned and walked back into the fold of the gemsbok. All of them shifted into the tall grasses, and everything was as before. Rachel looked in vain for the big fat-bodied eland, but it was gone. She felt the cape on her shoulders blending with the essence of her, lending her the nature of the animal once contained in these skins.

Standing tall, Rachel carried on, knowing that she walked now for all her family and people: past, present, and future. Yet there was something more: a dissolution. Her mortal body in its long trance grew nearer; she could smell the musty cave where it lay, and she could feel the agony of her body, her cancer's aggressive progression. Jan was there now, keeping watch. She felt herself leaving the cave and knew then that she was dying. Rachel returned to the veld of dreams, bowed her head, and walked on into the tall grasses where she belonged.

JAN

Across the country, in a painted cave hidden in the spine and bones of the red mountains, Jan sat back on his haunches, a man once more.

He was finished. Yolanda would survive, although he had drawn back from her any awareness or notion of his healing hands upon her shoulder and her mind. Jan looked at her mother and saw that Rachel was worn beyond salvation. Her journey had consumed everything she had to give. The cancer had taken the rest.

Voices from people forgotten to the underbelly of this place began to sing. As light touched the surrounding rock, Jan saw the host of Rachel's ancestors thronging the cave, her mother, Sara, standing at her feet. Her act was complete. Her children were on the path to freedom, each in his or her own way.

Jan sat until the voices and the light fell away. Bending forward, he began to pile stones upon Rachel's body. He arranged them delicately, each in its correct place. Upon leaving the cave as a leopard once more, he stood before the majesty of the red-stone mountains. In the distance, his land of fog and halfmens trees beckoned him north. Head heavy with sadness for his companion, he departed, for the work was done.

INGRID

Alone in a locked room at the police station, Ingrid rested her head on the table at which she sat. It had been six hours, maybe more, since the paramedics had eventually lifted Yolanda into an ambulance, refusing to allow Ingrid to ride along. In thick English, the police had said they had questions about the deceased and the injured white woman. They told Ingrid she was going where Litha had gone. They would not be dissuaded.

Now, they could come in again at any minute, push open the scuffed door, interrogate her about the dead man. Ask her questions she couldn't answer. She hadn't seen Litha since Stefan's house. She feared for him—and for herself.

For the longest time on this journey, the righteousness of her anger had held steady. But today, Yolanda had literally taken a bullet for her. How could she stand to lose her mother a second time?

The heavy door opened with a crack like a gunshot. Ingrid shot up at the sight of Philip's haggard, anxious face. Overcome, she ran toward him and held on to her uncle. A big man with a rifle stood beside him.

"Come," Philip said. "But listen to me: Don't talk to anyone, no eye contact, nothing; stay between this man and me. There's a car at the back door. Get straight in."

The handful of scattered personnel in the station fell quiet as they passed, Ingrid cowering behind her uncle's wide shoulders. Her heart pounded. She couldn't help glancing at one or two faces; she saw on them unwilling deference to Philip, bitterness at a world order changed. Striding behind, Philip's bodyguard cocked his weapon.

As they exited, bracing bodies and shifting figures nearby sprang to life. Ingrid was hastily piled into a car; driver in the front, it was already running. The sweet shut of its heavy doors and tinted windows cut her off from what those bodies wanted. The bodyguard was already in the passenger seat, gun at the ready, and her uncle pressed in beside her. There was a disturbing thud on the car's side, another. The driver pulled away with a screech, and Ingrid turned to the other person in the back seat: Litha, his face swollen. He gave her a small smile as she gasped. She threw her arms around him.

"Slowly," he said.

"They were just getting started on him," Philip said, shaking his head. "One dead white man and a living Black one, well . . ." He looked over at them. "They were going to make sure you slipped on a piece of soap or fell out of a window, my friend."

Heavy with guilt, Ingrid could barely look at Litha. He had been there with her. He had seen it all. When he said quietly, "I need to get home, Ingrid, back to my family," she nodded.

"I suppose it's time for me to do the same thing," she said. He squeezed her hand.

"Uncle Philip," she said, "where is my mother?"

"I got her airlifted earlier to a private hospital in Joburg. We're headed that way—not to the hospital but to Melville, where we'll be staying." Philip paused. Ingrid felt relieved; all was not lost after all.

"What happened, Ingrid? Do you understand that this was almost life or death for all of you? A white man dies, a white woman is blinded, and the trespassers are Black and coloured. Do you know how that looks? I had to pull out all the stops to negotiate for you three in this, of all places . . . you don't understand. The politics here is something else. The knocks on the car—those people were going to pull you two apart."

"But we didn't do anything. We were the ones who got shot at."

"Doesn't matter. There's an election in a week, the country is a tinderbox, and you're in the Free State."

They settled into a long drive through the dark. Litha stared out the window, not speaking. When Ingrid touched him lightly, he flinched. Where were they to find words for what they'd experienced together? She ran over every equation, trying to account for how her mother could have met her at that exact moment. How, despite being shot, Yolanda had thrown herself on Ingrid just before their attacker fired again.

A realization came upon her. She turned to Litha and whispered, "They didn't open the door."

Indeed, everything around Stefan was an unyielding, shut door, allowing for neither entry nor exit. Yet Ingrid knew that she had met her father. For a moment, when he'd knelt down beside her and Yolanda on the lawn, they had been a family, each wanting to save the other. But once again, Stefan had taken that away.

The rest of the experience came to her mind in fits and starts as they drove. Without warning, her body would stiffen with fear, as if the shooter she had watched go mad, who'd seemed to hate them so personally, would uncurl himself from one of the car's dark corners.

In the small hours, they arrived at the home of a friend of Philip's, a man wearing the yellow shirt of the Kaizer Chiefs soccer team. Ingrid sat in the kitchen with the men for an hour or two as they drank. She told them everything before returning to the room where Litha lay. She watched over him until she dozed off.

The driver took Litha to a doctor the next morning; by noon, he was stitched up and on a flight back to Umtata. He and Ingrid had agreed to talk in Cape Town when the time was right. Now, she had to reassemble the very idea of her family, her past, and herself. Questions needed to be answered. Her grandmother had not returned, but her mother had.

"Yolanda is being discharged," Philip told her in the midafternoon. "The hospital said she made a quick recovery, but she needed a blood transfusion. They couldn't find a bullet in her shoulder; looks like it went right through, and the wound had somehow started to close already. I didn't understand that part. Anyway, I'm leaving in an hour."

"Uncle Philip," Ingrid said anxiously.

He turned. She wasn't sure why she'd called out, what she needed from him to climb the mountain ahead of her. He came near and sat beside her with a sigh.

"When you say goodbye as often as I have, Ingrid," he said, "you learn that you're never ready for a hello with someone you missed. You don't know if it will happen, never mind how it's going to feel, so you don't think about it. In fact, you try your best not to. That way if it does come, that moment is glorious."

He gave her a slight smile and left. Staring at the clock in the kitchen, Ingrid wondered how to prepare for resurrection, twice over. She thought of all the Yolandas she'd encountered: the enigmatic artist, the fantasy of her own childhood, the unsettled memories lodged in the minds of her family. Her mother sat upon her heavily. Ingrid had held her near, and that sentiment wrung her most as she prepared to see her once again.

Later that day, with every step through the hospital ward, Ingrid tried to set aside the memory of the oil-painted face and the horror of seeing Yolanda shot. When her eyes fell upon the figure waiting for them, she immediately felt protective. Her mother's face was drawn, her eyes wide, seeking her out.

"I always thought I'd know what to say to you, at first," Yolanda said, while the nurse warned her not to get out of her wheelchair. Ingrid held her fast, grateful for the voice she didn't know but that she'd wanted to hear all this time.

Later, as the two of them had tea alone in the kitchen, Ingrid realized that Yolanda gave her the impression of being weathered, of a woman exposed, often at the mercy of the elements. She wore a loose linen shirt, borrowed from their host, over the bandages supporting her arm and shoulder. In the almond-shaped eyes, the pert nose they both shared, Ingrid found what she'd been seeking.

"I thought I knew you," Ingrid said through tears. The tension of the hours and days since Rachel's departure spilled out of her. "I knew enough to write you off; I thought it was deserved." She took her mother's offered hand. "It turns out I don't know you at all. I drove across the country so that a white man could exonerate himself. But you, I didn't want to hear what you had to say. I was wrong about you. I was so wrong."

Ingrid paused, and Yolanda looked at her gravely, leaning forward to squeeze her shoulder. Ingrid continued, "How did you know I was there, at his house?"

"Reuben. When I heard you were going there," Yolanda said softly, "I knew you were in trouble."

Mother gone, mother gained. Ingrid thought in the stillness that followed of what Yolanda had said and began to process what she had done. She wondered if it wasn't that Rachel had left her but instead that her grandmother had made room. Questions remained for Yolanda, but they would be asked at the right time.

For now, in that kitchen, a bond took root. The slow germination continued as they returned to Cape Town the next day. Both tried to find words to give form to a relationship so weighted down with the past, one ended and restarted in violence. Both of them had gazed down the barrel of the dead man's gun. Both were confronted with the loss of the woman they called *mother*.

YOLANDA

Yolanda observed Ingrid with grief, mourning the simple mother-and-newborn union they had had for only a moment. Ingrid looked to her as a fellow adult now, and Yolanda knew enough to treat her that way. Her lemon-blanket newborn was relegated to history. Yet any connection mattered.

One conversation awaited them. It required the right space and time. It was the one event Ingrid didn't ask after, although Yolanda knew she'd heard the shooter's words. Yolanda said nothing of it either, not yet.

The opportunity came a few days later, on the night before the elections. They were in Rachel's kitchen: Philip, Mark, Ingrid, and her, all together. Yolanda looked around at the stove and cupboards, the steel-legged table, the linoleum floor: a single unchanged room, the one in the middle of it all.

Mark appeared especially troubled, tapping a photo in his hand. Mark, her weary brother who did what he knew was right, no matter how challenging. She wondered if this was true courage: to stay and fight the fight, however ordinary and mundane the actions needed. To grow where you were planted alongside the people you loved. Yolanda knew what he had to say about the photo, but she knew, too, that she had to take this moment while she could. She wasn't ready for what

Mark would tell them, the gulf that would open up before them all. She might never be.

"They were after you, Philip," she began, hesitant at first. She stood at the kettle and the blue Cadac gas stove while the others sat at the table. "All they really wanted was you."

Philip had been preoccupied until now and had to leave soon. Hard-won democracy was less than a day away.

"All that time, with my head in my art, my heart in Stefan's hands, they wanted you."

"What are you talking about?" Philip gave her his attention, leaning back.

"I found out I was pregnant with you at four weeks, Ingrid. I remember telling Stefan, the shock on his face. We were frightened, both of us. Our relationship had been taking strain even before this. We truly didn't know what to do."

Ingrid's eyes widened. Of this period, Yolanda had told her nothing until now.

"Then, three or four weeks later, the cops came round. They knew where we lived 'cause they were used to trying to find you, Philip. They invited themselves in, ransacked my room, cuffed me, marched me to the station. Caledon Square, of all places, even though I wasn't political. I thought, I must really be in trouble if they're taking me there. Maybe someone saw me and Stefan. They held me for I don't know how many hours before bringing me to an interrogation room. I was terrified."

It pained Yolanda to see Ingrid's face fall. This was not the origin story her child had envisioned. Yolanda pinched her eyes shut. Instead of the usual terror, the suffocating sense that thinking of the attack brought in its wake, she felt stillness. She could do this, speak these words, without being entrapped by the ghouls.

"It was a gray room, with scratched walls like people had been trying to get out; I'll never forget it," Yolanda went on. On the table had been her underwear and some clothes, her journals, her photos, and some of her art. All neatly arranged in piles. She was directed to sit at the table across from an ugly, fat man with patches of hair. He'd looked at her with a sagging face and slid a pencil through a pair of her panties. He was grandfatherly, apologetic, and introduced himself as a detective. He went on about how much they knew about her and Stefan, recounted detail after detail. They'd collected information about them for a year. How unfortunate it was, he said at the end with a sigh, the case they'd have to make against them.

"All I know, Ingrid," Yolanda continued, "is that you're fluttering somewhere inside me. I'm a mother in that moment." Yolanda remembered trying to hide her fear, insisting on the lawyer she knew she wouldn't get. "He got up, reached the door, and said casually that they can make all of this go away, the whole mess, as long as I stayed away from Stefan, of course. But I had to do them one little favor, just one small thing. 'Where is your brother, Yolanda?' he asks. 'And what is he up to these days?'"

At the kitchen table, Philip drew back with folded arms, the frown on his face deepening. Mark had sunk down lower. Yolanda heard Ingrid's breath tighten. She didn't know if she was doing the right thing in letting Ingrid hear all this. But for too long they had all drowned in secrets.

"'We just want to have a chat with him,' the interrogator said. 'Find out what he's been up to. We know he's a terrorist. You don't want your brother to die, do you, Yolanda?'"

Yolanda shut her eyes to push back against the desperation that had come, then, with knowing she could be detained indefinitely without charge.

"I felt such hopelessness, because this was law and order in my country, mine. This was the police. They held me for a long time, tried to get to the same conclusion in different ways. Eventually I got sent home, frightened and exhausted; I don't know what their plan was with the charges. When I got home, Ma had a bag ready; she told me I was going up-country for a while. I stayed with Ouma. You were born there, Ingrid. Ma came up to stay with us, too, toward the end."

"I know that part," Ingrid said softly. Yolanda thought that more would need to be said of her time in that arid land, of how often Yolanda thought back to it fondly. But now she turned to Philip.

"After that . . . well . . ."

She watched her eldest brother's darkening face as she described the sexual assault. She directed her words at him, unable to look at Ingrid.

"But there was one thing after," she continued, holding on. "One thing among so many. Ma told me she found me on the sidewalk outside the house, and I smelled sharply of urine on top of everything else. One night, I don't know when, could have been weeks or months later—time was just swallowed by the attack—I was half-asleep. I was having so many nightmares; I've never slept well since—but I remembered the sound: a zipper, then this warmth that must have been someone pissing on me, and a voice near my ear, in my head, saying, 'Just cleaning you up. Listen, that, all of that, was for Philip. You be a good girl and go home and tell him.'"

Ingrid shifted her eyes from Yolanda to Philip, who sank his head down: a weary man.

"You've never asked me why I left, Ingrid," Yolanda said. "I've had many years to think about the reasons. At the time, it wasn't even a rational decision, and I left everyone here in an untenable position. But I knew that protecting you meant leaving you. If I couldn't even protect myself, how was I supposed to protect you? Soweto started to burn three months after I was assaulted. June of that year. The violence spread to here, and I knew then I had to go. It all ran so much deeper, though.

"I couldn't mother you anymore. And here, in this community, with the questions, the innuendo, it was assumed that you were born of the rape. I felt responsible. My own father, who believed that the system would take care of the good coloured people, who hated how his only daughter just wouldn't ever listen, made clear to me that I was responsible. I had engineered my own downfall by reaching beyond my station in life with a white man and had to pay the price."

Despite her hands over her face, Ingrid couldn't hide the tremors coursing through her body.

"I'm so sorry, Ingrid," Yolanda said. "For what I couldn't be, for what you didn't have." Yolanda went to embrace her as she saw on her child's face what her words had both given and taken away. Then she stood up to look out the small window at the empty yard, the lone mulberry tree that was a remnant of her childhood adventures and her daydreaming. Within, Yolanda felt a certain calm, history's hold loosened a little.

Philip slammed his fists on the table. "I'm going to find them," he said. "Every last one of them. They will pay."

"That isn't why I told you."

Yolanda exhaled and looked over at him. He was bent forward, and she could see clearly now how agedness marked the curve of his spine, the lines on his face. He couldn't look at her. Mark's head was in his hands. She regretted giving him another weight on top of the many he already carried.

"There's going to be a truth commission, Yolanda," Philip said. "I don't know yet if they'll offer amnesty, but that's a way to get to the bottom of this."

"I've been at the bottom of it for twenty years, Philip. I'm done. I just needed to say openly for the first time what happened to me. All of it. And I needed you all to hear it and know."

He came to stand beside her, raised a trembling hand, but put it down, unable to touch her. Though he held himself upright at the counter, his head fell.

"I heard some of it, Yolanda, I did, but I didn't want to know more. It was easier to say you brought this on yourself, to believe it." He softened. "How are you going to forgive me?"

289

He began to cry then, the long arc of his life in the struggle pouring out of him. She held him for a long time. Then she turned and rubbed Mark's back. Her eyes fell on the photo he'd brought.

Mark met her eyes, and Yolanda knew that the weeping was not yet done.

"There was a phone call," Mark said. "Here, yesterday. Mommy has cancer. They were phoning to make an appointment for her at Groote Schuur. She . . . she didn't tell anyone; I didn't know. How come I didn't know?" He shook his head, upbraiding himself. Yolanda sighed deeply. This was the missing piece about Rachel, the thing she'd sought since arriving in the Cape. But it was not what she'd wanted, not what she'd hoped for, not at all.

"Cancer?" Ingrid said. "But that's impossible. She's fine."

"She isn't," Mark said. "Wasn't. It's hard to know what problems were because of old age, what because of her visions, and what was the cancer. She had early-stage lymphoma, they said, a long, slow cancer." Standing beside Philip, Yolanda cast her eyes down. Only Ingrid and Mark could know this; only they had been here for their old mother. But she noted his words. *Wasn't. Had.*

"Well, when we find her, she can—" Philip said.

"We're not going to find her," Yolanda said quietly.

Mark sighed. "Do you remember Dinges?" His eyes were heavy. Yolanda walked over and rubbed his shoulders. He had already begun to mourn.

"The dog?" Philip asked.

"He was a little stray dog we adopted when we were children, Ingrid," Yolanda said, nodding toward the picture on the table. "That's his photo."

"He disappeared; I must have been eight or nine," Mark continued. "Do you remember, Philip?"

"We walked up and down, looking," Yolanda said.

"I remember," Philip said gravely. "We found him dead in a corner of one of the open fields."

"He was sick before he went away." Mark's voice shook. "Mommy said that he wanted to go and die in peace, that animals do that sometimes when they're not well." His crestfallen face, his body bent forward, was a terrifying sight, for Mark was the one who had stood, certain and present, through it all. "Our mother is gone, Philip. There wasn't a robbery; she's not lost. She left this photo and the other things for Ingrid and Yolanda to have. She left this as a message."

"She just left?" Ingrid said softly. "But where?"

"The north," Yolanda said, voicing what she'd long sensed. "Up-country. We won't find her. She knows that place like the back of her hand."

"How do you know?" Philip shot out. "How can you know?"

As she watched her eldest brother move away from them to lean against a wall, she settled at the table, consoling Ingrid and Mark. After a long time, Philip said softly, "I knew when I came to the house that nothing criminal had happened. It was obvious. But to accept all this . . ."

His words failed him; he curled forward, his shoulders shaking, and Yolanda saw with every sob how much he wanted to hold their mother, how much it pained him to have lost so many moments.

All she could think of was her father.

"There have been so many land mines scattered over my life," she began. She reached out and held Philip's hand, just held it, held on. "Some of them I just stepped around, delicately. Like Daddy, oh, Daddy." Philip's reddened eyes looked at her. He sat down. "I was a disappointment to him; he couldn't even look at me . . . after, and I don't know, Philip, I don't know where to begin accepting that Daddy has died without us ever making our peace. At least you got to do that; at least you got to spend time with Ma."

The siblings wept around Rachel's table.

Mark spoke. "It killed him, Yolanda—not you but the idea that he had chased you away when you needed him most. Every day, every day was a struggle for him, between his love for you and what he thought he was supposed to do."

There was much more to be said. The four of them shared the night together at the kitchen table. Tears came, but so did stories, some shared, some new. In the small hours, Yolanda followed Mark into the yard, concerned about her shaken brother. He was wringing his hands, sitting on the bench.

"I can't get over that I didn't know, Yolanda. 'Cause now I'm wondering, we were all so busy just carrying on, what else didn't I know that she was trying to tell me? She had so many stories; did she write them down? You said she went north; I know so little, almost nothing, about that part of her life. Now and then she told us about her mother, Sara, about the cart, the farm, and the way they lived. About being Nama. But Daddy dismissed it all, every single time. White history from textbooks was enough for him."

Yolanda let him speak, watched him grapple with a path he had never considered before—one that led back beyond the box apartheid had put them in, back to where they'd begun. They were more than could fit into a government box marked *coloured*.

"I can't even explain what I need, Yolanda, but I want to honor her in the place she came from. When tomorrow is over and things settle down, I want us to go north, to find that road back, even if it's only symbolic. Where was Sara from? Where was the farm? I know nothing about those roots, nothing about how they used to live. I can't just leave it like this, leave her. We don't come from nothing, after all."

Then her brother, the Gibraltar who had stood for them all, sobbed on her shoulder.

"We will find a way, Mark. A way forward through the past." This was truly Rachel's gift to them.

INGRID

Ingrid woke the next morning beside her mother, on Rachel's bed. Falling asleep, the two women had shared stories about her grandmother. Now, as the world woke, Ingrid lay, mindful that voting was unfolding in polling booths across the country. It meant something different to know the full scale of how difficult it had been for her family to get here.

"Come on, let's get ready," Yolanda said. "There's somewhere we must go before we vote."

Outside, Ingrid watched her mother select a handful of flowers from the garden before Yolanda drove them to Tokai Forest.

"We're going to Elephant's Eye," Yolanda said.

"Yes," Ingrid said. She understood why.

The scent of pine trees along the lower, forested section brought freshness to the air. Rising up from the city below felt like taking a big, welcome breath. This was the right place to be, Ingrid thought, especially now. Yet it was difficult to come to the mountain without Rachel.

Ingrid watched as Yolanda cast her eyes toward Silvermine's orange-and-white sandstone; at a troop of baboons scampering by, babies on their backs. She had a way of looking, her mother, an intensity that took her gaze beyond a casual glance. Yolanda studied the world, Ingrid realized. Nothing went unnoticed.

"Yes, I know this place," Yolanda said softly as they walked.

At the upper reaches, Ingrid took pleasure in her mother's joy at the sight of the False Bay coastline tapering off into the distance, at the Cape Flats showing its serene face. She watched Yolanda smile at a lone protea, a stark burst of blood red, as they walked the final stretch through the fynbos, toward the cave's open mouth. It was restorative, to have this shared moment, to have one of Rachel's favorite places elevate their spirits. Yet Ingrid felt grief and knew Yolanda did too.

They sat in stillness for a while until Ingrid spoke. "If I hadn't gone to Harrismith . . ."

"You're not responsible, Ingrid. Each of us in this family, as in any other family, made choices. We each did what we thought was right."

"Do you regret Stefan?" Ingrid watched the deep currents riffling on Yolanda's face. In that moment something lit up behind the tired eyes: a defiant light that made Ingrid think of Ouma: the picture of her great-grandmother that her mother had drawn in that old journal.

Middle age, Ingrid realized, was something she had always thought of as a state of pending stasis, of people settling into the ailments and accommodations that would see them through to old age. Looking at her mother in the morning light, she realized that this was a woman still in a state of becoming. Her clothes and jewelry painted a veneer of street sophistication over someone fluid, someone wrestling with herself, continually exhausted from the search for a place to simply be.

Yolanda pushed her hair back and smiled sadly. "I wish everything had unfolded differently for us. But do I wish we were never together? No, I loved him. He was my man; we belonged together. The two of us made sense when nothing else did. I know that's a difficult thing to believe in the uneven world of apartheid. But Ma taught me to stand up for myself, so I did. Being with him came at a cost that I could never have anticipated."

"What did you see in him?"

"Someone moved by something larger than himself. He wasn't just passing through life but wanted to experience it as fully as he could, on his own terms. We saw that in each other. It was part of why we were together. And love, we loved each other from the very start. But it wasn't enough, that love, not enough."

Ingrid gave her a long, seeking gaze. "Yolanda, you should have been enough."

Yolanda dropped her head and pinched her eyes shut for a moment, before stepping away to smoke.

Ingrid's eyes fell on the far-off mountain range she had driven through with Litha over a week before.

"He denied you," Ingrid said. "He lied to my face. I don't have a father."

"The one you have is imperfect, Ingrid. So was mine." Yolanda turned toward her.

"Pa loved us. Stefan doesn't." Ingrid clenched her hands as she told her mother about the confrontation with Stefan before leaving his house.

Yolanda fell still. The wind dried the tears springing to their faces, snatching them away before they could grow heavy. Coming to terms with Stefan was a task that would linger, Ingrid thought, unfinished.

Yolanda sat back down. "Looking at all this, I remember how I used to think that if only I could come back here, come home, then things would start again, be normal. I was just going overseas for a little while; that life wasn't the real one. But it was eighteen years of a life, and it was my life. I changed. I became someone else, someone who in some ways grew away from this place and in other ways never left." Ingrid heard in her tone that this knowledge saddened her. It was not what Yolanda had expected to encounter.

"But you, you have this home. You have what Ma gave you. What's happening in this country today . . . this is your country, Ingrid, and your future. It's been a battle to get to this day; it will be a battle after this day. That doesn't mean the fight isn't worth it."

Fear surged in Ingrid at the idea of motherlessness. "But this is your home, too; you must stay." She was a long way from reconciling with the painful loss of Rachel.

Yolanda held her, and Ingrid breathed in the welcoming amber scent she was growing used to.

"I'm not going anywhere right now," Yolanda said. "I waited too long to find you."

"Are you scared to be in Cape Town because of . . . what happened to you?"

"Yes, but love is greater than fear. Doesn't matter where I go; I'm always going to bring myself along. I'm tired of running."

"Uncle Philip wants to look for them, your attackers. Why don't you want to find them?" Ingrid asked.

Yolanda drew herself up tall. "People think pain moves in a straight line: you go through it, survive it, and then it's over. That's not how it works. The whole experience is circular, fluid. Over a month, a day, even a year, you can go through it all: reliving it, falling down, standing up, getting stuck on moments, staying on repeat. At some rare times, you even forget. But then you remember."

Ingrid saw Yolanda make a simple gesture: lifting her chin so that she faced the horizon, raising a hand to animate her words. Something Ingrid herself did without thinking. It drew her closer to her mother in a way she couldn't describe.

"Last night," Yolanda continued, "at Ma's house, I said what I needed to say to Philip. As a man, his suffering is seen as noble; as a woman, mine is treated as inevitable. But I need to let go of my rage toward him. Not because I owe that to him, but because it's toxic for me. What he does with that knowledge is up to him. For almost twenty years I've been stewing in shame, silent. I needed to be unsilent, need to." She inhaled sharply. "I survived rape. I have posttraumatic stress disorder. I'm an alcoholic."

In awe, Ingrid fell silent. "You should add that you smoke a lot," she said lightly after a minute, and Yolanda laughed, a pleasing throaty sound.

"I don't agree with you, though," Ingrid added. "I've lived with your art now longer than I've lived with you, Yolanda. That's how I got to know you. You can't leave being an artist out of the picture of who you are. You can't leave being my mother out either."

"Yes, but I failed, Ingrid, at those things."

"No, you didn't. Besides, we're made of stronger stuff than that. What would Ma say? *Môre is 'n nogge dag.* Tomorrow is another day."

Yolanda laughed again. "Yes, she would, my dear mother." She paused. "I don't need to find those men, Ingrid. They have never really left me. If anything, I need separation from them now. Everybody talks about forgiveness, as if it's a debt the victim has to pay, or they won't make it to kingdom come. Forgiveness is work, a privileged thing to be earned. I care more about myself and you, my family, than I do about amnesty for them. I don't want my pain to become a public spectacle. I owe them nothing. They have to live with themselves, answer for themselves. I will not shoulder that burden for them.

"But," Yolanda sighed, "we didn't come up here for me. I'm not ready to say goodbye to her."

"Neither am I. So we just won't," Ingrid said softly.

"She liked to say 'so long' instead of 'bye.' I remember that."

"Ja, she does. She did." Ingrid paused, the moment heavy, the women huddling close to each other. "So long, Ma." Her voice cracked.

"So long," Yolanda said.

The sun continued to light the world. They knew they should return to the bustle below, the lines where wide-eyed South Africans stood in wait for a future that was theirs to mold. Yolanda laid down the gardenias at the mouth of the cave. Then she and Ingrid walked slowly down the trail to the parking lot.

At Mark's house, he was gathering his children. Together, they all left to take their place in line at the local civic center; at least three hours of people ahead of them, many more behind. Past and future gazed at Ingrid with frayed, untidy ends, but there was more than that at play. Here, too, were faces among whom she belonged; here was the long and winding road taken to reach this point. Here was everything she held to her bosom: the lessons; the knowledge; the sense of who she was and, now, where she had come from and where she was going. She was humbled and heartened. Tomorrow would indeed be another day.

YOLANDA

Standing behind her daughter in the voting line, Yolanda clutched the little identification book that had been in the bundle left by Rachel. Philip was roving across voting stations and districts in Mitchells Plain. She imagined the euphoria and victory he felt, although this day was merely the start of the next leg.

Mark, standing before her, was solemn. As aware as she of the prices paid for today. Yolanda kept her eyes on her daughter, who would know nothing but this for the rest of her life. And she kept her mind on her mother, that inexplicable enigma who had drawn her back.

No more or less than any other South African, for the first time in their lives, the family waited and sang when the songs came. They watched people emerge with triumphant marks of blue ink on their thumbnails. They nursed their feet through the long day and held each other as they looked ahead to what this day would bring, and the next.

Afterward, Yolanda returned to Rachel's house. She attempted a bredie while thinking about the winding path to this day and back here, to this house. That night she curled up on Rachel's bed and rested peacefully for the first time in years.

In the morning, she lay silent for a long time. She felt her mother's presence around her, soft and tender as a glove. It was possible to be vulnerable now in this place of mothering, to be tender with herself in the same way Rachel had always been. Garrick lingered on her mind. It took her that night on into the next day to reach him at home.

"It's good to hear your voice," she began, before telling him what she was ready to of her journey. "I may never be whole like I was once, but I refuse to keep being broken." She wept on the phone.

"You have to accept the wounds," he said. "That's the only way you'll get to look past them and see what I see." She knew that he loved her. But neither would speak of it until they were ready to hear it and say it.

"Someone called for you," he said as they were finishing. "An old friend from England, said she had something for you, a letter. I told her to send it on to here. I'll hold on to it."

She smiled. Garrick had made no mention of the timing of her return. It was so like him to know that she would only do it when she was ready.

STEFAN

Harrismith was a small town: people talked. It was one of the things Stefan never got used to, everybody in your business. Since the shooting, rumors came and went, but Elsa had stayed with them to recuperate for a few weeks, and her presence quelled the gossip.

Now it was June. Life was back to the new normal: his mother was changed yet stubbornly the same.

Stefan closed up shop for the day and headed home. The open land of fields and sky was textured with gray cloud and distant patches of light. He decided to drive the long way, to take in the abundant space, which formed its own sea and tides. Every day since he'd seen Yolanda had brought the pinprick of a thought, a question, an undeniable longing. He'd run the math so many times, but still he was unable to understand how the pieces that had exploded that day had fit together. A memory cast a shadow: A quickly silenced conversation overheard when his mother's twin, Pieter, had visited her in hospital. Stefan had brushed it off, and yet disquiet lingered.

After pulling up in his driveway beside Katrina's car, he got a file of work orders from the trunk and entered the house. But before he could call out hellos, he saw her, his wife, seated primly on the couch with something in her hand. A single suitcase stood by the door.

"Trina? Are you OK?"

"My father, he came already to fetch the children. I wanted to talk to you before I go." She looked up, and he was startled by her somberness.

"Go? What do you mean, go? What is going on, Trina? Where are my children?" Stefan clicked the door shut, and the sound echoed through the silent house. Katrina jumped.

"I was so convinced in the hysteria of the whole thing that it was a mistake, something that went wrong between people we didn't know." She shook her head. "I looked outside in the middle of the panic and saw, just briefly. I saw how you touched that woman's face with my own eyes, and still I defended you; I said it proved you had sympathy for everybody. For days, for weeks, I wanted to believe. But then I couldn't anymore. I looked in the boxes you kept from Cape Town, all the way in the back of the shed."

Stefan's heart began to race. "Katrina, what are you talking about?"

She turned over the canvas in her hand and placed it on the coffee table. Watercolor flowers. Disas. He remained standing, feeling as if he was losing ground.

"Many things are breaking my heart as I sit here," Katrina said. "That you lied to me, that you chased your own child away like a dog, that your mother probably knew more than I did. But that isn't the worst, Stefan." She struggled to maintain her composure; he saw lines of strain upon her face.

She shook her head, his little wife with her tidy floral shirt and knees pressed together. "How come you're sitting with not one painting but three, and this one with that woman's name on it? Ulrika and Dikeledi told me what that young girl, what your child, said to you while I was getting your mother to the hospital. I know who Yolanda is now."

He stumbled through a few words, the memory of those halcyon days stirring up shame. Katrina stopped him.

"You know what I realized? That you couldn't tell me the truth when you hadn't even admitted it to yourself."

"Please stop." Stefan held up a hand. "What do you want from me?"

"Honesty."

It ran over him like a serrated blade, how difficult it was for her to do this. He sank into the sofa across from her.

"You, your mother, both of you lied to me," she said. "Look at the cost: a dead man in my garden, a woman shot, your mother's eye lost, an illegitimate child standing in our house." She paused. "And in the middle of all that, Pieter shows up suddenly."

"Oh, come now, Katrina. He's family, and her twin."

"Yes, but how many times did he visit her in hospital, Stefan? Once. He was here for a week. What was he doing the rest of the time? And I can't get anything from the police about who that shooter was, not even a name. No motive, nothing. He died on our property, and they're acting now like he doesn't exist. I know what Pieter is, Stefan; I know what he does. So do you."

"He's family."

"All the more reason to protect you."

Stefan swallowed. The timing of his mother's sudden visit; that moment of intense conversation shared between the twins. He was stunned.

"But whatever Pieter, your mother, whomever, concocted, Stefan, it doesn't explain this." She pointed to the painting. "You broke the law for this woman. Why? Just tell me why?"

The words did not come easily, but they came.

"To be with her was impossible. At first," he began. Katrina's back grew rigid. Her face fell; the last faint hope of something she'd held on to faded away.

He stood up, walked to the window. "You and the children are everything to me, Trina, everything. I would never do anything to change that. But the army changed me; you must understand. I went three times, between conscription and then call-ups. Three. At Caprivi, I watched a man getting blown up like tissue paper when he stepped on a land mine. I have never been able to get the sight of it out of my mind. At the border there were so many things that I couldn't talk about. I saw a Black man beaten to death for not giving us information he probably didn't have. Why didn't I defend that man?"

Stefan folded his arms. "Then I got called up again when Ulrika was small, off to Angola like a good *boereseun* and not a grown man with a life he's trying to get on with. Every day I spent there Yolanda was on my mind. Every day I had a nightmare that I was part of some operation that would get her brother killed."

Stefan turned to look at his wife. "But I come home from all this, and everything is the same: every Sunday lunch, every holiday, the same people from the same community. Going to the Cape, Amanzimtoti, Plettenberg Bay for holidays. We lived nice lives with everything we needed. We played rugby and had our braais, and it was like a dream. None of us spoke about what we saw, about the blood on our hands."

He paused, drew a long breath. "We are people in a bubble: nothing coming in, nothing going out. We get to take everything for granted without asking why it is that way."

Katrina gripped a tissue. The simple gesture made him turn his eyes away. "You're making your life, ours, sound so false," she said.

"Trina, you wanted the truth. This is what it was when I was in my twenties."

"So what was Yolanda? A way out of the bubble?"

He closed his eyes. "In a way, yes."

He didn't add that those days were bold and rich, filled with scents and words, sketches of plants and butterflies, the little things he and Yolanda had loved. It was a past frozen and lost. Gone like desiccated leaves and wings. Everything would go to mud now.

"How selfish of you." Katrina looked at him with large, sad eyes. "Did you know about the child?" she asked. "Did you know and walk away?"

He sat down again. "I knew, I knew that she was pregnant; we spoke about it a little but had no idea what we were going to do. She left me soon after that, just disappeared. Then I went to the border. It was over. I didn't know I had a daughter by her." He shrugged. "There was nothing for me to do. I admit that I didn't have the courage to go and find out more, but I can't change it."

"How long were you together?"

"Just on three years."

"So long? You and I married after one year. Did you want to marry her?" She asked it sharply, the impossible question. The anger he had skirted for decades made him stand up again. He folded his arms, set that emotion aside.

"How could we?" he said. "That was never an option in South Africa."

"But if you could have, would you have married her?"

He sighed heavily. "I married you, Trina, and I would never change that. Who knows how things would have turned out if apartheid hadn't been there in the first place. I might never have met her, maybe never have met you."

"Did you love her?"

"You're asking questions as if everything was simple, when it wasn't."

"You made a child; how difficult was that?" He watched her ball the tissue ever tighter. "I want to know. Did you love her? Do you still?"

"Why are you asking me about love? Of all the things you want to know, Katrina, why that?" He shut his eyes and thought of Yolanda's laughter, her embrace. He opened them to see Katrina solemn. She slipped a trembling hand over her mouth and stood up. Turning away, she dismissed him with her hunched shoulders like he was a condemned man.

"I had a picture, Stefan, of us. It was mine." Clutching her hand-bag, she walked a few paces toward the door before turning back. "I am what I am, Stefan, a boer, just a girl from the *plaas*. But I don't know now if you really even know me. I'm not *verkrampt* like Bram; I don't think the Blacks are subhuman. I'm not a snob like your mother, either, stuck in a different century. And still you didn't trust me; you didn't trust that I would love you enough to defend you. I don't know who I married. You are the father of my children, and I'm terrified; you don't understand how terrified I am. But I can't be with a man who lies like you can."

She walked out with her suitcase. She avoided his eyes and quietly shut the door.

He left the painting of the disas on the table, as if in orbit around all it implied. Afraid to peer too closely at his own heart, he returned to his routine. He went to work, came home, ran with his dog, hoped for restoration. He prayed for something more than the heavyhearted truth that his mother had lied to him, that it was entirely possible he'd been lying to himself.

But the following night the phone calls began. At first the caller simply hung up, but soon an angry voice declared him a *kaffirboetie*.

Then the night after, Katrina's eldest brother pulled up outside his house. All six feet of Bram jumped out of his truck. Another man followed him, head held low.

"Is it true?" Bram asked as Stefan opened the door. "You made a child with that hotnot—is it true?" He pushed Stefan backward. The other man cracked his knuckles. "My sister was pure when she married you, but you, you *Kaapse moffie*—"

The first punch came. Stefan tackled his brother-in-law, but he was no match for two. Soon he was pinned against a wall.

"You broke all the laws, hey," Bram said, disgust distorting his face into something hideous. "Just for a piece of pussy. *Kom,*" he said to the other man, who drove his knee into Stefan's solar plexus.

It would have been easier to let them have their way, but he fought back. His living room fell apart around him: glass broken, chairs turned up, cabinets toppled, curtains ripped.

Eventually they left. He lay sprawled across the coffee table where they'd thrown him. All he could do was shift at a glacial pace to the couch and lie there. His blood had marked and smudged the disas.

Hours later he heard a car and saw headlights beam. Adrenaline surged. Were they coming back to finish the job?

Thankfully, he knew her footsteps. Katrina put on the light as she entered, crying, "My God! Kom, Ma, kom help."

He reached for his wife. "Don't stay; it's not safe."

"You're still my husband, and this is my house. Bram said he taught you a lesson; I came because I knew what that meant."

Stefan could make out the form of his mother-in-law, who clucked her tongue, muttering in Afrikaans while she slipped a pillow under his head. Everything in him burned. Some of his ribs were broken; he dared not raise a hand to his face. Breathing was a fight, but still he spoke.

"Cape Town," he said with difficulty. "I must go, Trina. Can't be here anymore." He paused, inhaling as deeply as he could, tears swelling. "I must make it right."

As they cared for him in the hours that followed, Stefan realized how buried in shame he was. But the shadows around him shifted. A path was clearing, but there was one person who loomed in his way, who would have to be faced before he could go further. Elsa.

A week later, Stefan was at his sister Amanda's house in Cape Town's northern suburbs. Katrina had chosen to stay with her parents on the farm, and while he talked to her and the smaller kids on the phone, his daughter Ulrika refused to speak to him.

Upstairs in the guest room, he spent his second day lying in solitude. He was exhausted, as if he had carried an unwieldy load for too long. Eventually, his parents would find their way to him; he had not announced his arrival, but it wouldn't take them long. Their fall from grace had no doubt begun, corrosive gossip and chitchat picking Elsa apart. But it was Ulrika who stayed on his mind.

He remembered holding her for the first time, her fragility, his joy, and how he'd fallen in love with her. There had been a moment one night weeks after her birth, rocking her to sleep, when he had set aside a note of sadness that had hung over him. He'd thought about the baby he and Yolanda might have had. He'd known that he would have felt exactly the same way about that child. Now, he wondered if this was the course of his life: setting aside the uncomfortable, difficult, and unpleasant. Still, there wasn't a fear greater than for the safety and well-being of his children.

Shifting a pillow behind his head, he realized he had never been this alone, not in more than fifteen years. Children, wife, parents, customers, always someone needing him. The years of his marriage and running his business, going to war and coming home, had consumed more than an entire decade. Occasionally, in the early years after moving to Harrismith, he'd tried to get to the surf in Durban.

In the middle of all of that, they'd been trying and trying for the second child, his wife courting numerous prayers, and then: two little ones in the space of five years. Distantly, he remembered the fall of the Berlin Wall; his youngest had been two at the time.

South Africa had been moving inexorably toward what felt like chaos and bloodletting. The prospect of this had become real with the referendum, the white vote in 1992, on whether to retain apartheid. There had been much animated discussion in the Odendaal and Van Deventer households at the time. Stefan remembered shutting off the reflections he had gained while with Yolanda. It was better not to share too much.

As he shifted, relieving pressure on his ribs, another realization came upon him. There were many periods of contentment with his wife, of appreciation for her, but he couldn't think of a single time with Katrina that had felt like even a few moments with Yolanda had. In his little Muizenberg apartment flanked by the water, there had been so many moments when they hadn't needed to speak, their hungers the same, their silence sufficient. He had made Yolanda laugh; it was easy to, and she did so with abandon, as if the battering ram of apartheid weren't outside his front door, waiting, like a policeman with a baton.

Frustrated, angry voices drew him back to the present, voices downstairs. He heard a summons from his bellowing father, Danie. The time had come. Hobbling down into the living room, Stefan heard Elsa gasp with shock. But he held steady and watched her. This time he would not run.

ELSA

Elsa maintained her composure as she looked at her damaged son, his damaged life.

"Stefan, my boy, what happened?" She came closer, but he brushed her hand away. Everyone remained standing.

"Pa, Ma." He nodded. He was curt, dismissive.

"Stefan," Danie said. "What happened to you?"

"I don't want to talk about it."

She needed to control this. She stepped forward, cursing the slight speech impediment that tripped her words. "Danie, maybe we need to go—"

"No," his father growled. "I want answers."

"This, Ma," Stefan said, "is the end of what you started." He looked up at her and no doubt noticed what she saw every day now: the scars disguised under her makeup, the genteel eye patch making her look like a villain.

Danie spoke. "Did you know your mother had a long interview with the police? That she's out on bail? All because of this catastrophe. Ridiculous."

"Well, she brought that on herself. My life is a mess right now, Pa. My business has been vandalized; my house looks like a train ran through it. I have no income; my kids aren't even in the same province. What do you want from me?"

"I can't help you if I don't know the truth, and I want it from you." Danie stood with his hands on his hips. Elsa knew then that the ground she had fought to hold for two decades was eroding. "Is that girl, the one who came to your house, your daughter? Did you have a relationship with the woman who was shot?"

Stefan stood, silent. Elsa willed him to maintain the lie they all needed. They would not be able to turn away from this admission if it came.

"Answer me, Stefan."

"She is my child, and yes, I was involved with her mother when I lived in Muizenberg."

Danie's face fell. Silence reigned for a single strained moment. Then his father launched himself at Stefan, grabbed him by the shoulders, and shook him, cursing. Elsa pulled at him, her daughter helping to separate them.

"Stop, Danie, stop," Elsa thundered. "Leave him alone."

Her husband fell backward, enraged. Stefan bent over, clutching his ribs. Danie stormed out of the room toward the kitchen.

"Stefan, what the hell is the matter with you?" She feigned surprise, but Stefan shook his head.

"This is my business, Ma, not yours. This happened before I got married. But I think you already knew that."

She ignored his words. "This is our problem to fix now, do you understand? Why did you do this? Why? How could you?"

"Because I love her!" he erupted. The house filled with a long silence.

"Love?" Elsa didn't budge. "Love is standing here trying to protect you from yourself. Love is getting shot trying to protect your family. Don't you talk to me about love. What were you thinking?"

Stefan had nothing but a stony response. "All I did when I was with her, Ma, was think, think about everything you taught me, everything you expected me to be. Everything in its place, just right, prominent

312

gesiene mense, being a member of the kind of family you didn't have as a child."

"So now I'm responsible because you couldn't control yourself, couldn't use your own common sense? We gave you everything. You have no excuse for being such a disgrace."

"No, Ma, you took it all away. You hired him. You knew all these years."

"You with your imagination." Elsa clicked her tongue. "Stefan, you're going back to Harrismith; you're going to work things out with the Odendaals. I spoke with the lawyers; it's not too late to discredit that girl and put out this whole mess. If she ever comes back with this accusation, she has to go through the courts, paternity tests, the whole story. I will make her life hell. There won't be any talk of money."

Elsa chattered on but realized as she did so that her words no longer had power. Stefan remained still. She came closer, sizing him up. "You will stay away from those people. You're going to make up for this disaster you've brought into everyone's life. You're going to make this right."

But in that moment all was lost. She knew her son. He met her stare with one of his own. He had turned to frost. For the first time in his life, he raised his finger to her face.

"No," he said. "I am finished with you. Get out of my life, and stay out. For good." He shuffled as best he could toward the door, where he grabbed car keys.

It flickered like the static screen of a television, Elsa's sight. In that instant, so quick she did a double take, she saw with both eyes. But the Stefan she saw was different: a young man turning his head, a man in love, lit up with joy. A man complete, who had everything he needed and wanted.

She drew her head back in surprise, but the vision was gone. Stefan shut the door.

With a hand over her mouth, she remembered the dream of the old woman at the hospital.

STEFAN

Stefan walked out into the rain and wind of the Cape winter. He thought of his children, every single one of them. He loved them all. He loved them more than they could ever know.

He breathed in, smelling the rain and the clean, clear air. Then he fled down the highway, his world unmade around him.

The worst had happened, and now he had no choice but to face her. Order would only come from the point at which it had broken. He drove by memory to a house he hadn't seen in decades. The red path, the flower boxes, so similar to the other council houses, but he recalled the street and the number; he'd burned it in his mind once as a way to hold on to her. It was a long shot, but he had nowhere else to go.

Everything at the house was quiet. He came up the path and knocked. A middle-aged coloured man opened the door. Stefan stepped back when he saw the man's face change.

"What nerve. Now, now you come looking for her like a dog."

Yolanda appeared behind him. The small face of their daughter, his and hers, peeked out from behind her mother. The young Black man who had been with them in Harrismith stood behind them both.

"Mark. Stop," he heard Yolanda say.

But the coloured man pushed forward, his boiling anger carrying him onto the stoep. "All this time, while we raised your child, while my parents got old before their time and I spent my twenties looking after everybody, where the fuck were you? You couldn't come then, couldn't be bothered with the coloured girl you had a *lekker jol* with, hey?"

Stefan found himself midway down the red path, forced backward. It was over. There would be no order, no restoration. He had been naive to expect it.

"Take your sorrys and never come back here," he heard the man shout after him as he shut the gate and left.

There was only one place left to go: the place of beginnings. The sheltered cove of Muizenberg was an open arm welcoming him back. The **WHITES ONLY** signs were long gone. The beach was all he had left now: the tides; the rust rock of the mountain behind him; the places he'd walked in a different, fearless life. He settled on the sand and sat for a long spell. Salt water to salt water. The ocean. Tears. The wave here hadn't been his favorite—that lay along the long white beach on the other side of the mountain—but this was the place that reminded him most of that vibrant young life, the one he'd lived under the threat of censure, the one gone to dust. So bright and shiny, so taken for granted, so easily dismissed.

Surfers, who wore wet suits these days, lorded over the waters in front of him. For a brief spell, their sense of abandon and mastery had been his. But all that had been extinguished when Yolanda had gone away. She'd taken the light with her, left him hollowed out and ashamed. Ashamed to have been with her, ashamed that this was how it ended. Their love trampled on, treated like an act of depravity.

But it wasn't like that, he said to the waves. *It wasn't like that at all.*

"I knew I'd find you here." He turned with surprise as Yolanda sat down on the damp sand beside him. Those dark eyes, the curve of that chin. She offered him a cigarette, which he declined, before lighting one herself. Quiet filled the air between them.

"The swell looks good today," she said after a time. "Why did you come to the house?"

"I was looking for you." He paused. "I didn't hire that man, Yolanda. Please believe me. I would never hurt you." He met her eyes.

"What happened to you? Your face?"

"Family trouble." He looked back at the ocean, which could offer no ready escape, not this time. "Wherever I go, someone wants to fight me."

Yolanda flicked her hair back. "My brother has the right to be angry."

He met her eyes. "No one does more than your family, but she is my daughter."

"*Your* daughter? She has never been anything to you; you don't deserve her."

"I can undo nothing, Yolanda, nothing. I can't become a different man who made different choices." He paused before asking, "What's her name?"

"Ingrid Disa."

He smiled. "Does she know why she has that middle name?"

"She's smart. She'll figure it out."

"I'm sorry," he said.

Yolanda paused for a long time. "Stefan, for so long your love, ours, was the measure of my happiness, the measure of me," she said with finality. Stefan could tell that that time had long passed, that a life deep and wide as a valley stood between then and now. The wind pushed gray clouds overhead. Sunlight made a patchwork on the ocean. Yolanda met his eyes, for a flash, the same girl he'd met with the hippie skirt and hat. The eternal lay there under the wear of time, but there was more: a woman he didn't know, a woman looking back at him from over an abyss.

"Why did you come?" she asked again, softly this time.

"Why did you?" He looked away.

"I was arrested, Stefan. I was . . ."

"Because of us?"

When she nodded, his mind began to race to that period when separation had come between them so hard and fast. The immediate and lengthy call-up, justified under the pretext that he was an engineer.

"I got my papers out of the blue," he said. "I couldn't find you, didn't see you at the café; no one would tell me anything. I remember how your friends there looked at me. But I got the call-up and I had to go, and there was no way, no way to tell you I was going unless I came to your home. And I didn't want to do that to you, put what was between us out in the world like that." He shook his head. "My mother, her brother. What have they done?"

"Who we were was always out in the world, Stefan, just like our daughter is now."

He glanced over. "I'd like to meet Ingrid, if she wants to," he said. "My mother . . . I didn't hire that man; I know she did."

"There's so little that you know." Her words sounded like an accusation; he feared the portent.

"I kept the flowers you painted," he said instead. "From one of those walks we took."

"Suikerbossie."

"Suikerbossie. I kept them hidden, but they didn't stay that way." He felt longing for what had been lost, brief as the season of the disas.

"Do you want a paternity test?" she asked.

"No, I don't need it. She's mine."

"No, she's not. She is entirely her own person. My eldest brother, Philip, is pushing the investigation against your mother hard. He says I should lay charges, but I'm tired, Stefan." He looked at her tanned and lined face. Once again she was the girl in the café, looking at him with the same knowing with which he'd looked at her.

"Is your mother ever going to forgive you?" she asked.

"I don't know if I'll ever forgive her."

318

"She wanted what was best for you. Most mothers do."

"I knew what was best for me."

"Stefan, it wasn't so simple."

"Oh, Yolanda," he sighed. "Yes, it was." He paused. "I will never hurt our daughter."

"I know," she said, standing up. "I need to go."

Stefan nodded. "I need to let you go," he said softly. She walked away without looking back.

INGRID

Color had betrayed Ingrid. All her life, it had been a lived-in, lived-with thing, directing her to what was good or bad, right and wrong, to what was pure and what fell short.

But that old inherited logic had fractured. The white man, the one who was going to make everything right, was a coward. The Black man, that most feared of beings, was the safest berth she had. Her coloured mother, whom she'd written off as self-indulgent, had laid down her life for her. Her rural grandmother, uneducated, eccentric Ma, had possessed a complexity and mystery beyond anyone's understanding.

Distant cloud and rough surf mingled on the horizon. Seated beside Litha on the bench, Ingrid had watched Yolanda and Stefan: the stricken faces, the hands unheld. Her mother had shuffled them out of the house after her father's visit, told them they were taking a drive. But Ingrid saw the pain Stefan's visit had left Mark in and remembered all Mark had done for their family. There were loyalties at play now.

"He doesn't look like he did back in Harrismith," Ingrid said, nodding toward Stefan's visibly worn figure. "He looks older."

"Yes, like a man who is very tired," Litha said. He had returned to Cape Town, to Ingrid, impassioned and filled with as much desire to see her as she felt. He was marked, though, by the police's treatment of him. He didn't say much about his journey home. It was clear that his visit to Lusikisiki had been complicated by what had happened to him in the Orange Free State.

Still, he was the only one Ingrid could speak with about the shooting. And she was the only one he spoke with about what the police had begun to do to him. Present and unwavering, they were together. They spent nights and the small hours revealing their most private selves, although it could be a stumble through some insecurities and over others.

"Why don't you hate him?" Ingrid asked. "He's everything you want to get rid of in South Africa."

"I can't hate him, Ingrid. You come from him. Besides, he has come a long way from home to find you and your mother. And he can't go back. I have seen the worst of that place where he comes from. He can never go home again."

The simple truth lay before her: the pair in the sand. "This is what it was about all this time, the two of them," she said. "What about you and me, Litha?"

She had the impression that his family was biding time until he tired of her and came back to the fold. It could all end; it could all be snatched away.

"My son is OK for now, and Zintle is carrying on with her life, no matter what the families want. She is upset but moving on. I am here with you because I want to be." With a sharp breath, he drew away from her a little. "What about you?"

Ingrid was getting to know the guardedness in him, how it formed a shield to hide the rejection he had grown accustomed to in his life.

She leaned over, whispered her answer in his ear, and kissed him long and slow.

As her mother walked back toward them, Ingrid wondered if she had only just come upon the truth about racism: that it was no more than a series of judgments made without thought, a set of often-indiscernible devastations. If this was true, if color was no more than a masquerade for fear and ignorance, then what of her father? She rose.

"Should I go?" she asked Yolanda.

Her mother gave a small smile, considered her for a moment. "Only you can answer that," she eventually said.

Ingrid drew a deep breath. She strode over to where Stefan sat.

"Did you hire the shooter?" she asked, mustering as much ferocity as she could.

Her father stood up with difficulty, his eyes searching her face. She was surprised to see fear in him. "No." He shook his head. "It was my mother. But my sister says the case against her is weak, and she knows it."

"How do you feel about that?" Ingrid asked, trying to keep him on the defensive.

"Conflicted, angry. I've lost my mother, Ingrid. It doesn't matter if she goes to jail or not; it's over for me." He cast his gaze back to the ocean. The matter was serious, his words heavy. "How do you feel?" he asked.

Ingrid shrugged. "I didn't come to Harrismith expecting to die." She paused, then sat down gingerly. Stefan did the same. She saw him wince with pain.

"I don't know what I would have done if that happened," he said.

Ingrid frowned, taken aback. He was the one person she had cast as beyond redemption. But this man was out of kilter with the person she had constructed in her mind since the shooting.

"I know what you must think of me," he continued, as if reading her thoughts. "I didn't raise you, and my life is what it is. But I'd like to get to know you."

"How are we supposed to do that?" The past sat between them, an uncompromising and dense presence. Yet woven into it was a little girl who'd drawn pictures of a mother and father who were her very own.

"I can't be your father in the ways that you needed as a child. It's too late for that. But I'd like to know a bit about you, for you to know a bit about me."

Ingrid looked back at him. His gaze had traveled elsewhere, to a distant place.

"She wore a blue-and-yellow dress on our first date," he said spontaneously. "Your mother." He paused, drew in a breath. "We had tea together, Lemon Creams, yes. Biscuits and tea. It was at the house of the manager of the café where she worked; the woman lived in Harfield Village. I brought Yolanda flowers; she placed one behind an ear. I was already in love with her."

He continued to speak of their relationship gently, as if unfolding something precious.

"Could I have tried to find a way to help her, make things legal however I could, when she was pregnant? Probably, but it came with a cost, and at twenty-five I couldn't pay it. I just couldn't, didn't even know where to start. And I will live with that, always."

They sat in silence. Ingrid could tell that there was more: he was looking at the waves, too, like a lost lover. Glancing at her, he gave a clear gaze that hid nothing but offered instead all that he could give. "I'll be here. When you're ready for me, I'll be here."

She wanted to taunt, say that this was what it felt like to have things taken from you, to give up what you loved as her mothers had, Yolanda and Rachel both. But as she ran through the words in her mind, they fell flat. He already knew this. He was already there.

She remembered what it had been like to yearn for a family out of a magazine, different from what she'd grown up with. She understood now that her family had been people doing the best they could at often the worst of times, that maybe this was the nature of all families. It was a fact tinged not with pride but with sadness.

"You say that you're my father," she said to him firmly. "But I don't say that, not yet. I don't know what to do with that fact yet. You haven't earned me, Stefan," she continued. "So no, I am not going to come to you; you're going to do the work for us, for me. Yes, my uncle is going to detest you for a long time, but if you want a relationship with me, you need to go through him. You need to understand why." She paused.

Stefan turned to look at her. Of all things, she saw pride on his face. "You've given me a lot to think about," he said.

"So have you," Ingrid said with a sigh. "I suppose everything behind us is this family that didn't happen," she continued. "Maybe it was never going to, especially after the rape."

He froze. "What rape? What are you talking about?"

She snapped her eyes up to meet his. "You don't know?" Each looking at the other in disbelief, she told him of the vicious assault and watched as something, some ill-afforded innocence in him, shattered.

"Where were you when this happened?" he asked protectively.

"I was a baby, at home." She paused. "Where were you?"

Stefan folded, hands over his face. His lack of an answer would form the bars he'd be locked behind for the rest of his life. He had no right to sympathy, and yet Ingrid felt it.

"I probably shouldn't have told you," she said. "It wasn't my place."

They were silent for a long time. She watched him fight the urge to turn, to see her mother and go to her. "Yolanda doesn't need you, Stefan."

He gave a small nod. "I know, Ingrid. She never needed me as much as I needed her."

She stood up but lingered. There had to be something more than this wreckage, but she had gone far enough for now. One day, maybe, she would ask him to teach her how to surf. Yolanda had said he was proud and strong upon the water. Everything about her had lit up when she'd spoken those words, and Ingrid could see the purity of what had been there between them in that moment, how he'd made her feel. But this was not the day for all those words. She told Stefan to come to the house again only when he was truly ready to talk. Ingrid walked away slowly.

Driving in silence, Litha dropped Yolanda at home, then sat with Ingrid in his new car as it idled.

"Where do I go from here?" Ingrid asked, unsure of what she meant.

As he had so many months before when they'd first met, Litha put the car in gear and drove. They headed to Busy Corner in the nearby suburb of Grassy Park, where shops and fast-food take-out spots converged around the bus terminus and taxi rank.

"Come," he said. "Let's eat; then we can solve these big problems."

At a hole-in-the-wall they knew, they sat at a window, facing the main street. Litha soon set down their order between them: fried calamari falling from its foiled paper, slumping onto an abundance of vinegary soft *slap* fries piled in a heap.

Outside, taxi guards whistled and hollered, the minibuses stopping at will for passengers, music thudding. Ingrid spied a woman she knew on the sidewalk, knocked on the window to get her attention, and waved. They spoke briefly outside. The ordinariness of all this was just what she needed: space, a moment to think. The disruptions since April had extended her. Life's dimensions would never be what they were. But Yolanda was right: this was home, the place where she'd begun. It meant something, especially now, simply to be here.

Litha dug into the food as she did. They each sipped cans of Stoney ginger beer.

"So?" he asked. "Where do you go from here?"

Ingrid smiled. Here, at ease now in the world at the other end of the railway line, she thought of what was so palpable between Yolanda and Stefan. For a moment, light had hit the ocean. For a moment, something large and elemental yet soft and radiant had gathered in the space between her parents. It told Ingrid all she needed to know about whether they were meant to be and whether or not she had been a mistake.

"I guess I learn what it's like to have a mother and, later, when I'm ready for it, a father."

"It's not as bad as you think," he said, and they laughed.

"I have parents, Litha," she whispered.

"You do. You'll get to watch them grow up."

YOLANDA

It was the time of day that Yolanda liked best in the Appalachians: long August evenings, well after the humid heat of summer had settled upon the countryside. One chorus of cicadas picked up the symphony begun by another, wave upon wave of sound filling the sky as it settled into the navy lines of twilight.

She had returned to Virginia a month before. More than a year had passed since Rachel's voice had drawn her back to South Africa. During that time, Yolanda had taken an extended road trip north with her brothers and Ingrid, to say goodbye, as best they could, to Ma. The moment of letting Rachel go was not easy. It only came after all of them had reached a certain stage of acceptance and mourning. Eventually they held a memorial service, a small informal gathering atop Table Mountain, where Yolanda knew the old woman's spirit held steady.

That aside, the decision to stay in South Africa or leave was ultimately dictated by the state of Yolanda's credit card and the reality that she was struggling to belong in her mother's house, in an old life that no longer fit. Over several lunches and dinners, she and Philip spoke of how they envied Mark the continuity of his life. They in turn contended with the difficulties of coming home, of being exiles who belonged yet didn't. Philip found her a job. But she knew that the only way forward for her came from being true to herself.

In line with the politics of the day, there was an interest in South African art. Yolanda wrestled with establishing how and where to feel safe enough to create again; she knew she would not commit her soul to the canvas without it. Garrick came to mind when she thought of safety. And in truth, she longed for him.

She and Ingrid forged on. They both recognized that Yolanda could not replace Rachel, that they had to make their own terms. It had been effort, but they had built something over the course of the year, and Yolanda knew that it would hold despite the distance. Both were committed to the work.

It was Ingrid who settled the matter for her, saying that Yolanda should go back to where she needed to be. Ingrid would visit. In the meantime, Stefan had returned to Cape Town permanently. Time had softened everyone's sentiment toward each other, but the hard work of reconciliation was arduous and only just beginning. Yolanda had spent much time in the backyard with Mark discussing her brother's bitterness and how best to allow Ingrid's father the opportunity to set things right.

As a result, Stefan had made it as far as Rachel's kitchen table, where, Yolanda anticipated, much time would yet be spent having hard conversations. It had been difficult to see the person she used to be reflected in Stefan's eyes and remember the unfettered joy they'd snatched from the teeth of the police. Inasmuch as he was in her life again, she knew that they had to leave behind who they'd once been together, forever. They could not move forward otherwise.

Now, Yolanda lit another cigarette and walked into the yard to say goodbye to the stable hand. Garrick had been gone for a week with his kids on a fishing-and-camping trip, and he was due back today. Yolanda was overseeing the horses and helping but otherwise had free time. She'd used it to do what had once seemed insurmountable.

Inside her home, upon sheets of paper lying on her own kitchen table, were the outlines of the faces that had looked at her for nearly twenty years. She was separating them out from herself and her mind, able to look at them now as the damaged product of a damaged society. It was hard, intense work, to have light fall upon the darkness of these quarters.

But it all needed to be exorcised: the horrid hands, the spittle and urine, the torn clothes. Her body, violated and small on the ground. But her spirit never so. Through wails and trembles, she'd drawn the bleak world of that experience. Her torn-down heart. Her blown-up sky.

She understood that those memories would never be buried entirely, but she did not need to lie in the grave with them. She was creating space to breathe, space for something else to enter. "Come now," she'd said on this same porch last night, thinking of the young woman dragged into the car who lingered within, a ghost as weary as she was. "Dawn is coming."

As twilight fell, Yolanda played a new CD Ingrid had given her, a band called Tananas. The ubiquitous drum, accompanying a voice ululating in Shangaan, bled into the thick night air. Ingrid had taken her shopping for South African music before she'd left, and Yolanda found the sounds a restorative consolation for the daughter she missed greatly. She mulled, too, over the sound of African voices here, in the American South, where so many souls from the continent lay in the soil.

Back inside, she looked at the canvases and sketch pads scattered around her place. This, too, was a way of coming home. Feeding the dogs, then herself, she thought of how this was not the end of the journey but only another step.

Preoccupied with her work, she looked up later into a much darker night and saw the headlights of Garrick's truck. Pleased, she went outside. He pulled up near her place and hopped out of the old Chevy. His face was unshaven and tanned beneath a baseball cap.

"I wanted to see you so badly," he said. He collected her in his arms like a bundle, while the dogs yelped their happiness around them. Yolanda relaxed against him.

"Me too," she said. "How are the kids?" She offered him rooibos tea, which he'd taken a liking to.

"They're good. We stayed in West Virginia mostly, didn't make it down to Tennessee in the end, but they loved it. I was surprised their mother let me have them for so long. Speaking of kids, when am I going to meet this mysterious daughter of yours?"

"Thanksgiving, she's coming over for the holidays. She has a boy-friend; I'm so glad it's working out with Litha. Anyway, she has no plans to stay, but I can't wait to see her. I lined up some work, fall photo shoots. I need to make some money, follow my kid's example. Ingrid works so hard; she always has some exam or assignment coming up. Plus she's got a job she's really enjoying. She loves music, so her father's sister helped her get a job in a music store. She's saving money because she wants to have her own when she comes in November."

"That's timely, right. Thanksgiving."

They smiled at each other, then sat back on the porch, fingers inter-lacing lazily as they looked out at the night sky.

In the months that followed, the slow burn between them intensi-fied. They cherished Ingrid's holiday, and Garrick consoled Yolanda after the young woman returned home to get back to university. They agreed that Yolanda would return to Cape Town later in the year and stay a few months. Garrick might come too.

They resumed their evening walks. Through the hills and along the creeks, Yolanda paced beside Garrick, contemplating love, worth, and sacrifice.

Still, she was afraid. She waited for her past to reach out like a claw and claim the present. She kept him at bay, waiting for him to with-draw to a safer place than beside her. Maybe fear would lead her back to bitterness and self-loathing. Love was work, and it began within. He convinced her to visit a therapist. "If you don't treat PTSD like the seri-ous disorder it is, it will kill you like any serious illness would," he said.

She watched for a sign that being together was no more than con-venience for either of them. But none came.

Instead, as spring brought birds back to the verdant hills, she grew to love him more, to love the way he touched and spoke with horses. To see the way that profound loss marked him, but how he fought against it. How he was holding himself together much like she was.

Then one night, she led him to her room and showed him the flower of scar tissue on her shoulder, the tattooed letter on her waist. She saw the gashes and scars on his body where war had ripped through him and realized that he lived with constant pain in his own way. He bore his own burdens but did not turn away from hers.

After they made love, she bid him, "Come—if you really want to see me naked, then you should see this." She led him to the living room, where her art was laid out.

She drew a deep breath, then told him about the horse in the center of the room. She remembered, vivid still, the animal's muscles, a pulse from the earth's body, the bass thump of a gallop, hooves like a drum and dust like spray.

It all followed from there, the faces she would rather forget, the ones she held on to with all her might. She had brought many keepsakes of Rachel from the Cape but could not yet draw or paint her. Ma would be the center of a grand tattoo on her back, for it was true that Yolanda would always carry her.

In a corner of the wall, an inimitable shape.

"Table Mountain, right?" Garrick said. "I read a bit while you were gone, didn't want to sound like an ignorant American when you came back. So this is your South Africa."

"Yes. It's the sun like you've never seen it anywhere else and sky, blue sky, azure blue. It's smell: beautiful, deep *dhania* smell, turmeric, sticky chutney. The townships with no road signs or postboxes and stolen electricity; the chaos of the taxis; the nice leafy suburbs tucked against the mountain. It's silver birch trees winking in sunlight on Table Mountain. It's women ululating and singing in third class on the train at dawn. It changed. It didn't stand still and wait for me, and I had to begin my greetings all over again on different terms. It is my daughter, and it is my mother."

Tears pressed out of the corners of her eyes. She turned her head away. Garrick came up to her. She felt his calloused hands on her arms, a working man's hands, and released herself into them.

"Don't be afraid to show me who you are," he said. "I'll never turn away, if you'll do the same for me."

"I guess that's all anyone wants, right?" she said. "Someone who won't turn away."

Weeks later, an envelope arrived. It had been mailed more than a year ago by a woman who was old and wise but never frail. It had followed a circuitous path, from Cape Town to Manchester and on to Virginia, remaining stuck for a long period in the belt of a mail-handling system at the regional depot. A maintenance worker on the night shift, dismantling the system for cleaning, had noticed the bent envelope and put it back in the pile for processing.

Engaged in the industry of life, Yolanda opened it curiously. Tucked inside two envelopes was a child's drawing. Her own. It had been her first picture of her golden-eyed mother. Her mind racing, Yolanda pieced together the envelopes, the stamps, the language, the handwriting. There was a single handwritten note with the drawing that simply said, *You must make more.*

The words sank into her, the last of Rachel's gifts. She ran outside, as if she might see the messenger on the porch, in the yard; as if she could reach out and touch her. But all that greeted her were the breeze and the sun. Yolanda bent down until her forehead touched the ground and spoke a silent, grateful prayer to her mother.

The same sun that fell upon her set that day over a speck of land, a peninsula extending into an indigo ocean. A breath intermingled with the cool breeze that hung over the Cape. It wound and swirled, this last exhale breathed long ago in a mephitic enclave by an aged woman. The breath was with the southeaster and the northwester; it was everywhere and it was nowhere. It lingered between the buchu and the sandstone in this place that was both beginning and ending. The breath blew out on the salt sea air. It flowed over waves that came like the powerful eddy of love, constant as the tides.

ACKNOWLEDGMENTS

When I was six years old, my dad took me to a library in Wynberg, a Cape Town suburb where an inordinately large number of eucalyptus trees stood. There, as I was introduced to row upon row of books and vinyl records, the world opened up. I have, since that day, always been a library patron no matter where I've lived.

As such, thanks go firstly to my parents. To my late father, who, in offering me the simple guidance to eat slowly, be myself, read, and think critically, gave me words that I've held on to as best I can. To my mother, who taught me the pride and diligence that one should take with work and also how to make a good bredie, both of which turned out to be necessary skills in the decade it took to produce this novel.

Thanks to the public service offered by libraries and librarians everywhere. You have no idea what impact your work has.

This book wouldn't be in your hands without a wonderful conversation with Genevieve Gagne-Hawes and her early editing, nor without the steady guidance of Amy Berkower, my agent. Both of them saw what this story could be from the outset. I have been humbled by the care and thought shown by everyone at Little A: Hafizah Geter, Carmen Johnson, and the team committed to bringing this story forward in the best way possible. Eli Minaya, you've created a visual that captures the essence of this story—thank you.

Julie H. Ferguson and Joyce Gram, both of you were there when I said maybe I was ready to get this book out in the world, and I will always be grateful to you for the push. Without the superb guidance offered on surfing in the Cape by Sue and Antonio Tonin, as well as Kevin O'Sullivan, I wouldn't have known a shortboard from a long-board or Dunes from the Hoek.

Thanks, too, to the beta and critique readers who generously offered time, energy, insights, and encouragement, and to those friends and family who have stayed the course and shown care when that was needed. The most heartfelt thanks as always to the best of those friends: my husband, who has endured having a writer for a wife with such grace and patience.

To the Mother City and those with their roots in it, including my extended family and friends: your heart and irreverent humor, your slang and resilience, your cries of "Claremont, Mowbray, Kaaaaap," and your mountain are all here in my bones. This book, in the end, is yours.